6/20

Mrs. Lincoln's Sisters

Mrs. Lincoln's
SISTERS

A Novel

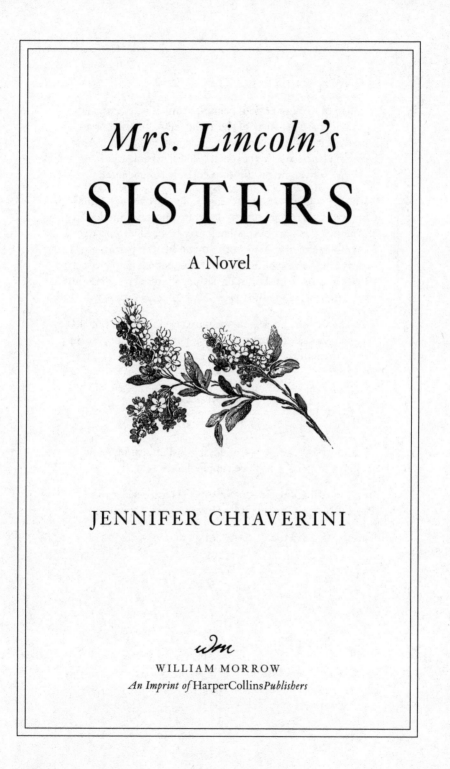

JENNIFER CHIAVERINI

WILLIAM MORROW

An Imprint of HarperCollins*Publishers*

MRS. LINCOLN'S SISTERS. Copyright © 2020 by Jennifer Chiaverini. All rights reserved. Printed in the United States of America. No part of this book may be used or reproduced in any manner whatsoever without written permission except in the case of brief quotations embodied in critical articles and reviews. For information, address HarperCollins Publishers, 195 Broadway, New York, NY 10007.

HarperCollins books may be purchased for educational, business, or sales promotional use. For information, please email the Special Markets Department at SPsales@harpercollins.com.

FIRST EDITION

Designed by Fritz Metsch

Library of Congress Cataloging-in-Publication Data has been applied for.

ISBN 978-0-06-297597-3 (Hardcover)
ISBN 978-0-06-303252-1 (International Paperback)

20 21 22 23 24   LSC   10 9 8 7 6 5 4 3 2 1

TO

HEATHER NEIDENBACH,

my own beloved Little Sister

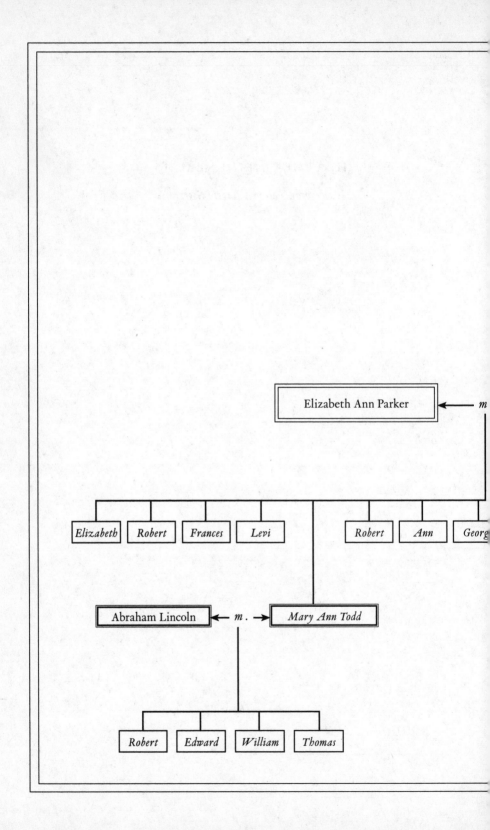

THE TODD FAMILY OF
LEXINGTON, KENTUCKY

| Robert Smith Todd | ← *m*. → | Elizabeth L. Humphreys |

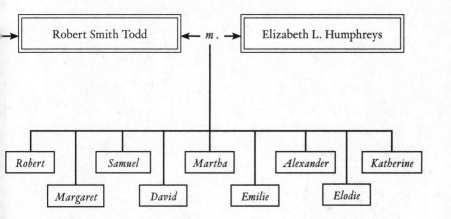

| Robert | Samuel | Martha | Alexander | Katherine |

| Margaret | David | Emilie | Elodie |

Mrs. Lincoln's Sisters

1

May 1875

ELIZABETH

A whimsical breeze rustled the paper beneath Elizabeth's pen as she wrote in the garden, but she held the sheet firmly against the table with her left hand and it was not carried aloft. She lifted her pen and waited for the gust to subside rather than risk smearing the ink, and in that momentary pause a light shower of blossoms from the plum tree fell upon her, the table, and the head of her sixteen-year-old grandson Lewis, sprawled in a chaise lounge nearby, so thoroughly engrossed in Jules Verne's *Around the World in Eighty Days* that he did not notice the petals newly adorning his light brown hair. She smiled, tempted to rise and brush the blossoms softly to the ground with her fingertips, but he looked so charming that she decided to leave them be.

It was to Lewis's mother she was writing—Julia, her eldest child and only daughter. Julia's husband, Edward Lewis Baker Sr., had been appointed United States consul to Argentina the previous year, and when the couple moved to Buenos Aires, Lewis came to stay with his grandparents. Ninian and Elizabeth's gracious home on Aristocracy Hill in Springfield had more than enough room for one much adored grandson, and they were delighted to take him while he finished his education, or indeed for as long as he wished.

The breeze subsided, leaving the delicate fragrance of hyacinth and narcissus in its wake, but before Elizabeth could again put pen to paper, the dull, chronic ache in her abdomen suddenly sharpened. She must have gasped aloud, for Lewis glanced up from his book. "Are you all right?" he asked, brow furrowing.

She managed a smile. "Perfectly fine, dear. I'm merely . . ." She inhaled deeply, ignoring the stab of pain, and forced a sigh of contentment. "Enjoying the lovely spring air."

He peered at her inquisitively, unconvinced. "Are you sure? Would you like me to have Mrs. Henderson or Carrie fix you a cup of tea?"

"I have one," she replied, gesturing to the cup on the table. A pale lavender petal floated upon the surface of the amber liquid, which was not proper tea but a tincture of ginger, willow bark, and raspberry leaf prepared for her by an elderly woman of color respected throughout the city for her knowledge of herb lore. No one but Elizabeth and her loyal housekeeper knew that she partook of the remedy almost every day, sometimes twice, morning and night. Although the brew temporarily relieved her symptoms and evidently did her no harm, she knew that Ninian and her sister Frances would chide her for wasting money on flavored water when her doctor had assured her that the aches and pains were all in her head.

At the time, knowing that a sharp rebuke would merely confirm for the doctor the accuracy of his diagnosis, Elizabeth had managed, with great effort, to nod politely and thank him. Although she had agreed to avoid strenuous activity, she had declined the laudanum he recommended. Only later, when she and Frances were alone, had she said what she truly thought. "And the droplets of blood on my undergarments, are they all in my head too?" she had demanded indignantly, albeit in an undertone, lest anyone overhear and be shocked by her impolite language.

Frances herself had looked somewhat shocked, but her late husband had been a doctor as well as a storekeeper, and she had probably heard far worse. She had assured Elizabeth that her pains and aches and blood were merely symptoms of the change of life, something all women must endure, and in time they would subside. Elizabeth hoped her sister was right, but feared she was not. At sixty-two, Elizabeth had passed through the change several years before, or so she had thought. This felt like something else, but if her doctor, her husband, and her closest sister said it was nothing, who was she to question them?

The pain faded back to a faint, dull ache. Setting down the pen and taking up her spoon, Elizabeth fished the plum petal from her teacup, set it on the saucer, and sipped the herb woman's brew. Even if unusually flavored, it was rather tasty, and made all the better with a spoonful of honey stirred in. The concoction did her no harm, she reminded herself, so no one else need know of it. If ever the time came when it failed to ease her pains, she would insist upon seeing another doctor.

As she set down her cup, the back door opened and Carrie emerged, small and fair in her gray dress and white apron and cap. "Mrs. Edwards, ma'am," she said, bobbing a curtsy, "there's a gentleman at the door who says he must speak with you most urgently."

Elizabeth was not expecting any callers. "Did he give you his card?"

"No card, but his name is Mr. Smith. Not *your* Mr. Smith," the maid added quickly, referring to another of Elizabeth's brothers-in-law, her sister Ann's husband. "I would have shown him in."

"Of course." Puzzled, Elizabeth rose. "I can't think of any urgent business I have with any Mr. Smith, or with any gentleman, for that matter."

"Do you want me to see to it?" Lewis swung his coltishly long legs over the edge of the chaise lounge and prepared to stand. "I can direct him to Grandfather's office or send him on his way, whatever seems best."

Elizabeth smiled indulgently, gestured for him to stay seated, and gave in to the impulse to brush the flower petals from his hair. "Thank you, dear, but I believe I can manage."

She accompanied Carrie back inside and through the house to the front entrance, where she found a slim fellow perhaps a decade older than her grandson standing on the doorstep, clutching his hat, and surreptitiously trying to peer through the front windows. Dismissing Carrie, she smoothed her skirts and opened the door. He brightened at the sight of her, and in the customary exchange of pleasantries that followed, he identified himself as Mr. Philip Smith of Elkhart. The unfamiliar name revealed absolutely nothing about his purpose in wanting to speak to her—and that, coupled with his keen gaze and palpable eagerness, made her instinctively wary.

"I regret that I cannot invite you in," she said. "Mr. Edwards is not at home presently, and I assume your business is with him. Perhaps if you leave your card—"

"Oh, no, I'm here to see you," the man interrupted, nodding for emphasis. "I must say, madam, I'm pleased to see you looking so well under the circumstances."

Her heart thudded. "Circumstances?" Her thoughts flew to Julia and Edward in far-off South America, to her beloved Ninian a few blocks away. "I don't understand."

"Surely you do." His gaze turned disbelieving, impudent. "You *are* Mrs. Lincoln's sister, aren't you?"

Of course. Why else would a stranger turn up uninvited at her door if not for Mary? Morbid curiosity-seekers did not plague the family as frequently as they once had, ten years after her brother-in-law's horrific assassination, but every so often a snake slithered out from beneath a rock. "I am one of her sisters," Elizabeth acknowledged, bristling. "I beg your pardon, but I was not expecting callers, and I must—"

"I won't need more than a moment of your time." He stepped forward as if he meant to block the door with his foot before she could close it. "Would you care to make a statement about Mrs. Lincoln's sad misfortune?"

"A statement?" Which misfortune? There were so many from which to choose, not that Elizabeth would know of any recent mishaps, not that she would ever confide in a random stranger who appeared on her doorstep without so much as a—

Then she understood. "You're with the press," she said, drawing herself up and fixing him with a withering look.

"Yes, as I said, Philip Smith, *Elkhart Gazette.*"

"You most certainly did *not* say." Grasping the doorknob, she said, "You have no honor, sir, but if you leave now, I won't summon the police and have you charged with harassment and trespassing. Good day."

She shut the door firmly and slid the bolt in place, heart pounding, mouth dry. Mr. Smith rang the bell and called her name as she shrank back into the foyer, bewildered and upset. Her family had been tormented by vile stories in the papers through the years, but rarely had a reporter violated the sanctity of their home or sought out Elizabeth in particular. How dare a reporter approach her now? She was a private citizen, not a politician who had deliberately chosen a public life. How could anyone think her so devoid of compassion and loyalty that she would conspire to dredge up ugly incidents from Mary's past? An estranged sister was a sister yet.

Unless—

Perhaps Mr. Smith was not looking into Mary's past but her present.

Elizabeth forced herself to take a deep breath, to think clearly, to remember precisely what he had said. He wanted a statement, not Elizabeth's reflections upon her sister's history but her reaction to some new incident. She pressed a hand to her forehead. Oh, Mary. What new scandal had she become entangled in, to the embarrassment and mortification of her family?

Whatever had compelled that reporter to visit Springfield, it was something so dreadful that he had expected to find Elizabeth in distress, and so significant that he assumed she already knew of it. And yet he had found her utterly unaware. How could this be? How had Mr. Smith outpaced the telegraph?

Unsettled, she went to the dining room in search of the morning newspapers, which her husband always read over breakfast. Elizabeth had slept poorly the night before, owing to the ache in her abdomen, and by the time she had risen and dressed, Ninian had already left for work. She did not remember seeing the papers folded on the table in front of his empty chair, and they were not there now. She went next to his study, but the papers were not on his broad mahogany desk. Nor were they in the library, where the tall bookshelves were neatly filled with law books and works of history and natural science, as well as a few popular novels and volumes of poetry. Nary a scrap of newsprint caught her eye.

She went to the parlor and rang for Mrs. Henderson, who had just returned from the market. The housekeeper confirmed that the papers had been delivered that morning as usual, and that she herself had glimpsed Mr. Edwards reading them at the breakfast table. She was as mystified as Elizabeth regarding their apparent disappearance, but she offered to search for them. In the meantime, Elizabeth returned to the garden to ask Lewis if he had any idea what had become of the papers. He had not seen them that morning either, nor had he spoken to his grandfather except to exchange hasty greetings as Ninian departed the house in a rush.

"Has something happened?" asked Lewis, setting his book aside and rising.

Before Elizabeth could reply, Mrs. Henderson emerged from the house steering a reluctant Carrie along by the elbow. Bringing the maid to a halt before them, she fixed the girl with a stern look. "Tell the missus what you told me."

Eyes downcast, the maid meekly said, "Mr. Edwards told me to burn the papers."

"What?" exclaimed Elizabeth. "And yet you watched me search the house for them and said nothing?"

"I'm sorry, ma'am. Mr. Edwards said to keep mum about it."

"Oh, for heaven's sake." Elizabeth felt a pang of distress. "Did he say why he wanted you to burn the papers?"

The young maid pressed her lips together and shook her head, but the only explanation was that there was something in the papers Ninian did not want her to see.

As Mrs. Henderson warned Carrie that they would have a serious discussion later about the consequences of keeping secrets from the missus, Elizabeth sent Lewis out to buy replacement papers. She paced in the garden as she waited, torn between annoyance with Ninian and apprehension for the dreadful news he had tried to conceal from her.

When Lewis returned, she knew from his stricken expression that he had paused to scan the front pages on the way home. "What is it?" she asked, a tremor in her voice. "What has my sister done?"

Lewis said nothing, but merely shook his head and held out the stack of papers. She took the *Chicago Tribune* from the top, unfolded it—and froze, breathless, when the familiar name leapt out at her in bold headlines.

CLOUDED REASON.

Trial of Mrs. Abraham Lincoln for Insanity.
Why Her Relatives and Friends Were Driven to This Painful Course.
Testimony of Physicians as to Her Mental Unsoundness.
Hearing Strange Voices—Fears of Murder—Sickness of Her Son.
What was Seen by the Employees of the Hotel.

Tradesmen Testify Concerning Her Purchases of Goods.
She Is Found Insane, and Will Be Sent to Batavia.
Scenes in Court.

Head spinning, Elizabeth sank down at the table where her letter to Julia lay forgotten, weighed down by her teacup. She could
scarcely breathe as she read of how Mary had become so feeble
of mind and so eccentric in her habits that a council of eminent
physicians and concerned friends had gathered to determine what
should be done to protect her from harm. A judge had ordered a
warrant for her arrest, and on Saturday last, she had been brought
unwillingly into court, "pallid, her eye watery and excited," accompanied by several unnamed friends. Also present, his eyes,
too, "suffused with tears," was Robert Lincoln, her eldest and
only surviving son, at whose behest the hearing had been called.
Word of the insanity trial had spread swiftly through the city, and
the courtroom had been densely packed with curious citizens and
members of the press. One by one, witnesses had been called to
the stand, where they had testified in lurid detail about Mrs. Lincoln's nervous derangement, her frenzied shopping sprees, her in-
explicable terrors and strange imaginings that her son was deathly
ill or that she herself was being stalked by sinister black-cloaked
men determined to murder her. The witnesses had agreed that the
poor, afflicted widow was not of sound mind, and that for her own
safety she must be committed to an asylum.

The jury had adjourned, and in the interim Robert had approached his mother, attempting to comfort her, but she had rebuffed him with the tearful exclamation, "Oh, Robert, to think
that my son would ever have done this!"

Only a few minutes later, the jury had returned with their
verdict: Mary Lincoln was insane and must be consigned to the
State Hospital for the Insane. The judge had quickly conferred

with her son and her friends, who had agreed that she would instead be admitted to Bellevue Place in Batavia.

"Oh, my poor sister," murmured Elizabeth, pressing her fingertips to her lips, heart aching. And poor Robert, to have watched in helpless horror as his mother's condition had become so desperate that he had felt obliged to pursue this heartbreaking course. But had it indeed been necessary? Mary was troubled, her behavior erratic, but was she insane? Surely not. Surely all she needed to ease a mind troubled by years of unmitigated grief was compassion and sympathetic companionship, nothing more.

But who would provide her with such spiritual comforts? Not the unnamed friends who had accompanied Mary to her trial; obviously they had not held her back from her precipitous fall and could not save her now. Nor could Elizabeth, even if she wanted to, for Mary had not spoken or written to her in years. Frances was kindhearted and dutiful enough to shoulder the burden, but Mary was estranged from her too, just as she was from her longtime rival Ann and even from dear Emilie, everyone's favorite. Of all their siblings and half-siblings still living, Elizabeth could not think of any who had not offended Mary, or been offended by her, and remained in her good graces. Perhaps a cousin or niece or childhood friend could be prevailed upon—

But no. It was too late for a loving friend to volunteer to soothe Mary's mental wounds with gentle ministrations and kindnesses. She had been committed to an asylum at the instigation of her own son. Elizabeth knew Robert well, and she was certain that her nephew never would have resorted to such drastic measures if he had believed any other treatment would suffice. All she could do now was pray for God's healing grace and hope that Dr. Patterson's sterling reputation was well deserved.

What else was there for a sister to do?

Anguished, she turned to the other papers in hopes of finding a more optimistic account of the trial, but each report confirmed the first one she had read. Lewis read silently beside her, taking up the pages as she discarded them, his youthful features clouded by concern. "Is there anything we can do?" he finally asked, raking a hand through his tousled brown hair.

"I don't know, dear," she said. "I need time to think."

"Shall I fetch Grandfather home at least?"

"No," she replied, her voice harder than she intended. "I'll see him soon enough."

Later that afternoon, when Ninian returned home from work, she met him in the foyer, wordlessly beckoned him to follow her into his study, and closed the door behind them. She had arranged the replacement newspapers on his desk, but he did not even need to glance at them to know that she had discovered what he had tried to conceal. "I had hoped to spare you grief," he said, without preamble, before she could properly accuse him. "It was a vain hope, I know that now. I knew it as soon as Carrie put the papers on the fire."

"Did you honestly believe that you could keep this from me indefinitely?"

"I hoped to delay the inevitable, to give you a few more hours' peace. I know you haven't been well."

"Indeed? I thought that you agreed with the doctor that my pain is only in my head—" Abruptly Elizabeth's words were choked off. The doctor's words took on an entirely new, foreboding meaning in the shadow of Mary's confirmed madness.

Ninian must have seen the frantic worry in her eyes. "You are not your sister," he said firmly, taking her in his arms and kissing her on the forehead. "You are not mad. You simply need a more qualified doctor and a better diagnosis."

"Oh, Ninian." Relieved, she closed her eyes and clung to him. "I'm glad you believe me, but . . . perhaps we should believe Mary too."

"You think the verdict is wrong, that she isn't insane?" He gestured to the newspapers on his desk. "I assume you read about her delusions of an Indian pulling bones from her face and wires from her eyes? That she hears raps on a table predicting the date and hour of her death? That she was wandering the hotel clad only in her nightdress? That she spied smoke coming from the chimney of a nearby building and became frantic that the city was burning down? That she accused a man of stealing her pocketbook, which turned up in her own bureau drawer?"

She held up a hand to interrupt him. "Yes, yes, I read the testimony. Every lurid detail is seared into my mind. I'm not disputing that Mary is deeply troubled, but I'm not certain that confining her to an asylum is the best way to help her."

"Several esteemed physicians were on that jury," Ninian reminded her. "We should trust their expertise. From everything I've learned—and I spent a good portion of my day investigating this very subject—Bellevue is no grim institution with scowling guards and bars on the windows, but a quiet, healthful resort in the countryside supervised by skilled doctors and devoted nurses. Mary will be well looked after there, and whatever her affliction may be, she will benefit from fresh air and rest. If your sister truly isn't mad but is merely exhausted, the truth will come out in time."

"I suppose—" Elizabeth inhaled shakily. "I suppose that's true. I hope it is."

Ninian looked as if he might say more, but he hesitated and took her hand. "Darling, whatever your sister's prognosis may be, the days ahead are going to be difficult. The press is certain to exploit Mary's misfortune for profit, and as her family, we may all find our names paraded before the public soon."

"Soon?" She offered a mirthless laugh. "I'm afraid the parade has already begun. While you were at the office, a reporter turned up on our doorstep and asked me for a statement. Thanks to your misguided attempt to protect me, I had no idea why he had come and made no comment at all. I can only imagine how he'll portray my confusion in his article: 'Mrs. Lincoln's Sister Utterly Indifferent to Her Plight.'"

"He wouldn't dare," said Ninian. "Even if you had known what he was after, a dignified silence still would have been the only appropriate response."

"Even so," said Elizabeth, "where news of my family is concerned, I'll thank you to protect me a little less vigilantly."

To her disappointment, he promised no more than to consider her words. She knew that meant he would rely upon his own judgment when deciding what to reveal to her, as he always had. Well, then. No more lying abed for her, regardless of poor sleep or discomfort the night before, if being informed meant racing him to the morning papers.

She slept no better that night, but nonetheless she woke with the sun, washed and dressed, and descended the stairs only a step or two behind her husband, who had risen later but needed less time to attend to his clothes and hair. The newspapers were folded neatly beside Ninian's plate, and after they were seated, Elizabeth raised her eyebrows at her husband, who sighed, kept the *Illinois State Journal* for himself, and passed her the *Chicago Tribune*.

She had prepared herself for the worst, and yet the article that immediately caught her eye rendered her stunned and breathless.

MRS. LINCOLN ATTEMPTS SUICIDE.

Chicago.—Between 2 and 8 o'clock yesterday afternoon Mrs. Lincoln attempted to commit suicide by poisoning. After being removed from the court room where she was adjudged insane earlier that day, her lunatic symptoms became quite violent, and she was put under the strictest surveillance, it being feared that she might do injury to herself. To-day she escaped from her room and hurried to the drug store of Frank Squair, under the Grand Pacific Hotel; she ordered a compound of camphor and laudanum, ostensibly for neuralgia. Knowing her mental condition, Mr. Squair pretended that he had none ready, and that it would take half an hour to put it up. She said she would call in again for it, and then walked out into the street, whereupon she took a carriage and drove to two other drug stores. Mr. Squair, guessing her intentions, had followed her, and in each case was able to warn the druggist not to provide her with the compound. Then, seeing that she intended to return to his own store, he hurried back and prepared a tincture of burnt sugar and water with a few drops of camphor. Supposing this harmless mixture to be what she had ordered, she left the store and immediately drank the entire bottle. She returned to her hotel, but upon discovering soon thereafter that the mixture had no effect, she tried to leave her room again to obtain a stronger dose, but was prevented. She will be removed to the private hospital at Batavia, Illinois, this afternoon, where she will have every attention.

"Ninian," Elizabeth gasped, "my sister—"

"Yes, I know." He set the *Journal* aside and reached across the table to clasp her cold and trembling hand. "It's terrible, but she's safe, unharmed. No doubt she's being watched very closely so that she won't be able to repeat the attempt."

"She was being watched very closely before, and yet she evaded her guards." Elizabeth shook her head, fumbled for her water glass with both hands, raised it to her lips, and carefully drank, wishing it was the herb woman's elixir. "How could a woman of her age and infirmity slip past her guards in broad daylight? How do we know she won't manage it again?"

"We both know how clever she is. Her guards underestimated her yesterday, but surely now they will be more vigilant." Shaking his head, Ninian took up Elizabeth's newspaper and scanned its version of events. "Your sister insists that she is sane, but this desperate act proves she is not. Thank God she was stopped before she harmed herself."

"Thank God," Elizabeth echoed. Sick at heart, she fervently hoped that those entrusted with Mary's safety would take their jobs far more seriously than they apparently had thus far.

Mary's suicide attempt confirmed the jury's verdict, or so Ninian believed. Elizabeth could not dispute the reasonableness of his conclusion, and yet she felt a stirring of doubt.

Was her sister's attempt to take her own life truly the impulse of a deranged mind, or was it the desperate act of a sane woman horrified to be confined to an insane asylum against her will?

How had Mary come to this?

Once they had been the Todd sisters, the belles of Lexington and Springfield. In the years that had unfolded since those bright seasons full of promise, they had all endured tragedy. Some of the sisters had lost homes, others fortunes, or husbands, or children. None but Mary had tried to take her own life.

But none of the Todd sisters had risen higher or endured more tragedy than Mary.

Could she be saved by the bonds of sisterhood, worn thin yet still enduring?

2

July 1825

FRANCES

Frances had not expected to spend the Fourth of July in her family's own garden, disconsolate, watching over her little sister Ann while she dozed on a quilt spread on the soft grass. Nearby, Elizabeth and Mary played Graces, tossing a hoop back and forth from a stick held in one hand, their laughter and playful teasing sounding forced, even from Mary, who reveled in merriment and fun. Like their brother Levi, who had gone off somewhere on his own after their plans were canceled, the sisters had expected to spend the warm, sunny day at the glorious Independence Day celebration now well under way at Fowler's Garden on the outskirts of Lexington. Nearly everyone planned to turn out for it, including all of Frances's school friends, wearing their prettiest summer frocks and hats, with their hair neatly brushed and curled or braided and adorned with ribbons of red, white, and blue. Roast pig and great haunches of beef would be sizzling on spits over a fire, and there would be pies bursting with fruit, sweet lemonade for the children, and whiskey by the keg for the grown-ups. There would be speeches and music, games and gossip, flags and bunting and fireworks. Best of all, Frances would have been free to run off with her girlfriends for the entire day, putting as much distance between herself and her little sisters as possible without leaving the fairgrounds.

She felt a pang of guilt for the disloyal thought. Little Ann wasn't so bad; it wasn't her fault she was still toddling around in diapers, a responsibility rather than a playmate. Six-and-a-half-year-old Mary, on the other hand, was insufferable. Pretty and charming, with a dimpled smile, clear, wide-set blue eyes framed by dark lashes, an abundance of cleverness and funny jokes, and an easy grace and daintiness that eluded Frances, she won the admiration of nearly everyone, from Mama and Papa and Grandma Parker to their neighbors and teachers. Even Frances's own best friends didn't mind if Mary tagged along after them, though she was two years younger. Mary made them laugh and invented the most amusing games, entertaining her friends until Frances felt quite forgotten.

It was exactly the same at home. Mary enchanted everyone so completely that they seemed not to mind, or even to notice, her determination to have everything her own way exactly when she wanted it. If Mammy Sally was braiding Frances's hair, Mary would dart over with her brush and wheedle and beg until Sally hastily finished with Frances so she could devote herself to Mary's long, silky locks of rich chestnut brown with flecks of gold. If Mama was reading Frances a story, Mary would squeeze in between them on the sofa and ask her to start over from the beginning, and of course Mama would smile and comply. If Auntie Chaney asked the children if they would prefer cornbread or beaten biscuits for breakfast, Mary would quickly call out her own choice and plead for it so sweetly that the temperamental but exceptionally talented cook would nod and get to work as if no one else had spoken. If Frances was confiding quietly in Elizabeth, their much-admired eldest sister, Mary would dart over to shoehorn herself into the conversation, even if Frances was in the middle of sharing a very private secret, which Mary would soon blab all over the neighborhood. Later she would feign surprise when Frances, furious and embarrassed, reproached her. "She didn't mean to hurt you,"

Elizabeth would say, excusing her when Mary grew tearful and begged forgiveness, as if Frances were the one at fault.

Frances struggled to forgive Mary when her younger sister wronged her, to be as tolerant and patient as Mama and Elizabeth, but Mammy Sally wasn't fooled. "You best snuff out that jealousy before it make you sour and mean," she warned Frances once, an amused glint in her eye. "You was the center of attention when you was the baby sister. Now it's Miss Mary's turn."

All Frances could do was nod and promise to try, but honestly, how was that admonition supposed to make her feel any better? What good did it do her now to know that she had once been the center of attention if she didn't remember how lovely it had been?

Anyway, Mary wasn't the baby sister anymore; Ann was, and newborn brother George Rogers Clark Todd was younger still. Sometimes Frances guiltily hoped that Mary too would soon find herself overlooked and forgotten as attention shifted to her younger siblings. Recently, as if sensing that possibility, Mary had taken to pretending that Ann did not exist—except when the younger girl wailed, impossible to ignore. Then Mary would grimace and stuff her fingers in her ears.

Frances smiled smugly to herself whenever she observed signs that Mary was becoming anxious about her place in the family, but almost immediately she would feel ashamed of herself. Mary was oblivious to her ugly thoughts, but even so, Frances would try to make up for them by inviting her to play dolls together or offering to read her a favorite story. Mary was unimpressed by Frances's generosity. "You hate dolls," she would reply, or, "I can read it myself." The rebuffs were insulting, but they made Frances feel vindicated for her unsisterly thoughts, so it wasn't all bad.

Still, no matter how much Mary provoked her, Frances knew it was a sin to take pleasure in a sibling's unhappiness. Brothers and sisters were precious. Accidents or illnesses could snatch away any of them at any moment, just as a fever had taken baby brother Robert three years before. Mama had been terribly sad for a very long time, until Frances had almost forgotten the sound of her merry laugh, once as clear and light as a silver bell. Blessedly, Ann had come along about two years later, and their cheerful, smiling Mama had returned to them from wherever she had gone, no longer lost to them. Surely, Frances and Elizabeth privately agreed, the new baby's arrival would drive any lingering sadness from the household.

So it had seemed, until that deceptively lovely July Fourth day as Frances sat on the quilt beside slumbering Ann, her gaze fixed on the house, on the window of the bedchamber where her mother burned with fever.

Just two days before, the reassuringly calm midwife—Mrs. Leuba, the watchmaker's wife from down the street—had arrived with her bag of instruments and poultices. She had smiled at the children and climbed the stairs to Mama's room, alone. Behind the closed door, Elizabeth whispered to Frances, their mother lay in bed with the windows shut and the curtains drawn, the air still and stifling. The precautions kept out harmful drafts but did little to muffle their mother's moans, which sent a shiver down the back of Frances's neck and made her faintly ill from worry.

She did not overhear her mother's ordeal for long, for soon after the midwife's arrival Papa told Mammy Sally to take the children up the hill to Grandmother Parker's house, where they were to remain until Mama had been safely delivered of her child. There Elizabeth dutifully helped their grandmother look after Mary and Ann, and Levi helped the servants with the outside chores, but Frances spent the hours pacing on the front porch and gazing intently down at her own home, built on the lower half of Grandmother Parker's lot. She tried in vain to glimpse signs of movement through the drawn curtains of her house, cringing whenever the wind carried a particularly sharp cry of pain to her ears. Grandmother Parker eventually called her inside for supper, but Frances returned to her post as soon as the table was cleared.

At dusk, she begged, "May I please run down to the house and find out what's taking so long?"

"Sometimes a woman's travail can last a day or more," Grandmother Parker replied, but she agreed to send her maid to inquire, since Papa had expressly asked her to keep the children away. The maid returned with the welcome news that everything was going as expected. Papa sent his love and told them not to worry, but how could Frances not?

The next morning she picked at her breakfast and halfheartedly agreed to mind Ann so her grandmother could finish sewing some garments for the baby's layette. It seemed ages until Papa finally strode up the hill—light brown hair tousled, cheeks ruddy, blue eyes shining with pride, tall and strong and handsome—to announce that the children had a new baby brother.

Levi, who had fervently prayed for another boy, cheered and punched his fist in the air, while Elizabeth, Frances, and Mary laughed with delight and hugged one another. Ann looked on, confused, thumb in her mouth, until Papa laughed and swept her up in his arms. "If you promise to be quiet and not tire your mother," he said, looking around at the older children, eyebrows raised for emphasis, "you may come see her now and meet your new brother."

They promised to be good, so Papa led them home and upstairs to Mama's bedchamber. They found her sitting up in bed supported by thick down pillows, her face pale but eyes shining, a tiny swaddled bundle in her arms. One by one she called the children forward and introduced them to little George, wrinkled and red-faced, his eyes squeezed shut. When it was Frances's turn to meet him, he gave a start and a tiny fist burst free from the swaddling blanket. "He's waving hello to you," Mama said, soft laughter in her voice.

Frances smiled, thrilled. Little George had not shown such favor to anyone else.

After Frances ceded her place beside Mama to Elizabeth, she watched Papa quietly confer with Mrs. Leuba as she packed her black bag. They smiled and nodded as they spoke, so although Frances couldn't make out their words, she knew all was well. Mrs. Leuba left soon thereafter, promising to return in the morning to check on mother and baby.

Eventually Mammy Sally shooed the children out of the room while Grandmother Parker settled down in the chair at Mama's bedside. Papa, who had stayed up all night, dragged himself off to Levi's bedroom, flung himself down on the bed, and quickly sank into a deep sleep. Frances and her sisters tiptoed off to the parlor, but although they thought they were playing quietly, Mammy Sally soon ordered them outside. Joyful and relieved, they ran and played on the shady hill between their house and their grandmother's, Ann alternately balanced on Elizabeth's hip or Frances's. Whenever they asked Mary to take a turn carrying her, she would recoil, shaking her head and protesting that Ann was too heavy for her.

"Just hold her by the hand then," said Frances irritably. "You should take a turn minding her."

"I minded you when I was your age," Elizabeth said, offering Mary an encouraging smile, as if it was worry rather than disinterest that kept Mary from eagerly volunteering. "You and Levi both."

Mary sighed and grudgingly let Ann cling to her hand as she unsteadily followed Elizabeth and Frances around the yard. Mary hated to be restrained from skipping along the stone paths or dancing over the lawn, free and unencumbered, and as soon as she could persuade Elizabeth to take over for her, she pried her fingers free of Ann's grasp and darted away.

Mama was too weary to join them for supper, but she was feeling so well that, as Papa assured the children, he could keep his promise to take them to the Independence Day celebration the next day. Mama would stay home and rest, with Grandmother Parker, Auntie Chaney, and Mammy Sally there to tend to her and the baby.

But the next morning, Frances discovered, Mama had come down with a fever in the night. Responding swiftly to Papa's summons, Mrs. Leuba had administered draughts and applied poultices, but when she left shortly after dawn, lips pressed together and strain evident in the lines around her eyes, Mama was no better.

The children were still at breakfast, pretending to be cheerful for little Ann's sake and murmuring worriedly among themselves, when Papa returned from fetching his friend Dr. Warfield, a professor at Lexington's Transylvania Medical School. "Papa?" Mary called, bolting from her chair, but the two men hurried past the kitchen and up the stairs without a word. Elizabeth lay a hand on Mary's shoulder, gently pushed her back into her seat, and encouraged her siblings to finish eating, but none of them were hungry anymore.

A faint tremor in her voice, Auntie Chaney scolded them for not cleaning their plates and sent them out to play. Neither she nor Mammy Sally nor Papa had mentioned the Independence Day celebration. Indeed, their agitated father had scarcely spoken a word to any of them as he raced in and out of the house on errands, and as they left through the back door, the silent looks they exchanged conveyed that they all knew their mother was very ill—much too ill for Papa to leave the house except to fetch another doctor.

As the day passed that was exactly what he did. After Dr. Warfield left, Papa summoned Dr. Dudley, a professor of anatomy and surgery at the university who was well liked by all and known for his cheerful manner. But he wasn't smiling when Frances glimpsed him approaching their front door with his black leather bag, then scarcely pausing to remove his hat as Papa grasped his arm and led him upstairs to Mama.

Auntie Chaney remembered to feed them lunch, but she made them eat outside on the veranda. They preferred eating on the veranda in the summer, but that day it seemed like a punishment, a means to keep them away from Mama. They picked at their food, but only Ann, unaware of the tension that gripped the rest of them, ate more than a mouthful.

"Do you think—" Frances hesitated, then rephrased the question she was afraid to ask. "Do you think Mama will get better?"

She had directed her question to Elizabeth, but Mary blurted, "Of course she's going to get better! What a stupid thing to say. She's just tired from having a baby."

Stung, Frances was about to retort when Levi said somberly, "Mama isn't just tired. Papa wouldn't call Mrs. Leuba and two doctors if she was only tired. He would just let her sleep."

"She has a fever," said Frances, knotting her fingers together in her lap. "I heard Mrs. Leuba tell Mammy Sally. A fever took baby Robert—"

"That's different," said Mary. "That was a baby sickness. Mothers don't get baby sicknesses."

"Sometimes they do," countered Frances. "Anyway, I'm not saying Mama has what took Robert, just that a high fever is very bad—"

"Let's not talk about it," Elizabeth interrupted, giving Frances a pointed look and tilting her head toward Ann, and then ever so slightly toward Mary, who had risen from her chair, face flushed, chin trembling, glaring at Frances as if daring her to speak another horrid word.

Resigned, Frances said nothing more about the terrible, cold, sinking fear in her stomach that seemed to spread throughout her chest and into her limbs as the day passed. By midafternoon, as she sat on the blanket minding Ann while Elizabeth distracted Mary with games and Levi wandered off to find some mischief, a third doctor had replaced the second—Dr. Richardson, a standoffish fellow less popular in Lexington than Dr. Warfield and Dr. Dudley, but a specialist in midwifery and women's ailments.

At least that was what Grandmother Parker told them when she arrived to look after them while their mother was subjected to complicated medical treatments they were too young to know about. But Frances knew something of this forbidden knowledge, for she had surreptitiously read a book Mrs. Leuba had left for Mama when she entered her confinement. She wondered if they had given Mama calomel for purging, or laudanum to reduce cramping, or if they would perhaps try bloodletting. The descriptions hadn't bothered Frances when she had read the words on the page, but when she imagined the treatments being inflicted upon her mother, she felt sick and wanted to sob. She couldn't seek comfort from anyone, however, because she wasn't supposed to have read that book and it was her own fault for doing it on the sly.

Grandmother Parker sent them to bed early, even Elizabeth, who crept from her own bed into Mary's when the younger girl began weeping into her pillow. Eventually Elizabeth was able to calm her, and to the sound of her younger sister's sniffling, Frances drifted off to sleep.

In the morning she woke to an unsettling silence. As she sat up in bed, Elizabeth stirred, one arm still around Mary's shoulders as she slept. Their eyes met, and they both knew that something was terribly wrong.

Slowly they washed and dressed, delaying the blow to come, then crept quietly from their room rather than wake their sisters. The door to their parents' bedchamber was closed, and from behind it came the sound of low, muffled weeping. Papa? Frances had heard him weep only once before, when baby Robert—

A chill swept over her, so cold she could scarcely breathe. She felt Elizabeth take her hand. "We must be brave for the little ones," her elder sister choked out in a whisper.

Frances's first contrary instinct was to think that maybe they wouldn't have to, maybe it wasn't what they feared. Her next thought was, *Who will be brave for me?*

They descended to the kitchen, where they found Auntie Chaney fighting back tears as she sliced and buttered bread for their breakfast as if it were an ordinary day and not the worst of all their lives. She and Mammy Sally abruptly broke off their hushed conversation when the children entered. "Poor little lambs," Mammy Sally said and held out her arms. They ran to her embrace, but Frances couldn't hear her words of comfort over the roaring in her ears. She didn't want to hear them. Until she did, she could cling to the hope that everyone was sad only because Mama was very ill, nothing worse than that, and in time she would get better and no one would need to be sad anymore.

But Grandmother Parker entered then, ashen-faced and trembling, George in his swaddling blanket in the crook of one arm. She grasped the back of a chair for support, inhaled deeply, and told them that their mother had passed away in the night.

Frances stumbled through the hours that followed in a daze, numbly looking on as Levi and then Mary joined them in the kitchen and absorbed the terrible news. Before long Ann's plaintive cry drifted downstairs to them, and since Elizabeth was holding Mary, tears streaming down her own face as she tried to soothe her younger sister, Frances was sent upstairs to get Ann. "Mama is gone," Frances told her as she changed her diaper and washed her face and hands, but Ann only blinked at her, uncomprehending. Lucky Ann, Frances thought, but immediately realized how wrong she was. Ann would have no memories of their beloved mother in the years to come. Even sad memories were better than none.

Frances carried Ann downstairs and fed her some bread and butter. Soon thereafter Papa appeared, eyes bloodshot, face pale and haggard, and told them in a husky, unfamiliar voice that they must all come upstairs and say good-bye to their mother. For a moment Frances felt a rush of hope: they could not say good-bye if Mama had already left them. But when her father and grandmother took them upstairs and arranged them around the bed and she saw her mother lying in repose on the pillows, her laughing eyes closed forever, her graceful hands folded upon her chest, Frances understood, and she felt a terrible surge of rage toward her father for unwittingly deceiving her.

The children said their hesitant good-byes, all save Ann, who frowned and repeated, "Mama? Mama?" as she looked from the still, silent figure on the bed to the faces of her father and siblings, uncomprehending. She dutifully kissed their mother's cheek when Frances held her near, but then her brow furrowed and she began to cry because everyone else was crying.

Papa's voice broke as he handed baby George to Mammy Sally and told her to take the children away. As soon as she led them from the room, Levi bolted down the stairs and out the back door, while the sisters went to the parlor, waiting for whatever would happen next, dreading it.

Sick at heart, Frances longed to rest her head on Elizabeth's shoulder and find comfort in her soothing words and gentle embrace, but Mary had gotten there first, scrambling onto Elizabeth's lap the moment she sat down, wailing and shrieking with grief so that Frances could barely hear herself think. There was nothing for Frances to do but find herself a place on the sofa opposite and cuddle Ann on her lap, since she absolutely refused to be put down. Frances glowered at Mary as she waited for her sister to calm herself and take a breath so that she could have her turn in Elizabeth's arms, but Mary would not be consoled. That was the moment when Frances knew that Mary would always—*always*—need Elizabeth more than she did, and that Elizabeth would always be there for her, trusting that Frances would be fine on her own.

She would have to be, Frances realized, hugging Ann a little tighter as she burned with grief and resentment. Mary would always come first.

3

May 1875

ANN

Ann did not quite know what to make of the note that Elizabeth's messenger delivered two days after Mary's trial. The elegant handwriting on the thick, creamy ivory paper was clear enough, but not her rationale for summoning the Todd sisters—those who lived in Springfield at least—to discuss what was to be done about Mary. What was to be done? According to the reports Ann had read in the papers, there was only one thing to be done, and their nephew Robert had done it.

Just that morning, the *Chicago Tribune* had published a sympathetic editorial—not to grieve the lady's friends or to pander to curiosity, they emphasized, but to assure the concerned public that Mrs. Lincoln had been treated in the most kindly and gentle manner throughout the proceedings, and that she had maintained her dignity and character as a cultivated lady. For years she had suffered under the mental strain of losing three sons to illness and having her husband cruelly assassinated before her eyes; the dreadful scenes playing over and over in her mind's eye ever since had worn away her reason. When her increasingly distracted thoughts and erratic behavior had suggested that she might come to some harm, Robert had finally had no choice but to seek to have her committed. "This proceeding, and the circumstances attending it, had long been foreseen by her intimates," the article concluded, "and it was postponed as long as affectionate regard could allow."

What intimates? Ann had wondered as she read the final lines. Mary's sisters certainly had not been consulted, and they knew more about her long, fraught history of "distracted thoughts and erratic behavior" than anyone. Ann could have shared a few significant facts with that panel of concerned friends and learned physicians, facts that might have swayed their decision. Not that Mary shouldn't remain exactly where she was for a while, if only to teach her a lesson. She had carried her ploys for attention and sympathy too far this time, and now she must suffer the consequences.

Mary was hardly the only woman to have lost children and a husband, Ann thought, stung by sudden contempt. Ann herself had lost her precious firstborn son, and the dreadful war had rendered their forcibly reunified country a land of widows and orphans and broken survivors. The other Todd sisters, though, like the vast multitude of women North and South alike, had never behaved as disgracefully as Mary had, embarrassing herself and shaming her family. Mary was always landing in the newspapers with some new, outrageous scandal: her pathetic pleas to Congress to provide for her as the widow of the great martyred savior of the nation; her restless wanderings from health spa to Spiritualist retreat in search of comfort; her defensive, very public responses to the offensive claims made by Mr. William Herndon in the biography he had written about Abe, his former law partner. Granted, the book and the many speeches associated with its publication were a disgrace to journalism, reeking with egregious lies and some of the most maliciously distorted scenes ever to travel from frenzied brain to poison pen, but the appropriate response would have been dignified silence. Mary had occasionally managed to act with dignity, but silence seemed beyond her abilities.

Except when it came to cutting out of her life someone whom she accused of wronging her. Then Mary could achieve perfect stubborn silence, even when the person in question was a once-cherished friend, such as Mrs. Elizabeth Keckly, her longtime dressmaker and erstwhile confidante. Even when the person was a sister.

What would the panel of distinguished gentlemen have made of that?

No examination of Mary's aberrant behavior could exclude that dreadful business in New York back in 1867 when she had enlisted Mrs. Keckly in her scheme to raise funds and public sympathy by selling off her wardrobe, a painfully embarrassing episode still snidely referred to as "the Old Clothes Scandal." Even that was presaged by her behavior as first lady, her spending sprees while the nation was engulfed in war, running up extraordinary debts buying lavish monogrammed china and fringed silk shawls while brave Union soldiers shivered in frosty encampments without blankets. Ann had found all too credible the rumors that Mary padded legitimate White House refurbishing bills with her own expenses, rumors that had run rampant almost from the beginning of her husband's administration. Ann had learned to avoid certain acquaintances whenever she went out in Springfield or visited family in Lexington because invariably they would interrogate her about Mary's latest antics. The inquisitors would frame their words in the guise of innocently polite inquiries about her family, but their eager glee never failed to reveal their true purpose.

Ann was tired of making excuses for or feigning ignorance about Mary's conduct. Why should she embrace the role of Mary's apologist? Mary apparently never once paused to consider how her behavior would reflect upon her sisters, the damage she would do to their prospects and fortunes. Never, it seemed, did she regret how poorly she repaid her family's love and loyalty, an affront Ann had experienced personally on more than one occasion. In those winter months before President-Elect Lincoln departed for Washington, for example, when throngs of ambitious office-seekers and newspapermen had descended upon Springfield, had it not been Ann and her husband, Clark Smith, who offered Abraham a quiet refuge in the backroom on the third floor of Clark's dry goods store so he could write his inaugural address in peace? Since the early days of Abraham's administration, Clark had displayed that desk in the large storefront window facing the courthouse square in his honor. It still drew curious passersby inside, where, after admiring the artifact of the martyred president, they often browsed and bought something. What if one day Mary's scandals obliged Clark to remove the desk from view? The store's receipts would drop precipitously, and even though Clark had four other successful shops scattered about the region, the Smiths could not take their income for granted. Had Mary given that a single passing thought? Could she not for once consider how her reputation affected them all?

As for the sage journalists' opinings that the tragedies Mary had suffered as a wife and mother had driven her insane, Ann could attest that her eccentricities had manifested long before she suffered these losses. Even as a child, Mary had desired fine things and the latest fashions more than modesty allowed, but more troubling was how she had always harbored excessive ambition and flaunted an unladylike interest in politics. When she was twelve years old, she had repeatedly begged their father to run for president because she yearned to live in the White House. At mealtimes and rare moments when their father relaxed with the family in the garden, Mary would pounce, imploring him to seek the office so earnestly that tears filled her eyes. Only when her father firmly, unequivocally refused did she join him in supporting his candidate of choice—Mr. Henry Clay, the former US senator, speaker of the House, and secretary of state, one of Lexington's leading citizens, and Papa's dear friend.

A year later, when Mary was a precocious girl of thirteen, she had ridden two miles from home to Ashland, Mr. Clay's gracious country estate. She had interrupted a dinner party, but Mr. Clay indulgently had led his guests from the table outside to admire her new pony and then invited Mary inside to join them at the table.

She was seated at his right hand, and during a lull in the conversation she said, "Mr. Clay, my father says you will be the next president of the United States. I wish I could go to Washington and live in the White House." She frowned, wistful. "I begged my father to be president, but he only laughed and said he would rather see you there than to be president himself."

"Well, if I am ever president," Mr. Clay had replied, charmed, "I shall expect Mary Todd to be one of my first guests. Will you come?"

Mary eagerly accepted, adding, "If you were not already married, I would wait for you."

The guests burst into laughter, and sensing that it was at her expense, Mary graciously excused herself and left the party. Thoroughly pleased with herself, she had trotted home and boasted to her sisters about the invitation. Elizabeth had smiled and congratulated her, but Ann and Frances, heaving sighs of exasperation, had declared that their father's esteemed friend was only being polite. He might be president one day, but he would never invite little Mary Todd to the White House.

"You'll see," Mary had retorted, tossing her head and looking to Elizabeth for reassurance. Elizabeth, smiling, had acknowledged that anything was possible.

Even now, years later, knowing how it had all turned out, Ann wondered how a young girl could have acquired such a strange, preternaturally ambitious obsession.

In the years that had followed, whenever the sisters or Mary's friends mused aloud about the sort of man they hoped to marry one day, Mary would state with all confidence that she intended to wed the president of the United States. "You wouldn't settle for a governor?" Frances had replied archly on one such occasion.

"Or a mere senator?" Ann had chimed in, shaking with laughter. "Perhaps he'll start as one of those, but he'll rise," Mary had said, her tone nonchalant but her expression hurt. At that, Frances had ceased teasing her, but Ann had found it far too amusing to let go. Whenever a new suitor called on Mary—and there were many as she grew to be one of the prettiest and most admired belles in Lexington—after his departure Ann would inquire, with feigned solemnity, whether Mary considered him worthy of the presidential chair. Mary would give her a withering look and flounce off, often noting airily over her shoulder that at least she *had* suitors.

A childhood fancy was one matter, but as the Todd sisters—who all eventually enjoyed the attention of an abundance of beaux—put away girlish ideals and regarded prospective husbands more pragmatically, Mary clung to her astonishing ambition to marry a president. Even knowing her as they did, the sisters were surprised, and Elizabeth was quite dismayed, when Mary declined several marriage proposals because the gentleman in question had no potential for or interest in becoming president. She even discouraged Stephen Douglas, a wealthy, well-educated rising star in the Democratic Party whom she liked very much, only because she did not think the American people would elect him to the highest office in the land.

"He is more likely than any of your beaux to become president one day," Elizabeth had protested when Mary confessed her feelings to her sisters. "No gentleman of your acquaintance since Mr. Clay has been so likely to rise so high."

"But Mr. Douglas will not rise high enough," Mary had replied, smiling to soften her words. None of them liked to disappoint Elizabeth, who had become a second mother to them all after Mama's death. "He will make someone else a wonderful husband someday, but he is not for me."

Not long thereafter, Ann and Frances had marveled that after so much calculation and with so strong a conviction, Mary had chosen a poor, self-educated, backwoods bumpkin of a lawyer who for all his reputed brilliance had no idea how to conduct himself in good society and surely would count himself very fortunate indeed if he managed to climb his way into the US House of Representatives. But fortune had favored Abraham Lincoln in those days, and off to Congress he went. Then, soon after losing a bid for the Senate, he had been elected president.

"Mary evidently saw something in him we did not," Frances had told Ann a few days after the election. "She has had the last laugh after all."

Ann had been too irritated to do more than press her lips together, force a smile, and nod. She liked Abe, and she and Clark had liked him even more after he became president, but she hated that Mary's astonishing childhood ambitions had proven not so ludicrous after all. Only a few short years later, however, Mary's glorious rise had ended in a devastating fall, and her old ambitions proved to be nothing more than hubris. All her life she had longed to be the wife of the president, but if her husband had not gone to the White House, he very likely would still be alive.

Perhaps that was enough to drive a woman mad, and yet Ann could not quite believe it of Mary. Surely this recent sound and fury was nothing more than another scheme gone terribly wrong, another ambitious plan that had collapsed all around her. And even if Mary had been knocked off her feet, she had certainly found a fine place to land. Ann had read up on Bellevue Place after the news had broken, and by all accounts it was a well-regarded private asylum on twenty secluded, picturesque acres on the banks of the Fox River thirty-five miles west of Chicago. The patients, no more than thirty-five at any one time, were ladies of quality, "nervous invalids" who were "not insane" or who occupied "a border-land between undoubted insanity and doubtful sanity." They were provided with the modern, moral treatment of "rest, diet, baths, fresh air, occupation, diversion, change of scene, no more medicine than absolutely necessary, and the least restraint possible." The three-story, ivy-covered, limestone main building was bright and spacious inside, with wide hallways, high ceilings, and large, well-lit rooms, each of which was decorated with elegant furnishings, vases of fresh flowers, and potted plants, all thoughtfully arranged to create a sense of restfulness, freedom, and seclusion. Surrounding the patients' residences were acres of gardens boasting manicured lawns, stands of mature evergreens and elms, ornamental shrubs, rosebushes, and flower beds, with smooth walkways winding throughout and hammocks and chaises lounges set in restful spots. In inclement weather, patients could wander through the vast greenhouses, forty thousand square feet of them, or make use of the carriages and sleighs provided, upon request, for daily outings.

Reading the brochures and descriptions in the papers, Ann could not recall having ever spent a holiday in such a lovely place as poor, dear, fragile Mary was forced to endure now.

She knew it would be unwise to express such cynical observations to her sisters when they met, for they were naturally inclined to sympathy, even though Mary had wronged them too. If they suspected Ann of schadenfreude, they would dismiss every word she spoke and make their plans without her. And if there was anything Ann dreaded, it was being excluded from her sisters' plans.

"Perhaps I should accompany you," Clark mused the next morning as they went down to breakfast, he attired in one of his better suits for a day at his flagship store, she in a brass-colored walking suit with a snug jacket and long, bustled skirt of wool muslin and ecru silk. "Someone needs to be there to represent the best interests of our family."

Ann regarded him from beneath raised brows as they entered the dining room. "I will be there for that."

He pulled out her chair and helped her seat herself at the table as the maid bustled in with the coffee tray. "Indeed, but it may be difficult for you to be entirely objective, since you and Mary are so much alike."

"What on earth do you mean?" protested Ann. "Perhaps we look more like each other than any of our sisters, taking into account the difference in our ages and the hardships Mary has suffered, but there the resemblance ends."

"I meant no offense," he said mildly, taking his place at the head of the table as the maid filled their cups and hastened back to the kitchen. "I rather thought that was why you two did not get along, because you're so similar."

"Nonsense. If Mary and I are not particularly close, it's because she's always resented me for usurping her place as the baby in the family." Just as Ann's own place had been promptly usurped by her brother George and the many half-siblings who had come after. "Mary was a moody girl, in temperament like our father but more capricious, a bundle of nervous activity. She was much like an April day, sunny all over with laughter one moment, then rainy the next as she cried as though her heart would break."

"Indeed," remarked Clark noncommittally. "Nothing like you at all."

She gave him a sharp look, but as the cook and maid entered at that moment with their breakfast, she did not rebuke him. "You couldn't come anyway. You're needed at the store."

"Edgar can manage quite well without me. He's proven time and again that he'll be a fine steward of my establishments when I entrust them to him for good—which I eventually shall do, sooner rather than later."

"You should still ask Allen if he wants any part of the stores," Ann reminded him. It was a familiar argument. "Edgar would not begrudge his younger brother a stake in the business."

"Allen seems inclined to choose another trade. Why he would

want to work for a stranger when he could manage an entire dry goods store with his own name above the door—" Her husband shook his head and picked up his fork. "He's young. I'll ask him again when the time comes, if it would please you."

"It would," Ann replied. How much more fortunate than Mary, Frances, and Emilie was she, to be mulling over simple domestic matters with a husband who contemplated retirement with every reasonable expectation of achieving it. She could afford to be generous of spirit, she chided herself. She must give Mary the benefit of the doubt and approach Elizabeth's conference with an open mind.

A few hours later, when the carriage left her in the raked gravel drive before Elizabeth's elegant home, she felt a faint echo of the awe and expectation she had felt thirty-three years ago to the month when, shortly after her eighteenth birthday, she had come to Springfield to live with Frances and William to seek a husband, although her stepmother and elder sisters would never have put it so indelicately. Mary had been living with Elizabeth and Ninian at the time, carrying the burden of the same unspoken but clearly understood mission. It was not considered ideal for younger sisters to marry before their elder sisters, but Mary was almost twenty-two, she had declined several proposals, and her understanding with Mr. Lincoln had fallen apart in January, much to the Edwardses' relief, for they had never approved of the match. It had been decided that Ann should not have to wait for Mary to be comfortably settled before securing her own happiness, not with Mary's prospects in decline and the family home in Lexington becoming uncomfortably overcrowded.

Then as now, the Edwards residence had been regarded as one of the finest in Springfield, well suited to the son of the former governor of Illinois, a successful lawyer who enjoyed great political expectations of his own, and his lovely bride. There the best society gathered for dinners, dances, and teas, politicians mingled with prosperous businessmen, and lovely young ladies and charming gentlemen discussed poetry, debated politics, and flirted with aplomb. Her elder sisters' own particular circle of close friends called themselves "the Coterie," and how thrilled and fortunate Ann had felt to find herself in the midst of such exalted company.

In the decades since, Elizabeth's home had become as familiar and as dear to her as any she had ever called her own, so it was with a wistful pang that she knocked upon the front door and waited to be admitted. How much nicer life would be if this were her home, hers and Clark's, and if her sisters were obliged to ride up the hill to visit her.

A maid showed her in and led her to Elizabeth's graciously appointed parlor, the same room in which Clark had courted Ann under her eldest sister's watchful gaze, the same room where Mary had wed Abraham after their fraught, intermittent romance had culminated in vows to love and honor until death parted them. Although the road Mary and Abe had traveled to matrimony had been rocky and winding, Ann had no doubt that they had truly loved each other. She had seen it in their eyes and had heard it in their voices. Anyone who made scurrilous claims to the contrary had not known Abe and did not know Mary.

She found Elizabeth seated with Frances on the sofa, the two of them clasping hands and murmuring earnestly to each other as if they were surrounded by eavesdroppers rather than alone in the house with only Elizabeth's staunchly loyal servants to overhear them. They looked up when Ann entered and fell silent so abruptly that for a moment Ann feared they had been discussing her fate rather than Mary's.

Frances rose to embrace her. "How are you, Ann?" she asked, taking her hand and leading her to an armchair by the window, the one she knew Ann favored.

"I'm well." Ann looked from one sister to the other and amended, "As well as any of us can be, given the circumstances."

Elizabeth sighed mournfully, while Frances nodded and regarded Ann knowingly through her spectacles, which lent her narrow face with its sharp features and distinctive nose the aspect of a wizened bird. "As heartbroken and anxious as we sisters feel, Robert is suffering far worse," she said, reclaiming her place on the sofa beside Elizabeth. "He did not come to this decision easily, and he expects the public to condemn him for it."

"From what I've read in the papers, public opinion seems to be in his favor," Ann replied, surprised. Robert should not be blamed for responding to the problem Mary had created the only way any reasonable person could. That Mary disliked the outcome was not his fault. "Every editorial I've read portrays him as a dutiful son who bravely confronted an impossible situation. I haven't read a single word of condemnation."

"In his last letter, Robert told me that he expects condemnation to follow once word spreads that the judge appointed him conservator of his mother's estate," said Frances. "He is steeling himself for accusations that he had her committed under false pretenses so that he could gain control of her fortune."

"He shared the same worries with me," said Elizabeth. "As I told him, he had no choice. Mary's irrational fear of poverty was so profound that she carried tens of thousands of dollars in bonds about her person. What if she had lost them? What if she had been robbed? She would have been rendered as destitute as she always wrongly feared she was."

"Her attempt to take her own life proves that Robert was right to consult the doctors and that they were right to declare her insane," Frances added. "He had to have her committed for her own safety."

Ann felt heat rise in her cheeks as she observed the back-and-forth conversation, and she fervently hoped her sisters would mistake her hurt and disappointment for some other emotion. Robert had not bothered to write to her. Why not? She was no less Mary's sister and Robert's aunt than Elizabeth and Frances were.

"What's done is done," she said, keeping her voice steady, betraying none of her hurt feelings. "The question remains, what do we do now?"

"To help Mary?" asked Elizabeth.

"Yes, of course," Ann quickly replied, although that was not what she had meant. "But also, how do we keep this quiet?"

Frances shook her head bleakly. "Any hope of keeping this quiet was lost the moment the press was allowed into the courtroom."

"How do we manage the scandal, then, before it ruins the rest of us?"

"I don't care about scandal," said Elizabeth, brow furrowing. "We've weathered scandals before. I care about Mary."

"We all care about Mary," said Frances, glancing at Ann, "but Ann makes a fair point. Mary is safe and is being well looked after. Now that we know she's receiving the care she needs, perhaps we should turn our thoughts to Robert and his family and consider how we can best console and hearten them."

Once again Ann found herself not quite understood by her sisters, but before she could explain, Elizabeth spoke. "But do we know that?" she asked pensively, knotting her fingers together in her lap. "I don't mean to suggest that Bellevue is unsuitable or that Dr. Patterson is not eminently qualified, but is that the best place for Mary?"

"What do you mean?" asked Ann. Could it be that Elizabeth too suspected Mary of feigning her affliction?

Frances peered at their elder sister. "Surely you wouldn't rather see her committed to the State Hospital for the Insane, as the judge originally ruled?"

"Absolutely not! I simply wonder if it is truly necessary for her to be committed at all. Perhaps she would be better off in a familiar place where she could be attended to by devoted family."

Ann and Frances exchanged a look of alarm. "You mean here," said Frances carefully, "attended by you."

Elizabeth nodded, a flush rising in her cheeks.

"Oh, Elizabeth," said Frances, in a tender but exasperated tone. "You take too much upon yourself. How long has it been since Mary last spoke to you or wrote you a letter? Months? Years?"

Ann knew it was the latter, and Elizabeth's wince confirmed it. "Our reconciliation is long overdue," she said, her voice quietly insistent. "The time has come to forgive past injuries and come together as sisters."

"You've done nothing requiring her forgiveness," said Ann, a trifle sharply. "It is she who has wronged you. If you forgive her, that's all well and good, but you cannot seek her forgiveness for something you haven't done."

"I sided with my daughter after Julia offended her."

"As any of us would have done in your place," said Frances. "Julia's insult was nothing, a trifle. She apologized, and that should have been the end of the matter."

"Instead, it was the end of any sisterly feeling Mary once felt for me. However, I have not lost my love for her, nor my sense of my duty as a sister. I feel that I should offer to take her in—" Abruptly Elizabeth fell silent as she winced and pressed a hand to her abdomen.

"Are you still in pain?" asked Frances. "You said you were going to see your doctor again."

"I did see him. He confirmed his original diagnosis that it's all in my head."

"What nonsense. If he can't find the source of the problem, you must consult someone else more capable."

As Elizabeth nodded and promised that she would, Ann observed the scene, unsettled, and more than a little lost. "Have you been unwell, Elizabeth?"

"Yes, a bit," said Elizabeth, exchanging a cautious look with Frances, "but not so bad that I thought it necessary to worry everyone."

But it was bad enough to tell Frances. "I'm not 'everyone.' I'm your sister."

"Of course. I should have told you. I'm sorry."

"You should see another doctor."

Elizabeth held up her hands and managed a smile. "I will. I promise. Between the pair of you, I am duly scolded and convinced."

"Good, but in the meantime, you are in no condition to take on nursing Mary," said Frances emphatically.

"She might not accept your hospitality even if you offered," Ann pointed out. "For all you know, she might burn your letters unread."

"I should hope not," said Elizabeth, visibly hurt. "We're sisters."

Ann muffled a sigh. What did sisterhood mean to Mary anymore?

"I for one believe Mary should remain at Bellevue where trained physicians and nurses can properly care for her," said Frances. "Elizabeth, my dear, sweet sister, you have an abundance of love and compassion, but no medical training in diseases of the mind. In this regard, Dr. Patterson and his staff surpass you."

Elizabeth mulled that over. "I suppose you're right. I've always tended her before, but this—perhaps this is beyond my poor abilities." Suddenly she looked up and held Ann's gaze. "What do you think, Ann?"

Ann hesitated, surprised to be asked, reluctant to share her honest opinion, certain they would think less of her for it. How it would shock them to hear that she did not believe Mary was insane at all, but merely needy and selfish, indulging in dramatics to get what she wanted. Mary had always manipulated her sisters by professing to suffer more, grieve more, deserve more than they did. Mary had long felt abandoned and neglected, not only by Robert and his family but by her sisters, by Washington society, by all those who had profited from her late husband's political largesse, and most of all by an ungrateful public who would allow the wife of the great martyred president to live humbly, alone, and quite forgotten. So Mary had feigned illness, and when that did not get her the attention and financial reward she so desperately craved, she had embellished her performance until it was impossible to ignore her. But she had overshot the mark. Instead of convincing her would-be benefactors that she was ill enough to deserve their support, they had decided to lock her up.

"I am not convinced that Mary is mad," Ann admitted. "But I believe she should remain where she is, just in case I'm wrong. Time will tell."

"Ninian said much the same," said Elizabeth, resigned. "Very well. I will not invite her here."

Frances clasped her hand. "It's for the best," she assured her elder sister.

On that point, Ann agreed. Mary ought to stay exactly where she was—not because she needed medical treatment, but because she needed to learn some humility. Let her stay at Bellevue until its bucolic beauty grew stale, until the peaceful isolation became annoying, until she found herself bored and frustrated without an audience. Then she should stay a few months longer, until she had learned her lesson.

They were all suffering, Mary no more than anyone else. When her shameful little game did not get her what she wanted, she would abandon it and find herself miraculously restored to reason. Ann knew it was only a matter of time.

4

1825–1826

ELIZABETH

A fter Mama died, her spinster sister, Aunt Ann Maria Parker, moved in to manage the household and care for Elizabeth and her siblings, but their mother had been unique in all the world to them and no one could hope to fill her role completely. Fortunately, Aunt Ann Maria was not alone. Grandma Parker often welcomed the heartbroken children into her home up the hill, and one of Papa's sisters, Aunt Eliza Todd Carr, came to Lexington to help out as much as she could. The household slaves comforted and cared for Elizabeth and her siblings with more tenderness than before, especially Auntie Chaney and Mammy Sally, and a wet nurse was hired for baby George. But despite the circle of sympathetic affection surrounding them, the children were bereft, keenly aware of the gaping, aching, unfillable void left in their lives by their mother's death.

Though Elizabeth was not yet twelve, her younger siblings instinctively sought from her all the intangible things their mother had once provided. Her place in the family inexorably shifted, and she found herself assuming the roles of consoler, adviser, confidante, and mediator of disputes. She accepted her new duties without complaint, even on long days when she wanted to fling herself into a comforting embrace and sob out her own sorrows rather than be strong for everyone else.

Papa could not offer her the consolation she longed for, not because he was cold or uncaring, but because he struggled with his own grief, and because he was so often away. He had always been preoccupied with his businesses, his elected office as clerk of the Kentucky House of Representatives, and the many society obligations of a scion of the proud Todd family, but after Mama's death, he threw himself into his work as if only exhaustion would bring him untroubled sleep. The children missed him desperately and could not help feeling doubly abandoned, but when tears threatened, Elizabeth would lift her chin bravely and remind her siblings that he worked as hard as he did to provide for them. They would be silly to feel neglected with Grandma Parker, their aunts, and the slaves seeing to their every need, and how could they ever feel lonely with a houseful of brothers and sisters for company?

Sometimes they believed her. Sometimes Frances would study her dubiously, Levi would scowl and go off on his own to throw rocks at birds or commit some other act of boyish cruelty, and Mary would burst into tears.

Autumn came, then winter, and with each passing month the sharp edge of Elizabeth's grief wore down until it had faded to a dull, persistent ache that never entirely went away. The family celebrated Christmas at Grandma Parker's house, where Elizabeth helped the adults make the occasion festive for the younger children. They all tried not to dwell too much upon memories of happier Christmases past, when Mama had made the holiday season merry and bright for them all.

Early in the New Year, Elizabeth was carrying her schoolbooks from room to room, seeking a quiet corner to study in, when she heard conversation down the hall. Drawing closer to the parlor doorway, she heard Grandma Parker and Aunt Ann Maria chatting over tea with another lady whose voice she did not immediately recognize. Reluctant to be drawn into a dull conversation when she had work to do, Elizabeth decided to tiptoe away before they beckoned her in to sit and chat.

Just as she turned to go, she heard the visitor say, "I assure you, this is not mere gossip. I myself saw him calling at the young lady's house, and my cousin saw them sleigh-riding together a few days later."

Elizabeth froze.

"It is far more likely that he was calling on her mother," said Grandma Parker. "Mrs. Humphreys is one of the most esteemed ladies in the capital, and Robert knows the family well. Two of her brothers taught at Transylvania University. Two others served in the US Senate."

"And yet this might explain why Robert so frequently travels to Frankfort," said Aunt Ann Maria tentatively, "and why he is so distracted and restless when he comes home."

"He goes to Frankfort often because his legislative duties require his presence," said Grandma Parker. "No, I cannot believe it. Robert adored my daughter. She has been gone less than six months. I cannot believe that he would seek a new wife so soon."

A new wife? Elizabeth's heart plummeted. Instinctively she drew back from the doorway, nearly dropping her schoolbooks.

"Not even to find a new mother for the children?" prompted the neighbor.

"The children have my daughter and me," said Grandma Parker. "His sister Eliza stays with them from time to time and Mammy Sally rarely lets them out of her sight. They have no need for a stepmother."

"As you say," replied the neighbor, a trifle affronted. "I'm only telling you what I would want to know in your place. Folks say he is courting Miss Humphreys like a lawyer determined to win a lawsuit and that they already have an understanding."

"Impossible. Robert would never disgrace my daughter's memory so. It would be unforgivable."

Holding her breath, Elizabeth backed slowly away down the hall, unwilling to hear any more. She did not want to believe that her father would put aside his mourning so swiftly, and yet the details their neighbor had shared were unsettlingly specific. Why would she spread rumors certain to cause injury if they were not true?

With so little to go on, Elizabeth dared not share the dreadful secret with anyone, especially her sisters. All she could do was wait and watch and listen, catching clues as the grown-ups let them fall.

One morning a few days after the neighbor's visit, Elizabeth came down to breakfast to find Papa and Grandma Parker sitting alone at the table, cups of coffee cooling before them, the air thick with tension. They broke off their hushed conversation when she entered, but before she could bid them good morning, Papa shoved back his chair, rose, and quit the room, brushing past Elizabeth with little more than a curt nod.

Elizabeth turned to her grandmother, bewildered. "What's wrong?"

Grandma Parker studied her for a moment, a flush in her cheeks, tight lines around her mouth. "Where are the other children?"

"Baby George is with the nurse, Mammy Sally is getting the girls dressed, and I thought Levi was down here with you." Elizabeth glanced around. "Maybe he's in the kitchen?"

"Getting in the way, no doubt. Why don't you hurry back upstairs and help Mammy Sally with your sisters? I'm sure she has her hands full."

The mild rebuke stung. "Yes, Grandma." And yet she lingered, then carefully rephrased her question. "Is something wrong with Papa?"

"Nothing that a good shake and a dose of common sense wouldn't cure," her grandmother retorted, but her tone softened as she added, "Go on, Elizabeth."

Elizabeth nodded and hurried off, a sob catching in her throat.

She knew then that her father truly was courting this Miss Humphreys of Frankfort, and that it was only a matter of time before he won her heart. They would have a new stepmother before long, whether they wanted one or not.

This was too troubling a burden to carry alone, so Elizabeth swore Frances to secrecy and confided what she knew. Frances's eyes grew wide and anxious, but she said, "He might like Miss Humphreys, but we don't know that he's going to propose, and she might not accept even if he does."

"Why wouldn't she? Papa's very handsome, he's successful, and he's a Todd. Who would refuse him?"

Frances made a face as if surprised that Elizabeth hadn't grasped the obvious. "He's old and he has six little children."

"Thirty-four isn't old."

"He'll be thirty-five next month."

"That still isn't *old*." But Frances was right about one thing: few young ladies pictured six young stepchildren gathered around when they imagined themselves as blushing brides. Fewer still would find the situation agreeable, even for a man as wonderful as Papa.

As the winter passed and neither Papa nor Grandma Parker said a word about an impending marriage, Elizabeth dared to hope that perhaps Frances was right. Maybe the lady from Frankfort had declined their father's proposal, or maybe he had decided not to make one. Papa was traveling less frequently to Frankfort, she observed, but he seemed more distracted and irritable. Three times a week, when the stagecoach brought mail to the Lexington post office, Papa would send Nelson to collect the family's letters and pace in his study until he returned. Then Papa would practically snatch the letters from his hand, leaf through them with his jaw clenched, and either clasp one to his chest and sigh with relief or thrust the envelopes back at Nelson and storm off in a fury. If

Nelson did not react quickly enough, the mail would scatter like autumn leaves upon the foyer floor.

Once, in late February, Elizabeth was about to carry Ann upstairs for her nap when she came upon Papa and Nelson only moments after the taciturn slave had returned from the post office. "It is no great difficulty for an educated lady to write letters with reasonable frequency," Papa grumbled. "Have they run out of ink and paper in New Orleans?"

"Who's in New Orleans, Papa?" asked Elizabeth, shifting Ann onto her other hip as she stepped into the foyer.

Her father gave a start and turned around. "No one you know, child. A business acquaintance."

"You said an educated lady."

"So I did." Papa glanced at Nelson, who gave him the barest shrug but otherwise offered no assistance. Squaring his shoulders, Papa turned back to Elizabeth. "Well, my dear girl, as it happens, I was referring to Miss Humphreys, a lady from Frankfort whom I hope to persuade to join our family as my wife and as a mother to you children."

Elizabeth clutched Ann a trifle too tightly; the little girl squirmed and mewed a complaint. "Why?" she asked faintly. If the lady required persuasion, why not leave her alone?

"Why? Because—" His voice broke, and his expression grew agitated. "Because my domestic circle is broken, and when I am worn down by the cares and perplexities of the world, I long to retire into the sanctuary of an unbroken home. I feel more unsettled and afloat than I ever have before. A sun is wanting to complete the system of which I compose a part." He paused, cleared his throat, and studied her, uncertain. "I suppose you're too young to understand."

Miserable, she merely nodded. She didn't understand him, but not because she was too young. She patted Ann gently on the back and continued upstairs, wondering how she was going to break the news to Frances.

As it happened, she did not need to. That evening before bedtime, Papa called the children together in the parlor, and with Grandma Parker looking on, steely-eyed, he told them that he had proposed to Miss Humphreys, and that she had accepted, and now all that remained was to set a date and bring their new mother home.

"I don't think I want a new mother," said Mary in a small voice, her blue eyes pensive.

"From the mouths of babes," grumbled Grandma Parker.

"Mary," Papa protested, drawing her onto his lap, ignoring her grandmother. "Is that how you all feel?"

Scowling, Levi nodded emphatically, but Elizabeth and Frances merely hung their heads and looked away. Ann clung to Elizabeth's skirts and gazed up at her worriedly, while George dozed in his nurse's arms, blissfully unaware of how their lives were going to be turned upside down once again.

Papa heaved a sigh and told them firmly that they must give Miss Humphreys a chance. She was a lovely, accomplished young woman from an exceptional family, much like their own, and a maternal presence would restore the comfort and happiness they had lost. At that, Grandma Parker made a disparaging noise in her throat and shifted in her seat, resting one elbow on the arm of her chair and touching a forefinger to her temple. Her steely gaze, which never shifted from Papa's face, turned blisteringly contemptuous.

When Papa asked them to promise to welcome their stepmother with loving hearts and open minds, the children obeyed, but Elizabeth saw her own uncertainty and hurt reflected in their eyes, and she knew that keeping that promise would be easier said than done.

Winter passed and spring blossomed, but still Papa and Miss

Humphreys did not set a wedding date. Elizabeth and Frances, eavesdropping together and separately, soon pieced together that their father wanted to marry immediately, but again and again his bride-to-be demurred, driving him to distraction.

"Six children," said Frances sagely when she and Elizabeth pondered her delay while picking strawberries one warm afternoon in June. "That's reason enough to wait."

"I suppose," Elizabeth replied, doubtful. Grandma Parker said that Miss Humphreys was already twenty-five, practically a spinster. It was cruel to keep Papa on a string while waiting for a gentleman unencumbered by children to come along, if that was what she was doing. There were days when Elizabeth thought it might be nice to have a stepmother, someone to gladden Papa's heart and nurture the younger children so she could be a simple schoolgirl again. More often, she was grateful that the engagement was prolonged, for the longer the wedding was postponed the less likely it seemed that it would happen.

Grandma Parker made the most of the months of suspense and uncertain waiting. She had never met Miss Humphreys, but she didn't need to know her daughter's would-be successor to be absolutely certain she was unworthy of the role. At odd moments, she would make disparaging comments about the dangers of indolent wives and wicked stepmothers. Elizabeth and Frances politely ignored her remarks, out of loyalty to Papa, but Levi, Mary, and Ann gleefully joined in, with as little genuine malice as if they were mocking an evil witch from a fairy tale. Their grandmother's displeasure with their father spiked whenever a new letter from Miss Humphreys filled him with elation and hope, just as her satisfaction rose when the post brought no word from his intended for a week or more and he sank into perplexed despair. Observing the ebb and flow of her father's and grandmother's moods, the happiness of one in inverse proportion to the other's, Elizabeth discovered another reason to dread the marriage: Grandma Parker's resentment would surely only worsen when Papa brought Miss Humphreys home as his bride.

Summer passed, autumn came, and then the prolonged uncertainty that had enveloped the household for nearly a year abruptly ended in mid-October when Papa announced after supper one evening that he and Miss Humphreys would marry in Frankfort on the first day of November. They must all prepare to welcome their new stepmother into their home, which would thenceforth be hers as well. The children absorbed the news in various ways, according to their personalities: Elizabeth with dutiful resignation, Frances skeptically, Levi with a shrug and feigned indifference, and Mary with tears and frantic pleas to their father not to go through with it. This endeared her to their grandmother, no doubt, but Papa regarded his favorite child sorrowfully and told her that he expected her to treat her new stepmother with respect and kindness, assuring her that affection would come in time.

Elizabeth was surprised, a few days later, when Aunt Ann Maria mentioned that none of the Parkers or Todds would attend the wedding, not even the children. "It seemed unwise, given the circumstances," she added vaguely, but she refused to elaborate.

A week after the wedding, Papa brought Miss Humphreys home—but of course she was not Miss Humphreys anymore but Mrs. Todd. She was quite pretty, the Todd sisters agreed when they conferred in whispers in their bedroom later that evening. She was poised and graceful too, more reserved than their warm, affectionate Mama, but they could not blame her for that, since she hardly knew them. Frances noted that she had taken George in her arms as if she were accustomed to cuddling babies, and she had not recoiled when he spat up on her dark blue, elegantly tailored traveling dress, but had calmly asked Mammy Sally for a wet cloth to wipe up the mess. "Maybe that's a good sign that she likes children," Frances added.

"Maybe she only likes babies," said Mary glumly, rolling on her side and kicking at her quilt.

She had better like babies, Elizabeth thought, with a sudden wrenching sensation in her chest, for she might have some of her own before long.

Their new stepmother, who instructed the children to call her Ma, had not come to Lexington alone. In addition to several large trunks of fashionable clothes and new linens and housewares, she had brought several of her mother's slaves, whose attempts to settle into the roles they had filled in Frankfort were met with resistance by the Todd family's servants. Mammy Sally's resentment of Judy, the young slave nurse whom Mrs. Humphreys had sent to relieve her daughter of the burden of raising six stepchildren, was so tangible that it seemed to make the very air between the two women seethe and spark. A young maid, Mary Jane, was too timid and eager to please to offend anyone, but Jane Saunders, the imperturbable housekeeper Mrs. Humphreys had personally trained to run a household and serve in the dining room, sparked acrimony with Auntie Chaney and Nelson every time she usurped one of their usual chores rather than deferring to their seniority and asking them for an assignment. Not that any of the slaves openly complained in front of the white family, of course, but their mistrust and animosity simmered just beneath the surface, and Elizabeth was sure they had plenty to say among themselves when they were unobserved.

Papa had warned the children that it might take some time for them and their stepmother to get to know one another before they began to feel like a real family, and that they must be patient and not judge one another on first impressions. Elizabeth dutifully made every effort, but for all the things she liked and admired about her new stepmother, one dismaying truth that soon became evident made all the rest seem unimportant.

Ma did not like Mary.

At first, she had seemed charmed by Papa's favorite, as most people were, by her beauty, her smile, and her seemingly boundless energy. She was clever and precocious, and though she spoke to adults with respect, something in her manner suggested a lack of deference, as if she believed she was addressing her equals. She could be moody and capricious, as the new stepmother of six soon learned, cheerful and laughing one moment, throwing a bitter tantrum the next. Ma had been given a very proper upbringing, and she seemed at a loss for how to manage a willful girl who could not be controlled and did not know her place. And with Mammy Sally unwilling to trust Judy with anything more important than washing diapers, and Auntie Chaney and Jane Saunders engaged in a constant struggle to prove who was more essential to the household, Elizabeth could understand why their stepmother so often seemed overwhelmed, and why she would so often gather herself up, scold Mary for some wrongdoing, and send her up to her room alone to pray that Jesus would help her become a good little girl.

Months passed with conflicts smoldering and Papa alone seeming content with the new domestic arrangements. Frances and Mary often fled to the refuge of Grandma Parker's house up the hill, but Elizabeth felt obliged to stay behind and keep Ma company and help with the youngest children. The house had become so crowded, even more so than the addition of four souls could account for, but she did her best to help, tamping down squabbles between the siblings, giving Ann and George an extra cuddle when they needed one, promising her dear Mammy Sally and Auntie Chaney and Nelson that no one could take their places, that they need not fear being sold off, because they were part of the family too. "Thank you for the kind words, Miss Elizabeth," they usually replied, as if by rote, and she knew she had failed to reassure them.

Then one afternoon Papa, his face radiant with joy, announced that a new baby brother or sister would be joining the family in a few months. Flooded by painful memories scarcely a year old, Elizabeth wondered how he could be so happy, knowing how they had lost Mama.

A new baby was coming, and perhaps more after that. And the house was so crowded already, Elizabeth thought worriedly, even with Mary so often being sent up to her room or fleeing to Grandma Parker's house.

They must draw closer to one another, or someone would have to give way.

5

July 1875

EMILIE

After her last piano student of the afternoon departed, Emilie went to the kitchen to pour herself a cool glass of water. She drank deeply, yet found no refreshment. Brooding, she wandered outside to the garden, seeking solace in the fragrance of verbena and pink dianthus, the warm colors of calla lily and zinnia, and the song of wood thrush and chickadee. The excessive heat and humidity of the day had stirred wistful memories of bygone summers at her mother's country estate about twenty miles west of Lexington on the Frankfort Pike. In her memory, Buena Vista had been bathed in gentle sunshine and refreshing breezes from April through September, year after idyllic year. She knew, of course, that it must have rained sometimes, and that occasionally the weather must have been as sweltering and humid as the weather in Louisville that week, but such oppressive days never came to mind when she reflected upon the Buena Vista of her early childhood. After Papa had passed in the cholera epidemic of 1849 and their reduced circumstances had obliged her mother to sell their house in town and move Emilie and her siblings out to their erstwhile summer retreat to economize—well, those were different times, evoking memories of an altered, more complex hue.

How heartbroken Emilie had been, at the tender and complicated age of thirteen, to have lost her childhood home so soon after suffering the devastating loss of her beloved Papa! She had been born in that elegant brick residence on Main Street, and unlike her elder half-siblings, she had never lived in the house on Short Street, the one her mother had tried to make her own as a young bride and new stepmother. Her parents' first child together, a son, had been born there a year after they were wed, but he had passed away in Ma's arms a few days later. Soon thereafter, Ma began urging Papa to move the family to another home, one not shadowed by sad memories of lost loved ones.

Some acquaintances and gossipy neighbors murmured that Ma had really wanted to put some distance between herself and Grandma Parker, who glared down judgment upon her daughter's successor from her hilltop home on their shared lot. Emilie had never heard her mother admit as much aloud, but if indeed it were true, who could blame her? It was difficult enough to embark on married life, raise six grieving stepchildren, and endure the loss of her firstborn without a jealous matron hovering nearby, watching her every move and assuring her she was doing everything wrong.

Papa must not have been willing to let go of the Short Street house, for he kept the family there even as it grew, with baby Margaret arriving in 1828, Samuel in 1830, and David in 1832. It was when Ma was expecting David that she began to suggest more emphatically that they find a larger home. Perhaps eager to escape his former mother-in-law's scrutiny himself, Papa had bought the house on Main Street in 1832, and it was there that Ma brought five more Todd offspring into the world: Martha in 1833, Emilie in 1836, Alexander in 1839, Elodie in 1840, and Katherine in 1841. Though the new house was full of children, every so often Ma planted her hands on her hips, looked around, and remarked with great satisfaction that the house was spacious enough for them all, a claim impossible to make about their former home. As if to prove it, she had invited her niece and namesake, Betsey

Humphreys, to live with them. Betsey and her half-sister Mary were the same age and quickly became inseparable playmates, with Mary as the instigator of merriment and mischief and Betsey her admiring companion. At first Ma had looked askance at their friendship, but she had eventually resigned herself to it, perhaps hoping that Betsey would be a good influence on her most willful stepdaughter.

Although Emilie had not come along until years later, she knew about Mary's success at school and many other aspects of her childhood because amusing stories and cautionary tales featuring her escapades had become part of family folklore. Emilie recalled almost as vividly as if she had witnessed the events herself when ten-year-old Mary, tired of her girlish pinafores and longing for the more fashionable attire of a young lady, decided to improve her muslin skirt with the addition of a homemade bustle. Knowing Ma would never allow it, Mary enlisted Betsey to help her secretly gather willow branches from a neighbor's yard. Mary then wove and tied the branches, contriving a makeshift bustle for each of them. They stealthily discarded the scraps and hid the bustles in their room until Sunday morning, when they rose early, donned their refurbished dresses, and slipped from the house to walk to church before anyone in the family saw them. Mary, the swifter of the pair, would have escaped, but Ma caught Betsey in the foyer, called Mary back into the house, looked them over from head to toe, and burst into laughter. "What frights you are," she exclaimed. "Take those awful things off, dress yourselves properly, and go to Sunday school." The girls obediently went upstairs to change, mortified and chagrined, with Mary weeping in anger over their ill treatment and ruined plans.

Mary's girlhood passion for politics was also legendary among the Todds, Parkers, and Humphreyses, as well as most of their neighbors. Her ambition to live in the White House one day had seemed preposterous at the time but in hindsight had proved remarkably prescient. Her pony ride to Ashland to secure an invitation to the White House should Mr. Clay be elected still evoked chuckles from some of her siblings and exasperated sighs from others, but Mary's spat with a friend during the election season of 1832 was less amusing, as it foreshadowed estrangements yet to come.

President Andrew Jackson had come to Lexington to campaign for reelection, and a grand procession through the city planned for the occasion would culminate in an enormous rally and barbecue at Fowler's Garden. The entire city turned out for the parade. Democratic supporters lined the streets, cheering, shouting, unfurling banners plastered with political slogans, waving handkerchiefs, and holding up hickory twigs in honor of "Old Hickory" as he passed in an open carriage. Even staunch Whigs like the Todds and Parkers came out for the spectacle, for it was not every day that a president came to Lexington. Mary, observing through narrowed eyes the man whom her friend Mr. Clay hoped to unseat, remarked to a young Democratic friend clapping wildly beside her that she would never vote for General Jackson, but at least he was not as ugly as she had heard. When her friend protested that President Jackson was not any uglier than Mr. Clay, Mary coolly replied, "Mr. Henry Clay is the handsomest man in town and has the best manners of anybody—except my father. We're going to snow General Jackson under and freeze his long face so that he will never smile again."

"How dare you?" protested her companion. "Andrew Jackson with his long face is better-looking than Henry Clay and your father both rolled into one!"

That was too much for Mary. She and her erstwhile friend did not speak to each other again for several years.

Frances and Ann used this incident as evidence of Mary's temperamental and obdurate nature, but Emilie sympathized, not only because the insult to their father offended her, but because she had suffered a humiliating incident of her own on Mr. Clay's behalf. Twelve years after Mary's altercation, when Mr. Clay was again attempting to unseat an incumbent president, Emilie was playing dolls with a friend when they overheard their parents in the other room discussing politics. Emilie mentioned how much she liked Mr. Clay, her friend spoke up for President Polk, and both insisted that her own favorite would win. Then Emilie's friend said, "I bet you your doll that Mr. Polk will be reelected."

This was a very special doll, the most beautiful doll either girl had ever seen, a gift Emilie's father had purchased for her in New Orleans. Yet so certain was Emilie that the better man would triumph that she agreed to the bet. A few weeks later, after Mr. Polk won and her friend showed up to claim her prize, Emilie refused to give it to her. The ensuing argument brought Papa into the room to investigate, and when the girls tearfully explained the conflict, Papa solemnly said, "Emilie, you must give her the doll. It is highly dishonorable not to pay your debts." Beaming jubilantly, her friend carried off the precious doll, while Emilie flung herself into her father's arms, sobbing inconsolably. "This will teach you the dangers of gambling," he told her, and although some might look at the choices she had made later in life and disagree, Emilie believed that she had taken those words to heart.

Mary would have sympathized with Emilie that day, no doubt, but she was eighteen years older and had already left home. Emilie had not yet turned three years old when Mary went to Springfield to live with Elizabeth and Ninian, where she would enjoy the lively social and political milieu and, everyone hoped, she would find a husband. In those days, traveling was arduous, and Mary had little reason to return to Lexington to visit, since, as even the youngest children knew, she and Ma did not get along. Thus, Emilie's earliest memories of Mary were vague, built on stories shared by her elders and excerpts from her four married half-sisters' letters home—Mary's own words as well as passages written by Elizabeth, Frances, and Ann about her in tones that could be loving, exasperated, amused, or annoyed, depending upon the circumstances.

Emilie was almost eleven years old when Mary returned home for her first visit since her marriage, which none of the Lexington clan had attended, so swiftly had it been arranged. By then, Mary was a wife and mother of two young sons, and her husband was the newly elected representative of the Illinois Seventh District to the United States Congress. The Lincolns planned to spend three weeks with the Todds before continuing on to Washington, DC, so Abraham could assume his office, and the entire household had been bustling and bursting with excitement as they prepared to welcome them. Even seventeen-year-old Sam came home from college in Danville to meet his brother-in-law and young nephews.

The day of their arrival was cold and blustery, so when the train whistle sounded in the distance, they lined up inside the wide front hall rather than outside on the front porch—family in front and servants in the back, except for Nelson, who waited at the front door, ready to open it at the sound of the travelers' approach.

When he opened it at last, bowing formally, a gust of wind seemed to sweep the Lincolns inside. Mary entered first, with eighteen-month-old Eddie in her arms. One glance at her elder half-sister and Emilie was awestruck by her loveliness. Mary's clear, sparkling blue eyes took in the scene, and when she smiled, a fresh, faint wild rose color appeared in her smooth, fair cheeks. Her glossy chestnut brown hair was swept back from her lovely, smiling face, except where it fell in soft, short curls behind each ear.

A taller—*much* taller—dark-haired man with prominent cheekbones and depthless eyes followed Mary into the foyer carrying four-year-old Robert. The man crouched low to set the boy gently down, and when he rose and straightened and seemed to continue to stretch to ever greater heights, Emilie's heart pounded and she almost could not breathe. All she could think of was the ravenous giant from the story of Jack and the Beanstalk—surely this stranger was that same giant, so tall was he and so big, with a long, full, black cloak over his shoulders and a fur cap with ear straps drawn around his head so that little of his face could be seen. Expecting any moment that he would bellow that he smelled the blood of a little Kentucky girl, Emilie shrank close to her mother, hiding behind her voluminous skirts and squeezing her eyes shut. But instead of a fearsome roar, she heard the voices of her family raised in warm greetings and merry laughter. Trembling, she slowly opened her eyes and peered around her mother's skirts only to discover her loved ones exchanging handshakes and embraces not only with sister Mary and the children but with the fearsome giant as well.

When he had greeted everyone else, the man turned, crouched on one knee before Emilie, and smiled, looking at her with eyes so warm, kind, and gentle that in an instant she forgot that she had ever feared him. When he held out his arms, she obligingly let him lift her high, high in the air as he stood, so that if she had not been clutching him tightly, she might have reached up and brushed the crown molding with her fingertips.

"So this is Little Sister," he said, amusement adding an undercurrent of laughter to his mellow tenor voice.

After that, he always called her Little Sister, and soon Mary too adopted the nickname. Emilie had never feared him again, not even when he rose to become the most powerful man in the land and held the power of life and death over those she loved most. He called her Little Sister even after her husband refused his offer of a commission in the Union Army and joined the Confederates instead. And she would never forget how he and Mary both had welcomed their Little Sister to the White House in those terrible weeks of anguish after Ben died.

Would Mary fondly call her Little Sister still, if Emilie reached out to her? Was Mary in any state to speak to her or read a heartfelt letter and respond in kind?

At thirty-eight years old, the last twelve lived as a widow, Emilie would have thought herself capable of bearing the news of Mary's misfortune with more womanly stoicism and grace, but the latest revelations in the press had unsettled her deeply. Earlier that morning, after seeing her own three children well started on the day but before her first pupil arrived, Emilie had pored over Robert's recent letters, searching for euphemisms and deflections, anything that would explain the discrepancy between what she had *believed* about Mary's condition, and about Bellevue Place, and what her circumstances actually *were*, according to a certain Mrs. M. L. Rayne, correspondent for the *Chicago Post and Mail*. How a reporter, a stranger, had been allowed to see Mary when Dr. Patterson strongly advised friends and family not to visit out of concern that seeing them might agitate the patient and delay her recovery, Emilie could only wonder.

She would have traveled to Illinois to see Mary several times by now if she had known that visits were not harmful after all. She and Mary were estranged, but they were still family—and unique among all the Todd sisters, Emilie had distanced herself from Mary rather than the other way around.

How her choices tormented her now! She had always loved Mary, and Abe too, and indeed her quarrel had been with him, not with her sister. But after his assassination, when Mary had not responded to Emilie's tentative letters of condolence, she had found herself at a loss, uncertain what to do. Should she persist, or should she wait patiently until her elder sister reached out to her? Eventually, preoccupied by her own grief and hardships, Emilie had stopped trying to find the right words to break the chilly silence that stretched between them.

Although she had severed ties with his mother, Emilie had kept in touch with Robert, her adored nephew and dear friend. As he was only seven years younger than herself, he had always felt more like a cousin than a nephew, and even when they had been on opposite sides of the war, their bonds of affection had not shattered. Unfortunately, the same could not be said for other members of their family: some remained irrevocably estranged a decade after the war ended, and others had left this earth, taking all hope of reconciliation with them.

But since she and Robert were close, Emilie trusted him—his judgment in correctly evaluating his mother's condition, and his honesty in sharing his observations with her. Two weeks after the trial, he had written to assure her that his mother was receiving the best medical care and was as happily situated as possible, and that he was determined that she should have everything for her comfort and pleasure that could be safely provided. His mother resided in a private suite of two rooms with a bath, on the second floor in the same section of the building where the Patterson family's quarters were located. Mary slept in the larger bedroom, while her personal attendant, a young former schoolteacher selected for her kindness and intelligence, occupied the smaller. Rumors that Mary was restrained by barred windows and locked doors were absolutely untrue: the windows were fitted with light, ornamental wire screens to prevent falls, and her door was locked only at night; during the day, she herself kept the key. As for her angry accusations at the trial, she was no longer furious at Robert for, as she had seen it then, his unfilial betrayal. "The expression of surprise at my action which was telegraphed in all the papers, and which you doubtless saw, was the first and last expression of the kind she has uttered and we are on the best of terms," he wrote. "Indeed my consolation in this sad affair is knowing that she is happier in every way, in her freedom from worry and excitement, than she has been in ten years."

Emilie knew that those ten years referred not to the end of the war but to the ill-fated day of his father's murder. That day marked the crux of Mary's life; thenceforth, everything belonged either to the hopeful Before or the wretched After.

In letters that followed, Robert informed Emilie that he visited his mother every week, often bringing along his five-year-old daughter Mamie. Without exception, Mary was delighted to see her grandchild, and in every regard she was cordial and welcoming to her son. Or so Robert's letters reported well into June. Then—and here Emilie detected a pattern of troubling changes she had not noticed before—Mary went out walking less frequently and canceled nearly as many carriage rides as she scheduled, until apparently she was rarely leaving the building. "Today Mother was not quite so friendly in her manner to me as in previous visits," Robert had written on June 17, and a week later, he had passed on a remark from her personal attendant that Mary had been sleeping restlessly of late.

The signs were subtle, but when Emilie purposefully searched Robert's letters for them, they leapt off the page. Although Mary had appeared to be settling in well at Bellevue Place when she had first been committed, over the past few weeks she had become restless and aggrieved.

That altered disposition was likely what had informed the account Mrs. Rayne presented to the *Post and Mail*. The reporter met first with Dr. Patterson, who had been reluctant to discuss his patient's condition, but either he had overcome his reticence or Mrs. Rayne had later found an orderly more willing to talk. Mrs. Lincoln gave the staff little trouble, but she was capricious in her walking and riding, scheduling a carriage ride for midday, then postponing it until the afternoon, and then until after supper, and then canceling it altogether, only to start over again the next morning. She had brought ten large trunks of clothing with her, but despite that abundance, she had ordered elaborate morning dresses of black French cambric and white striped lawn, which she never wore; soon thereafter, when she requested samples of black alpaca to have a suit made, she "was diverted from this, as it was only a form of her malady to accumulate material." More distressing yet, Emilie read that often Mary would sit alone in her room and imagine herself at the White House entertaining senators and ambassadors with her beloved husband at her side. On other occasions, she would sit at her table and converse with her deceased sons—a symptom of her illness, Robert assured Emilie, and not to be confused with a sudden escalation in her belief in Spiritualism.

Ordinarily Mrs. Lincoln refused to see any visitors, "even declining to leave her room when they are in the house or on the grounds," so Mrs. Rayne had been pleasantly surprised when her request to meet was accepted. A doctor escorted her up to Mrs. Lincoln's suite, where the former first lady welcomed her cordially, shook her hand, and invited her to sit. She was dressed in an ordinary black dress, half worn; her glossy chestnut brown hair had gone mostly gray and was carelessly arranged in a coronet braid coiled into a knot in back. "She looked worn and ill," Mrs. Rayne wrote, "and her hands, ringless and uncared for, were never at rest. I could plainly see in her lusterless eyes and in the forced composure of her manner evidences of a shattered mind. She was perfectly ladylike in manner, but rambling and diffuse in her conversation." Even so, she spoke tenderly of her late husband, and upon learning that her visitor was from Chicago, she inquired politely about several friends residing in the city.

In parting, Mrs. Lincoln took a lovely bouquet from a crystal vase on her table and asked the reporter to accept it. "I thought I could perceive in the diplomatic bow and smile a return of the old society manner," Mrs. Rayne wrote, "and my heart was full for the woman who sat down silent and alone in her solitary room to keep imaginary company with Senators and Ambassadors in the light of that gracious, kindly smile long since hidden beneath the coffin lid." No encouragement was held out that Mrs. Lincoln would ever become permanently well, the sympathetic reporter concluded, but there was no better asylum than Bellevue Place for the attempt to restore her reason to be undertaken.

Emilie had been shaken by the article, which left her bewildered and worried. The distracted, pathetic, delusional woman portrayed in its columns bore no resemblance to the confident, clever, gracious elder sister she had admired since childhood. Nor did that unhappy woman resemble the unwell but cooperative and steadily improving mother Robert had described with tender frankness in his letters.

Had this Mrs. Rayne observed the real Mary Lincoln? Had Mary allowed a stranger a glimpse behind the brave mask she maintained for those who loved her most faithfully? But no, that wasn't Mary either. Her sisters and closest friends had seen her at her best and at her worst, when she had shone radiantly as the first lady of the land and when she had lain prostrate in bed, keening with grief. She would not conceal her true self from them now. Even her suicide attempt—Emilie's heart thudded at the thought of it—had been made in plain view of dozens of witnesses.

Who was this reporter who had either observed a Mary none of her sisters knew or fabricated a pitiful tale for unfathomable reasons of her own? What was true, and what was falsehood? Were greedy opportunists manipulating Mary for their own gain, or was Mary somehow orchestrating it all, whether to secure her release or win public sympathy or something else entirely?

One matter was certain: Mary needed her loved ones to put past grievances aside, to help her make her way through this dreadful chapter of her life and find the path to a more hopeful future. The Todd sisters all had survived tragedy. They all had endured loss—parents, husbands, children, whole nations and noble causes, all had fallen away, lost to time. If they could not rise above their old resentments to help a sister in need, would it not be said that they had learned nothing from their own suffering?

Emilie was neither a philosopher nor a physician, just a music teacher, a widow, a sister, a mother. She could not claim any particular knowledge of the diseases of the human mind, but she did know how the accumulation of sorrows could burden the spirit.

She also knew that she could not help Mary from the other side of an unbroken silence.

6

February 1832

FRANCES

A light flurry of snow danced past the windows of the front parlor, but the fire on the hearth warmed the room and enhanced the lamplight, banishing the false twilight. The noises of the younger siblings playing in the nursery were pleasantly distant, so Frances was able to work in peace, enjoying the quiet industry of the winter afternoon. If only Elizabeth were there, with her pleasant conversation and generous encouragement, Frances would have been perfectly content. But Elizabeth had already gone to Aunt Eliza and Uncle Charles's country house to prepare for the upcoming festivities, and although the rest of the family would soon join her there, her absence was keenly felt. They had better get used to it, Frances thought hollowly, certain that she never would.

It was on Elizabeth's behalf that Frances, Mary, and cousin Betsey labored on a Sunday afternoon when they might have been out sleigh-riding or reading a delightful novel. In two days, Elizabeth would marry Ninian Edwards, the handsome, dashing Transylvania University law student who had won her heart. Like his bride-to-be, the groom came from a prominent political family, and he brought to their union an impressive lineage, substantial wealth, and important connections. His father was the former governor of

Illinois, and Ninian had great expectations of enjoying an equally brilliant political career. Since he was still in his third year of law school, the newlyweds planned to remain in Lexington while he completed his degree. After that, they would move to Belleville, Illinois, to be near his family.

Frances felt a lump in her throat imagining the four hundred miles that would all too soon separate her from her dearest sister. They had never been so far apart for more than a few days at a time. Who would comfort Frances when she was melancholy, or encourage her when she felt dispirited, or advise her when Mary got on her last nerve? Elizabeth promised to write often, but a fond smile and a warm embrace between sisters conveyed so much more than could ever be put down on paper. It would be bad enough when Elizabeth left home to live with Ninian in his boardinghouse near the university. How would Frances bear it when she moved to another state?

She rested her hand, holding the needle, on her lap, closed her eyes, and inhaled deeply, quietly. It would not do to become so upset that she pricked a fingertip and ruined the lovely lace and silk illusion headpiece and veil she was making for her sister. Frances had less than forty-eight hours to finish it; there was no time to spare for picking out stitches and replacing bloodstained fabric. None of her sisters would be able to assist her if she fell behind, for they too were hurrying to finish essentials for Elizabeth's trousseau. Mary, the most gifted seamstress of the Todd sisters despite her young age, was finishing a fine wool suit Elizabeth would wear when she traveled to Belleville to meet more of Ninian's relations and their expansive circle of family friends. Cousin Betsey was putting the last stitches into the binding of a wedding quilt, a collaborative project the women and girls of the Todd, Parker, and Humphreys families had begun soon after the couple announced their engagement. Every member of the household except for the boys and the younger children had some wedding work to complete and very little time left in which to do it.

Aunt Eliza had the most demanding role of all, for she was hosting the wedding and the reception at her spacious home in Walnut Hill, seven miles southeast of Lexington. Through the years, the elder Todd children had spent many joyful weeks in the countryside with Aunt Eliza, Uncle Charles, and their children. Their aunt Hannah Todd Stuart, her husband, and their children also lived nearby. All of the cousins had played happily together, enjoying merry games of tag and hide-and-go-seek in the adjacent woods; going on picnics in sun-splashed meadows and shady groves; picking berries, walnuts, and chestnuts as they came into season; going on hay rides in fair weather and sleigh rides in winter; roasting apples and telling stories around the fireside. Frances cherished her memories of those visits, which had lasted weeks or even months at a stretch, but she knew now—and had sensed even then—that the real purpose had been to get the stepchildren out of Ma's way so she could attend to her own.

Ma's only regret about their lovely home on Main Street— the only regret she had ever mentioned in Frances's hearing anyway—was that it was simply too crowded for a family of eight children with another on the way—ten including cousin Betsey. Those very lamentations, in fact, were what had prompted Aunt Eliza to offer to host Elizabeth's wedding at her home instead. Frances was pleased for Elizabeth that such an agreeable solution had been found for her special day, but that did not resolve the ongoing problem of Ma's dissatisfaction with the increasingly crowded conditions at home. Frances was nagged by a troubling suspicion that, rather than find a way to make more efficient use of space, Ma preferred to scatter her stepchildren among the extended family.

Perhaps Elizabeth's departure would make enough room in the

house to soothe Ma's discontent, a very good thing considering her delicate condition. A new brother or sister would be joining the family in about six weeks, and the fewer cares burdening Ma until then, the better it would be for everyone.

Muffling a sigh, Frances took up her needle again and resumed working on a particularly complicated section of the bride's headpiece. She had just tied a knot and snipped the trailing threads when she heard a quiet rapping sound from elsewhere in the house: three knocks, a pause, two knocks, a pause, and one.

She turned her ear toward the sound and listened, but when only silence followed and none of her companions glanced up from their work, she threaded her needle again and resumed sewing. Barely two minutes later, the knocking came again, this time slightly louder, and yet restrained.

This time Mary looked up. "Did anyone else hear that?"

Frances nodded, but Betsey said, "Hear what?"

"A rapping sound, like knuckles on glass." Mary repeated the pattern on the arm of her chair. "I've heard it twice, repeated in the same pattern."

"It's probably just the little ones playing jacks," said Betsey, her gaze focused intently on the quilt.

"They're upstairs in the nursery," said Frances. "This sounded like it came from the kitchen."

"Then it's probably Aunt Chaney cooking."

Mary shook her head. "No, Ma gave Aunt Chaney permission to visit her husband this afternoon. That's why we're having a cold supper."

Just then the knocks sounded again—three, two, one.

Betsey's eyebrows rose, and her hands, still clasping the edge of the quilt and the needle, fell to her lap. "Perhaps it's a deliveryman, or Levi playing a prank."

"A deliveryman would go to the back door," said Mary. "This sounded like a knock on a window."

Frances carefully set the headpiece aside and rose from her chair. "There's only one way to find out."

She meant to go alone, but Mary and Betsey promptly abandoned their work and followed her across the hall, through the empty kitchen, and to the rear entry. When Frances opened the door, a gust of wind blew icy crystals into the air around her, but no one stood on the back stoop.

"Look," said Mary, ducking past Frances to bend for a close look at scuff marks in the thin trace of snow. "Footprints. Someone was here."

"It would be just like Levi to distract us with a fright when he knows we're busy," said Betsey.

Frowning, shaking her head, Mary drew back into the kitchen. Closing the door firmly against the cold, Frances turned in time to see her younger sister striding toward the pantry. Frances and Betsey hastened after her, only to round the corner and halt abruptly, as Mary had, in front of Sally. Slowly their mammy turned toward them, her expression wary, a piece of cheesecloth and a coil of smoked sausages in one hand and a thick piece of cornbread in the other.

"We thought we heard rapping on the kitchen window," said Mary, her gaze traveling from Sally's face to the food she carried, "but no one was at the back door."

"Only footprints in the snow," Betsey added.

Sally's guarded expression drew Frances's sympathy. "Obviously someone came on an errand and Mammy Sally took care of it and sent him on his way," she said, dismissing the mystery with a shrug.

Sally's mouth pressed into a grim line. Silently, Frances willed her to play along, but she said nothing.

"Is that what happened, Mammy Sally?" Mary prompted. "If not, I suppose we'll have to tell Ma that there are prowlers about. She'll tell Papa, and he'll have to—"

"No prowlers around here, Miss Mary," Sally broke in. "No need to tell nobody."

Mary cocked her head to one side and planted a hand on her hip. "What is it then? Levi playing pranks?"

Sally held each of them in her gaze for a long moment. "Can you keep a secret?"

"If necessary," said Mary, while Frances and Betsey nodded.

"Then you best promise to keep this one." Sally gestured, quick and defiant, toward the cloakroom. "Go fetch your wraps and hurry back. Quiet, now."

Quickly the girls dashed off to pull on their boots and coats and mittens, then hurried back to Sally, who waited resignedly at the door, the cloth-wrapped bundle of sausages and cornbread tucked under one arm. Stepping outside, Sally drew her shawl closer around herself and jerked her head to the west to indicate that they were to follow. The girls trailed after her through the back garden to a stand of evergreens some distance from the house, where a few weatherworn oak posts, the remnants of an old fence, stood sentinel in the snow.

Sally gestured to the middle post. "See this here mark?"

The girls drew closer to study a knot in the wood. After a moment, Frances discovered a curious pattern almost hidden within the wood grain, not a natural variation of the bark but a symbol carved by hand. "What is it?" she asked. "Did Indians carve it?"

"Indians," Sally echoed, scornful. "I left that mark myself. It tells runaways that if they hungry they can get vittles from this kitchen. All of them runaways know this sign, and I have fed many a one."

"Runaway slaves?" Betsey gasped. "Here?"

"That rapping you heard was likely someone trying to get my attention. Probably too hungry to wait in the woods until nightfall."

"Do Papa and Ma know about this?" asked Frances.

Sally eyed her sharply. "What do you think?"

"I expect not," she replied, chagrined.

"Mammy Sally," said Mary, "you know it's against the law to help runaway slaves. You could get in a lot of trouble. I'll go into the woods and give him the food myself."

Some of the tension around the older woman's eyes eased. "No, honey. He would hide from you like a scared rabbit. No hand but a black hand can give him this food, no matter if he be starving." She sighed and flipped the corner of her shawl toward the house. "You girls go back inside and finish your sewing. Remember you promised to say nothing to no one. If you break your vow, that old blackbird over there will fly down to hell tonight and tell on you to the Devil."

They were too old to believe their mammy's superstitious tales anymore, and yet Frances felt a pang of foreboding, and the two younger girls shivered.

Wordlessly, they hurried off to the house while Sally made her way into the woods, stepping on bare patches and broad stones to avoid leaving a trail through the snow. They said nothing, not even in whispers, as they put away their boots, hung up their wraps, and settled back down to work. Mary eventually began chattering away about a poem she had recently read, and for once Frances was grateful for her sister's gift of gab, which allowed Frances to mull over the morning's events without feeling obliged to join in the conversation.

Later that night, when the little ones were asleep and the older children were preparing for bed, Mary caught Frances alone in the hall outside their bedroom. "Do you think Mammy Sally will run away?" she murmured.

"I don't think so," said Frances, taken aback. "Helping a hungry runaway is one matter. Running away oneself is quite another."

"Do you think she and Auntie Chaney and Nelson and the others are happy here?"

For a moment Frances could only look at her, bemused. "Do you really want to know what I think?" Mary so rarely did.

"I wouldn't have asked if I didn't."

"Well, Mary—" Frances hardly knew where to begin. "How would you feel in their place?"

Mary regarded her, uncomprehending. "I'll never be in their place."

"All the more reason you should think about it. Auntie Chaney has to get permission to visit her own husband. Mammy Sally hasn't seen her family since Christmas. Every slave in this household has family somewhere else, and Papa and Ma keep them apart."

"Papa can't afford to buy them all, and even if he could, Ma would say there isn't enough room."

Frances sighed, exasperated. "That isn't the point. Look, I'm tired. My eyes ache from sewing. Please get out of the way so I can go to bed."

"I can't believe Mammy wants to be free," said Mary plaintively. "How could we do without her, and how could she manage without us? She loves us."

"I'm sure she does, but—"

"None of our slaves need fear Papa would ever sell them." Mary's voice had risen, but she quickly caught herself, glanced over her shoulder, and lowered her voice to a whisper again. "It would be like selling off a member of the family. We love them and they're happy here. Our family isn't cruel to slaves, not like those horrid people you read about in the papers. Didn't Grandma Parker and Grandma Humphreys both put in their wills that after they pass on, their slaves are to be freed?"

"If Grandma Parker and Grandma Humphreys love their slaves so much, why not free them now? It's no sacrifice to free your slaves when you've passed beyond needing them." Sharply, Frances added, "Don't you dare repeat what I've said to them or to Papa, Ma, or anyone."

"I won't say a word."

"You'd better not. If I get in trouble, I'll know it's you who tattled."

Mary drew herself up, affronted to have her integrity questioned but pleased to be included in an elder sister's secret. "I said I won't."

Frances nodded and went off to bed, hoping Mary would keep her word. It was good, she supposed, even at the risk of displeasing Papa and Ma, that Mary was questioning the way things were, when slavery contradicted many of the principles they had been brought up to revere about their country and their faith.

In truth, Mary was not the only Todd sister who knew of Frances's deep ambivalence about their family's slaveholding, past and present. She and Elizabeth had talked it over many a time, their conversation always in secret, always conflicted and impassioned. Perhaps their family's servants were treated relatively well, but they were still enslaved, unable to make simple choices for themselves. For example, as proven that very day, they needed permission to visit their own families, from whom they were forcibly separated. Who could ever be truly happy in such circumstances, even with plenty to eat and a roof over their head?

Every year tensions over slavery seemed to grow, not only in Lexington but throughout Kentucky and beyond. Stories filled the newspapers and the rumor mill about masters brutalizing their slaves and slaves suddenly fighting back, with deadly consequences. Not three years before, slaves bound for the Lexington market had turned upon their captors, leaving corpses scattered on an old country road; the shackled men, unable to flee, had been swiftly caught and hanged. Two years later, at a dance for colored folk held outside of town, a white patrol had descended with guns and torches, killing one slave and wounding several others. From other states came frightening, sickening stories of vicious slave-owners beating or killing slaves and slaves rising up in murderous revolt. Recently Elizabeth had confided to Frances that it would be a relief to leave Kentucky for Illinois so that she need no longer witness slaves being marched in chains through Lexington on their way to the auction block, nor would she be pricked by guilt whenever she was waited on by servants who had no choice but to serve her.

Frances understood why moving to a free state would be a great relief for Elizabeth, if a small comfort to compensate for the distance from home and the absence of family. In a way, Frances envied Elizabeth that liberty to not witness slavery at close hand, even if, as she took over her sister's place as the eldest at home, she would remain ever mindful that slavery continued to cause tremendous suffering. Moreover, as disagreements within their family and community grew more heated, and as violence broke out more frequently wherever slavery abided, it seemed impossible to hope that free states could remain untouched by the conflict forever.

Frances slept restlessly, troubled by thoughts that Mary's questions had provoked and by bittersweet anticipation of Elizabeth's nuptials. Upon waking, she resolved to put aside gloomy reflections for her elder sister's sake. Mary queried her no more about slavery that day or the next, and neither she nor Betsey nor Sally spoke a word about the runaway or the curious mark carved into the old fencepost. Sewing with renewed determination, Frances finished the headpiece and veil with hours to spare before the family departed for Walnut Hill on February 14.

Elizabeth was a radiant bride, Ninian a most handsome and gallant groom. The wedding ceremony was poignant and joyful, and the reception Aunt Eliza had masterfully put together was merry, full of laughter and warmth. Frances hoped with all her heart that Elizabeth and Ninian would carry the love so fulsomely shared that day in their hearts for the rest of their lives.

Later that night, as the newlyweds bade their guests good-night and farewell, Elizabeth shared a few private words and an embrace with each of her sisters. To Frances she said—clasping her hands, eyes shining—that she prayed Frances would soon know the bliss and joyful anticipation she herself felt at that moment. "And if you can't find a worthy gentleman here," she added, smiling, "you'll have to come to us in Illinois. I've no doubt Ninian has many friends who would be honored to take a Todd sister as a bride."

"Be sure to save the most handsome one for me," Frances said lightly, although her heart trembled a bit at the thought of marrying anyone anytime soon. She would turn sixteen on her birthday three weeks thence, and crowded though some might call it, she was not ready to leave home quite yet.

Six weeks after the wedding, Ma gave birth to a son she and Papa named David. As soon as Ma recovered from her ordeal, she redoubled her efforts to convince Papa to move. He soon acquiesced, and in May he purchased a grand home only two blocks away on West Main Street, a large, double brick residence with a wide center hall, four chimneys, and numerous rooms with high ceilings, tall windows, and elegant, tasteful architectural embellishments. Large formal flower gardens surrounded the house, a small conservatory stood along the left side, and stables and slave quarters were a discreet distance away behind the house. Elkhorn Creek wound through the property, promising relaxing strolls along its banks and hours of play and exploration for the children.

The new house, a former inn, was wonderfully spacious, large enough to accommodate them all, even with the new baby. Thus it came as a surprise to all the Todd sisters when, in late summer, Ma announced that Mary would be enrolled in boarding school in the fall.

Madame Mentelle's Ladies' Academy was only one and a half miles down the Richmond Pike, quite near Mr. Clay's Ashland estate, but the proximity only made the arrangement more curious. Most of the academy's Lexington girls attended as day pupils, but not Mary. Every Monday morning, Nelson would drive her in the carriage to the school, where she would reside in the dormitory with girls from distant farms and towns until he brought her home again on Friday afternoon.

If Mary was displeased with the arrangement, or if she sensed that she was being removed for any reason other than to further her education, she never admitted it aloud. She was bright, intellectually curious, and sociable, and she soon emerged as one of the brightest and most popular students at the school.

Frances envied Mary her education, but not her living arrangements. Although on her weekend visits home Mary described Madame Mentelle's school as a kind of heaven on earth for clever girls, Frances wondered how she felt to be sent away when the move to a larger house plus Elizabeth's departure had made room enough for all. Even if, for the sake of argument, Frances conceded that someone had to leave, shouldn't cousin Betsey have returned to her own family before Mary was sent away?

Mary was too proud, so Frances would not ask her, but she could not help wondering how her sister endured it, knowing she was the one child for whom there was not enough room.

7

August 1875

ANN

In Elizabeth's well-ordered kitchen, Ann instructed the cook to prepare a pot of the ginger and raspberry leaf tea her sister insisted upon drinking and to set a few slices of lemon cake on a plate in hopes of tempting her appetite. Elizabeth had lost weight since her surgery, but in recent days she had been resting well and eating better, and color was returning to her wan cheeks. Her new physician assured the family that she would be restored to full health within a few weeks, but Ann did not trust the household servants to care for their mistress as assiduously as a sister would. Thus, every day for the past three weeks, after seeing her husband and eldest son off to work and Clara, Allen, and Minnie off to school, she had come to the gracious Edwards residence to watch over her eldest sister as she recuperated. Had Elizabeth not done as much for Ann during her own travails of the body and spirit?

When the tray was prepared, Ann carried it outside to the summer porch, where Elizabeth reclined on the chaise lounge, a gardening book momentarily forgotten on the cushion beside her, although she still marked her place with a finger.

"I promised Ninian you would eat something midmorning to make up for the breakfast you neglected," Ann said, mildly scolding, as she set the tray on the table beside her sister. "Don't make a liar of me."

Elizabeth smiled as she pushed herself up to a seated position, and Ann leapt forward to prop her up with pillows. "How are you feeling?" she asked, even though Elizabeth had sighed wearily not one hour before that she was tired of the question. How thankful the sisters were that Elizabeth had heeded Frances's advice and obtained a second opinion about the pains that were allegedly a figment of her imagination.

How shocked and frightened they all had been when Elizabeth's new doctor acknowledged that he had discovered growths in her womb, and how tremendously relieved they were when, after a second examination, the doctor assured them that the growths were neither cancerous nor likely to become so. He would have been inclined to leave them alone except for the pain, bleeding, and pressure on the bladder they caused. Privately, Frances had told Ann that she expected him to recommend a hysterectomy, which had become a considerably safer but no less drastic operation since it had been first attempted in America about thirty years before. To Frances's surprise, he instead proposed that he remove only the fibroids, surgically detaching them and leaving the womb otherwise intact. With the aid of chloroform, he promised, Elizabeth would sleep peacefully through the entire operation. If the relatively new procedure proved to have failed, she likely would have to endure a hysterectomy after all, but thus far all indications were that it had succeeded beyond expectations. Now all that remained was for her to heal and regain her strength.

"I'm feeling better than ever," she said as she reached for the teapot. Ann beat her to it and poured her a cup, which her sister accepted with a smile. "The pain of the surgery has passed, my original symptoms are gone, and every day I feel stronger. I think tomorrow I may work in the garden—"

"You may go for a brief stroll in the garden," Ann interrupted, "but work is out of the question. Not until the bleeding has stopped entirely."

"Yes, nurse," Elizabeth replied meekly, but when she sipped her tea, her eyes shone with amusement as she met Ann's gaze over the rim of her cup. Her good spirits were very reassuring, something their other sisters would want to know, which meant an evening of letter-writing for Ann. She need not write to Frances, of course, for she planned to stop by later that afternoon and would see for herself how well their eldest sister was faring. As for Mary, Frances saw no need to break their mutual silence to inform her of Elizabeth's steady recovery from an affliction about which Mary knew nothing. Elizabeth would not want her to do so, and Robert would probably object on the grounds that the news of her sister's infirmity would upset his mother. Ann reminded herself to warn Emilie not to mention Elizabeth's condition in her letters, but perhaps caution was unwarranted; the last Ann had heard, Emilie had written twice or thrice to Mary at Bellevue but had not received a single word in reply.

"Has the mail arrived yet?" asked Elizabeth, as if she had read Ann's thoughts. "I haven't heard from Julia in more than a fortnight."

"I'll check," said Ann, rising. "I wouldn't worry. You've said yourself that letters take an age to travel all the way from Buenos Aires. Several letters are undoubtedly on their way to you at this very moment."

She returned inside and passed through the house to the foyer. The morning post had arrived only moments before, and Ann found the housekeeper arranging the letters on a slim silver tray to carry out to her mistress. Ann completed the errand herself, pausing just inside the back door to leaf through the envelopes. There were three—none from Julia, sadly, nor did Ann recognize the other addresses.

The moment she stepped outside, Elizabeth's eyes met hers, and even before Ann shook her head, her sister knew that no word from Julia had come that day. "I'm sure you'll hear from her soon,"

Ann said, handing Elizabeth the tray and seating herself in the chair nearest her sister's.

"Perhaps I should send a telegram, just to be sure," murmured Elizabeth, thinking aloud as she opened the first envelope. "But the expense . . ." Her voice trailed off as she unfolded a single page and began to read. Her brow furrowed in puzzlement, and then she frowned, and by the time she reached the bottom of the page, she was shaking her head.

"What is it?" prompted Ann, impatient. "What's wrong?"

Sighing, Elizabeth held out the letter. "My words will not do it justice."

CHICAGO LEGAL NEWS COMPANY
151 & 153 Fifth Ave.

Chicago, July 30, 1875

Mrs. Edwards.
Dear Madam:
I have just returned from a visit to your dear sister, Mrs. Lincoln. She desires me to write to you asking you to come up and visit her and expresses a wish to return with you to Springfield. She feels her incarceration most terribly and desires to get out from behind the grates and bars. *I cannot feel that it is necessary to keep her thus restrained. Perhaps I do not look at the matter rightly, but let this be my excuse—I love her most tenderly and feel sorry to see one heartache added to her already overburdened soul.*

She has always spoken most tenderly of you and I do believe it would do her good to meet you and receive a sister's loving tenderness.

Pardon the liberty I have taken in addressing you and believe me, your sister's friend

Myra Bradwell

"Myra Bradwell?" said Ann, bewildered. The name seemed vaguely familiar. "Who is this woman that she has visited Mary when even Emilie was not welcome, and what is the Chicago Legal News Company?"

"The *Chicago Legal News* is a prestigious and widely read newspaper in law circles," said Elizabeth, gingerly picking up her teacup but forgetting to drink. "Ninian subscribed for many years. Mrs. Bradwell is the founder, publisher, and editor-in-chief of the paper, and she's considered the first lady lawyer in the United States. She's also a rather outspoken activist for numerous causes—woman's suffrage, legal rights for women—"

"And our sister has become her latest cause?"

"Apparently so." Elizabeth sipped her tea and returned the cup to its saucer. "My goodness. 'Grates and bars'? 'Incarceration' and 'heartache'?"

"A lawyer's rhetorical exaggeration, surely." Ann studied the letter again, shook her head, and returned it to Elizabeth. "Why does she write to you on Mary's behalf? Why didn't Mary write to you herself? Robert said that she's free to send and receive as many letters as she likes." And yet she had sent none to any of the Todd sisters. Ann attributed this strange reticence from a once-prolific letter-writer to both her illness and their estrangement.

"I don't know." Pensively, Elizabeth scanned the page. "How strange to hear that Mary speaks of me tenderly and wants me to visit, when we have not exchanged a word in ages."

"Stranger still that she wants to come here." Ann regarded her sister quizzically. "You aren't thinking of inviting her?"

"No, certainly not." Frowning, Elizabeth shifted in her seat, adjusting a pillow. "If she were well enough to leave the asylum, wouldn't Robert have told us? Wouldn't Dr. Patterson have written to inquire? Remember that Mary used to say that she could never return to Springfield, for it was haunted by too many memories of Abraham and her poor lost sons. In her present fragile state of mind, Springfield might be the very worst place for her to visit."

"Let's not forget about your own fragile state," said Ann, folding her arms, leaning back in her chair. "You're in no condition to play hostess to our troubled sister." Nor would Ann volunteer her own home, not that this Mrs. Bradwell had mentioned either her or Frances, or Emilie, Elodie, or Martha for that matter. Apparently, it was Elizabeth or no one.

"If Mary had written to me herself, perhaps I might be reassured that she is of sound mind and does indeed yearn to come here . . ." Elizabeth's voice trailed off, but then she added, "But she did *not* write to me, and so I cannot truly know what she wants. I have only the word of Mrs. Bradwell, whom I've never met. She calls herself Mary's friend, but how do I know what she is?"

"So many people have exploited Mary, or have tried to," said Ann. "If I were you, I'd proceed with caution."

"Certainly, and yet this letter requires a prompt reply."

Ann rose. "I'll fetch pen and paper."

Elizabeth held out a hand to stop her. "No, not just yet. I'll need time to think. Tomorrow will be soon enough. I'll want to speak with Ninian first, and with Frances."

Ann nodded and sat down, a trifle vexed that her own counsel would not suffice.

The rest of the day passed uneventfully. Ann saw to it that Elizabeth ate a healthy portion of a nourishing lunch and escorted her on a gentle stroll around the garden. She departed in the late afternoon, before Frances arrived and Ninian returned home from work, but not without admonishing the housekeeper and the maid to send a messenger immediately if her sister required anything at all from her. The maid replied that they had matters well in hand, her deferential curtsy taking none of the sting from her impertinent tone.

Upon returning to the Edwards residence the following morning, Ann saw to her sister's needs before broaching the subject of Mrs. Bradwell.

"I've written a reply," said Elizabeth, rising from the sofa. It was raining, so they sat in the parlor rather than on the summer porch. She disappeared down the hall toward the library, from whence she soon returned with a sheet of creamy, heavy paper embellished with her fine script. "I read it over to Frances and Ninian. They agree that it's an appropriate response, but if you dissent, please tell me."

"Oh, never fear," said Ann dryly, taking the letter. "I certainly shall."

Springfield, Aug. 3 1875

Mrs. Bradwell,
Dear Madam:

I haste to reply to your kind note, relative to my unhappy sister. My heart rebelled at the thought of placing her in an asylum; believing that her sad case merely required the care of a protector, whose companionship would be pleasant to her. Had I been consulted, I would have remonstrated earnestly against the step taken.

The judgment of others must now, I presume, be silently acquiesced in, for a time, in the hope that ere long, her physical and mental condition will be improved by rest and medical treatment. The sorrows that befell her in such rapid succession and the one, so tragic, was enough to shatter the nerves, and infuse the intellect of the bravest mind and heart. I regret to say that I cannot just now visit Mrs. Lincoln, being prostrated from the effects of a recent surgical operation. But I will at once write to her, and soothe her burdened heart, if possible, with words of love and sympathy.

It is my opinion that she should be indulged in a desire to visit her friends as the surest means of restoring her to health and cheerfulness.

Accept my thanks, for your interest in my sister, and the suggestions you have made me.

Yours truly

Mrs. N. W. Edwards

"Hmm," murmured Ann when she had finished.

"By which you mean . . ." prompted Elizabeth.

"It's a fine letter. I think 'haste' should be 'hasten,' but never mind."

Elizabeth laughed. "Surely you have more to say than that."

"Well, to begin, would you really have remonstrated against commitment if Robert had asked your opinion? Even though the panel of learned physicians recommended it?"

"Indeed, I would have."

"And whom would you have chosen as her companion and protector?"

"Why—" Elizabeth hesitated. "Perhaps her former companion, Mrs. Keckly."

"Former *friend* as well. I think you forget that Mary cut her off after that scandalous memoir." *Behind the Scenes*—what an apt title for a book that exposed their sister's private moments in the White House and reprinted her private letters without permission. "Do you truly believe Mary would ever welcome her back into the fold after that betrayal? Could you blame her?"

"No, I suppose not."

"There is no one suitable to serve as her constant companion and guardian—unless you mean to volunteer yourself, which I strongly discourage. You are barely out of a sickbed yourself."

"How carefully did you read?" protested Elizabeth, gesturing to her letter. "I wrote nothing about taking Mary into my home, only that I think she ought to visit friends. I believe that would do her good." She plucked the page from Ann's fingers. "Unless you have anything else to contribute, I shall send it."

It was true that Elizabeth must reply to Mrs. Bradwell, and Ann could think of nothing better to say, so she made an acquiescent bow and fetched her sister an envelope and a pen.

Several days passed, marked by gratifying signs of Elizabeth's steady recovery. If she did write to Mary with words of love and sympathy to soothe her burdened heart, as she had told Mrs. Bradwell she would, Ann did not witness the writing or the posting of any such letter.

Neither sister said anything more about Mrs. Bradwell until the second week of August, when Ann arrived at the Edwards residence at noon to find Elizabeth, her expression drawn, pacing in the garden and clasping and unclasping her hands, betraying her agitation. "Are you unwell?" asked Ann, fearing a relapse.

"Stronger every day," said Elizabeth, brushing aside her sister's concerns with a wave of her hand, "but greatly distressed. Oh, Ann, Mrs. Bradwell called on Mary again, and she showed my letter to Dr. Patterson. She argued that it was evidence that Mary's family condemns her commitment."

"What nerve," exclaimed Ann. "It is no such thing."

"She insisted that Dr. Patterson show the letter to Robert, which he did, and now—" Elizabeth wrung her hands. "Robert is quite displeased with me, as his most recent letter makes clear."

"He should save his displeasure for Mrs. Bradwell. How is this affair any of her business?"

"Mary reached out to her for help, and to her husband. You may have heard of Mr. Bradwell. He's a former county court judge and is currently a state legislator. I don't believe he represents Mary officially, but he does advise her on legal matters from time to time."

Ann felt a stirring of unease. First Mrs. Rayne from the *Post and Mail*, then the lawyer and gadfly Myra Bradwell, and now her distinguished husband. Mary was clearly rallying her troops. "How is it that Robert is displeased with you," she asked, "when he has so many others from whom to choose?"

"I did say that I would have objected to committing her to an asylum had I known in time, and Robert set that process in motion. I don't blame him for feeling obliged to defend himself."

Ann's eyebrows rose. "That must have been some letter."

With a wry twist to her mouth, Elizabeth withdrew a folded paper from her pocket and handed it over. While Ann sat down on a nearby bench to read, Elizabeth resumed her circuit of the garden, pausing now and then to pluck a faded blossom from a flowering shrub or to uproot a weed, or perhaps she was merely disguising the need to pause to catch her breath.

Robert's letter was not nearly as fiery as Ann had expected, given Elizabeth's distress. "There is no need for me to recount the past ten years of our domestic history. If it has caused you one tenth of the grief it has caused me, you will remember it," he began, but to Ann her nephew sounded more weary than angry. He described the facilities, staff, and programs of Bellevue in greater detail than she had yet read in any brochure or previous letter, and indeed she understood why, as he said, he considered it a great blessing that his mother was in a restful place where she could receive the attention and medical treatment she needed. He was certain that the tranquility of the estate and the absence of vexation had enabled his mother's condition to improve, but Dr. Patterson had warned him that Mr. and Mrs. Bradwell's visits threatened to undo all the good that had been accomplished. "What trouble Mrs. Bradwell may give me with her interference I cannot foretell," Robert added. "I understand she is a high priestess in a gang of Spiritualists and from what I have heard it is to their interest that my mother should be at liberty to control herself and her property." He had long been concerned that unscrupulous acquaintances would take advantage of his mother in her distress, which was one reason why he had wanted her removed to a more protective environment. Mrs. Bradwell seemed determined to extricate his mother from Bellevue before her reason was fully restored, a scheme that would prove dangerously reckless. In a recent conversation, his mother had implied that if she were released, she would immediately go abroad, where Robert would be unable to assist her should her debilitation return.

"I have no objection should my mother wish to visit you in Springfield," he concluded. "In fact, I believe this would benefit her significantly. In the meantime, I invite you to visit my mother and see Bellevue for yourself, rather than rely on the dubious claims and exaggerations of Mrs. Bradwell."

Sighing, Ann rose, folded the letter, and returned it to her sister. "Our nephew is upset, but not at you. Mrs. Bradwell is the object of his ire, and with good reason."

"Nevertheless, I owe him an apology." Elizabeth sank down upon the bench Ann had vacated. "I must write to him and explain that I regret questioning his decision, especially in a letter to a stranger—for Myra Bradwell is a stranger to us, despite her notoriety and her claims upon Mary's friendship."

Carefully, Ann prompted, "And his suggestions about an exchange of visits?"

Elizabeth spread her hands, a gesture of futility. "As you yourself have told me, I am in no condition to travel or to entertain Mary, in her present state. Robert will understand."

Ann was quite sure that he would, but before Elizabeth's reply had time to reach him at his home in Chicago, another letter from Mrs. Bradwell arrived.

CHICAGO LEGAL NEWS COMPANY
151 & 153 Fifth Ave.

Chicago, Aug. 11th, 1875

Dear Mrs. Edwards:

I came in from Batavia last Saturday afternoon. Stayed with your sister Friday night. Slept with her and saw not one symptom of insanity. She slept as sweetly and as quietly as a kitten. Robert tells me if you will take her, he will bring her down to Springfield. I do hope you will for she must be at liberty. Do please take her and love her and I am sure you will not have any trouble with her for Dr. Patterson told Mr. Bradwell and myself that he never had a patient that made him so little trouble.

I am so sorry for the dear woman, shut up in that place. When they tell me she is not restrained, I want to ask how they should like it themselves?

I hope to hear from you soon,

Kindly,

Myra Bradwell

The implication that Elizabeth would not love her sister without explicit instructions to do so from Mary's relentless advocate so upset her that a good measure of the vitality she had regained after her surgery dissipated. Ninian was so alarmed by her sudden relapse that he considered writing to the Bradwells to threaten legal action if they did not extricate themselves from what was a private, family matter. His brother-in-law Clark persuaded him to hold off, for the time being; Robert was Mary's executor, and it was up to him to order the Bradwells to leave his mother alone, if that was what he wanted and Dr. Patterson recommended.

Elizabeth felt obliged to inform Robert that Mrs. Bradwell had contacted her again. In the same letter, she explained that while she was willing to consider allowing Mary to come for a visit, it must be precisely that, a stay of limited duration, and a Bellevue nurse must accompany her. "The peculiarities of Mary's whole life have been so marked and well understood by me, that I have not indulged the faintest hope of a permanent cure," she confessed, astonishing Ann, who had believed her eldest sister to be far more optimistic about their sister's condition.

In closing, Elizabeth astonished Ann again. "I am unwilling to urge any steps, or assume any responsibility, in her case," she wrote. "My present feeble health, causing such nervous prostration, would render me a most unfit person to control an unsound mind. I am now satisfied, that understanding her propensities as you do, the course you have decided upon is the surest and wisest."

Ann had never known Elizabeth to absolve herself of responsibility for her younger siblings, and she would not have believed it had she not seen it written in Elizabeth's own hand.

Yet, soon thereafter, Elizabeth confessed that although she could not visit Bellevue herself, she would feel greatly relieved if someone she knew well and trusted implicitly would call on Mary and report back to her. Emilie was proposed, but Mary's lack of response to her letters had hurt and bewildered her, and she was reluctant to make the trip, not knowing whether she would be admitted. The sisters had no reason to believe Mary would welcome Ninian or Clark, and as for Ann, she did not want to go and made excuses why she could not.

In the end, they decided to send two of their daughters—Elizabeth's daughter and namesake, Lizzy, a widow thirty-two years old, with Ann's seventeen-year-old Clara as a traveling companion. According to Robert, Mary delighted in her granddaughter Mamie's visits, so perhaps she would be pleased to see her grandnieces as well.

Ann was satisfied, and Elizabeth was greatly relieved, when the two younger women returned from Batavia to report that

Great-Aunt Mary had welcomed them cheerfully. Before and after taking tea with her, they had toured the facilities and the grounds and had found everything to be exactly as their cousin Robert had described it. "There is nothing wrong with Bellevue that would not be mended if Mrs. Bradwell and her husband would simply mind their own business," Lizzy said. "Their meddling does no good and may do great harm, if it persists."

Ann and Elizabeth could not agree more, but what could mere sisters do to keep the interlopers at bay?

8

1832–1839

ELIZABETH

Elizabeth and Ninian spent their first few months as newly-weds living modestly in Lexington, enjoying the novelty of life as an ordinary law student and his devoted wife rather than a son of the former governor of Illinois and a daughter of the illustrious Todd family. Elizabeth had little housekeeping to do in their boardinghouse suite, so when she was not helping Ninian by keeping his clothes in order, fetching books from the library, or taking dictation while he worked out essays and legal theses aloud, she had plenty of leisure time to devote to reading, calling on friends, and visiting her family's luxurious new residence on Main Street. Knowing that Grandma Parker had taken her father's removal of her grandchildren from their shared lot as a personal offense, Elizabeth took care to call on her at least once a week too. She often brought Frances along, and Mary as well, on weekends when she came home from Madame Mentelle's Ladies' Academy.

Although her younger sisters endeavored not to complain, Elizabeth knew Frances and Mary were unhappy at home. The house on Main Street was their stepmother's domain, where the offspring of Papa's first marriage were tolerated but never made to feel as if they truly belonged. Frances and Mary sometimes argued about who suffered more: Frances, permitted to live at home with the family but expected to help keep house and mind the children, or Mary, singled out as the least wanted but provided with an excellent education to compensate. She was learning to speak French fluently, starring in school theatricals, and studying the classics, history, natural science, and dancing—and when not engrossed in her books and lessons, she enjoyed the company of many new friends. After these ongoing debates, Frances and Mary usually concurred that Mary was the more enviably placed of the two. Even so, Frances looked smug as she acknowledged that at least she was wanted at home, and Mary looked forlorn, knowing she was not.

Elizabeth gave her sisters a sympathetic ear and a place of refuge for as long as she could, but in due course her darling Ninian earned his degree and moved them to his hometown of Belleville, Illinois, across the river from St. Louis, where he worked as a lawyer and dabbled in local politics. Elizabeth had scarcely settled in when Ninian's father unexpectedly passed away, a victim of a deadly cholera epidemic that swept through the frontier states in that terrible summer of 1833. Although the Todd family was spared, in large part because Papa evacuated Ma and the children to the resort town of Crabb Orchard Springs when the first rumors of disease began to circulate, Lexington suffered a dreadful blow. In the span of ten days in June, fifteen hundred citizens fell ill and nearly fifty a day perished. In a heartrending, terrifying letter, a friend of Elizabeth's who had lost her parents and two brothers described the prohibition of public gatherings, the scarcity of coffins that was forcing mourners to bury their loved ones in old trunks and boxes brought down from attics, and the silent streets deserted except for horses slowly pulling carts stacked with the dead.

In Springfield, the disease had not been nearly as apocalyptic, but the Edwards family had lost its patriarch, and although Elizabeth had not known her father-in-law long, she mourned him sincerely. Governor Edwards had been a generous father, and as his eldest child, Ninian received a substantial inheritance. When his father's successor appointed him attorney general in 1834, Ninian purchased a magnificent home on Aristocracy Hill in Springfield. Splendid and spacious, the house had well-appointed parlors and dining rooms for entertaining, as well as numerous spare bedrooms for guests. The residence quickly became a hub of society's younger set, and as Ninian achieved one political advancement after another and Elizabeth forged many close friendships, invitations to dinners, balls, teas, and soirees at the Edwards residence became highly sought after among the Springfield elite.

There were, of course, sorrows to temper their joys. They were three years married when Elizabeth gave birth to their first child, a precious babe who died in her arms a few days later. Elizabeth wept and grieved, longing for her child, for her absent sisters, but she was comforted by the kindness of friends and by Ninian's steadfast love and assurances that they would try again.

By spring, Elizabeth had recovered from her physical ordeal, although a heaviness lingered in her heart, sometimes present only at the edge of her awareness but always with her. In the forge of loss, she had become more empathetic to others' unhappiness, and when she contemplated her younger sisters' difficulties at home, she resolved to help.

"I'd like to invite Frances for an extended visit," she told Ninian one morning over breakfast. "Ma has nine children at home with another expected in November, and next month Mary completes her studies at Madame Mentelle's and will move back home for good. The overcrowding will be unbearable, and the burden of keeping the peace will fall upon Frances's shoulders."

Ninian smiled and reached for her hand across the table. "And who better than a doting older sister to offer her refuge?"

"I'm not thinking only of her," Elizabeth admitted, clasping his hand in hers. "I long for my sister's company. It will do my heart good to see her enjoying herself for a change, to be merry and smiling among young ladies and gentlemen her own age, instead of constantly surrounded by the clamor of small children."

What she did not say was that Frances was nearly twenty, and if she was going to find a husband among the young gentlemen of her acquaintance in Lexington, she likely would have done so already. She could not bear to imagine Frances as a lonely spinster living in her stepmother's shadow for the rest of her days.

"How long would you like Frances to stay?" asked Ninian.

"As long as she likes," replied Elizabeth. "Indefinitely. Until she has another home to go to and need not return to Papa and Ma, where they have no room for elder siblings."

Ninian's eyebrows rose, and she knew he understood that the object was to find Frances a good husband. It was well that he did not object, for Elizabeth expected him to steer his most eligible bachelor friends in Frances's direction.

Frances eagerly accepted her sister's invitation, and as it turned out, by the time she came to them in October of 1836, Elizabeth had happy news to share: she was expecting again. "How glad I am that you will be here to help me through my ordeal," Elizabeth told her after divulging the wonderful secret.

Frances glowed with the happy pride of knowing she was needed and wanted. "No gladder than I am to be here. I promise to help you however I can."

"I didn't invite you here only to wait on me," said Elizabeth, nudging her playfully. "I've arranged a very full social calendar for you, and I insist that you thoroughly enjoy yourself."

Frances laughed and promised she would try.

True to her word, Frances reveled in parties, dances, and dinners throughout the autumn and into the winter, striking up friendships with young ladies in the Coterie, as the members of their clique called themselves, and making the acquaintance of many charming young men. But the sisters also enjoyed quieter, companionable hours sitting together in the parlor or conservatory, reading, sewing, or knitting, reminiscing about bygone days and gossiping about new acquaintances. Their conversations often turned to politics. They were Todds, after all, and since childhood they had been offered a healthy portion of political talk with nearly every meal at their father's table.

Ninian, a Whig like Papa and Mr. Clay, was serving in the state legislature, and the summer leading up to the August elections had been especially contentious. In June, Colonel Robert Allen, a Democrat of Springfield running for the legislature, had announced in a campaign speech that he possessed certain shocking facts that, if known to the public, would destroy Ninian's chance for reelection, as well as the chances of two other Whigs, the sisters' cousin John Todd Stuart and John's junior law partner, Abraham Lincoln. According to Ninian, Mr. Lincoln had written an eloquent letter to Colonel Allen urging him to divulge the alleged facts, "whether they be real or imagined," so they could be examined and their veracity determined. In July, another Democrat, Dr. Jacob Early, brought up the mysterious facts in a debate; when Ninian shouted him down and declared his charges absolutely false, Dr. Early challenged him to a duel. Thankfully, Mr. Lincoln spoke next, and he handled the subject in dispute with such eloquence and clarity that his listeners were astonished, and all thoughts of a duel were abandoned. Ultimately, Colonel Allen's specious allegations had done lasting damage: both Ninian and Mr. Lincoln had easily won reelection in August, but cousin John, who had forgone the state legislature in a bid for Congress, lost his seat.

"You and Ninian are always speaking of this Mr. Lincoln," remarked Frances one evening as she and Elizabeth were relaxing by the fireside before bed. "You all seem very impressed with him. Why have you never had him up the hill for dinner?"

Elizabeth hesitated before explaining, for when she tried to frame it in words, the omission seemed terribly snobbish and unkind. After all, Mr. Lincoln was their cousin's law partner, and like Ninian he was one of the famed "Long Nine," a group of nine senators and representatives, each over six feet tall and sharing similar political philosophies, who represented Sangamon County in the Illinois General Assembly. Their most ambitious endeavor was their effort to move the state capital from Vandalia to Springfield, a measure that naturally was very popular with their constituents. By those measures, he seemed a natural fit for the Edwardses' dinner table.

But while Mr. Lincoln was a brilliant lawyer, a skilled politician, a gifted orator, and a man of sterling character, he was also uncultured and roughly hewn, a self-educated backwoodsman and veteran of the Black Hawk War who had risen above his humble origins by sheer force of will and native intellect. Although no one doubted the quality of his mind, his intelligence, or his amiability, he had no family connections to recommend him, his attire and grooming were astonishingly careless, and he displayed none of the habits or the demeanor expected of a gentleman. He seemed uncomfortable and awkward in society, unfamiliar with the customs and norms that Ninian and the other men of their class had learned as boys. For a man of renowned eloquence in the courtroom and on the political stump, Mr. Lincoln struggled to engage in pleasant small talk with the ladies, with whom he seemed embarrassed and tongue-tied. He also had a gloomy aspect that his jokes and tall tales could only momentarily dispel, a perpetual melancholy that some attributed to the tragic loss of his beloved fiancée, Miss Ann Rutledge of New Salem, Illinois, who had succumbed to typhoid less than a year before. And yet, despite his ostensible shortcomings, Ninian and his acquaintances never spoke of Mr. Lincoln with anything but admiration and respect. Everyone believed he could go quite far, and since he had already exceeded all reasonable expectations, no one could predict how high he might climb.

"He seems a worthy gentleman, despite his rude origins," said

Frances, her tone mildly scolding, after Elizabeth tried to explain. Abashed, Elizabeth promised to invite Mr. Lincoln to join them at their next dinner party.

He accepted with a note that was gracious, eloquent, and self-deprecating all at once, confirming Elizabeth's misgivings that an invitation had been long overdue. On the night of the dinner, he amused the men with humorous stories and jokes, endeared himself to most of the ladies with his bashfulness and unmistakable kindness, and charmed Elizabeth herself without apparently trying to do so. He evidently made a fair impression upon Frances as well, for she agreed to let him call on her, twice coming for tea in the parlor. She accepted his invitation to escort her to an academic lecture in town, and he kept company with her at a levee at their cousin John's home. But the spark, if such it was, never quite caught fire, and by spring it was evident that Frances had lost interest.

"He's a good man, an excellent man, but—" Frances paused to search for the words. "I'm abashed to say it, but he is deficient in the little niceties of romance that warm a woman's heart. Is it shallow of me that I mind this? He pays no attention to his appearance, he has made no effort to improve his shabby clothes or his unkempt hair, and the art of flirtation is utterly lost on him. And—well, he isn't what one would call classically handsome, is he?"

"No, he is not, at that," admitted Elizabeth, without noting that other qualities—his integrity, intelligence, and kindness— were far more important in a marriage than fine clothes and debonair manners. She kept this observation to herself, because in truth she was relieved that Frances had not formed an attachment to him. Despite his many fine qualities and great potential, he was quite poor, and he simply did not come from the same exalted sphere that the Todds, Parkers, and Edwardses inhabited. She could not imagine that Frances, brought up in the same genteel fashion as all the Todd sisters, would be content as the wife of a penniless country lawyer.

Thus, Mr. Lincoln returned to what he had formerly been to the family: Ninian's Whig colleague in the legislature and cousin John's law partner, but a potential suitor to a Todd sister no longer.

In April, Elizabeth gave birth to a beautiful daughter whom she and Ninian named Julia. Soon thereafter, Mary came to visit for the summer and helped with the baby, while also enjoying the whirl of social gaiety, as Frances had done before her, and reveling in the political discussions that filled every dinner and levee at the Edwards residence with crackling energy and great expectations for the future. The mix of intelligent, ambitious men and beautiful, clever women created an intoxicating atmosphere in which even Elizabeth, a respectable wife and mother, thrilled to partake.

At the end of the summer, Mary returned rather reluctantly to Lexington to live at home and pursue an advanced course of study with her former teacher, Dr. Ward. Having heard so many stories about the remarkable and peculiar Mr. Lincoln, she regretted that she had not had the opportunity to meet him during her visit. They might have crossed paths at any number of society gatherings, but Mr. Lincoln had been too busy with his burgeoning law practice and with serving in the Tenth Assembly to be out and about.

"I'll introduce you the next time you visit," Elizabeth promised. "I hope you are not disappointed if he does not live up to his billing."

"May the day of that visit come soon," Mary replied fervently, with a forlorn little smile.

Elizabeth understood that it was Springfield Mary would miss, not the introduction to Mr. Lincoln that she regretted deferring. Embracing her, Elizabeth murmured soothing reassurances, pained to see her vivacious younger sister's light dimming at the prospect of returning to their stepmother's household. Madame Mentelle's school had always felt more like home to her than Ma's house on Main Street, but her years there had come to an end.

Elizabeth resolved to invite Mary back for a lengthier visit as soon as Frances was properly settled.

Months passed before Elizabeth glimpsed any sign that such a day was on the horizon. Frances enjoyed flirtations with several young men in the Coterie, but it was some time before her heart warmed to any one gentleman in particular. Dr. William S. Wallace, a native of Pennsylvania who had studied at Jefferson Medical College in Philadelphia, had come west intending to embark on a new career in land speculation, but after he settled in Springfield, the need for doctors had been so great that the citizens had prevailed upon him to return to the practice of medicine. He had done so willingly and had opened a drugstore as well. The Golden Mortar was located on the first floor of an office building just below the law practice of cousin John Todd Stuart and Mr. Lincoln. The two lawyers frequented the shop often, especially Mr. Lincoln, who enjoyed passing idle hours entertaining the men who gathered around its potbellied stove with jokes and stories. It was through their friendship that Frances became acquainted with Dr. Wallace, and what a momentous introduction it proved to be.

Neither Elizabeth nor Ninian saw their romance coming. Dr. Wallace was intelligent and amiable, but he was fourteen years older than Frances, with no political ambitions and only modest skills as a businessman. Yet he was admired as a physician and respected as a gentleman of the community, and he must have been proficient in "the little niceties of romance that warm a woman's heart," for he certainly warmed Frances's.

On a lovely spring day in May 1839, Frances married William in the flower-bedecked parlor of the Edwards residence, surrounded by her friends from the Coterie and his from the Springfield business community. If Frances had any misgivings about leaving her comfortable suite in her sister's home on Aristocracy Hill for a modest room at the Globe Tavern, a humble, two-story, wooden inn near the statehouse, she was too much in love to dwell upon them. Besides, Elizabeth assured herself, their new lodgings were only temporary. Eventually William would save up enough money to move his bride into more suitable accommodations. Such a move would be necessary, in fact, once children came along.

Soon after the wedding, Elizabeth wrote to Mary to tell her about the ceremony; about Frances's lovely white satin gown; about the warm, loving looks the couple shared as they spoke their vows; about the excellent wedding supper, for Elizabeth's cook had absolutely outdone herself for the occasion; about the merriment of the assembled guests; and about the certain hopes the couple had of future happiness.

And now, since Frances was settled and their best guest room was vacant, Elizabeth concluded her letter with an invitation. "Come and make our home your home," she wrote, fulfilling a promise she had made two years before.

Mary was already twenty-one, and although she had entertained many ardent suitors in Lexington, none of them had been intelligent, witty, or intriguing enough to hold her interest long. "Among her beaux are many scholarly, intelligent men," cousin Betsey had written to Elizabeth not long before, her dismay and exasperation evident in every line. "Yet she never at any time shows the least partiality for any of them. Indeed, at times her expression indicates a decided lack of interest, and she endures their attention without enthusiasm. Without meaning to wound, she often cannot restrain a witty, sarcastic phrase that cuts deeper than she intends. There is no malice in her heart, but she is impulsive and makes no attempt to conceal her feelings. Indeed, that would be impossible, for her face betrays every passing emotion."

Cousin Betsey despaired that Mary might never find a husband if she did not temper her wit and learn to say more with a demure glance than a sharp tongue. Elizabeth had to laugh to imagine her sister, skilled at school theatricals though she had been, attempting such a ruse. Mary simply had not yet met the man who could adore her as she was, who could match her wit for wit.

Perhaps she would meet that man in Springfield.

9

August–September 1875

EMILIE

Emilie was grateful that Robert and her sisters in Springfield kept her informed about Mary's condition, since Mary would not or could not reply to her letters, but as the summer passed their piecemeal reports became increasingly frustrating to her. Assembling a complete picture of Mary's circumstances from the details scattered among so many different letters became a nearly impossible task when one sister would unwittingly contradict something Robert had written, or when vague ellipses in their letters suggested they were not telling her all that they knew or suspected.

Perhaps her sisters held back out of kindness, to spare her feelings. They must have guessed how it had wounded her to learn that Mary frequently begged the bedridden Elizabeth to visit—never directly, always using Robert or Mrs. Bradwell as intermediaries—while Emilie's offers to come to Bellevue had been rebuffed by silence.

Hurt and bewildered, Emilie had mulled over the snub and eventually had concluded that Mary meant no offense. Elizabeth and Emilie simply filled very different roles in her life, and at the moment, in her fragile condition, she needed Elizabeth—the eldest, the caregiver, the sister whose embrace they all sought in times of fear or sorrow. To Mary, Emilie would always be the

Little Sister, lost and needing protection, even though she was a woman of almost thirty-nine years with children of her own. Her elder siblings' inability to see her as more than a helpless child vexed Emilie beyond measure, especially since she had more than proven herself by successfully raising her three children, using her musical training to support her family, and managing a household quite capably, all without a husband by her side.

Perhaps their delusions persisted because Emilie was the second-youngest of all the Todd siblings and it was hard to think of her as anything but the baby. Perhaps it was because she had been widowed so early in her marriage and, at the time, her circumstances had been so desperate that she had indeed needed her mother and sisters to rescue her.

Perhaps it was because they had never forgotten how, years before, she had almost been lost to the family forever, and their excessive vigilance now was their unwitting attempt to atone for their neglect then.

Elizabeth was already married and William was courting Frances the day two-year-old Emilie went missing. One minute she was in Mammy Sally's care, and the next she had vanished. When a search of the house and garden turned up no sign of her, Papa contacted the police. The alert was sounded, and nearly everyone in Lexington turned out to search. Levi, George, and Nelson joined the groups combing the nearby fields and creek banks, while Papa, Mary, Ann, and hundreds of others scoured the city, fanning out from the Todd residence to knock on doors, alert neighbors, and query other children they encountered along the way. They went down alleyways and peered into dark, filthy places a sweet little girl never would have entered of her own volition. All the while, Ma remained at home with the younger children and the servants, pacing, increasingly frantic, awaiting word, fearing the worst.

By midafternoon Papa had made his way nearly a mile from the house, much farther than toddler Emilie could have wandered on her own. He was searching down a narrow alley when he glanced up and spotted her watching him through a window. Racing to the stoop, Papa pounded on the door until it opened and the occupant emerged—a man a few years older than himself, his eyes red-rimmed, his mouth twisted in grief. Pushing past him, Papa snatched up Emilie, confirmed that she was unharmed, and then turned upon the man furiously, demanding an explanation. Shaking, the man replied that he had found Emilie wandering the streets, and since he and his wife had no children, he had decided to bring her home to raise as their own. "The child is so uncommonly beautiful," he said as tears flowed down his cheeks. "It overcame my sense of right."

Moved by pity, Papa had declined to press charges. Back at home, the family, shaken but relieved, rejoiced to have Emilie restored to them, and she was watched very carefully from that day forward.

Years later, when Emilie was home during a break between terms at the conservatory, she had asked Frances about that day. "My own memories are quite vague," she had admitted. "I remember playing with a doll while a woman sang to me, and I remember Papa shouting at the man, but I don't recall being carried off or how I came to be wandering alone on the streets."

"We were never certain how you were lost," Frances had replied. "I've always supposed that Mammy Sally had taken you out on some errand or to play at the park, and in one of her drunken spells, she misplaced you."

"Mammy Sally had drunken spells?"

"You don't remember?"

Emilie had shaken her head, taken aback. Her beloved mammy, an irresponsible drunkard? The very thought of it had been utterly incongruous with every childhood memory.

"She got drunk whenever she had the chance, which fortunately wasn't often. Auntie Chaney kept Papa's liquor under lock and key, and Mammy Sally rarely scraped together enough money to buy any herself."

"I don't understand. Why would she have taken to drink?"

Frances had fixed her with a level gaze. "You really can't imagine why? Perhaps it was the only escape she had."

Immediately Emilie had recognized the point her abolitionist half-sister was trying to make, but she could not believe it. The Todd family was kind to their servants. They were a beloved, essential part of the family. How on earth could Mammy Sally be so unhappy that she would drown her sorrows in drink?

She had decided that Frances must have been mistaken—after all, she had been in Springfield at the time—but Emilie had never found any other reasonable explanation for how she came to be on the streets alone. Thank God Papa had found her and thwarted her kidnapping, not that the sad, childless couple had meant her any harm. Her parents and elder siblings never forgot how close they had come to losing her, and their instinct to protect her had endured until the present day—which might explain why they withheld from her the more upsetting details of Mary's confinement at Bellevue.

If not for Robert, Emilie might have felt completely in the dark. Throughout the summer, he had written her long letters freely confiding his increasing concern about the Bradwells. His mother had been content at Bellevue until they began visiting her, he complained, and their clamoring for her release made her nervous and excitable, undoing all the progress she had made earlier that spring. Robert was furious when he discovered that on one visit the Bradwells had brought an acquaintance along: Mr. Franc Wilkie, the lead writer for the sensationalist *Chicago Times* newspaper, and a complete stranger to Mary, Robert, and Dr. Patterson. That the Bradwells had chosen a Saturday for their visit, when they knew Dr. Patterson would not be at the asylum, was especially outrageous. Afterward, Dr. Patterson had warned

Mrs. Bradwell that she must thereafter obtain Robert's permission to visit Mary, especially if anyone unknown to the family accompanied her. To make this point unmistakably clear, Robert had met with her in person and, after politely thanking her for her concern, had told her to visit less often, never to bring along people whom he did not know, and not to carry letters from his mother to anyone other than family.

Regrettably, the meeting did nothing to deter Mary's determined self-appointed advocate. When Robert and his family departed for a much-needed vacation in Rye Beach, New Hampshire, Mrs. Bradwell set her sights on Elizabeth. In the third week of August, she turned up on the Edwardses' doorstep to argue the case for Mary's release—which, as a skilled, highly motivated lawyer, she did with aplomb. That very afternoon, Elizabeth wrote to Robert claiming that she had not expressed herself well in her previous letters, and that in truth she did not object to Mary leaving the asylum. "It may be that a refusal to yield to her wishes in this crisis will greatly increase her disorder," she pointed out. "I now say, that if you will bring her down to Springfield, and are feeling perfectly willing to make the experiment, I promise to do all in my power for her comfort and recovery."

That same day Robert received an unsettling letter from Dr. Patterson, written after the Bradwells' most recent visit to Bellevue. They had met with Mary privately for an hour and then, upon leaving, had stopped by the doctor's office to declare that she ought to be released to her sister in Springfield immediately, for confinement was injuring her health. When Dr. Patterson showed them a letter Elizabeth had written to Robert explaining that she could not take Mary into her home owing to her recent surgery, the Bradwells insisted that "improper influences had been brought to bear upon Mrs. E.," or she never would have refused to take Mary in.

"So much discussion with Mrs. Lincoln about going away tends to unsettle her mind and make her more discontented, and should be stopped," Dr. Patterson had concluded. "She should be let alone and this I have told Judge Bradwell. She should never have been subjected to this unnecessary excitement. It is now apparent that the frequent visits of Mrs. B. have stirred up discontent & thus have done harm."

Robert could endure no more. First, he telegraphed Dr. Patterson, instructing him to keep his mother in treatment at Bellevue and to cut off "absolutely all communication with improper persons." Next, Robert wrote to Elizabeth to inform her of the doctor's opinion that the Bradwells' interference was harming Mary and to urge her not to entertain them or their notions any longer. Lastly, he wrote to Emilie to tell her about his communications with the others and to fume about the whole exhausting, unnecessary affair.

"Surely this will be the end of it," Emilie had written back. "At the very least, you have won a respite. The restrictions you have imposed will give your mother time to recover from the setbacks the Bradwells have caused. Upon your return to Chicago in September, they may again demand to see her and prevail upon you to secure her release, but until then, they can cause you, and her, no more trouble."

Her letter was probably still on its way to Robert when she learned how very wrong she was.

One warm late August morning between breakfast and the arrival of her first pupil of the day, Emilie was practicing a particularly challenging section of the *friska* of Liszt's Hungarian Rhapsody No. 2 when she sensed rather than heard someone just beyond her peripheral vision. Everyone knew not to interrupt her at the piano unless it was very important, so after finishing a measure, Emilie lifted her hands from the keys and turned on the bench to discover her daughter Katherine lingering in the doorway, holding a newspaper, her expression uncertain.

For a moment Emilie's breath caught in her throat. Sometimes Katherine so strikingly resembled her dear Ma, who had passed away little more than a year ago at the age of seventy-four, that Emilie was overcome by sudden emotion, a cascade of love and wistfulness. "What is it, darling?" she asked, beckoning her daughter forward.

"You must not have read the papers this morning or you would know." Katherine folded the paper in half as she approached and indicated a column just beneath the masthead. "If this is true, then it's wonderful news, but why didn't cousin Robert telegraph to tell us?"

Emilie hesitated before accepting the paper, then braced herself and began to read.

MRS. LINCOLN RECOVERING HER REASON.

Mrs. M. L. Rayne writes to the Chicago *Post and Mail* from St. Charles, in the vicinity of Bellevue Hospital, to which Mrs. Lincoln was sent from Chicago, as follows:

You will be glad to learn—and this is the first public intimation of it—that Mrs. Lincoln is pronounced well enough to leave the Asylum and visit her sister Mrs. Edwards, of Springfield. It is not likely she will return to Bellevue Place, as there is some feeling evinced in the matter of her incarceration, by friends who refuse to believe her insane. A leading lady lawyer, of Chicago, has been with her much of late, and, with the assistance of her legal husband, will assist Mrs. Lincoln's restoration to the world. She is decidedly better, sleeps and eats well, and shows no tendency to any mania, but whether the cure is permanent or not, the test of active life and time will prove.

"'A leading lady lawyer,'" Emilie read aloud. "Who else but that dreadful Mrs. Bradwell? Robert has prevented her from appealing for his mother's release privately, so the Bradwells will force a hearing in the press." She set the paper on the far end of the bench, resisting the temptation to fling it aside. "Katherine, dear, I'm afraid your aunt Mary is still very much unwell. The Bradwells are simply trying to force your cousin Robert and Dr. Patterson to release her with this very premature announcement. When your aunt Mary does not appear in Springfield soon, the Bradwells expect the public to demand why her release was suddenly canceled."

"What is wrong with these meddlesome people?" asked Katherine. "Don't they realize the harm that could come to Aunt Mary if she leaves the asylum before she's cured?"

"Perhaps they sincerely believe that she is not and never was insane." Emilie sighed and rubbed her forehead where a slow, dull ache was forming. She could only hope that the Bradwells did not have a more sinister motive.

By now Robert surely knew of the Bradwells' leak to the press; newspapers in the East had undoubtedly reprinted the *Post and Mail* piece, just as the Kentucky papers had. Emilie could image her nephew striding along a forest path in New Hampshire, quietly furious, considering how to respond, or whether it would be best to maintain a dignified silence. Her heart went out to him. The burden of his mother's illness was enough to bear without the Bradwells and Mrs. Rayne casting aspersions and attempting to force his hand.

Two days later, Katherine was waiting for her at the breakfast table, her expression anxious as she slid a newspaper closer to Emilie's plate.

"What is it now, my love?" asked Emilie wearily. She beckoned the maid to pour the coffee. Bad news was best taken on an empty stomach, but she could not face whatever awaited her without coffee.

"A second salvo," said Katherine, indicating a column in the center of the page above the fold.

Emilie took her time stirring cream and sugar into her coffee, raising the cup to her lips, and taking a deep drink. Then she could delay no longer.

MRS. LINCOLN

Judge Bradwell Tells a Post and Mail Reporter
What He Thinks of Her Confinement

Chicago, August 23.—Judge Bradwell to-day said to a *Post and Mail* reporter: I have no hesitation whatever in saying that Mrs. Lincoln ought not to be where she is now, and never ought to have been placed there. It was a gross outrage to imprison her there behind grates and bars, in a place understood to be for mad people. Why, to be so shut up and guarded, and locked up at night, with the feeling that it may last for life, is enough to make almost any aged and delicate woman crazy. She is no more insane today than you and I are. I am as thoroughly convinced of it as of my own existence. I have had several business letters from her since she has been there, and Mrs. Bradwell has had letters of womanly friendship from her repeatedly, and she writes as straight and intelligible a business letter as she ever did and as good friendly letters as one need ask for. There is not the slightest trace of insanity or of a weak mind about any of her writings. When I last visited her, one week ago to-day, she sighed and pleaded for liberty like a woman shut up without cause. Said she to me: "Mr. Bradwell, what have I done that I should be kept here in this prison, behind these grates, my footsteps followed, and every action watched by day, and my bedroom door locked upon the outside at night, and the key taken away by my jailer? Surely 'I am not mad, but soon shall be.' I want liberty to go among my friends."

Emilie was trembling from outrage by the time she reached the last line. What a brazen ploy, to declare before the public that Mary was the victim of unjust imprisonment! How dare they accuse Robert and Dr. Patterson—indeed, the entire panel of learned physicians who had appeared at the trial—of incompetence at best, malice and cruelty at worst?

Yet amid her distress and indignation, Emilie also felt a prick of envy. Mary had evidently written a great many letters to the Bradwells. Emilie wished her sister had spared a moment to send one to her too, if only so that she might see for herself whether Judge Bradwell's claims about the quality of Mary's writing—and by extension, her mind—were true.

Lest anyone doubt the Bradwells' resolve, the very next day Franc Wilkie, the *Chicago Times* reporter who had accompanied the couple when they visited Mary earlier that month, published an exclusive interview beneath the cumbersome headline, "REASON RESTORED: Mrs. Lincoln Will Soon Return from Her Brief Visit to the Insane Asylum; for Her Physicians Pronounce Her Sane as Those Who Sent Her There; and She Is Only Awaiting Robert's Return from the East to Set Her Free Again." The rest of the column ostensibly offered an objective analysis of Mary's health based upon scientific facts and the personal observations of a disinterested third party. The conclusion was that Mary, unjustly imprisoned, was no more insane than the men who had condemned her to the asylum.

It was too much, and yet it was far from over.

In the days that followed, as Judge Bradwell's interview and Mr. Wilkie's falsely optimistic article were reprinted in papers across the country, other reporters pounced on the story, embellishing the original with biographical details about the persons involved, speculating about Mary's condition, questioning Judge Bradwell's role in the case, and defending Robert as an upstanding citizen and dutiful son who would not, under any circumstances whatsoever, have his mother committed without just cause. Several editorials indignantly questioned why the Bradwells had involved themselves so intimately in a private matter, especially since the family had clearly expressed their desire to be left alone. One newspaper referred to the Bradwells as "Intermeddling Mischief Makers," a title that fit them as well as any Emilie could devise.

Eventually Dr. Patterson felt compelled to set the record straight in a letter to the editor of the *Chicago Tribune*, because, he said, "now that so many incorrect statements have been made, I deem it proper to correct some of them." "Mrs. Lincoln is certainly much improved, both mentally and physically," he noted, "but I have not at any time regarded her as a person of sound mind. I believe her to be now insane." Even so, he did not object to her visiting her sister in Springfield, but he did not believe this would restore her reason. As for charges of false imprisonment, his accusers were free to pursue options other than castigating him in the press: "Mrs. Lincoln has been placed where she is under the forms of law, and, if any have grievance, the law is open to them."

Dr. Patterson's letter was such a thorough and well-reasoned refutation that it should have brought the all too public dispute to an end, and the growing disgust with the Bradwells on the part of the press and the citizenry should have further induced them to withdraw. But Emilie had come to expect the worst from the Bradwells, so she did not allow her hopes to rise too high.

Thus, she was appalled but not surprised the following morning when Mary's would-be champions published their most brazen and salacious article to date: "MRS. LINCOLN: Is the Widow of President Lincoln a Prisoner? No One Allowed to See Her Except by Order of Her Son." The so-called "entirely truthful eyewitness account" that followed, a description of a visit to the tormented and pitiful former first lady, was clearly the work of Myra Bradwell. Emilie was so sickened and outraged by the heavily fictionalized narrative depicting her nephew Robert as a cruel gaoler and ungrateful son that she could not finish reading it.

In early September, Emilie received another letter from her nephew, this time posted from Chicago. Robert had returned home after a holiday that had proved far less restful than he and his wife had hoped, he noted wryly, and he had scarcely had time to unpack before he had been confronted by "the extraordinary performances of the Bradwells."

"After assuring you of my safe arrival home, my next duty will be to write to Dr. Patterson to inquire if it would be safe to grant my mother a visit to Aunt Elizabeth in Springfield," he wrote. "My mother has worked herself into such a state of agitation in the expectation of a visit, once the idea was impressed upon her by her misguided advocates, that even if all contact with them ceases, the agitation will persist. I am concerned that if her state of continuous ferment and dissatisfaction persists, not only will her health fail to improve, but she may be worse off than before."

The Bradwells had ruined Bellevue as a peaceful, quiet retreat where his mother could rest and be fully restored to health, Robert explained. Now she perceived it as a prison, and it was difficult to imagine how she could regain her reason in such conditions. Therefore, if Dr. Patterson confirmed that she could safely leave, and if Elizabeth agreed to take her in, Robert would arrange for his mother to leave the asylum and return to Springfield.

He had sought to have his mother committed for the sake of her health and safety, and now the same concern obliged him to consider withdrawing her—despite his grave worries that she remained as insane as the day she had been committed.

10

1839–1842

ELIZABETH

When Mary crossed the threshold of the house on Aristocracy Hill in October 1839, having eagerly accepted Elizabeth's invitation to stay indefinitely, her clear blue eyes shone with delight and her smooth cheeks flushed rose pink from expectation. "Ann is absolutely green with envy that I am here and she is not," Mary confided as she and Elizabeth settled her in the best guest room. "Not merely green, but an entire palette of emerald, olive, and chartreuse!"

"Ann will have her turn soon enough, if she wishes to come," replied Elizabeth mildly, sighing over the unconcealed glee in Mary's voice. Was it too much to ask for a little sisterly compassion for poor Ann, the only stepdaughter left to squirm and fume beneath Ma's watchful, critical gaze?

Mary had plenty of reasons to be joyful, and her rival's unhappiness should not have been one of them. Even in sophisticated Springfield, the Athens of the West, Mary's arrival created quite a stir. Everyone in the Coterie—as well as a great many on the fringes longing to be invited in—were eager to meet the most recently arrived Todd sister. Ninian had established himself as a young politician on the rise, Elizabeth was now regarded as one of the city's most gracious hostesses, and Mary's status as a Todd enhanced their anticipation.

Elizabeth was pleased and proud to observe that her sister did not disappoint. Mary swept into society with charm, grace, and poise to spare, delighting the young ladies and winning the admiration of the gentlemen. Soon everyone in Springfield had seen or heard about the beguiling intensity of her clear blue eyes fringed in dark lashes, the allure of her flawless complexion, and the silky richness of her chestnut brown hair flecked with gold, which she often adorned with flowers. She embraced the gaiety of balls, dinners, and soirees with abandon, sparkling on the dance floor as brilliantly as she did in the animated political discussions and debates, in which intelligence and wit were essential. In no time at all, Mary had accumulated an abundance of admirers, and it was obvious that she enjoyed the art of flirtation, teasing and enticing, encouraging many without relinquishing her heart to any particular one.

"She could make a bishop forget his prayers," Ninian remarked dryly to Elizabeth one evening as they observed her holding court in a senator's drawing room, her hair artfully coiled atop her head and embellished with hothouse flowers, her neck smooth and elegantly turned, her beautifully sculpted shoulders shown to their best advantage by the low, curved neckline of her claret watered silk gown. Elizabeth might have been jealous except that Ninian did not sound as if he approved of his sister-in-law's popularity—unless it was her outspokenness, her headstrong nature, or her evident desire always to be the center of attention that vexed him.

As for Elizabeth, it did not trouble her in the least that her sister reveled in the attention. Mary had spent far too many years feeling unwanted in her own home for Elizabeth to begrudge her this brief, precious time as the most desirable belle in Springfield. Wasn't the point of her visit to make her an excellent match, and wasn't a charming, lovely, witty young woman at least as likely as a shy, demure girl to attract a good husband?

And indeed, Mary did draw the eye of practically every eligible bachelor in Springfield. State legislator Stephen Douglas became a particular favorite, even though, regrettably, he was a Democrat and supported President Jackson. Aside from that significant drawback, he was intelligent, ambitious, and exceedingly clever, so Mary enjoyed his conversation and spent more time in his company than with any other member of their set. But Mary also showed favor to a gentleman from Missouri, a congenial lawyer and grandson of Patrick Henry, as well as other handsome fellows who impressed her with their dancing or their wit.

For a time, Elizabeth—and quite a few other observant members of the Coterie—thought her sister might be hoping for a proposal from another legislator, Mr. Edwin Webb. Elizabeth had often seen them engrossed in conversation at soirees, their heads bent close together, their voices earnest. She had also overheard Mary and Mercy Levering, their next-door neighbor and Mary's closest friend in Springfield, refer to him as "the winning widower." When Ninian mentioned that Mr. Webb's name and Mary's were being linked in gossip and conversation about town, Elizabeth decided to ask her sister outright if they had an understanding.

"Goodness, no, we have nothing of the sort," Mary replied, laughing. "Mr. Webb is indeed a widower of merit, our principal lion of the legislature, but a match between us is out of the question, there being a slight difference in our ages of some eighteen or twenty years!"

"Many successful marriages have been made of such matches," Elizabeth pointed out.

"Yes, but for me, such a vast difference would preclude the possibility of congeniality of feeling." With a wry smile, Mary added, "And let us not forget his two adorable little objections."

Elizabeth nodded, understanding and not judging her. Given Mary's history with Ma, Elizabeth could not blame Mary for her ambivalence about raising stepchildren.

Another young man who sought to win Mary's favor but

failed utterly was William Herndon, an innkeeper's son who had attended college in Jacksonville about forty miles to the west, although he had dropped out after a year. He was a member of the Young Men's Lyceum and aspired to become a lawyer, but in the meantime he clerked at Mr. Joshua Speed's store and honed his legal arguments in debates around the potbellied stove with men like cousin John Todd Stuart and Abraham Lincoln. He was not really included in the Edwardses' illustrious set, but he and Mary did cross paths from time to time, and that was enough for him to develop quite an infatuation with her. Nothing came of it, however, for early in their acquaintance, when they danced together at a party, he stammered out that she seemed "to glide through the waltz with the ease of a serpent." He had meant it as a compliment, but Mary took offense and retorted, "Mr. Herndon, comparison to a serpent is a rather severe irony, especially to a newcomer." She wanted nothing more to do with him after that, and her rebuff quickly cooled his ardor.

But aside from the unfortunate Mr. Herndon, Mary charmed a vast majority of Springfield's eligible bachelors. She even brought out previously unseen qualities in Mr. Lincoln, whom Frances had dismissed as lacking all refinement and romance. He seemed intrigued by Mary's conversation, which was ever graced by wit and intelligence. They shared a passion for poetry, literature, and Shakespeare, and both enjoyed reciting lengthy passages from memory. Mary's ability to debate the finer points of politics impressed him, and she was personally acquainted with Henry Clay, a Whig leader he had long admired. It was little wonder they enjoyed conversing so much, Elizabeth thought, since intellectually they had much in common, although they came from such different stations in life that they could never be more than friends. Frances had discovered this, and eventually Mary would too, especially since she was surrounded by so many other more attractive, more suitable gentlemen.

But as winter passed and their acquaintance seemed to deepen rather than fade, it was Frances who first noticed that Mary seemed more affected by Mr. Lincoln's opinion than that of any other suitor. If she teased him for failing to observe some convention of society, his look of gentle reproof made her blush furiously. If he came upon her in the midst of making fun of an absent acquaintance, or addressing someone with unnecessary sarcasm, she would abruptly fall silent, mortified that he had overheard. "I have never seen Mary so eager to impress a gentleman," Frances mused for Elizabeth alone. "Usually she stands aloof and waits for them to attempt to impress her."

Mildly alarmed, Elizabeth passed on Frances's observations to Ninian, who told her not to worry. Mary was clever, he reminded her unnecessarily, and it was unimaginable that a genteel young woman like her would abandon the luxury and prestige to which she was accustomed to share poverty with even the kindest and most eloquent of men. Elizabeth wanted to believe her husband, but all chance of that fled one evening in early spring when their cousin Stephen Logan called on them at home and proceeded to tease Mary about her popularity.

"I hear the Yankee, the Irishman, and our rough diamond from Kentucky were here last night," he said, throwing a sidelong grin to Elizabeth and Frances. "How many more have you on the string, Mary?"

"Are they not enough?" she replied archly. "Which of them do you fear the most?"

Cousin Stephen folded his arms over his chest and pondered the question. "I fear I am in grave danger of having to welcome a Yankee cousin."

"Never," Mary exclaimed. "The Yankee, as you call Mr. Douglas, differs from me too widely in politics. We would quarrel about Henry Clay. And James Shields, the Irishman, has too lately kissed the Blarney Stone for me to believe he really means half of his compliments. As for the rough diamond—"

"The rough diamond," their cousin interrupted, "is much too rugged for your soft little hands to attempt to polish."

"Ah, but to polish a stone like that would be the task of a lifetime," said Mary, her voice taking on a new warmth. "What a joy to see the beauty and brilliance shine out more clearly each day! The important thing is the diamond itself, clear and flawless under its film."

Elizabeth exchanged a quick, alarmed glance with Frances.

Cousin Stephen regarded Mary, astonished. "You don't mean that you would seriously consider it?"

"Why not?" she countered. "He is one of your best friends. You have told me time and again you never met a man with more ability, more native intellect."

"Mary is not thinking of Mr. Lincoln in the light of a lover, cousin," Elizabeth broke in hurriedly. "He is merely one of her most agreeable friends, and not one whit more agreeable than Mr. Douglas or any other."

Mary said nothing, but only pressed her lips together in a stubborn little line, and cousin Stephen good-naturedly changed the subject. That was all well and good for one evening, but from that day forward, Elizabeth and Frances both observed that Mary flew to Mr. Lincoln's defense the moment anyone spoke critically of him, even in the smallest degree, while she herself still made harmless, amusing jokes about him when he was not present.

Even Ninian agreed that these were troubling signs.

By the spring of 1840, within the Coterie and throughout the concentric circles of society emanating from it, there was a widespread understanding that Mary and Mr. Lincoln were engaged, or soon would be. Determined to put such speculation to rest, Elizabeth and Ninian agreed that as her guardians in Springfield, it was their responsibility to make her see reason. One afternoon in late March, they summoned Mary into the parlor, where they sat her down, informed her of their strong objections, and pointed out, since she seemed determined to ignore it, the incongruity of such a marriage.

"Although Mr. Lincoln is honorable, able, and popular," said Ninian frankly, "his future is nebulous, his family relations on an entirely different social plane."

"I am aware of his humble background," said Mary. "That only makes his accomplishments all the more impressive."

"His education, unlike your own, has been desultory," Ninian continued, as if she had not spoken. "He has no culture, he is ignorant of social forms and customs, and he is utterly indifferent to social status."

"Why could you not fancy some gentleman possessing the qualities Mr. Lincoln lacks?" asked Elizabeth, disliking the cajoling tone in her voice but unable to quash it. "Why not Mr. Douglas or one of the other promising young men in love with you?"

Mary's gaze held a challenge. "Mr. Douglas has no wealth to speak of either."

"Perhaps not," said Ninian. "But he's an educated and polished young man, a rising young politician with a future bright enough to satisfy the most ambitious woman."

"He's four years younger than Mr. Lincoln, and yet he has already achieved great political honors and is spoken of as a potential candidate for Congress." Remembering her sister's childhood vow, Elizabeth added, "He could become senator, perhaps even president. From every perspective, nothing could be more desirable or more likely to secure your future happiness than to marry him."

Mary listened impassively, but a resolute thrust to her chin told Elizabeth that her entreaties were wasted words.

Increasingly worried, Elizabeth confided to her sisters and to other Todds and Parkers in Springfield and Lexington that she feared Mary was on the verge of making a dreadful matrimonial mistake. At first they were amused, certain this was just another of Mary's many inconsequential flirtations, but when Elizabeth insisted that her relationship with Mr. Lincoln was of a different sort altogether, their alarm surpassed Elizabeth's own. They inundated Mary with letters full of advice and warnings and objections, disturbing anecdotes and tearful lamentations, until she began to meet the daily delivery of the post with an expression of grim fatalism.

An unforeseen and regrettable consequence of the ongoing dispute was that eventually word circulated through the Coterie and on to Mr. Lincoln that the Todds did not consider him a desirable addition to the family. But what could be done about that? Elizabeth's duty was to her sister, and if saving her from a bad match came at the expense of Mr. Lincoln's pride, so be it.

Elizabeth waited in dread for Mary to announce their engagement. She did not fear that the couple would elope, for Mr. Lincoln was too honorable and Mary would insist upon a proper wedding with all the trimmings, but instead, like a prayer answered, the danger receded.

In mid-April, Mr. Lincoln embarked on his annual spring tour of the Illinois Eighth Judicial Circuit, following the circuit court judge as he traveled from town to hamlet through nine counties, taking on clients, arguing cases, and soliciting future business for Stuart & Lincoln. Along the way he campaigned for the Whig candidate for president, William Henry Harrison, making speeches and winning over voters with eloquence and humor. He and Mary exchanged occasional letters—Mary naturally refused to divulge the contents to her sisters—but in his absence Mary enjoyed dances and soirees as much as ever, and she did not shun the company of other gentlemen. In this, Elizabeth found reason to hope.

Her hopes soared higher yet in midsummer, for by the time Mr. Lincoln returned to Springfield in June, their separation had been prolonged by Mary's departure for a lengthy visit to their uncle David Todd in Columbia, Missouri. Elizabeth and Frances agreed that the two surely continued to exchange letters, and their uncle mentioned that Mr. Lincoln had visited Mary after attending a Whig convention in Rocheport, fifteen miles due east, a significant distance out of the way for a man on horseback. Still, the elder sisters assured each other, time and distance would allow passions to cool and reason to resume control.

And then, another gift of fate: when Mary returned to Springfield in September, she discovered to her dismay that Mr. Lincoln had set out on another long trip through southern Illinois. When he returned at the end of the month, they had only a few days together before he departed on the fall county court circuit, from which he would not return until November.

Elizabeth hoped that this time Mary would tire of waiting for Mr. Lincoln and turn her attention to another gentleman, but this she adamantly refused to do. She and Mr. Lincoln continued to correspond, and in late October, when Elizabeth steeled herself and demanded to know whether, against the advice of all her family, Mary had formed an attachment to him, Mary fixed her blue eyes upon hers and said, "We have an understanding. When Mr. Lincoln returns, we will resume courting."

"Very well," said Elizabeth, exasperated. "Do as you please, and bear the consequences."

Things were icy between them for some days, but the chill thawed when Ninian's cousin, Matilda Edwards, arrived for a visit. Beautiful and beguiling at eighteen years old, Matilda became the most admired young lady of the Coterie, enchanting with her novelty as much as her loveliness. Elizabeth half-expected Mary to become jealous, but instead the young ladies became fast friends, perhaps because Mary had given her heart to Mr. Lincoln and was confident that he was too honorable a man to betray her trust.

Elizabeth and Ninian resigned themselves to a betrothal when Mr. Lincoln returned to Springfield in early November, but to their relief, the couple did not hasten to make their intentions known. Rumors circulated that they were secretly engaged, but when they met at society functions, they made no overt displays of affection. By early December, Elizabeth began to wonder if their affections had cooled, so little did they resemble a couple passionately in love.

"Do you think Mr. Lincoln fancies Matilda?" Frances murmured in Elizabeth's ear at a Christmas party where Mary held court at one end of a ballroom and Mr. Lincoln regaled a cluster of young lawyers with tales from his circuit court travels on the other.

"Everyone fancies Matilda," replied Elizabeth, searching the crowd for her husband's young cousin. "She is the most beautiful and charming young lady in Springfield. All the men are at least half in love with her, except your husband and mine."

"I believe she means more to Mr. Lincoln than that," said Frances, cupping her chin in her hand as she pondered the scene before them—ladies in beautiful gowns of velvet and silk flirting with gallant gentlemen, ingenues and youths mingling with matrons and statesmen, music from a string quartet serenading them all. "Or perhaps he simply dislikes that Mary has gotten so fat."

"Frances!"

"I'm not trying to be cruel, but look at her. She's become corpulent. She's straining the seams of her gown."

"That's a dreadful thing to say." Yet Elizabeth could not deny it. "I might expect as much from Ann, but not from you."

"Others have said far worse, though apparently not in your hearing." Frances put her head to one side, considering. "However, I suppose Mr. Lincoln is too decent a man to break off an engagement because of her looks, if they *are* engaged and it is not merely wishful thinking on Mary's part."

"Enough," said Elizabeth sharply in an undertone. Bickering between sisters tried her patience. They were no longer children competing for attention from Papa and approval from Ma.

But something *had* altered between Mary and Mr. Lincoln;

that much was evident. Mary was still lovely, if a bit plump, and if Mr. Lincoln gazed admiringly at Matilda, so did nearly every other man in the city. Elizabeth longed for her sister to confide in her as she once had, but Mary had been deeply offended by the confrontation in the parlor the previous March, and she refused to reveal anything about her feelings or their understanding, or to divulge when, or if, a betrothal would be forthcoming.

Then, on the first day of the New Year, Mr. Lincoln called unexpectedly at the Edwards residence, his voice low with regret, his expression somber. Mary received him in the parlor, while Elizabeth, Matilda, and Ninian withdrew to give them privacy. They knew not what to expect, but the sound of raised voices through the closed door made them wary, and the high-pitched sobs that followed were more foreboding still. After a lengthy interval of quiet, the sound of footsteps in the hall and the closing of the front door indicated that Mr. Lincoln had departed without bidding them good-bye. They hurried back to Mary, who sat crumpled on the settee, tears streaming down her face. In a voice choked by grief, she told them that their engagement had ended.

"He asked me to release him," she said as Elizabeth swiftly sat beside her and took her in her arms. "I told him that I would do so, but I declared that my heart is unaltered, unlike his, and he is duty-bound to marry me."

"Oh, sister," said Elizabeth, exchanging an anguished look with Ninian. "It would be better just to let him go."

"I've no doubt you would think so," said Mary, pulling free from her sister's embrace. "I'm sure your disapproval of the match was at least in part what compelled him to end it."

Pained, Elizabeth put her arms around Mary again, gently, and this time her sister allowed it. "All will be well in time," she said, holding her close, swaying slightly from side to side as if she were comforting her own young daughter. "All will be well."

In the months that followed, Mary gradually recovered from

her broken heart. She returned to society almost immediately, to dispel gossip, and was thankful that they had never publicly announced their betrothal so she need not explain what had happened to it. At first her laughter and gaiety had a forced, hollow quality, but soon she seemed to be genuinely enjoying herself, if not with the same lightheartedness as before.

Mr. Lincoln, quite to the contrary, looked dreadful and undone, like a man on the brink of losing his reason. Ninian confided to Elizabeth that his friends worried he was suffering a nervous breakdown from which he might not recover. Rumors swirled that he met with his physician daily and described himself as the most miserable man living. He missed a legislative roll call, and when he finally emerged after a week's self-imposed confinement to his rooms, witnesses observing him on the street said that he looked haggard and emaciated. He never came by the Edwards residence anymore, of course, but mutual friends kept Ninian informed. By spring, Mr. Lincoln was apparently recovering from his profound distress. Later that summer, a five-week stay at Mr. Speed's country estate in Kentucky was said to have done him a world of good.

A year passed. Life went on for Mary and Mr. Lincoln, separately.

Frances and William had long since moved from the small room at the Globe Tavern to a charming home on Sixth Street, and it was there that Frances gave birth to a precious daughter they named Mary Jane. Soon thereafter, the Wallaces invited eighteen-year-old Ann to live with them, ostensibly to help with the baby, but also to seek a husband. Though Mary was yet unmarried, and it was generally desirable for elder daughters to marry before younger, Papa and Ma thought it unfair to make Ann wait. Also, Ma had birthed two more children since Mary had gone to Springfield, and the house on Main Street was too crowded yet again.

To Elizabeth, Mary seemed ever mindful that her twenty-fourth birthday was swiftly approaching, and that with each passing year she would become less likely to marry. Her mood was either in the garret or the cellar, blissfully happy or profoundly depressed. As for Mr. Lincoln, according to the rumor mill, he struggled even to climb out of the cellar. It was impossible not to hear news of him from time to time, not only because they had many mutual friends, but also because cousin Stephen Logan had taken him on as a junior law partner earlier that spring.

For months, Mary mingled in society while Mr. Lincoln avoided it, focusing on his law practice, his legislative responsibilities, and the company of sympathetic friends. Mary was occasionally heard to say that she wished Mr. Lincoln would rejoin society, for his intelligent conversation and tall tales were greatly missed, and his acquaintances wanted reassurance that he was well. Elizabeth was proud of Mary for maintaining a tone of sincere friendship when she spoke thus, betraying none of the sadness or regret that surely lingered in her heart.

Then, in September 1842, Mary and Mr. Lincoln met by chance at the wedding of mutual friends. Elizabeth observed them from a discreet distance as they chatted amiably, shared a dance, and parted with cordial smiles. A wave of relief swept through the gathered throng; Miss Todd and Mr. Lincoln had reconciled, and no longer would mutual friends be obliged to keep them apart or side with one or the other.

After that, Mary never spoke of Mr. Lincoln at home among the family except with casual indifference. Thus, it came as a complete shock one afternoon in early November when Ninian rushed home from work, burst in upon Elizabeth in the parlor, and declared, "Mary and Lincoln are getting married!"

"What?" exclaimed Elizabeth, rising. "They are betrothed?"

"Yes, and not only that, they are marrying today. I ran into Lincoln on the street just as he was leaving the home of Reverend Dresser, and he informed me that they had arranged for him to perform the ceremony at his residence this evening."

"Marrying—today? It cannot be!"

"Naturally I insisted that the vows would be exchanged here, at our home, instead." Ninian ran a hand over his beard, grimacing. "How would it look otherwise?"

Elizabeth nodded, her thoughts in a whirl. How could she possibly pull together a proper wedding with only a few hours' notice? "We must prevail upon them to postpone, if only for a day."

Ninian agreed, so Elizabeth gathered up her skirts and raced upstairs to her sister's bedroom, where she discovered Mary singing happily to herself as she packed her trunk. "You are engaged?" Elizabeth managed to say. "Without a word to me, to Ma, to anyone?"

Mary offered a coy smile and a little shrug. "After all that happened, we believed it was best to keep the news of our renewed courtship from all eyes and ears."

"What courtship? When did you ever see each other?"

"We met at the home of Mrs. Francis. It was she who brought us together at the wedding of Martinette and Alexander, and she who offered us her parlor and companionship so that we might talk and rekindle our affection." She smiled, her gaze turned inward. "Only we two knew that the embers had continued to burn all these long months."

Elizabeth shook her head and clasped a hand to her brow, exasperated. She pleaded with Mary to delay the wedding one day, and although at first Mary regarded her suspiciously, she eventually consented. Then Elizabeth sprang into action, swiftly sending out three dozen invitations, engaging three bridesmaids and a best man, selecting a simple white muslin dress from Mary's wardrobe for a bridal gown, and putting the parlor in proper order.

"There is hardly time to arrange a wedding supper," said Elizabeth peevishly as she and her sister passed on the stairs, rushing about on separate errands. "Instead of baking a cake, I may have to send out for gingerbread."

"Gingerbread is good enough for plebeians," Mary snapped

back, referring to the Edwardses' previous objections to Mr. Lincoln's humble origins.

Elizabeth bit back a retort, and she did attempt to bake a proper wedding cake, but in her haste and distraction she made some error and it turned out badly, sinking in the middle and drying out around the edges. There was nothing to be done for it.

Rain fell in torrents on the wedding day, pounding against the parlor windows as the couple exchanged vows from the *Book of Common Prayer* before their hastily assembled friends and family. Abraham—for that was what Elizabeth must call him now— slipped a gold ring on Mary's finger inscribed with the phrase, "A.L. TO MARY, NOV. 4, 1842. LOVE IS ETERNAL."

Mary was radiant, Abe smiling and yet solemn. It was an unexpected end to a tumultuous courtship, but they loved each other, the deed was done, and her sister was immeasurably joyful at long last, so Elizabeth pushed her lingering worries to the back of her mind and wished the couple every happiness.

11

September 1875

Frances hoped Elizabeth knew what she was doing.

Robert believed that the Bradwells had ruined Bellevue as a place of healing for his mother, and although Dr. Patterson had asserted in his letter to the *Chicago Tribune* that he believed her still to be insane, he was willing, even eager, for his patient to depart. Frances suspected that his agreement with Robert's assessment was for his own comfort rather than Mary's well-being, but she could not blame him for desiring a respite from the Bradwells, their persistent agitating, and the onslaught of publicity they had brought down upon him.

Even though Dr. Patterson believed Mary ought to depart at once, Robert prudently sought a second opinion. At his request, Dr. Andrew McFarland, the superintendent of the Jacksonville, Illinois, State Hospital for the Insane, traveled to Bellevue to examine his mother. Dr. McFarland insisted that Mary required the serenity, quietude, and expert care of an asylum for at least a few more months if there was to be any reasonable hope of restoring her sanity. He perceived no good that could result from a visit to Springfield other than to gratify her ardent wish to go, the seed of which apparently had been planted in her mind by others. "My fear is that as soon as she is beyond the control of the present guardians of her safety, the desire for further adventure will take possession of her mind," Dr. McFarland warned. "Desires which, if acted upon, may prove hazardous to the patient."

Robert had sent a copy of the doctor's report to Elizabeth and Ninian, and they in turn had shared it with Frances and Ann. Given Dr. McFarland's emphatic recommendations, Frances assumed that Robert would decide to leave Mary where she was until she was completely recovered, while also banishing the Bradwells so they could no longer influence her. To her astonishment, he instead arranged for his mother to travel to Springfield, and for Elizabeth to receive her. Still cautious, Dr. Patterson imposed two conditions before consenting to her release: Mary would remain under a nurse's care while traveling and throughout her visit, and she must sever all communications with the Bradwells.

Privately, Frances and Ann agreed that moving Mary from the asylum to the Edwards residence was reckless and potentially dangerous. "Must Mary always have everything she wants, even if it is harmful to her?" said Ann, exasperated. "If Dr. Patterson can no longer help her, then send her to another asylum, but don't make her poor Elizabeth's burden."

"Elizabeth has always believed that Mary would be better off in a private home," Frances reminded her, "where she can be cared for by someone who loves her."

"Well, that leaves only Elizabeth, doesn't it?" Ann retorted.

Frances recoiled, stung. She too loved Mary, and she had to believe that deep down Ann did as well. Frances had not offered to take Mary into her home only because she believed her sister was better off at Bellevue. She was motivated by love as much as Elizabeth was; they simply disagreed about what was best for Mary.

Sometimes Frances wondered if she was the only Todd sister who remembered how Mary had agonized over where to go after Abraham's tragic death ten years before. His successor, President Andrew Johnson, had allowed the grieving widow to remain at the White House for more than a month after the Executive Mansion passed to him—an act of great courtesy, Frances had thought at the time, and still believed, even though subsequent events had sparked her keen dislike of the man. Estranged from her sisters, Mary had not summoned any of them to comfort her in her distress, so they learned secondhand that when obliged to leave Washington, she had adamantly refused to move back into the house she still owned on Eighth and Jackson in Springfield, where she and Abraham had embarked upon married life. The house was too full of memories of happier years with her husband, she had written to their cousin Betsey, and if she tried to live there, "deprived of *his* presence, and that of the darling boy we lost in Washington, it would not require a single day for me to lose my reason entirely." A few years later, Mrs. Keckly had recorded in her memoir— which Frances and Ann had secretly read, against Mary's wishes and Robert's—that Mary had vowed never to return to Springfield until she was wrapped in a shroud to be laid to rest in the tomb beside her husband. "May heaven speed that day," she had added fervently, words that had pained Frances to read. She too had lost her husband and had buried two children—her youngest, dear fifteen-year-old Charles, only a year before—yet she did not yearn for death. How could two sisters face similar heartbreak so differently, one with resigned determination to press on, the other with a melancholic longing for it all to be over?

Mary's claims about her circumstances, then and now, were full of contradictions. Frances knew for a fact that not all of Mary's memories of Springfield could be happy—far from it—nor was the house on Eighth and Jackson the first that Mary and Abraham had shared as husband and wife. That abode, which Mary euphemistically called "cozy" and "quaint" in letters to distant friends who would never see it, was the same humble room at the Globe Tavern that Frances and William had rented as newlyweds. At four dollars a week for lodging and board, it was inexpensive and clean, but those were its only redeeming qualities, for it was neither private nor comfortable, nor quiet. Several stagecoach companies rented offices in the building, and whenever a stage arrived, a large bell on the roof would peal loudly just above the startled tenants' heads. Legislators and lawyers who had come to town for the season gathered in the public rooms downstairs, loud and gregarious from morning until late into the night. Lodgers were required to take their meals together in a common dining room at specific hours, regardless of individual schedules or preferences. Frances and William had tolerated the Globe with good humor and by assuring each other that it was only temporary, but Mary had loathed the place as much as Abraham had enjoyed it, accustomed as he was to hard travel and the communal board of the circuit court.

Although they could not afford a fine home, Mary had resolved to appear in society as if a hilltop mansion like her eldest sister's was the Lincolns' natural habitat and destiny. Within days of their wedding, she had commenced polishing her rough diamond of a husband, sending him to the tailor to have new clothes made— better-fitting than any he had purchased before, made of finer fabrics—and endeavoring to rid him of his gauche country manners, such as eating butter with his knife, coming to the dinner table in his shirtsleeves, or putting on his hat "country fashion," with his hand on the back of the brim. Abe had earnestly tried to go along with her plan to remake his "outward show," but he had often reverted to his old habits, making the aristocratic Mary's temper flare. Once, after she had spoiled an afternoon tea with her sisters at Elizabeth's house with her interminable complaints, Ann had interjected sharply, "If I had a husband with a mind such as his, I would not care what he wore or which fork he chose."

"You're right, of course," Mary had said, contrite. "It *is* foolish, the way I complain about very small things."

And yet after a respite of hours or days, her exasperated lamentations would resume.

Frances thought that both of her sisters were correct, up to a point. It seemed petty to complain about Abe's occasional irksome, homespun turns of phrase when virtually every man in the legislature marveled at his eloquence when he spoke on matters of law, and yet without the attire and manners of a cultivated gentleman, he would not be taken seriously and it would be far more difficult for him to rise. And rise Mary had been determined to do, perhaps as high as Aristocracy Hill, perhaps higher.

Despite her aspirations, it was at the Globe that, in August 1843, Mary had borne their first child—Robert Todd Lincoln, Papa's namesake. Frances would have helped her with the baby, but she had a young child of her own by then and William had often been ill. If she and Mary had been closer, Frances probably would have found a way to care for Mary too, and in hindsight she wished she had, for it might have brought them closer together. Instead, Mary had relied upon a hired girl and the wife of one of Abe's friends, who had visited every now and then to tidy up or to watch the baby while Mary rested or caught up on other chores. Their help had been even more essential after Abraham had set out on the court circuit again, leaving Mary almost entirely alone with a newborn for more than six weeks.

She must have been terribly lonely, Frances reflected guiltily. She wished she had not been so absorbed in her own cares and had found time to attend to her sister. It was entirely possible that Mary would have gratefully accepted assistance, or even simple companionship, but had been too proud to ask for them.

As autumn had turned to winter, little Robert's nighttime cries, though no louder or more frequent than any other baby's, had begun to annoy the other residents of the boardinghouse, mostly single men unaccustomed to children. In January 1844, aware that they had worn out their welcome and badly needing more space and a kitchen of their own, Abraham and Mary had purchased a modest home from Reverend Dresser, a five-room Greek Revival cottage only a few blocks from Abraham's law office, with a wood-shed, a privy, and space for a carriage. It boasted none of the lux-uries of Elizabeth's home or even Frances's, but it was sturdily built and a place of their own where Mary at last had room to breathe.

Once she was fully the mistress of her own home, Mary had set about redecorating the cottage—a more compliant subject for her improvement schemes than her husband had proven to be. Frances remembered being impressed by how Mary had transformed the cottage into a genteel, comfortable home with shrewd purchases of furniture, household goods, and yards of inexpensive calico from which she herself sewed curtains, tablecloths, and the like. Twelve years later, when Abe's legal practice was thriving, the Lincolns had enlarged and remodeled their home, transforming it into the gracious showplace Mary had long desired. Of all the places she had called home, only the White House was grander.

Frances knew that despite what Mary had said as she reluctantly prepared to leave Washington, the memories she, Abe, and their children had forged in the cottage were not all happy but rather a mix of sunlight and shadow. They had celebrated the glorious news of Abe's 1846 election to Congress in the parlor, but they had also returned to it, discouraged and facing an uncertain future, when he had lost his bid for reelection after a single, disappointing term. Their second child, a son they named Edward, had been born in 1846 in the cottage, the same place where, three and a half years later, he died of diphtheria. And then, a year later, the home witnessed the return of hope and happiness when Mary birthed another son, named William Wallace after Frances's husband, who had tended Eddie so tirelessly throughout his fatal illness. A little more than two years after that, they had welcomed their fourth and last son—Thomas, soon to be nicknamed Tad—in the same room where two of his elder brothers had been born. Their happy, rambunctious brood was complete, and the indulgent parents had watched their boys grow, full of hope and worry and anticipation for their future.

Happy memories indeed had been made beneath that roof, but Abe had been gone ten years, and Willie and Tad too had joined their father and elder brother Eddie in death. It was little wonder that Mary, shattered by grief and facing a bleak future, had so adamantly refused to return to the cottage after leaving the White House—and stranger still that she dared to return now to Springfield, with her nerves in as fragile a state as they had been since that terrible April of 1865.

Frances pondered the curious contradiction. Perhaps, despite what Mary had said a decade before, it was only her former home she dreaded, not Springfield itself. The once-cherished house would remind her too painfully of the loved ones she had lost, while the Edwards residence had only happy associations, as it had been the scene of her glorious coming out in Springfield society and of her wedding, where she had pledged her heart forever to her one great love. As for Elizabeth, despite their estrangement, she surely remained a figure of maternal love and consolation for Mary, as she did for all the siblings she had helped raise after their mother's death.

If regarded from that perspective, Mary's urgent need to seek refuge at Elizabeth's house, which she had once been invited to consider her own for as long as she liked, was entirely logical and rational, not the strange, urgent impulse of a deranged mind, but a natural yearning to come home. Elizabeth's willingness to take in a troubled, fragile sister from whom she had long been estranged was more difficult to understand.

But coming Mary was. Frances and Ann were uncertain how to help Elizabeth manage. When they hesitantly asked if she wanted them to be present to welcome Mary when she arrived, Elizabeth pondered the question before shaking her head. "I believe we should allow her to settle in quietly, with as little excitement as possible," she said. "Too much fanfare might overexcite her."

"But Mary always liked to have a fuss made over her," Ann objected mildly, but Frances agreed with Elizabeth, so it was decided that Frances and Ann would come for tea on the second day after Mary's arrival. If Mary seemed well enough to attempt a more ambitious gathering, Ann's husband and the sisters' adult children could join them for dinner the next week.

On September 10, after four months at Bellevue Place, Mary left the asylum in the watchful care of a female attendant. They traveled by coach to Chicago, where they met Robert at the station and boarded the train for Springfield. Dr. McFarland had arranged for a nurse to come to the Edwards residence the next day; she would sleep in the room next to Mary's and care for her throughout her visit. For this *was* a visit, everyone involved emphasized; it was not a relocation, but an experiment to see how Mary fared outside the sheltering walls of the asylum.

Later that day, Frances heard the train whistle, glanced at the mantel clock, and felt her heart thud at the realization that Mary and Robert had arrived. The rest of the day passed in curiosity and apprehension as she tried to imagine what was going on at the Edwards residence at various hours. Would Mary be calm or distraught? Had she and Elizabeth reconciled on sight, or were their conversations strained and redolent of old bitterness? Torn between impatience and dread, Frances was grateful for the message Elizabeth sent over later that evening to assure her that Mary had arrived safely and had settled comfortably into her former room. The next morning her thoughtful eldest sister sent her maid with another note to report that Mary had slept well, had eaten a healthy breakfast, and looked forward to seeing her and Ann the next day.

Frances's nerves fluttered at the very thought of it.

On the afternoon of September 12, Ann came by for Frances in her carriage; it was out of her way, but a light rain was falling, enough to make Frances's walk most unpleasant. The sisters said little as they rode through the city and up Aristocracy Hill to the Edwards residence, which they knew almost as well as their own. "Do you think she'll make a scene?" Frances asked nervously as the carriage halted in the raked gravel drive.

"Mary always makes a scene," said Ann, adjusting her gloves. "The only question is how dreadful it will be."

"Or how pleasant," protested Frances. "Mary can be very charming when she wishes."

Ann gazed heavenward and stepped down from the carriage. "That was years ago, when it was necessary," she said, turning around to see if Frances needed a steadying hand as she descended.

So helpful to one sister, so contemptuous of the other. Frances muffled a sigh as they approached the front door. She regretted that she had ever teamed up with Ann in teasing Mary or gossiping meanly about her behind her back. Frances had grown out of it, but apparently Ann never would.

If Ann had hoped to find Mary raving or in a stupor, she must have been sorely disappointed by the calm, quiet scene that unfolded in Elizabeth's parlor when the four eldest Todd sisters took tea together for the first time in years. Mary's lustrous chestnut brown hair had gone gray, and her once-sparkling blue eyes seemed tired and puffy. She greeted them kindly, but with reserve, somewhere between the familiarity of a sister and the gracious condescension of a first lady. Ninian had forewarned Frances not to mention the asylum, so instead she asked Mary—carefully, obliquely—how she was feeling.

"A bit tired from travel," Mary replied, offering a wry smile, "but otherwise, perfectly sane."

Heartened by the bit of humor, Frances smiled back.

Mary inquired politely about their children and grandchildren, and they asked about hers. When Mary mentioned that Robert had departed on the morning train to Chicago due to an urgent matter at his law office, Frances detected not a trace of resentment or hostility in her sister's voice. Mary smiled and even laughed when she recounted an amusing anecdote about Robert's eldest, Mamie, and she listened with keen interest to news of old friends from Springfield with whom she had lost touch. Sometimes she fidgeted or wrung her hands, and twice she started in her chair and looked over her shoulder as if she had heard a door slam or a glass shatter, but otherwise she seemed mostly fine, albeit tired, as she herself had admitted.

They parted with embraces and promises to meet again soon. Since the tea had gone so smoothly, Frances was not surprised when the next day she received an invitation summoning herself, Mary Jane, Will, Fanny, and Ed to a family dinner at the Edwards residence the following Tuesday.

Robert returned to Springfield for the occasion, which, defying expectations, turned out to be a perfectly delightful evening. True, Robert kept a watchful eye on his mother throughout the evening, as if he feared that at any moment she might burst into a frenzy of accusations or weeping, but Mary remained composed throughout, an ideal guest, grateful to be among the company and to receive such kind attention from her hostess.

"Her good behavior cannot last," Ann predicted as Clark helped first her and then Frances into their carriage for the ride home. And yet one day passed and then another without any sign that it would not. With her grandnephew Lewis as her escort, Mary took walks and went for carriage rides; she delighted in visits from extended family and a few trusted, longtime friends; she came to tea at Frances's house and was invited to dine with Clark and Ann at their home. All the while, it seemed to Frances, she, her sisters, and their husbands held their breath and hoped that everything would continue to go well. To their surprise and relief, everything did. In fact, Mary seemed to improve day by day.

"You could not have known this visit would go so well," Frances said to Elizabeth one afternoon. She had arrived early for tea on purpose, so that she might speak to her elder sister alone. "After everything we had read in the papers about her condition, as well as the doctors' recommendations that she remain in the asylum, why did you allow her to come?"

Elizabeth spread her hands, brow furrowing. "Habit, I suppose? I'm the eldest. I've looked after her since I was little more than a child myself. Why not now, when she most needs me?"

"You had every reason to decline," Frances countered. "Two expert doctors advised against allowing her to travel. There must have been more to your decision than mere habit."

Suddenly, tears sprang into her elder sister's eyes. "Perhaps I am more inclined to sympathize with Mary because I believe that insanity, while new to our family line, is not restricted to her."

"What do you mean?"

"No one ever speaks of it, but our grandfather, Levi Owen Todd, died in an asylum."

Frances studied her, uncomprehending. "No, he died in a hospital, of consumption."

Elizabeth shook her head, her expression bleak. "That is the most widely known story. Papa and Grandma Parker shared a different version with me. I thought perhaps they had told you as well."

"They never breathed a word, not to me." Frances pressed a hand to her brow, shaken. She would have gone to her grave believing a lie.

Elizabeth clasped her hands together at her waist, bracing herself. "I have also observed signs of madness in my own dear Julia."

Frances gasped and reached for her hand. "No, not Julia?"

Elizabeth squeezed her hand tightly and nodded, a tear trickling down her cheek. "I suspected it first when she was only thirteen," she said, her voice barely above a whisper. "Melancholia and mania that came and swiftly passed, only to return as if with the seasons. Her symptoms worsened with the birth of each child, and they were severely felt by all those around her, particularly by her husband and myself."

"But—but she must be doing well, if she has been allowed to accompany Edward to his posting abroad, so far from home—"

"Yes, truly, she has been quite well in recent years." Elizabeth took a deep, shaky breath. "But one never knows. I live in dread that her dark moods will come upon her again and this time linger forever. How can I abandon Mary when one day I might need a sister or a cousin to do for my own beloved child what Mary requires of me now?"

Wordlessly, Frances embraced her, stroking her back soothingly so that Elizabeth could compose herself before their other sisters arrived. She had never imagined that such unhappy secrets afflicted Elizabeth. Now her decision to take Mary in made perfect sense—and yet it did not make it seem any wiser. Had Elizabeth put emotion before safety in disregarding the explicit warnings of Dr. Patterson and Dr. McFarland?

Throughout Mary's visit, Elizabeth kept Robert apprised of his mother's condition through daily letters describing her habits and moods. "I can truly say that she has not appeared to better advantage in years than she does now," she wrote to him at the end of the first week. The experiment appeared to be succeeding, and Frances knew that Robert had begun to wonder whether perhaps his mother would be more likely to recover her reason at the Edwards residence than at Bellevue Place.

On September 20, he asked Dr. Patterson to reexamine his mother and advise him.

"I am not able to report much change in the mental condition of Mrs. Lincoln since you last saw her," Dr. Patterson wrote in a letter Robert later shared with his aunts. "I do not hesitate to say that as a result of her communication with Judge and Mrs. Bradwell, she became worse; and since they have ceased their visits and letters, she is again better and improving." With regard to her permanent transfer from Bellevue Place to her sister's home, since Mary had complied with all of the conditions imposed upon her for the visit, Dr. Patterson acknowledged that an extended stay ought to be attempted.

With that, Mary's return to the asylum was postponed indefinitely—even though, as Frances noted apprehensively, not once had Dr. Patterson claimed that she was cured.

12

1854–1856

EMILIE

Although Emilie felt perfectly content and cherished at Buena Vista with her Ma and her siblings, she longed to follow her elder half-sisters to Springfield, just as she had followed Mary to Madame Mentelle's Ladies' Academy, albeit as a day student. For years her half-sisters' stories of the Coterie and Springfield society had enchanted her, filling her imagination with scenes of lovely young ladies in exquisite gowns mingling with handsome gentlemen at balls and parties—the music, the dancing, the flirtation, the lively conversations about literature and politics. Emilie had little interest in politics per se, but she respected men with the ambition to seek political office, and she admired women who could discuss policy and debate points of law as cleverly as any legislator.

Emilie had adored Mary and Abe ever since they visited the Todds in Lexington en route to Washington for his first—and thus far only—term in Congress. When Mary made a second visit to Buena Vista in the summer of 1851, she impressed and delighted Emilie with her wit and vivacity. Flattered by the attention and charmed by Emilie's prettiness, Mary took a special interest in her, and their bonds of affection grew. On the eve of Mary's departure, she embraced her beloved Little Sister and promised that when she came of age, she could come to Springfield and stay with her and Abe and their three young sons for as long as she wished.

Thrilled, Emilie longed for the months to fly swiftly past until she turned eighteen, at which time Ma had promised to consider Mary's invitation. Three years had passed since Ann, the last of the Todd sisters to move to Springfield for some sisterly match-making, had married the merchant Clark Moulton Smith. In their fine house on South Fifth Street on the same block as the Governor's Mansion, Ann had borne two children, an eldest son named Lincoln and his younger brother, Edgar. The time seemed ripe for another Todd sister to take Springfield society by storm. With rising anticipation, Emilie counted the days until her eighteenth birthday, but Ma needed some persuading before agreeing to let her go. Once Ma's blessing was secured, Emilie sent word to Mary that she was accepting her invitation at long last. She packed her trunk and boarded the train to Springfield, full of soaring hopes and fond wishes she could not wait to fulfill.

It was a cold, brilliantly sunny day in December when Emilie crossed the threshold of the Lincoln residence, where Mary greeted her with a cry of joy and a heartfelt embrace. Brother Abe followed by clasping her hand and welcoming her warmly, his dark eyes beaming with kindness and affection. Robert was attending prep school, but Willie and Tad ran to greet their aunt, delightfully noisy and cheerful and rambunctious, before racing off again.

Elizabeth, Frances, Ann, and their husbands would join them for dinner that evening, but Emilie had time to warm herself by the fire with a cup of tea before Mary showed her to her room and helped her settle in. "You have arrived in the midst of a very busy season," her elder sister said happily as she helped her unpack. "So many Christmas parties and balls and dinners await you! Tonight's dinner will seem quiet in hindsight."

But the social calendar was not all that kept Mary occupied those days, she explained. Abe was in the midst of another campaign.

"I thought he had left politics to focus on his new law practice," said Emilie, surprised. She knew that after his single term in Congress, he had hoped to be appointed to certain political patronage positions; the posts he was interested in had gone to other men, however, and instead he had been offered the position of governor of the Oregon Territory. Mary frequently had intense flashes of intuition that had proved true more often than not through the years, and she had insisted that accepting that post would ruin any chance he had of becoming president one day. Whether Abe had trusted her clairvoyance or simply had not wanted to uproot the family, Emilie could only guess, but he had declined the appointment. As far as Emilie knew, he had not actively sought any role in government since then.

"It's true that the law has taken up most of his time," said Mary. "He grew tired of working as our cousin's junior partner, so he decided to start a new firm and hire a junior partner of his own." She made a face. "Regrettably, he chose that dreadful William Herndon, the one who tried to flatter me by saying I danced with the grace of a serpent."

Emilie laughed. "I hope Mr. Herndon is more eloquent in the courtroom than in the ballroom."

"Even if he were not, I don't think Abe would mind. He insists upon splitting all his fees with Mr. Herndon fifty-fifty. And yet when Abe was my cousin Stephen's junior partner, his cut was only a third."

"Your Abe is very generous."

"To a fault. Mr. Herndon does not deserve half the fees. He is not half the lawyer my Abe is, nor one-quarter the man."

Emilie glanced up from arranging folded stockings in a bureau drawer, her eyebrows rising. Apparently, Mr. Herndon's clumsy remark still stung, years later. Ma had said that Mary never forgot an affront; perhaps that was no exaggeration.

Dismissing Mr. Herndon with the wave of a hand, Mary resumed hanging Emilie's dresses in the wardrobe and explained how the passing of the Kansas-Nebraska Act had rekindled Abe's interest in seeking political office. The act overturned the ruling of the Missouri Compromise of 1820, which had restricted the spread of slavery to territories south of Missouri's southern border. For decades, the nation had been divided by a line running east-west between Southern slave states and Northern free states, and the status of new states depended entirely upon geography. The Kansas-Nebraska Act instead decreed that new states forming from territorial land would decide by popular vote whether to forbid or allow slavery.

"But isn't that desirable?" asked Emilie. "It's democracy, is it not, to put such decisions in the hands of the people?"

"Not if the people desire to perpetuate a monstrous injustice," declared Mary, closing the wardrobe door firmly. "Slavery must not be permitted to spread beyond its current borders. Abe calls it a cancer."

"My goodness," said Emilie, sitting down on the edge of the bed. "A cancer?" What must Abe think of the Todds back in Lexington, of Emilie herself, for perpetuating it?

Mary regarded her levelly. "I was raised in a slaveholding family, as you were. I daresay I have more experience and knowledge about the 'peculiar institution' than my husband does. And I say he is not wrong, and we both believe that the majority of the people share his opinion. Even Ninian remains firmly against slavery, despite switching parties to become a Democrat, more fool he."

Emilie managed a shaky laugh. "Ma would not like to hear that Abe is an abolitionist."

"I see no need to tell her." Mary shrugged indifferently. "It would not change a thing. We are not ruled by her opinions."

She went on to explain that Abe had been inspired when another Todd cousin, Cassius Clay, had campaigned against the Kansas-Nebraska Act in Illinois, declaring that Whigs, Free-Soilers, and like-minded Democrats must unite in order to prevent the insidious spread of slavery. He had been moved, too, by transcripts of speeches by Frederick Douglass, the former slave turned abolition activist, who lamented that his people had no Stephen Douglas on their side, only truth, justice, and their humanity. For as it happened, Mary's former beau and Abe's longtime rival had become one of the act's fiercest advocates.

In late summer, Abe had embarked on a speaking campaign to denounce the expansion of slavery, and the reception to his speeches had convinced his supporters in Springfield to put his name forward as a candidate for state representative. More than that, they had published an announcement of his candidacy, without his knowledge or consent, while he was out of town and unable to intervene. He had had other ambitions, but when the unendorsed announcement had met with great enthusiasm, his friends and supporters had prevailed upon him to keep his name in the race. On November 7, he had been elected to the Illinois legislature once more.

"Why, that's wonderful, Mary," exclaimed Emilie. Although they disagreed on the slavery question, she knew Abe to be a man of unmatched intelligence and integrity, well deserving of such a distinguished position. "When will he be seated?"

"He won't be," said Mary. "Not three weeks later, he formally declined the office. You see, it is against the law in our state for a legislator to be elected to the United States Senate, and that is the office to which he aspires."

Emilie gasped. "He turned down the seat he won in the Illinois legislature so he may campaign for senator?"

"It is a risk," Mary acknowledged, but her face glowed with the certainty that it was a risk worth taking. "He may end up with nothing, having sacrificed one office to pursue the other. And yet, the enthusiastic crowds he meets on his speaking tours are so strongly with him that he believes he has an excellent chance to win."

The question would be settled in a special legislative election to replace the incumbent senator at the end of January. In the meantime, the work of winning over the legislators who would choose the next senator of Illinois awaited. Fortunately, brother Abe would not have to toil alone. In addition to his friends and political colleagues, he had Mary, who brought pertinent newspaper articles to his attention, discussed the issues with him, and helped him clarify policies and create strategy. When he traveled, she kept her ear tuned to gossip, distinguished between truth and rumor, and briefed him on relevant matters upon his return. Abe preferred to rehearse his speeches aloud, and Mary, who would listen intently, pose insightful questions, and offer suggestions, was the ideal first audience. She could not accompany him as he worked the halls of the statehouse, garnering support and observing the competition, but she could help him prepare.

Emilie often sat in on these practice sessions, and she marveled not only at Abe's masterful oratory and Mary's keen grasp of complex issues, but at the way the couple worked together, so different in personality and yet so harmonious. She could not imagine Papa and Ma collaborating in this way, and it made her wonder if she should not aspire to a more egalitarian marriage than theirs, the example she knew best and, until now, had assumed she would emulate.

As fascinating as it was, Emilie spent relatively little time observing Abe and Mary prepare for the election, for as Mary had promised, she had arrived when the social season was in full swing. With Mary as her indulgent chaperone and adviser on everything from attire to hairstyling to witty conversation, Emilie embarked on a delightful whirlwind of balls, dinners, soirees, and sleighing parties. She befriended several charming young ladies and found herself much admired by many young gentlemen, all of whom were pleasant enough, and handsome enough, and good enough dancers, but none of whom made her heart beat faster or became the subject of pleasant daydreams.

As much as she enjoyed being, as Mary proudly proclaimed her, the loveliest belle in society that season, Emilie also welcomed quieter, more intimate gatherings with her sisters and their families. The Todd sisters met at least one afternoon a week for tea in Ann's parlor, and every Sunday the sisters, husbands, and children met for dinner in Elizabeth's grand dining room. Emilie delighted in her young nieces and nephews, and she cheerfully took her needle in hand to help prepare the trousseau for Julia's June wedding.

"By then you may have your own betrothal to announce," Ann teased as the sisters sat together sewing one snowy afternoon in mid-January. Emilie blushed and her sisters smiled, but her heart sank a little too. She had met nearly all the eligible young gentlemen in Springfield, and while many of them were perfectly adequate, she did not truly fancy any of them, not in the way she had so romantically imagined when she was counting the days until her eighteenth birthday and the commencement of her glorious adventure in Springfield.

Meanwhile, the election provided a fascinating distraction. The sense of anticipation that had graced her visit from the beginning intensified as the end of January approached. On the day of the election, Emilie woke to discover a blizzard raging outside her window, but her distress quickly eased when Abe told her that the vote had been postponed a week and a day. The interval dragged by, provoking anxiety and dread in the household where there had been almost none before.

Finally, on February 8, Emilie joined Mary to observe the election from the statehouse gallery, which fairly crackled with eagerness and urgency intensified by the delay. By his best estimate, Abe judged himself a few votes shy of the majority required, but he hoped to gain support from one round of balloting to the next.

After the first ballot, Mary squeezed Emilie's arm and pressed her lips together in a valiant effort to contain her jubilation. Abe was only six votes shy of victory, and since no candidate had claimed a majority, another vote would be called, in which he was sure to acquire more support. After the next round, however, as legislators' loyalties shifted, he tallied a net loss of two votes. In the third round, he lost two more. On and on it went for hours, the atmosphere increasingly tense and frantic, as candidates lost and gained ground and one and then another seemed moments away from capturing the majority.

Then, on the seventh ballot, one of the four candidates withdrew from the race and pledged his votes to Lyman Trumbull, who, like Abe, was against the Kansas-Nebraska Act. Trumbull now commanded more votes than Abe had ever won on any balloting, and in the eighth round he received eighteen more. All the while, Governor Joel Matteson, the leading Democratic candidate, was steadily gathering more votes from the act's advocates. It seemed inevitable that if the anti–Kansas-Nebraska Act voters could not consolidate their support behind a single candidate, the proslavery candidate would win.

"My husband is going to sacrifice himself," Mary murmured tensely near Emilie's ear, a catch in her voice. Moments later, he did precisely that, pledging his fifteen votes to his rival Whig to ensure that an abolitionist would achieve a majority and win the election.

Even Emilie, political neophyte that she was, recognized this as a tremendous show of party loyalty and a significant personal sacrifice on her brother-in-law's part. It was only afterward, as the session was adjourned and the men were leaving the statehouse, that he learned how his opponents had arranged their sudden shift of votes to a single candidate ahead of time, hoping that it would be enough to capture the majority. Their gambit had failed, but only because Abe had put the greater good ahead of his own advancement.

He had bet his seat in the state legislature on the senatorial election, and he had lost both.

In the days that followed, Abe seemed more relieved that the ordeal was over than regretful that he had not won. "The agony is over at last," he said ruefully the next morning when Emilie gently asked him how he was feeling. "It was rather hard, but perhaps it will be better for the cause that Trumbull was elected."

"Take heart, brother Abe," Emilie consoled him. "From the ashes of disappointment, a great triumph may yet arise."

"I'll keep that in mind, Little Sister," he said, a fond smile slowly brightening his face.

She reminded herself of that aphorism as summer came and she was no closer to a betrothal than the day she had arrived. In June the Todd sisters and their families celebrated Julia Edwards's marriage to Edward L. Baker, a lawyer, a friend of Abe's, and the editor and co-owner of the *Illinois State Journal*. After that, in her letters from home, Ma began hinting, and then plainly declaring, that Emilie had perhaps overstayed her welcome. Although Mary insisted that she had not, Emilie realized that her visit to Springfield must draw to a close.

She returned to Lexington without a promise of marriage, without even the likelihood of a proposal. In the weeks that followed, Mary sent her many long letters full of news about the family and her new acquaintances. She never failed to conclude with an invitation for Emilie to return to Springfield whenever she wished, whenever Ma consented.

As it happened, she did not need to, at least not for the reasons implied.

Soon after Emilie settled back into life at Buena Vista after so many months away, she was introduced to a young man at a ball, a gentleman who, in her eyes, surpassed all those she had met in Springfield. Benjamin Hardin Helm, a graduate of West Point from Hardin County, Kentucky, was so handsome—six feet tall, strong and fit, with a military bearing, ruddy complexion, attractive features, and penetrating blue eyes—that when he bowed over her hand for the first time, she was rendered nearly speechless. They began courting, and within a few months he declared himself to be deeply in love with her—not one bit more, she secretly believed, than she was in love with him.

They married at Buena Vista less than a year later, in March 1856, and were certain that joy and contentment would fill their hearts and their home for the rest of their lives. As brother Abe had once done, Ben served on the county circuit court. He and Emilie enjoyed each other's company so much that they decided she would accompany him when he traveled rather than allow the circuit to part them, as it had too often parted Abe and Mary.

Thus from the ashes of her disappointment in Springfield arose the glorious triumph of marriage to the man she loved most dearly in the world.

Emilie fervently prayed that the old saying would prove as true for brother Abe as it had for her.

13

October–November 1875

ANN

Mary had been so pleasant, cheerful, and friendly to Ann since her return to Springfield that naturally Ann's suspicions soared. They had never been as congenial as sisters were supposed to be, although they had become friendlier during the years Mary and Abe were married. Ann had always liked Abe, even when Elizabeth had her convinced that he was an unsuitable match for Mary—an absurd worry, as it had turned out. As for her own husband, Clark had admired Abe almost to the point of idolatry, especially after he ascended to the presidency. Perhaps, Ann mused, their fondness for Abe had helped her see Mary in a new light. She and Mary might have become quite close if Mary had not spoiled it by assuming an insufferably imperial manner after becoming first lady. Ann had complained to mutual friends that Mary expected them to address her as if she were Queen Victoria. Word eventually got around to her sister, who took great offense and assumed even more regal airs.

Now Ann did not know what to think. Earlier that spring, she had believed that Mary was feigning her illness in order to win sympathy from her family and the public, but especially from Congress, so that it would be moved to increase her pension. But upon seeing her after her release from the asylum, Ann had been shocked by her wan, aged appearance and subdued manner. Mary had always been vain and would not have let herself go, even to further a profitable scheme. The only plausible explanation was that she was too depressed to bother with the outward show that had once meant so much to her.

Granted, Mary still cared about fashion, but her desire for new dresses and fine fabrics seemed obsessive to Ann, a symptom of her mental illness. She ordered dresses made up and never wore them, and then she turned around and purchased yards of fabric—always mourning black—and never had it made up into dresses. But when Ann suggested to Elizabeth that Mary's urgent and persistent need to shop could be a mania, Elizabeth emphatically disagreed. "Her acquiring items, even if they're unnecessary, is not excessive, considering what she can afford," she said. "If we would all simply adopt a position of indifference to her spending, she might become less defensive and more willing to discuss it."

When Ann remained skeptical, Elizabeth hastened to remind her how far Mary had come since she left the asylum. Her color was much better and her eyes were clear. She no longer fidgeted in her chair or jumped at the slightest sound. She enjoyed visiting friends and family, she was cordial and lucid when chatting with callers, and with her sisters she was more reasonable and gentler than she had been in years. "I have no hesitation in pronouncing her sane," Elizabeth declared.

Ann let the argument drop. Elizabeth seemed determined to see only the good in Mary. Robert, on the other hand, was inclined to doubt that his mother was any better than when she had left Bellevue. "Her demeanor since the trial has shown that in general she is able to control her impulses if she has a reason to do so," he replied after Ann wrote to warn him of Elizabeth's revised assessment of his mother's sanity. "She will appear rational until you bring up the subject of money, which draws her mania to the surface."

Ann agreed with her nephew, but apparently he was unaware

that there was another subject besides money about which Mary was not entirely rational. Recently, Ann had noticed, even if none of her sisters had, Mary became vexed whenever Robert's name came up in conversation. Vexation was not mania, but it seemed irrational enough. But if Ann conceded that Mary was not entirely rational now, would she not also have to admit that the same had been true back in the spring? Only a fool would believe that Mary had been pretending to be mad in the spring but was genuinely mad today.

Bemused, Ann mulled over the disturbing events that had led up to Mary's insanity trial, not only the strange visions she had confessed to her doctor and her suicide attempt, but the bizarre frenzy of fear that had come over her a month before Robert first consulted Dr. Patterson, and two months before the panel of learned physicians had declared her insane.

In January 1875, Mary had gone to Jacksonville, Florida, to spend the winter. A nurse had traveled with her to tend to her various ailments, and Mary's first letters home had been entirely lucid and conversational, describing her travels, the weather, the landscape, and her health. She had enjoyed the benevolent climate, gone sightseeing, and received callers in the elegant parlor of her boardinghouse suite.

According to Robert, and to the many newspaper reports Ann and Clark had read with fascinated horror in the days that followed, all had seemed well until mid-March, when Mary suddenly and inexplicably became convinced that Robert was deathly ill, and no reassurances from her nurse or from her Jacksonville acquaintances could disabuse her of her fears. She sent a frantic telegram to Robert's law partner asking about his health and declaring her intention to depart for Chicago immediately. Ninety minutes later, she had telegraphed Robert directly: "My dearly beloved son Robert T. Lincoln rouse yourself and live for my sake all I have is yours from this hour. I am praying every moment for your life to be spared to your mother."

Immediately wary, Robert telegraphed the Jacksonville Western Union office to ask, discreetly, if Mrs. Lincoln seemed to be in any difficulty, "mentally or otherwise." The manager promptly responded that she seemed "nervous and somewhat excited," and that her nurse companion believed that she ought to return home as soon as possible. In the meantime, Mary sent Robert another telegram, saying, "Start for Chicago this evening hope you are better today you will have money on my arrival."

Dismayed by his mother's excessive anxiety and irrational behavior—including her apparent conviction that if she promised him wealth, he would find the will to live—Robert realized that his experience with all her eccentricities and manias in the past had not prepared him for the difficult choices that would soon confront him.

When he met his mother at the station in Chicago, she seemed shocked to see him in perfect health. He invited her to come home with him, but she declined, as she and Robert's wife were estranged. Instead, Robert escorted his mother to the Grand Pacific Hotel, where he arranged a room for her and ordered supper; while they ate, she lamented that a man on the train had poisoned her coffee. Deeply troubled, Robert reserved the room next to hers so that he would be near if she became distressed in the night.

He had intended to take his mother home the next morning. Instead, they had remained at the hotel for two weeks.

Every night Mary had woken from a restless sleep, and, terrified to find herself alone, she had knocked on Robert's door and tearfully asked to stay with him. One morning she tried to descend in the elevator half-dressed, and when Robert and a hotel employee prevented her, she fought them, screaming, "You are trying to murder me!" When they managed to get her back to her room, she told them an outlandish story about a man who had stolen her pocketbook on the train and planned to return it to her that afternoon. Later that day she accosted the hotel manager, telling him that something was wrong with the building: she heard strange sounds in her room at all hours, and she was afraid to be alone. She complained that people were speaking to her through the walls; she insisted that the South Side of the city was on fire and that their lives were in danger; she believed that a strange man in the corridor intended to molest her. When the hotel staff reported other bizarre behaviors they had observed, the manager warned them that she was deranged.

With each passing day, she became more agitated and paranoid, and as the tenth anniversary of his father's assassination approached and terrible memories resurfaced, Robert feared that she might break down completely. Erring on the side of caution, he hired a pair of Pinkerton agents to shadow his mother whenever she left the hotel. Whenever Robert was absent, Mary hurried out to the nearby stores and indulged in a frenzy of reckless spending, purchasing forty pairs of lace curtains for $600, three watches for $450, soaps and perfumes for $200, and $700 worth of jewelry. Since she had no home to furnish and wore only mourning black without jewels, Robert condemned the bulging parcels as entirely unnecessary and returned as many of the items as the merchants would accept.

On and on it went, until Robert could bear no more. Resigning himself to his utter lack of options, he consulted expert physicians and began the process to have his mother tried and committed.

As always was the case with Mary, the entire painful, heartrending, embarrassing episode had been thoroughly examined and adjudicated in the press. Ann remembered well the pitying looks and sidelong glances she had received as she went about her errands and calls in Springfield, as if acquaintances wanted to offer consolation but assumed that she would prefer they not acknowledge the incidents, as if strangers wondered whether Ann might suddenly go mad like her sister right before their eyes.

If Mary never had been insane, as she claimed, how did she

account for her deranged behavior in those terrible weeks? And if it had all been an act, would that not reveal a derangement of a different sort?

Harassed by unslaked curiosity, Ann finally decided to come right out and ask Mary to explain herself.

She posed the question one afternoon as they walked together in the Edwardses' gardens, luxuriant in autumn blooms and fall foliage. To her surprise, Mary did not take offense, but pondered in silence for a long moment. "The signs of derangement I exhibited last spring must have arisen from a physical disorder," she eventually replied, her voice low, her expression pensive. "My health was poor before I went to Florida—hence the hiring of a nurse as a traveling companion—and it worsened after I was caught out in a rain shower and developed a dreadful cold. I was conscious of a fever, and at the time I was taking chloral hydrate very freely, to induce sleep. Those causes had much to do, undoubtedly, with producing the untoward behavior."

Ann studied her sharply, unable to discern whether Mary was telling the truth—or rather, whether to believe she was. Mary's cheeks were flushed, suggesting she had indeed just made an embarrassing confession. Ann was on the cusp of accepting her sister's explanation, but then she considered that Mary had no fever at the moment, and she was not taking chloral hydrate as far as Ann knew, and yet she still displayed signs of mania. Perhaps this so-called explanation was no more than an elaborate lie deftly woven to ensnare the most skeptical of the Todd sisters. If Mary could convince Ann, the others would be easily won.

If Mary could pretend, so could Ann. She would act as if she believed her elder sister, yet all the while, she would watch her surreptitiously for signs of madness.

By the end of October, Ann still could not decide whether Mary's increasing annoyance at Robert qualified as mania or was merely an ordinary, regrettable quarrel between a mother and a son.

The crux of the matter was the control of her property.

Although Mary had secured her release from the asylum, she remained legally insane, and Robert remained her conservator. According to state law, she could not appeal to change her status until at least one year after her commitment trial. This immutable fact gnawed at her. Robert hadn't written the law, but she blamed him for her legal circumstances, and as the weeks passed her resentment steadily and visibly grew. Mary was proud and liked to think of herself as independent, and it galled her that her son controlled her bonds and had been given most of her trunks and possessions for safekeeping.

Her discontent surfaced with greater frequency from late October into November. She would seem perfectly amiable, polite, cheerful, and affectionate in company, but if the subject of her property was broached, she suddenly became agitated and irritable. She disparaged Robert to her sisters as she rarely had before, provoking mild remonstrances from Elizabeth. "I am convinced that the only alternative, for the sake of peace and quiet, will be for Robert to yield to Mary the right to control her possessions," she told Ann and Frances wearily one afternoon when Mary was not there to hear.

"Do you mean her bonds and accounts too?" asked Frances.

Elizabeth hesitated. "Yes, I believe so. Regardless of her legal status, Mary is no longer insane—"

"In your opinion," said Ann pointedly, her tone conveying that it was something less than an informed medical judgment.

"In my opinion, based upon close observation," Elizabeth emphasized. "In such altered circumstances, Robert ought to let Mary do whatever she chooses, whether it be shopping, traveling, living where she likes, or managing her money. Mary has suggested that if her bonds were returned to her, she would entrust them to Mr. Bunn at the Springfield Marine Bank. He was a close friend of Abe's, someone she trusts. She isn't planning to carry the bonds about with her as she did before."

"I see nothing wrong with letting Mary have her trunks and belongings, but her money is another matter," said Frances, brow furrowing. "She'll spend it all on frivolities and clothes she'll never wear. There will be nothing left for her to live on in the years to come."

"If I've learned anything in life, it's that once you have done all you can for people, you ought to let them be," said Elizabeth, lifting her chin. "I am going to write to Robert and tell him so."

Frances regarded her levelly, a faint frown turning the corners of her mouth. "Then you oblige me to write to him as well, to give him *my* opinion."

Elizabeth inclined her head, acknowledging her right to do so.

Ann looked from one sister to the other, wary and wondering, until a faint stirring of anger took greater hold. The three Todd sisters who called Springfield home had always shared a particularly close bond, not only because they saw one another more often, but because of a deep affinity borne of similar perspectives and shared experiences. Mary had always lived outside their small circle—or, as she probably preferred to believe, above it.

Mary had disrupted nearly every relationship in her life. Would she now come between her sisters, setting one against another, their longtime amity forgotten?

14

April 1856–November 1860

After suffering the bitterest loss of his political career, Abe "picked up my lost crumbs of last year," as he ruefully put it, and committed himself to his law practice. His prospects and earnings rose as his career flourished, and in April 1856, Mary arranged for significant expansions and renovations to the Lincoln cottage. An entire second story was added, with additional bedrooms for the family, a guest room, a maid's room, and a servants' staircase in the back. The first floor was thoroughly redone as well. The front entrance opened into a wide stair-hall, with a formal parlor on the left and an informal sitting room for the family on the right. Double sliding doors led from the parlor into Abe's library and study, across the hall from an elegant, spacious dining room where Mary could at last entertain in fine style. Every room was also lavishly redecorated with floral carpets, luxurious floor-to-ceiling drapes with heavy swags, and ornate wallpaper.

How Mary relished shopping and decorating, and how immeasurably pleased with herself she had been on the evening she celebrated the completion of the project with a party for three hundred! As they toured the house among a throng of friends, family, and distant acquaintances who had somehow finagled invitations, Frances and her sisters admired Mary's work and agreed that the renovations had been beautifully and tastefully done. The

Edwards residence remained the larger of the two and, in Frances's opinion, the more elegant, but in the interest of family harmony, she did not share her observations.

The first visitor to use the new guest bedroom on the second floor was, quite unexpectedly, Benjamin Hardin Helm, who had come to Springfield from Kentucky on business for his law firm. Mary and Abe were eager to meet the husband of their beloved Little Sister, and upon learning that he had taken a room in a boardinghouse for the week, they insisted he stay with them instead. As Mary told Frances afterward, although they were twenty-three years apart in age, Abe and Ben immediately became close friends, with a bond of affection as strong as between brothers. Ben admired Abe's kindhearted nature, eloquence, intelligence, and wit, while Abe appreciated Ben's thoughtful and scholarly demeanor. They were both sorry when Ben's business concluded and he returned home to Kentucky, but he promised to return with Emilie for a longer visit after their baby was born.

Emilie would have been pleased to see brother Abe undaunted by the painful defeat she and Mary had witnessed from the statehouse gallery two years before. Just as the Kansas-Nebraska Act had inspired him to reenter politics in 1854, so did the *Dred Scott* decision and the election of James Buchanan as president compel him to strengthen his commitment to the burgeoning Republican Party. He decided to challenge the incumbent US senator, his old rival Stephen Douglas, and in June 1858 he received the unanimous support of the Republican Party.

Frances, Elizabeth, and Ann joined Mary in the gallery of the Hall of Representatives to observe Abe make his acceptance speech to the more than one thousand delegates who had met for the Republican State Convention. Ninian and other friends had warned Abe that the speech was too radical—his law partner, William Herndon, declared that he was being morally courageous but politically imprudent—but Abe decided to deliver it as written.

And what a speech it was—meaningful, prophetic, logical, and profound, a warning about the steadily rising tensions between slave states and free that transfixed Frances the way no other oratory on the subject had before. "A house divided against itself cannot stand," Abe declared in the early moments of his address. "I believe this government cannot endure, permanently half slave and half free. I do not expect the Union to be dissolved—I do not expect the house to fall—but I do expect it will cease to be divided. It will become all one thing or all the other."

From August through October, Abe and Mr. Douglas traveled throughout the state together for a series of debates. A throng of newspapermen from around the country accompanied them, so their speeches were often printed verbatim in cities throughout the land. Not only did the debates allow Illinois voters to understand the candidates' opinions thoroughly, but they also brought the controversy about the expansion of slavery to the attention of a national audience. Frances and William agreed that the national attention made Abe familiar to that same vast audience, which included powerful political groups in the East. Most resided outside of Illinois and would not be able to vote for him this time, but Abe was sowing seeds to harvest in the future.

Frances and her sisters followed the debates in the press, excited, hopeful, and apprehensive. On November 2, 1858, Abe won the popular election by four thousand votes—but in Illinois the state legislature chose the US senators, and although they were supposed to be guided by the citizens' vote, they were not bound to it.

Unfortunately for Abe and the Republicans, the Democrats held a majority, and they promptly reelected Stephen Douglas to a second term.

Perhaps it was a foreseeable defeat, but as Frances and William had noted months before, Abe remained very influential in his home state, and now the rest of the country knew his name too.

He continued to make speeches and to support other Republican candidates, and by early 1860, he was being spoken of as a candidate for president in the same breath as the renowned statesmen William Seward, Salmon Chase, and Edward Bates. While Mary reveled in the possibilities, Frances was amazed to think that her younger sister's childhood wish might be on the verge of coming true.

In April, the city of Springfield officially declared that Abraham Lincoln was their first choice for president of the United States. "We deem ourselves honored to be permitted to testify," the proclamation read, "our personal knowledge in everyday life as friends and neighbors of his inestimable worth as a private citizen, his faithful and able discharge of every public trust committed to his care, and the extraordinary gifts and brilliant attainments which have not only made his name a household word in the Prairie State, but also made him the proud peer of the ablest jurists, the wisest statesmen, and the most eloquent orators in the Union."

Mary fairly swooned with delight.

In the second week of May, the delegates at the Illinois Republican Convention in Decatur not only nominated Abe—dubbing him the "rail candidate for president" and with great fanfare carrying into the hall two fence rails he had supposedly split as a youth—but also passed a resolution stating that "the delegates from this State are instructed to use all honorable means to secure his nomination by the Chicago Convention, and to vote as a unit for him."

"I cannot emphasize enough how essential this is to his success," Mary told her sisters over tea a few days later. "Abe knows he cannot win the nomination on the first vote. William Seward is the front-runner, and his lead is substantial. However, the senator of New York is not universally beloved. If Abe survives the first ballot, delegates from other states might rally to him as an alternative to Mr. Seward."

On May 16, the Republican Convention opened in Chicago. As Abe intended to follow the established custom of not attending in person, he and Mary and the rest of the extended family were obliged to wait for news to reach Springfield by telegraph.

Other relevant party business took up the first two days. When the floor was opened to nominations on the third day, Abe was nominated and seconded, along with Mr. Seward, Mr. Chase, and several other worthy gentlemen.

Then the voting began.

Knowing that Mary was likely to be nervous and excitable throughout what was expected to be a long day with multiple rounds of balloting, her sisters took turns keeping her company. Frances was home with the children when word of the first ballot came through: Seward 173$^{1}/_{2}$, Lincoln 102, Cameron 50$^{1}/_{2}$, Chase 49, Bates 48, McLean 12, Collamer 10, Wade 3, Sumner 1, Fremont 1.

"Uncle Abe is second only to Mr. Seward," Mary Jane marveled, shaking her head prettily. "All those important men, and he beat them all."

"Loyalties will shift now," Frances explained. "If defeat seems inevitable, a candidate's supporters may vote for someone else in the next round."

Later, it was Ninian who came by with news of the second ballot: Seward 184$^{1}/_{2}$, Lincoln 181, Chase 42$^{1}/_{2}$, Bates 35, Dayton 10, McLean 8, Cameron 2, Clay 2. "Abe gained ground, but so did Seward," Ninian remarked.

"Yes, but observe how much Abe narrowed the gap," Frances exclaimed. "He may overtake Seward yet."

"The third round will decide it," said Ninian. "The other nominees are too far behind. Their supporters will surely choose between the two leaders with their next ballot. The question remains, which of them will reach 231 votes first, Abe or Seward?"

Soon thereafter, Frances went to Mary's house to attend her until word of the final balloting arrived. Frances found her sister alone, except for the children and servants, for Abe had spent the day in the telegraph office awaiting news and election returns. The hour grew quite late. They chatted and kept their hands busy with sewing or knitting until their eyes grew tired from the strain of working by lamplight. The children were put to bed, the house grew silent, but in the lovely sitting room of the Lincoln home, Mary and Frances were wide awake, listening for the sound of Abe's arrival and trying not to watch the clock.

It was nearly nine o'clock when Mary sat up in her chair, suddenly alert. "Do you hear that?" she asked.

Frances listened carefully until a faint melody drifted to her ear. "Music?"

Pressing a hand to her heart, Mary nodded and bolted to her feet. Frances followed her to the front entry, where her sister paced back and forth, wringing her hands and smiling tremulously, until they heard Abe's distinct tread on the front porch.

Mary flung open the door, and there stood her husband, eyes beaming, a faint, melancholic smile on his face. "I told the fellows waiting outside the telegraph office that there was a little woman at home who was probably more interested in this dispatch than I was." He held out a telegram.

Mary gasped and snatched it from his hand, and Frances read over her shoulder the results of the third ballot: Lincoln 231^1/$_2$, Seward 180, and Chase 24^1/$_2$, with the remaining few votes distributed sparsely among the others. Then, once Abe had won the majority, all of the delegates immediately switched their votes so the choice would be unanimous.

Abraham Lincoln had won the Republican Party nomination for president of the United States.

As Frances marveled and Mary cried for joy and embraced her husband, the faint music they had heard from afar swelled as an impromptu marching band approached the house, playing jubilant, patriotic tunes. A vast crowd soon gathered, and Abe stepped outside to address them, accepting the honor of their visit, which he assumed was not so much for himself as for the representative of their great party. After a loud burst of applause, Abe thanked them again and remarked, "I would invite you all into the house if I thought it were large enough to hold you."

"We will give you a larger house on the fourth of next March," a man called out. The crowd laughed and cheered and clapped.

"As my current home could not contain more than a fraction of you," Abe continued, "I will merely invite in as many as can find room."

Immediately a shout went up and there was a rush for the door. Frances and Mary had a moment to exchange a look of panicked dismay before they hastened to welcome the unexpected guests.

By the time the last well-wisher drifted away, it was too late for Frances to return home, so she stayed overnight in the guest room, her head still buzzing from wonder and excitement. The next morning she and Mary slept late. After waking, they chatted happily over a leisurely breakfast—the last leisurely morning her sister was likely to have for a while, Frances supposed. She returned home after breakfast, so she was not present when the official delegation from Chicago arrived to formally inform Abe that the Republican Convention had selected him as their candidate for the presidential election. Soon thereafter, Abe formally accepted.

Republicans across the land reveled, virtually all of Springfield rejoiced, and Frances thought Mary should too. The Todd sisters read in the papers how the delegates in Chicago had celebrated after nominating Abe, how cannons had been fired and nearly thirty thousand people had filled the streets, shouting and cheering, how the *Press* and *Tribune* buildings had been illuminated from foundation to rooftop, and how bands had played triumphant marches as Republicans paraded through the streets with fence rails on their shoulders in a nod to Abe's humble origins.

Soon thereafter, the press shifted its focus to Springfield. Reporters raced to learn more about the Western lawyer who had astounded the country by defeating the presumptive nominee. Mary well understood how important it was that her husband make an excellent impression on the writers who would soon describe him for millions of curious and skeptical readers. Treating them as honored guests, Mary graciously entertained the journalists who crossed their threshold, making them comfortable in her beautifully decorated home, offering them delicious food and drink, impressing them with her grace, knowledge, and charm, and quickly dispelling the notion that the Lincolns were country bumpkins. Most of the subsequent articles praised her lovely manners and stylish appearance, but one earned her eternal enmity by describing her as "squatty," and a few others indignantly noted that she was too free with her opinions and had an "unwomanly" interest in politics.

Others who descended on Springfield to meet their nominee included politicians, party leaders, and other prominent Republicans who held no official office but were respected for their ability to make or break a candidate. Despite the publicity of the Lincoln-Douglas debates two years before, Abe remained a stranger to a vast number of men he urgently needed to vote for him. He was so little known even within his own party that after the convention there had been some confusion within the Republican press about whether his given name was Abraham or Abram.

Most of these political men requested a private meeting with Abe and came away impressed with his intelligence and astute grasp of the rising tensions between the North and South, as well as the dwindling number of options to resolve the conflict peacefully. Dozens more came to introduce themselves and to pledge their loyalty, some out of a sincere belief that he was the best man to bear the standard of the Republican Party, others in the hope of receiving a patronage position after he took office. The majority left Springfield with a favorable opinion of the candidate and his wife, but some looked askance when Mary listed her ideal choices for cabinet positions or queried leaders about campaign strategy. Their pointed looks conveyed as emphatically as words that her role was to be the devoted, selfless angel of her husband's household, not his political adviser.

Frances was aware that Mary was working tirelessly to support Abe by winning over the press and the Republican establishment. This was the role Mary had prepared for all her life, and she embraced it with great enthusiasm. But in the weeks following the convention, Mary's great endeavor receded into the background for Frances as other concerns occupied her thoughts. Ann's ten-year-old son Lincoln had fallen ill from typhoid, and for many long days he suffered from burning fevers, headaches, lethargy, and terrible stomach pains. William attended him several times a day, examining him carefully and offering him the best remedies known to medical science. Frances did all she could to assist her husband, while Elizabeth visited daily to take Ann's place at Lincoln's bedside so she could steal a few hours of sleep. When the boy's symptoms precipitously worsened, Elizabeth moved into the Smiths' guest room and managed the household so her sister could devote herself to nursing her son. But despite their vigilant care and William's renowned skill, Lincoln grew weaker day by day. On June 12, he died as his weeping parents clasped his hands and prayed until all hope was lost.

Frances knew that nothing she could say would ease her devastated sister's pain. What else could she do but embrace Ann and let her weep in her arms until exhaustion overcame her and she was able to sleep?

Mary, who knew too well how Ann suffered, came by every day to sit with her when Ann could do no more than recline in a darkened room and grieve. On better days, if Ann responded to her coaxing, Mary escorted her on slow, quiet walks in the sunshine to keep up her strength. Elizabeth and Julia looked after the household and the younger children, while William and Frances saw to the funeral arrangements. Even Abe's crucial political activities came to an abrupt halt while the family mourned.

On the day of the burial, Frances sought comfort in the words of scripture the minister intoned, and she tried to take heart from observing how the family had come together to show their deep and abiding love and support for the grieving parents. But as the small coffin was lowered into the ground, a strange, grim premonition came over her that one day all of Springfield would be clad in mourning black and the Todd sisters would grieve anew—not together, but separated by immeasurable distances.

The presidential race would not pause for the family's mourning. In keeping with established custom, Abe did not campaign for himself. Instead, other prominent Republicans stumped for him—Charles Sumner and Cassius Clay, as well as his erstwhile rivals for the nomination, Salmon Chase, Frank P. Blair, and William Seward. Restrained from using his most powerful means of persuasion—his own extraordinary oratorical skills—Abe knew he needed help if he was to win the national election.

Some help came to him from an unlikely quarter—the Democratic Party. Their national convention in Charleston had ended in shambles in April, when outraged Southern delegates had walked out after a heated dispute over the party's official platform regarding slavery. When the Democrats officially reconvened in Baltimore on June 18, the disgruntled delegates' states had replaced them with more cooperative men. To no one's surprise, Mr. Douglas was chosen as the party's nominee. Five days later, the excluded Southern delegates defiantly held their own convention elsewhere in the city and nominated former congressman and current vice president John C. Breckinridge, a Kentuckian who adamantly insisted that the Constitution permitted slavery throughout the states and new territories. Further crowding the slate of presidential candidates was Mr. John Bell of Tennessee, the nominee of the Constitutional Union Party, an alliance of conservative Know-Nothings and Whigs whose simple platform suggested that their approach to the slavery question was to ignore it altogether. With the Democrats splintered, the outlook for a Republican victory in November seemed promising, but Ninian, who had remained a Democrat even though switching parties in 1851 had failed to win him a seat in Congress, held out hope for the Democrats. He believed that the battle for electoral votes would break along geographic lines, with Abe battling Mr. Douglas for the Northern states and Mr. Breckinridge and Mr. Bell splitting those in the South. "Douglas has trounced Abe before," Ninian said, more cheerfully than Frances thought polite. "The Republicans should take nothing for granted."

Even with the Democrats splintering into factions, Frances and Elizabeth privately agreed that Abe had his work cut out for him. According to the press, news of his nomination had met with incredulity in Washington, and Democratic newspapers gleefully ridiculed his humble origins, calling him a "third-rate Western lawyer" and a "fourth-rate lecturer who cannot speak good grammar" and whose illiterate speeches were "interlarded with coarse and clumsy jokes"—a claim that anyone who had ever heard him speak would recognize as patently untrue. Not surprisingly, the Southern press provided the most blistering vitriol, mocking not only Abe's intellect, which they wrongly assumed to be quite insignificant, but also his appearance. "Lincoln is the leanest, lankest, most ungainly mass of legs, arms and hatchet-face ever strung upon a single frame," the *Houston Telegraph* declared with fascinated horror. "He has most unwarrantably abused the privilege which all politicians have of being ugly." Remarking upon Abe's image in *Harper's Weekly*, the *Charleston Mercury* proclaimed, "A horrid looking wretch he is, sooty and scoundrelly in aspect, a cross between the nutmeg dealer, the horse swapper, and the night man, a creature fit evidently for petty treason, small stratagems, and all sorts of spoils." Elizabeth knew Mary took great offense at such depictions, and she too found the lurid prose utterly unfair. Abe might not be what most people would consider handsome, but he was not the grotesquerie depicted in the papers either. And what did his looks have to do with his ability to govern?

Unfortunately, petty mockery of Abe's appearance proved to be one of the more benign aspects of press coverage in the South. Editorials in papers in nearly every Southern city warned of the dreadful consequences that would befall the nation if he were elected, not the mere policy disputes of bygone days, but violent confrontations in the halls of government and cataclysmic upheaval in Southern towns and homes. Although Frances could not prove it, she was sure the fearmongering in the press was what inspired the malicious, cowardly death threats that began arriving at Abe's law office and the Lincoln family home. Her heart went out to poor Mary, who daily swung between elation and terror, depending upon the papers and the post.

As November approached, the results of early fall elections boded well for Abe, with sweeping Republican victories in local and state elections in Vermont, Maine, Pennsylvania, Ohio, and Indiana. Then, at long last and yet before Frances felt quite prepared for it, election day arrived. The morning dawned lovely and clear, and to Frances the crisp autumn air seemed to hum with tension and expectation. Mary had told her sisters that Abe planned to spend the day with his friends and supporters in a room reserved for him at the statehouse, and that the first returns were not expected until after seven o'clock in the evening. Knowing that Mary would fret and worry at home alone with only the children for company, Frances and Elizabeth promised to join her there after supper and to remain with her until the end.

Not long after they settled down in Mary's sitting room, preparing themselves for a long, anxious wait, a messenger boy arrived with word from Abe, who had left the raucous statehouse for the telegraph office to await the national returns in relative quiet. He had won the New England states and Pennsylvania, the boy reported; a few hours later, he returned to announce that Abe had won the Northwest and Indiana. He had not taken a single Southern state, nor was he likely to, for several had left his name off the ballot altogether.

Frances silently tallied the electoral votes, and when her eyes met Mary's, she knew they had been struck by the same dreadful thought: Abe must win New York, for without the state's precious thirty-five electoral votes, he would fall seven short of a majority.

The hours passed slowly, fatigue and tension draining them of the desire to chat. Then, around two o'clock in the morning, the sisters heard a brass band approaching, heedless of the late hour and slumbering neighbors likely to be startled awake by the rousing, cheerful march.

It was then the sisters knew that Abe had taken New York, and therefore the entire election.

Soon thereafter, the front door opened and Abe strolled in. Hurrying to meet him, Mary threw herself into his arms in a passion of tears. "Why, Mary," said Abe, patting her shoulder and smiling over her head at Frances and Elizabeth, "I thought you wanted me to be president."

"I do," said Mary, smiling up through her tears, "and I am very happy—that is why I am crying."

As she and Elizabeth congratulated Abe and bade the couple good-night, Frances thought that, despite his smile, her brother-in-law seemed as somber as she had ever seen him.

From the moment dawn broke, Springfield was filled with celebration—marching bands, impromptu parades, speeches at the statehouse. Frances joined in some of the festivities, but for the most part she spent the day at home, overjoyed for Mary and Abe but exhausted from excitement and dazed from the sudden release of tension. The next morning, feeling better rested, she called on Mary to find her sister shaken and drawn, her abundant joy of the previous few days utterly gone. "What's wrong?" Frances asked, placing her hands on her sister's shoulders and looking her over. "Are you ill? Should I fetch William? Have you received bad news?"

Mary tried to smile, but grimaced instead. "You will think it's all nonsense."

"Tell me anyway."

Mary sighed and led her to the sitting room. "Last night, Abe lay down to rest on the lounge in his office." She seated herself on the sofa and, with a gesture, invited Frances to sit beside her. "He saw his image reflected in the mirror, but with two faces, one much paler than the other. The sight unsettled him, and he told me so."

"It was a trick of the light, or a badly formed mirror. What is so upsetting about that?"

"I think it was a vision," said Mary. "A prophetic sign that he will be elected twice, but will not live out his second term."

"Oh, Mary." Frances reached out to clasp Mary's hand, cold and trembling, in both of her own. "It is no such thing. Abe was tired. He glimpsed himself in the mirror from an odd angle. You're giving it too much meaning."

"I've had prophetic visions before."

"This isn't one of them," said Frances firmly. "This wasn't even your vision, but Abe's. Why spoil this triumphant moment with false fears? Don't you have enough to worry about, what with preparing to move to Washington and become mistress of the White House?"

Mary smiled wanly and acknowledged that Frances made a fair point.

In the country beyond Springfield, the response of the press to Abe's election was swift and unambiguous, whether for good or ill. One Kansas paper referred to the news of his victory as "glorious tidings," while the *Richmond Dispatch* gloomily intoned, "The event is the most deplorable one that has happened in the history of the country." The *Courier* of New Orleans agreed, warning that the election had "awakened throughout the South a spirit of stubborn resistance which it will be found is impossible to quell." The *New York Enquirer* paid homage to the spirit of democracy and took a conciliatory approach, proclaiming, "Stretching out our hands to the South over this victory, we have no word of taunt to utter for the threats of disunion which were raised for our defeat. Let those threats be buried in oblivion." The editor of the *Semi-Weekly Mississippian* would have none of that, and beneath a headline declaring, "The Deed's Done—Disunion the Remedy," he called Abe and the vice president–elect, Hannibal Hamlin, "both bigoted, unscrupulous and cold-blooded enemies of the peace and equality of the slaveholding states, and one of the pair strongly marked with the blood of his negro ancestry." More upsetting was the editor's conclusion that since the election proved the intention of the Northern states "to wield the vast machinery of the federal Government to destroy the liberties of the slaveholding states, it becomes their duty to dissolve their connection and establish a separate and independent government of their own."

Frances knew that the South had been threatening to secede for decades, and that a certain amount of heightened agitation and a frenzied clamor for secession could be expected in the aftermath of such a hard-fought election. She wanted to dismiss these fiery diatribes as more empty threats—and yet they seemed to represent a new mood in the nation, a strange distemper that threatened an untenable peace.

In late November, Frances was at Mary's home helping her send out invitations for a dinner party when a parcel arrived. "Another unexpected gift," Mary said, pleased, as they carried the flat, rectangular parcel into the sitting room, where Mary took scissors from her sewing basket and began to cut the twine and brown paper wrappings. "This one is from South Carolina, of all places. Since the election, gifts have been arriving from all across the country—"

Her voice choked off as the paper fell away to reveal a painting on canvas—a crude likeness of Abe, tarred and feathered, a rope around his neck and chains binding his feet.

Frances gasped. Blanching, Mary dropped the painting and drew back in horror, a hand pressed to her heart. "Who would paint such a monstrous thing?" she exclaimed, voice shaking, tears in her eyes. "Who would send it here—here, where his wife and children—"

"Don't look at it," Frances said, snatching up the horrid painting and carrying it from the room. "Never think of it again."

But she knew the dreadful image would be forever seared into her sister's memory, as would the malevolent threat it implied.

15

November–December 1875

Throughout November, letters and telegrams flew between Springfield and Chicago, between three concerned sisters and their increasingly exasperated nephew. Whether his mother was mad or sane was an open question, and also beside the point. Robert did not trust Mary's judgment in financial matters, not because of a doctor's diagnosis but because of her impulsive behavior. As the conservator of her estate, as well as her son and the head of the family, he was responsible for her conduct, her physical safety, and her financial security. "There is no person upon whom lies the responsibility and duty of protecting her when she needs it, except myself," Robert wrote to Ann in the middle of the month, and also to Frances, as they discovered when they compared letters afterward. "I want to do everything in my power for her happiness, and I have no wish to interfere with her expenditures other than to ensure that she will have enough money to last the rest of her life."

Frances agreed that in her fragile mental state, Mary could unwittingly impoverish herself. Ann thought that it was far more likely that she would deliberately go bankrupt in order to humiliate her son, for the public would surely blame him if his unwell, widowed mother was allowed to squander her fortune.

Ann sympathized with Robert, who carried several major responsibilities: for his resentful, possibly mad mother; for his law practice; and for his family, which included a newborn son, his third child. He did not need the additional distraction of a prolonged battle with his mother over her assets. Nor was he certain whether he was legally permitted to turn over the bonds and other accounts to his mother, as she demanded, since the entire point of a conservatorship was to protect such assets from a person declared legally insane.

A week after his son was born, Robert wrote to his Springfield aunts to say that he would make no decisions without consulting his most trusted advisers. These included David Davis, a close friend of Abe's since his circuit court days and the man most responsible for Abe's nomination in 1860. In 1862, Abe had appointed him to the Supreme Court, and three years later he became the executor of Abe's estate. In late November, Robert wrote to inform the Springfield family of Justice Davis's recommendations, sending one letter to Elizabeth, which he asked her to share with the others. Justice Davis believed that Mary should have remained at Bellevue until she had recovered completely, and that the Bradwells' meddling would prove disastrous to her. However, since the deed was done, he recommended that Robert remove all restrictions on his mother's travel and residence and return her belongings, but rather than turn over her bonds, he should pay her a monthly income, which she would be free to spend as she wished. "This advice I intend to follow," Robert wrote.

Soon thereafter, boxes and trunks full of his mother's possessions arrived at the Edwards residence, including a jewelry box and eleven trunks of clothing. When Ann stopped by to help Mary, Elizabeth, and the housekeeper and maid find places to store everything, Elizabeth, much perturbed by the enormity of the task, wearily concluded that most of the clothes and trinkets would have to remain in the trunks, for there was not enough wardrobe and bureau space in the house to allow them to unpack everything.

At first Mary seemed delighted to have her belongings back, but as the afternoon wore on and she completed a cursory examination of the trunks, her face clouded over with suspicion and disappointment. "This is not everything," she fretted. "He kept back some of my most precious items, my most sentimental favorites."

"Isn't this enough for the present?" asked Ann, gesturing around the once-tidy guest room, now crowded with cartons and trunks. "You have more dresses here than you can possibly wear in a year, and you keep buying new ones. You're going to squeeze Elizabeth's family out of their own home."

"It's the principle of the thing," Mary retorted. "None of this would matter if Robert would simply yield up my bonds."

This, Ann and her other sisters knew, Robert had no intention of doing. "Mary has become very much embittered against Robert over the past fortnight," Elizabeth confided to Ann in a murmur later that day as she was seeing her to the door. "The more he yields, the more she demands."

"Then let's hope our nephew will stand firm this time," said Ann, "or soon you won't be able to walk around your house without tripping over a trunk."

Elizabeth's forlorn look suggested that she had considered this possibility but did not see how to forestall it.

When Ann next called on her eldest sister at the end of the month, Elizabeth confessed that matters had only worsened. Mary continued to demand that Robert increase her monthly stipend and send her the rest of her trunks, even though Elizabeth protested that they did not have enough room to store them and that Mary did not truly need them. "More troubling yet," said Elizabeth, pursing her lips and glancing over her shoulder to make sure Mary was out of earshot, "she has been giving away an astonishing number of her possessions and money to old friends and acquaintances."

"The money is a concern," mused Ann, "but isn't it good that she's getting rid of things she no longer wants or needs? If she gives away enough, eventually you may have your house back."

"It isn't good at all," Elizabeth protested. "Many of the items she's given away actually belonged to Robert. I know for a fact that she gifted them to him and his wife years ago. As for the rest, those things ought to be considered part of his eventual inheritance. Ninian and I are shocked that Mary would rob her son of his future."

"Robert has never counted on a future inheritance to provide for himself and his family," Ann said. "His career is flourishing, for which he deserves all the credit, and he's built up his own wealth."

"That doesn't make Mary's actions any less wrong." Elizabeth held up her hands and shook her head. "I'm not talking about a gown she will never wear again, or a shawl ten years out of style. She should be free to dispense with such things as she wishes. My concern is about precious family mementos, artifacts of Robert's late father. Don't you agree those ought to go to Robert and his children?"

Ann hesitated, her uneasiness rising. For the past ten years, Mary had occasionally gifted a dear friend or a loyal colleague of Abe's with one of his possessions—a walking stick, for example, or a top hat or book. But to give away trunks full of belongings out of spite was quite another matter. Even if Mary had the legal right to dispense with the items as she wished, Robert deserved to be informed.

"I have no interest in an inheritance," Robert responded to Ann's urgent note. "Indeed, I had assumed that my mother had already cut me out of her will. When it comes to the ultimate disposition of her property, I do not want my best interest or that of my children to be a factor in the decision. The only objective I wish attained by any plan that may be devised is her own protection."

Ann considered this very generous of her nephew, far more generous than his spiteful mother deserved. Her indignation rose in December when Mary, increasingly incensed by Robert's refusal to return her bonds, threatened to hire an attorney to overturn his conservatorship. Mary warned her son that the legal process would oblige her to divulge the truth about the past ten years of their relationship, details that, if made public, would embarrass him more than herself, both personally and professionally.

Elizabeth told Ann that she and Ninian had talked themselves hoarse trying to dissuade her. Patiently and clearly, Ninian had repeatedly explained the rules of conservatorship to his sister-in-law, but she simply refused to believe that Robert had no legal discretion to restore her control over her assets as long as the judicial system still considered her legally insane.

"She's going to tear this family apart," Ann lamented to Clark one evening as they prepared for bed, shivering from upset nerves as much as from the cold. "Has she not dragged our reputation through the mud enough for one lifetime? What could she possibly gain by revealing private conversations with her son—highly fictionalized conversations, I'm quite sure—to shame him before the public? The people respect him and dislike her. She will never win them over, and she will convince absolutely no one that she should be in charge of her fortune. She will only prove that she ought never to have left Bellevue."

"She must think it won't come to that," said Clark as he turned down the lamp. "She must assume that Robert would rather give in to her demands than have her make a public spectacle of them both."

"But he cannot legally give her what she wants."

Clark sighed and climbed into bed beside her, drawing the quilts over them. "Someone needs to convince her of that, before this goes too far."

The room fell dark and silent, but her brooding kept Ann awake for a while. When she woke the next morning, she decided that since no one else seemed likely to convince Mary to relent, she might as well try. It was unlikely she could make matters worse.

A few snowflakes drifted past the windowpane as Ann put on a warm wool dress and went down to breakfast, nodding along to the children's chatter as she mentally rehearsed what she ought to tell her sister. It was late morning before she had the opportunity to put on her boots and wraps and venture out to the Edwards residence.

When she arrived, the housekeeper informed her that her mistress was resting and Mrs. Lincoln had gone out for a walk with her grandnephew Lewis. Invited to wait in the parlor, Ann decided to meet her sister and grandnephew along the way, the better to let Elizabeth sleep undisturbed.

Breathing deeply of the crisp air, which carried a faint hint of snows to come, Ann set out in the direction the housekeeper had indicated. She had gone only two blocks when she spotted Mary's familiar figure, cloaked and hooded, coming up the sidewalk toward her, alone. Lewis was nowhere to be seen.

Immediately suspicious, Ann lifted her skirts and hurried toward her sister. She reached Mary before she could duck away, not that Ann couldn't easily overtake her in a footrace. "Where is Lewis?" Ann asked, trying to sound merely curious.

Mary drew herself up imperiously. "I wanted to be alone with my thoughts."

"I was told he went out walking with you."

"He had business of his own to complete, so we parted company."

Ann could only imagine how Mary had managed to elude her grandnephew, and how embarrassed the young man would feel later when he discovered that he had been duped. "I see you had errands too," Ann said, eyeing the thick envelope her sister clutched under her arm. Quickly she stepped forward, and although Mary turned to block her view, she was not fast enough to hide the name of the sender.

"Judge Bradwell?" Ann exclaimed. "You have been communicating with the Bradwells?"

"What if I have?"

"You know very well that cutting off all contact with those two was a condition of your release!"

"Ceasing contact was a condition of my *visit*," Mary retorted, her voice steely. "Once I was permanently discharged, such conditions no longer applied."

"I doubt Dr. Patterson or Elizabeth or Robert would agree." Glimpsing a cagy look in her sister's eye, Ann added, "If you didn't think it was wrong, you wouldn't be keeping it secret, or lying about your errand and abandoning Lewis along the way."

"Judge Bradwell is my legal adviser. If you must know, I asked him to send me my will so that I may amend it."

To cut Robert out, Ann had no doubt. "Is this the only contact you've had with Bradwell or his wife?" she queried. "If obtaining your will is all that has passed between you, and you have no intention of writing to either of them again, then I will not feel obliged to tell Elizabeth and Robert what I know."

"Nonsense," said Mary, brushing past her as she continued on her way back to the Edwards residence. "You'll tell them whatever you please, embellished beyond recognition."

Greatly vexed, Ann turned and followed her sister home, reluctant to leave her alone but unwilling to walk beside her. Mary immediately went upstairs to her bedchamber, while Ann went to Elizabeth's room, relieved to find her awake. Elizabeth was so astonished and troubled by the news of Mary's subterfuge that she sent word to Ninian to come home from work immediately. Conferring in his study with the door closed, Ann, Elizabeth, and Ninian quickly deduced that Mary's anger at Robert had begun to surge right around the time she had resumed her correspondence with the Bradwells. They also agreed—grudgingly, on Ann's part—that clandestinely resuming contact with the meddling pair was not grounds for returning Mary to Bellevue. Even so, Elizabeth considered it a personal betrayal. Severing contact with the Bradwells was a condition not only for Mary's release but also for her acceptance into the Edwards household. That the short-term visit had turned into an indefinite stay mattered not at all. By going behind Elizabeth's back, Mary had betrayed her sister's trust.

Of course Robert had to be informed, though doing so incensed Mary all the more.

In late December, over her sisters' pleas and protests, Mary hired an attorney, former Illinois governor John M. Palmer, to appeal Robert's conservatorship. Mary became increasingly excitable and contentious during the few days the governor investigated the legal statutes, and she eagerly awaited the day when the facts of the case would be presented to her. As her guardians, Elizabeth and Ninian were obliged to attend the meeting, which convened in Ninian's study one frosty afternoon. At Elizabeth's request, Ann and Frances came too, ready to help however might be necessary, depending upon the governor's findings and Mary's reaction.

Mary's expression was bright with anticipation that slowly faded as Governor Palmer informed her that Robert's understanding of the law was sound. The conservatorship could not be dissolved until she was no longer considered legally insane, and that appeal could not be heard until a year after her insanity trial.

At first Mary did not understand him, but sat wringing her hands, only asking when her bonds would be restored to her. Ninian took Governor Palmer aside and asked him to explain the principle of conservatorship to her, showing her references from law books if necessary, for she would be more likely to accept the unhappy truth from her own lawyer than from her son, her sisters, and her brothers-in-law.

Eventually Mary inhaled deeply, fixed a steady gaze on her lawyer, and said, "One year from the date of that abhorrent trial?"

"Yes, Mrs. Lincoln," her attorney replied. "One year."

She rose stiffly, sweeping her skirts behind her. "I shall note the date and the hour." Shoulders squared and head erect, she left the room without a glance at her sisters, at Ninian, or at anyone else.

Upon receiving a report of the meeting, Robert wrote to Governor Palmer offering to resign as his mother's conservator if the governor was willing to take his place. Governor Palmer declined.

"I am not interested in her property now, nor do I desire an inheritance later," Robert wrote to Ann soon thereafter, his weariness and frustration evident in the strokes of his pen. "She has always been generous to me in the past. I am exceedingly gratified to her for it all, and I shall never hesitate to acknowledge it, but my gratitude will not discharge my duty to her. I will do what I believe is best for her, even, if necessary, against her will."

As the year waned and she observed Mary's antipathy toward him steadily increasing, Ann suspected that anything Robert did short of returning her bonds would be precisely that: an action taken against her will, and to be resisted with all her strength and cunning.

16

December 1860–March 1861

ELIZABETH

A few days before Christmas, at a state convention held at Saint Andrew's Hall in Charleston, the delegates of South Carolina voted unanimously to secede from the Union.

Although warnings of secession had appeared with increasing frequency in Southern papers after Abe's election, many people in the North, including Elizabeth and Ninian, were astounded when South Carolina finally made good on the threat. The stock market roiled, politicians debated to no avail, and citizens North and South wondered with trepidation or fervor which state would be next to secede. Any hopes that South Carolina could swiftly be restored to the Union through negotiation were dashed when its newly appointed leaders declared that the three federal forts within its borders fell within their jurisdiction. While President Buchanan dithered over the appropriate response, perhaps wishing that Abe could replace him immediately and relieve him of the responsibility, the federal officer in charge of one of the forts took action. On the night of December 26, Major Robert Anderson moved his troops from their vulnerable position at Fort Moultrie on the mainland to the more defensible Fort Sumter in Charleston Harbor. The next day the South Carolina militia seized Fort Moultrie and Castle Pinckney and demanded Major Anderson's surrender. Major Anderson declined and resolutely held his post while the South Carolina military settled in for the siege.

In the midst of unprecedented national turmoil and alarm, Abe remained obliged to continue the work of his fledgling administration, and appointing a cabinet was foremost. He invited his former rivals for the Republican nomination, including Mr. Chase, to meet with him in Springfield, while others, such as Mr. Seward, sent proxies. Much to her chagrin, Mary was not allowed to sit in on their private meetings, but at the dinners and receptions she hosted during their visits she had many opportunities to speak with the potential cabinet secretaries and to weigh their merits. Elizabeth understood why Abe was obliged to consider his former rivals and other prominent party men for these important posts, but she hoped he did not overlook loyal, eminently qualified men closer to home—namely, her own dear Ninian. It would be bad form if Ninian came right out and requested a position, but he could, and did, intimate that he was ready and eager to serve in whatever capacity his brother-in-law deemed fit. Between themselves, Ninian and Elizabeth agreed that attorney general would be a high honor for which his skills and experience well suited him, but postmaster general was also prestigious enough.

Their anticipation was overshadowed by dire reports from the East. On January 5, the *New York Herald* reported that a steamship called the *Star of the West* had set out from New York for Charleston with supplies and troops to relieve Major Anderson at Fort Sumter. Other newspapers confirmed the story, noting where and when the merchant vessel had been spotted as it journeyed south along the coast. "I would feel reassured by President Buchanan's long overdue action," said Mary disparagingly, "except that the people of Charleston can get the news from Eastern papers as easily as we do. Surely their military forces will be ready and waiting when the *Star of the West* arrives. I can imagine all too well what a horror it would be if Americans turned their weapons upon their fellow Americans!"

Her words proved terribly prescient.

On January 10, Mary departed for New York—escorted by Clark, who knew the city well and could bring his merchant's skills to bear—so that she might purchase a wardrobe befitting the wife of the president-elect. After that, they would continue on to Cambridge to visit Robert at Harvard, and then bring him home so that he could accompany the family on the presidential train to Washington the following month. Mary confided to her sisters that along the way she intended to meet with prominent Republicans at levees and dinners, ostensibly so that they could pay their respects, but also so that she could evaluate their loyalty to her husband and raise support for her favorite candidates for his cabinet.

Elizabeth could not imagine that Abe knew anything about Mary's plans to go politicking, and she was quite sure he would not approve.

Mary and Clark boarded the eastbound train even as newspapers blazed with alarming new reports from South Carolina. The previous day, the *Star of the West* had sailed into Charleston Harbor and had been fired upon by militia and young military cadets. Struck in the mast but not seriously damaged, the steamer nonetheless had been forced back into the channel and out to the open sea.

On that same day, far to the south, delegates in Mississippi voted in favor of secession. The next day Florida seceded from the Union, and the next day Alabama followed suit. One after another the Southern states fell, like books carelessly arranged on an unsteady shelf. Former president John Tyler, living in retirement in Richmond, Virginia, published an appeal for a peace conference to make one last great effort to resolve the crisis without bloodshed. In unwitting mockery of Mr. Tyler's plea, Georgia seceded two days later, and two days after that five senators from Alabama, Florida, and Mississippi rose to offer farewell speeches before resigning their seats in the Senate and departing Washington for their homes in the South.

The papers somberly described how Senator Jefferson Davis, the last to speak, reiterated his opinion that states had the constitutional right to leave the Union and that his home state of Mississippi had justifiable cause for doing so. Even so, he regretted the conflict that had divided them. "I am sure I feel no hostility toward you, senators from the North," he said. "I am sure there is not one of you, whatever sharp discussion there may have been between us, to whom I cannot now say, in the presence of my God, I wish you well; and such, I feel, is the feeling of the people whom I represent toward those whom you represent." Weary from illness and strain, he expressed his hopes that their separate governments would eventually have peaceable relations and offered a personal apology for any pain he might have inflicted upon any other senator in the heat of debate.

Five days later, Louisiana seceded.

Mary had returned to Springfield by then, still glowing from her marvelous shopping excursion and the attention she had received in the press, although not all of the coverage was favorable. Even so, when the Todd sisters met in Elizabeth's parlor to share news of the family, Elizabeth could see that Mary was as anxious as she. Their half-sister Martha had married a doctor and settled in Selma, Alabama; their half-sister Elodie was living with her and intended to remain in the South. Their brother George and two of their half-brothers, Samuel and David, were living in New Orleans. Elizabeth had received one letter from Elodie since secession fever had taken hold of the South, but nothing from their brothers.

Her brother Levi urged her not to worry. "Our half-brothers have never been avid letter-writers," he noted. "They're likely chagrined that they didn't support Abe in the election, and now that he's won, they're keeping quiet so they don't appear hypocrites. They'll come around in time, when they see Abe isn't one to hold a grudge."

Elizabeth wanted to believe him, but their half-brothers in the South were not like Levi, who admired Abe and had campaigned for him in Lexington. Recently Levi had even pledged to give up liquor, the better to impress and emulate his brother-in-law, who never drank. Elizabeth fervently hoped Levi would remain sober, for he could be an angry, neglectful drunk, and his marriage had suffered for it. His voice no longer slurred, and he seemed to have acquired a renewed interest in life, but his hands trembled slightly and his skin had a tinge of jaundice. Perhaps, if his sobriety endured, those telltale signs of a chronic drunkard would fade in time.

Amid a shifting whirl of emotions—tremendous pride as Abe prepared to ascend to the highest office in the land, anxiety over their splintering nation, happiness for Mary as her childhood dream came true, worry for their loved ones who had apparently thrown in their lot with the secessionist South—Elizabeth and her sisters helped Mary prepare for the journey to the White House. There were trunks to pack, possessions to store, private family papers to burn, arrangements to rent out their home to make, guests to entertain, gifts to acknowledge, countless letters to write. So many well-wishers and office-seekers sought out Abe at home or at his law office that he was obliged to withdraw to a backroom on the third floor of Clark's dry goods store to write his inaugural address undisturbed. Mary was in her element, shopping and packing and issuing orders with unbridled delight, but whenever she heard of a new threat against her husband, she grew pale and trembling. Tearfully she begged Abe to travel with a bodyguard, but this he was loath to do. He was among friends and family in Springfield, he said, and he emphatically disagreed that his life was in any danger there.

The day was swiftly approaching when the Lincolns and their

entourage would leave Springfield for Washington. Mary's sisters assured her that even if Abe did not see to his own safety, his campaign manager, Judge David Davis, and Mr. Norman Judd, who had been placed in charge of Abe's security for the trip, would make any necessary arrangements. Mary frowned a little at the mention of the judge. When Abe had stopped listening out of courtesy whenever Mary suggested certain gentlemen for various cabinet posts, she had written to Judge Davis to persuade him of their merits, hoping he would present her recommendations as his own. Thus far it did not appear that the judge had interceded on her behalf.

In the first week of February, their half-sister Margaret, now Mrs. Charles Kellogg, traveled to Springfield from Cincinnati so that she might join them for the journey to Washington; a day later Martha arrived from Selma. Elizabeth was delighted to see them both, but Martha's presence brought a particular sense of relief, for she had imagined secession as a violent earthquake tearing an impassible rift between Union states and those that had seceded, as if Alabama had been torn from the map. Elizabeth hoped the nascent rebellion would be put down quickly, before it could complicate travel between North and South, preventing the sisters from moving freely between their households as they pleased.

Now the Todd sisters who had reunited in Springfield were preparing for another journey, and on February 5 they helped Mary host a grand farewell celebration at her home. Family, friends, political supporters, and a few members of the press were invited to visit between seven o'clock and midnight to make a parting call on the president-elect and his wife. Hundreds were expected, but thousands came. Abe himself received the guests as they entered and introduced themselves, then passed them on to be introduced to Mary, who awaited them in the parlor. Elizabeth thought she looked absolutely radiant in her rich white moiré antique silk gown with a full train and a small French lace collar. Her lovely neck and shoulders were adorned by a string of pearls, exquisite in their simplicity, and her rich chestnut hair was elegantly coiled and dressed with a slender floral vine. Her eyes sparkled and her smile beamed as if she felt nothing but joy and anticipation for the years to come, and in that perfect moment, with her sisters basking in her happiness and the toast of Springfield at her home to pay their respects, perhaps she did.

At half past seven on the morning of February 11, Abe and his entourage of advisers, secretaries, and friends boarded the Inaugural Express, a special train that would carry him on a roundabout, twelve-day journey from Springfield to Washington. In fact, he would not travel on one train but on several bearing that title in turn, for the varying rail gages along the route would oblige the party to change trains several times. The Inaugural Express, the first of its name, was an exquisitely wrought, modern marvel of gleaming brass and iron, with a powerful engine and a towering funnel stack puffing steam into the air. Directly behind it was the baggage car, and last of all came a yellow passenger carriage festively draped with bunting and flags, its wooden trim varnished until it gleamed. The Inaugural Express would stop at numerous cities along the way so that Abe could thank his supporters, receive their accolades, participate in various civic ceremonies, and make speeches promoting national unity.

Elizabeth was thrilled to be included in Mary's entourage, along with her daughters, Julia and Lizzy; her sisters Frances, Margaret, and Martha; and their cousin Lizzie Grimsley. Owing to the inconvenient early hour, Mary, Willie, and Tad and her ladies would not depart on the train with Abe and his gentlemen—an entourage that included Robert, William, Levi, and several other friends and advisers—but would join them the next day at their first stop, in Indianapolis.

That was why, as the hour of Abe's departure approached, Mary, Elizabeth, and Frances were not aboard the Inaugural Express but rather standing on the platform of the Great Western Depot. Well bundled up against the cold amid the bustle and excitement of the exultant crowd, the Todd sisters awaited Abe's parting speech, which was sure to be a poignant moment even though they would see him again very soon.

The crowd quieted as their president-elect emerged onto the rear deck of the railcar. "My friends, no one not in my situation can appreciate my feeling of sadness at this parting," Abe began, his voice carrying over the gathering. "To this place, and the kindness of these people, I owe everything. Here I have lived a quarter of a century, and have passed from a young to an old man. Here my children have been born, and one is buried. I now leave, not knowing when, or whether ever, I may return, with a task before me greater than that which rested upon Washington."

As he continued to speak, Elizabeth stole a glance at Mary and felt a pang of sympathy at the sadness and uncertainty she saw clouding her sister's expression. To be the wife of the president was all Mary had ever wanted, and yet almost daily, horrid, threatening letters and reports of assassination plots arrived at their door. Abe tried to shield her from the worst of it, and yet she knew.

Elizabeth reached out and took her sister's hand, and when Mary gave a start and turned to her, Elizabeth offered an encouraging smile. Mary seemed to take heart, and when Abe finished his remarks, she smiled with genuine happiness and clapped her small, gloved hands as enthusiastically as the rest of the cheering crowd.

When Mary, her two younger sons, and her other companions joined the president-elect's party in Indianapolis the next day, they boarded an even more opulent train. Like the first Inaugural Express, it was an impressive work of modern engineering, draped with flags and bunting. The engine's smokestack was embossed with thirty-four white stars—one for each state in the Union, regardless of any declarations of secession—and lithographic portraits of Abe's presidential predecessors lined its sides. Aboard this gleaming, powerful wonder, they traveled on to Cincinnati, where a marching band welcomed them to the city and a full day of speeches, appearances, and events awaited. After spending the night in Cincinnati, the president's party continued on the next morning to Columbus, making frequent stops along the way so that Abe could address the cheering, flag-waving crowds eagerly awaiting him. That evening in Columbus, there were more speeches, a party at the home of Governor William Dennison, and a military ball, at which Mary danced and chatted and charmed everyone she met late into the night.

So it continued, day after long, wondrous day, from Columbus on to Pittsburgh and through Pennsylvania to Buffalo. Although Elizabeth was enchanted by the unfamiliar scenery and the joyful celebrations at small towns along the route—and took great delight in watching her daughters reveling in the experience—eventually she began to find the routine grueling. She knew Mary did too. At some stops, Mary would stand in a receiving line at a reception, smiling and shaking hands for hours; on other occasions, she complained of headache and remained in her train carriage to rest on the sofa with her eyes closed and the curtains drawn against the thin winter sunlight. In Ashtabula, Ohio, when she failed to appear on the railcar deck at her husband's side, the crowd called for her until Abe smiled good-naturedly and held up his hands to quiet them. "I should hardly hope to induce her to appear," he said, "as I have always found it very difficult to make her do what she did not want to." The crowd roared with laughter, and even Elizabeth found herself smiling at the little joke made at her sister's expense.

The Todd sisters knew that the Inaugural Express had taken such a long, circuitous route through several cities and towns not only to allow Abe to greet as many supporters along the way as possible but also to thwart anyone who might wish to do him harm. When Mary learned that the Philadelphia, Wilmington, and Baltimore Railroad had hired the Pinkerton National Detective Agency to investigate a plot to vandalize railroad property during their stop in Baltimore, Elizabeth concealed her own nervousness as she and the other ladies comforted Mary.

"Detective Allan Pinkerton knows about the threat," the eminently rational Frances noted. "Every guard, police officer, and agent will be prepared and alert for any sign of danger."

"I'll still feel better once we pass through that city," said Mary tremulously, wringing her hands, cheeks flushed with worry. "Maryland is still in the Union—for now—but it is a slave state, and Baltimore has been particularly hostile to my husband."

"All will be well," Elizabeth said soothingly, hoping she spoke truth. "What could go wrong, with so many gallant protectors surrounding us?"

On February 21, the president-elect's party left New York City, aboard the most luxuriously appointed train yet, and made several stops in New Jersey before arriving in Philadelphia to a tremendous welcome of cheering crowds, brass bands, and artillery salvos. Later, Abe addressed a vast throng from the balcony of their hotel, then withdrew to a private room to enjoy a quiet dinner with the family before receiving well-wishers at a public reception in the hotel's drawing room. After nightfall, the city celebrated Abe's election with a glorious pyrotechnics display, the grand finale of which presented a red, white, and blue wall of fire surrounding the phrase, written in illuminated silver letters, "WELCOME, ABRAHAM LINCOLN. THE WHOLE UNION."

As soon as the bright spectacle faded, Mr. Judd drew Abe, Judge Davis, and a few other gentlemen aside into a private room. Mary managed to slip inside before the door closed, and Elizabeth, after waiting to see whether her sister would promptly reappear, peremptorily excluded from the meeting, retired to her suite, where her daughters were preparing for bed and reminiscing in awestruck tones about the day's events.

More than an hour later, Elizabeth was settling down to sleep herself when she heard a rap on the door and opened it to find Mary in the corridor, face pale and eyes shining with tears. "Dreadful news, simply dreadful," she choked out, twisting a handkerchief so tightly the fabric strained.

Quickly Elizabeth ushered her inside to the sitting room and softly closed the door to the hallway as well as to the adjoining chamber where her daughters slept. "What's wrong?" she asked, seating herself on the sofa beside her distraught sister.

"You recall, of course, the scheme to damage the railroad as we pass through Baltimore."

"Of course."

"The Pinkerton agents have since discovered a more sinister plot." Mary inhaled shakily and dabbed at her eyes with the handkerchief. "The station in Baltimore is strangely, most inconveniently configured. To transfer from inbound to outbound trains, passengers have to cross through a narrow pedestrian tunnel, the same tunnel our carriages will use to take us to our lodgings in the city. According to the detectives, after our train halts, Southern sympathizers intend to create a diversion further down the tracks to draw the police escort away. When we enter the tunnel"—Mary choked out a sob—"at least eight men will be waiting to stab or shoot my husband!"

"Goodness," Elizabeth exclaimed. "How certain are the detectives that this is no idle rumor?"

"Certain enough that the military has urged—no, demanded—that Abe leave us and travel through Baltimore under the cover of night, in disguise and accompanied by Pinkertons." Mary shook her head, mouth pursed. "I am entirely against it. I refuse to be separated from my husband, and I am certain that this timorous, clandestine entrance into Washington will make him appear weak before the public and all those dreadful secessionists."

"Perhaps, but his safety must be the primary concern," said Elizabeth. "What does Abe think?"

Mary frowned. "He said that unless there are other reasons besides incurring ridicule that make the plan unwise, he is inclined to approve it."

If Abe thought that was best, Elizabeth would trust his judgment. The next morning, when she confided in Frances, Margaret, and Martha, they too agreed with Abe that the military likely knew best. The sisters' words were brave and their voices determined, but their eyes revealed their worry.

Over Mary's objections, Abe did continue ahead without them. Conveyed by less ostentatious vehicles, he slipped through Baltimore clad in a Scotch cap and a tartan cloak, stooping to conceal his remarkable height, a disguise he abandoned well before he reached Washington. Mary and the rest of the party departed later, continuing on the Inaugural Express and pulling into the depot at New Jersey Avenue and C Street at about four o'clock in the afternoon, ten hours after Abe had entered the city.

"See who has come to meet us," Mary murmured to Elizabeth as the train came to a halt. She nodded through the window to the platform below. "Do you recognize the gentleman on the left, Congressman Elihu Washburne? It's good to see an old friend from Illinois here. The slight man standing beside him, the one with silver hair and a cane, is Senator William Seward. Abe has chosen him for secretary of state—over my strong objections. He has no principles, and he aspires to be the power behind the throne, but he'll soon discover that my husband is no callow boy to be molded."

Despite her disparaging tone, when Mary and her entourage descended from the train and Mr. Washburne and Mr. Seward came forward to welcome them to the capital, she accepted their compliments graciously and chatted amiably as the two gentlemen escorted them to the carriages that would take them to their hotel. Elizabeth rode with Mary, the boys, and the two gentlemen, while Frances, William, Levi, and the other ladies followed in a second carriage and the rest of Abe's companions in a third.

Elizabeth's first incredulous, appalled impression of Washington City was that it was a squalid rural village where cows, pigs, and geese roamed freely through the streets, which Mary had warned her were cloudy with dust on dry days and ran thick with mud when it rained. Pennsylvania Avenue and a few adjacent blocks of Seventh Street were paved, but the cobblestones were broken and uneven, and mud oozed up between the cracks. The 156-foot stub of the Washington Monument stood forlornly in the midst of an open field where cattle grazed, its construction halted by political squabbling, financial uncertainty, and vandalism. The Capitol, too, was unfinished, but there at least construction continued; the incomplete, truncated dome loomed above the landscape, hemmed in by derricks and scaffolding, flanked by bare, unadorned marble wings, and surrounded by workers' sheds, tools, piles of bricks, and blocks of marble scattered on all sides.

"It is not as dreadful as it looks," said Mary in an undertone. "When Abe was in Congress, I discovered that Washington City offers a peculiar mix of grandeur and squalor side by side. I've always chosen to focus on the city's more pleasant attributes— the elaborate mansions and lovely gardens, the grand estates in the surrounding countryside, the opulent marble edifices that house the various federal departments, and let's not forget the splendid, extravagant levees, dinners, and balls. It does take a bit of care to navigate the city without ruining one's skirts and shoes in the mud, but that's what carriages are for."

When Mary smiled brightly, Elizabeth smiled back, but she found herself suddenly relieved that she was only visiting. Only Abe's offer to Ninian of a cabinet position could extend her stay indefinitely, but that was an increasingly unlikely prospect.

The carriages took them up Pennsylvania Avenue, lined with trees that lifted bare branches to the overcast sky, past the State Department, the more massive Treasury Building, and, at a distance so they only caught a glimpse of it, the Executive Mansion. Mary had been invited to call there on March 1 so that Miss Harriet Lane, President Buchanan's niece and hostess, could offer her a guided tour of the White House. Elizabeth longed to accompany her sister, but Mary herself would welcome the Todd ladies to her new home soon thereafter.

They arrived at the Willard Hotel, a rambling, six-story edifice that was not only the city's finest and largest hotel but also a nexus of Washington society and politics. As Mr. Washburne helped them down from the carriage, he remarked that it would not be wrong to call the Willard more the center of the federal government than the Capitol, the White House, or the State Department, as so many policies were debated and compromises worked out in its storied parlors and corridors. Recently the Willard brothers had gamely endeavored to maintain peace between contentious factions by assigning Southern guests to rooms on a single floor and urging them to use the ladies' Fourteenth Street entrance, while Northerners were encouraged to use the main doors on the Pennsylvania Avenue side. Even so, rivals were bound to encounter each other in the hotel's public rooms, which were illuminated by gaslight, opulently furnished in rosewood, damask, lace, and velvet, and redolent of cigar smoke and spilled whiskey. One quick look and Elizabeth resolved not to let her daughters spend any time there unaccompanied. Her heart sank when she observed Levi hanging back and ducking inside when he thought no one was watching.

As soon as they were shown to their rooms, Mary's first desire was to reunite with her husband. Then, and in the days that followed, while Abe organized his government, Mary embarked on her own campaign—helping her entourage settle in, welcoming family and friends, and accepting calls from diplomats, statesmen, and their ladies. Elizabeth and Frances observed a troubling absence of the most prominent ladies of Washington society, most of whom were Southerners, but they said nothing to Mary, hoping that she would be too busy to notice and would not consider it a snub.

Southern ladies tended to show up in greater numbers at events where Abe would appear too, drawn by curiosity, Elizabeth supposed. At one reception, where Abe and Mary received callers for more than two hours in a crowded, humid parlor on the second floor of the Willard, a waiter spilled coffee on Mary's dress, a favorite lavender silk she had intended to wear to a party after the inauguration the following week. "What shall I do?" Mary fretted as Elizabeth and Martha swept her into an adjacent lounge where no one could gawk as they frantically blotted her dress with their handkerchiefs. It was all to no avail, for the stain had set. "I have nothing else suitable to wear."

Elizabeth heard the frantic note in her voice and realized that Mary must have detected the snub from the Washington ladies after all. They had all read the snide remarks in the papers, the speculation that the Lincolns were uncultured hayseeds and bumpkins who would bring down the quality of the social scene with their unrefined Western ways. Mary absolutely must appear elegant and stylish whenever she appeared in public or she would never win them over.

"You'll need an entirely new gown," said Mrs. McLean, the wife of Colonel Eugene McLean of Maryland, who had followed them unnoticed into the lounge. "I know just the dressmaker— Mrs. Elizabeth Keckly. She's the most acclaimed modiste in Washington City. She creates all of my fine dresses, and those of other fashionable ladies—Mrs. Douglas, for one."

"Stephen Douglas's wife? She's quite lovely, and always beautifully attired." Mary considered. "Your dressmaker's name sounds familiar."

"She came to Washington from St. Louis," said Mrs. McLean. "Perhaps she sewed for your acquaintances there. If you wish, I'll invite her to call on you so that you may interview her."

This plan was quickly agreed to, and Mary returned to the reception in the ruined gown, a fan artfully held open to conceal the stain.

Mary's tour of the White House on the first of March went well, or so she told her sisters afterward. Miss Lane promised to arrange for a meal to be prepared for the Lincolns and their guests at the White House following the inauguration, when the Executive Mansion would pass to their custody. The staff had provided Mary with a detailed list of protocol regarding management of the White House, which she was sure would be very useful. Yet a tightness around Mary's eyes suggested that, however courteously Miss Lane's household had welcomed her, they had conveyed no warmth or genuine friendliness. "A certain coolness is to be expected, I suppose, since she is a Democrat and I am a Republican," Mary confided to Elizabeth and Frances. "I am, after all, replacing her as the first lady of Washington."

Perhaps that was not the only reason for Mary's chilly reception. The next morning Frances came early to Elizabeth's room to show her the most recent *Harper's Weekly*, which included an article describing "Mrs. Lincoln's sisters" as "the toast of Southerners."

"To Washington's social elite, who are predominantly of Southern extraction, we Todd sisters are uncouth Westerners," said Frances, frowning. "To Yankees we are Southern belles clamoring for secession."

"I don't believe this piece goes quite that far," said Elizabeth, skimming the article. "But don't show it to Mary."

"This piece isn't the first to cast doubt on Mary's loyalties, nor will it be the last," said Frances. "I fear that until this rebellion is put down, she'll find herself caught in the middle, claimed by neither side, mistrusted by both."

"I do hope you're wrong," said Elizabeth, but her heart was troubled.

On the morning of the inauguration two days later, Elizabeth rose early, a thrill of pride and expectation chasing away sleep as surely as the first pale rays of dawn peeking through her window. She washed and dressed with care, then woke Julia and Lizzy and set them to the same task, lingering in the doorway until she was convinced they would not crawl back into their beds. She ordered breakfast sent up to the room, and after they had eaten, they finished their toilettes, helped one another into their fine new dresses, took turns arranging one another's hair, put on jewelry, reconsidered, traded around earbobs and necklaces, and considered their reflections in the mirror. When they were finally satisfied, they heaped praise upon one another with great enthusiasm and sincerity, confident that they would be equal in appearance to the most disdainful snobs of the Washington elite.

They left their suite and joined the other Todd ladies in Salon Number 6 to help Mary prepare for the momentous day. She looked resplendent in an ashes-of-rose sateen gown, with an elaborate headdress of flowers and ribbon upon her shining chestnut hair and diamonds sparkling from her earlobes. They were such a merry group, all in good spirits, pleased with how lovely they looked together, and dressed becomingly for the events at the Capitol that were soon to begin.

Then a knock sounded on the door. "Enter!" Mary called out cheerfully.

A lovely colored woman entered, her dress stylish and beautifully made, perfectly fit to her elegant figure. She carried herself with almost regal dignity, and when Mary rose to greet her, she inclined her head in a graceful acknowledgment of Mary's status as the first lady of the land.

"You are Elizabeth Keckly, I believe," said Mary. "The dressmaker that Mrs. McLean recommended?"

Mrs. Keckly bowed her assent. "Yes, madam."

"Very well." Mary returned to her dressing table and examined her face in the mirror, touching the delicate skin beneath her eyes, frowning at what might have been newly discovered or newly imagined lines. "I have no time to talk to you now, but at eight o'clock tomorrow morning, I would like you to call at the White House." Turning in her seat, she held Mrs. Keckly's gaze and added portentously, "Which is where I shall then be."

"Yes, madam." Mrs. Keckly bowed again and saw herself out.

"Who was that enchanting woman?" asked Martha, who had been standing at the window on the other side of the salon and had missed the brief conversation. "Such noble bearing! Is she a foreign princess?"

"Mrs. Keckly is the dressmaker Mrs. McLean recommended last week. I was told she might call today. I wish I could have interviewed her now, but we haven't the time. I do hope I wasn't too abrupt." Studying her reflection in the mirror, Mary gave her coiffure one last gentle pat, rose from her chair, and gazed around the room, smiling affectionately at each of them in turn. "My dearest ones, I cannot fully express how overjoyed I am that you came so far to share this glorious day with me. Now, shall we go see Mr. Lincoln become Mr. President?"

Elizabeth and the other ladies all agreed that this was a very fine idea.

The morning had dawned chilly, damp, and overcast, but by the time Mary, her sons, and her ladies arrived at the Capitol, a gusty, intermittent wind had blown away the clouds. Thousands of spectators lined the parade route President and Mrs. Lincoln would take to the White House after the ceremony. Elizabeth had not yet seen her brother-in-law that day; Mary had explained that Mr. Buchanan was picking up Abe in his gleaming black barouche and escorting him to the Capitol.

Inside the Senate chamber, a guard escorted them to their seats in the diplomatic gallery, from whence they observed the last oratory of the Thirty-Sixth Congress. An expectant hush fell over the chamber as outgoing vice president Breckenridge—another Todd cousin from Kentucky—rose and offered a pleasant farewell address to the Senate, after which he summoned Mr. Hannibal Hamlin to the Senate floor and administered his oath of office. Applause and cheers filled the chamber as the new vice president took the chair and called the Thirty-Seventh Congress to order.

One by one, the newly elected and reelected senators took their solemn oaths of office. When the last of the senators had been sworn in, the entire assembly proceeded outside to the eastern portico, where a platform had been erected for the conclusion of the ceremony. Elizabeth linked arms with her daughters in the crush, grateful for the military guard who kept a path clear for Mary and her companions.

Shortly before one o'clock, the central door was opened for them and Mary emerged onto the portico accompanied by her sons, the Todd ladies, and several gentlemen. The sky had cleared, and the sun shone brightly down upon the crowd of roughly thirty thousand people who had packed the muddy Capitol grounds below to witness the historic occasion. As they were led to their seats, Elizabeth spotted other dignitaries seated in places of honor closer to the front, shaded beneath a wooden canopy near a small table where Abe would soon stand and address the crowd.

After the Todd entourage seated themselves, the portly clerk of the Supreme Court appeared, carrying a Bible in one hand and leading the elderly, frail Supreme Court chief justice, Roger Taney, with the other. When Abe appeared upon the platform, Mr. Buchanan looking pale, sad, and nervous at his side, deafening cheers greeted him and continued until nearly the entire Senate and all other dignitaries had taken their places. Then Senator Edward D. Baker of Oregon stepped forward and announced, "Fellow citizens, Abraham Lincoln, president of the United States, will now proceed to deliver his inaugural address."

Abe rose, serene and calm, putting on his spectacles as he approached the canopy. He removed his hat, and then suddenly halted, looking around with a self-deprecating smile as if he had only then realized that he had no place to put his hat while he took his oath. His former rival, Senator Douglas, promptly came forward, took it, and held it on his lap while Abe addressed the crowd.

And what an address it was. Elizabeth had heard her brother-in-law speak many times before, but this time she found herself profoundly moved by the simple eloquence of his words, the clarity and compassion of his thought.

He began by attending to the fears of the Southern people, emphasizing that he had no intention of interfering with slavery where it existed, for although the Fugitive Slave Law deeply offended a great many Americans, he felt bound by the Constitution to enforce it. Then, using simple, articulate, and evocative phrases to lead the audience logically from one truth to another, he asserted that despite claims to the contrary, according to the Constitution, the Union was not and could not be broken. "I shall take care, as the Constitution itself expressly enjoins upon me, that the laws of the Union be faithfully executed in all the States," he vowed. "Doing this I deem to be only a simple duty on my part, and I shall perform it so far as practicable, unless my rightful masters, the American people, shall withhold the requisite means, or, in some authoritative manner, direct the contrary. I trust this will not be regarded as a menace, but only as the declared purpose of the Union that it will constitutionally defend and maintain itself."

The North and South could not physically separate, he reminded them, and must not spiritually. "We are not enemies, but friends," he said, with lyrical power that enthralled his listeners. "We must not be enemies. Though passion may have strained, it must not break our bonds of affection. The mystic chords of memory, stretching from every battlefield and patriot grave to every living heart and hearthstone, all over this broad land, will yet swell the chorus of the Union when again touched, as surely they will be, by the better angels of our nature."

While all around her, and throughout the grounds of the Capitol, men raised their hats, women waved their handkerchiefs, and everyone roared their approval, Elizabeth sat motionless and transfixed, riveted by the unexpected power of Abe's words. When Julia nudged her, she promptly rose, tears gathering in her eyes as the chief justice made his slow and unsteady way to the table where Abe stood. There the elderly jurist conducted the official rite, and Abe placed his hand on the Bible, recited the oath of office, bowed, and kissed the holy book.

It was done. A fanfare of brass and a thundering of cannons announced that Abraham Lincoln had become the sixteenth president of the United States.

17

January 1876

FRANCES

"It is impossible to reason with your mother on the subject of her bonds," Frances wrote to Robert early in the new year. "She is much exasperated against you."

If anything, that was an understatement. Although Mary was affable, cheerful, and friendly in every other regard with any other person, she fumed daily over her bonds and railed against the ungrateful, disloyal son who kept them from her. Whenever Frances protested that Robert was nothing of the sort, Mary would fix her with a baleful stare and say that she knew secrets about her son's business affairs that would change Frances's opinion of her nephew utterly if she knew. Frances did not ask her to divulge those secrets, for she knew they would be distortions of the truth, if not entirely fictitious. Robert was a scrupulous, highly principled young man, and it was obvious that Mary only wanted to punish him for having her committed.

"Perhaps you could stop referring to your mother's insanity in your letters and conversations with others, for such remarks invariably make their way back to her," Frances suggested to Robert in the same letter. "She despises all references to her sanity, even when well-meaning friends express their joy that she has regained it. She has never considered herself insane, and hearing others, especially you, speak to the contrary aggrieves her."

Frances did not know how else to advise him. She and Robert agreed that Mary never should have left Bellevue until she was entirely cured, but now that she had been released, it was impossible to imagine that she would submit to being returned there—or being sent anywhere else she did not wish to go. Elizabeth and Ninian were unlikely to be much help if Robert decided to try. They believed that Mary's reason was entirely restored, and except for the estrangement between her and her only surviving son, they seemed unperturbed by her behavior. They both repeatedly told Robert that his mother would surely remain upset and embittered toward him until he returned her bonds, but this observation was entirely unhelpful, since he was bound by law not to do so for at least five months more.

Ann believed that Mary ought to be watched every moment and her choices restricted, while the Edwardses thought she ought to be able to do as she pleased and given whatever she wanted. Frances could not see how either controlling her or indulging her was likely to help her, and shouldn't that be their objective, helping Mary? There had to be some middle way between those two extremes that would restore Mary's reason and tranquility. She had made a great deal of progress at Bellevue before the Bradwells interfered. It was hard not to blame Mary's renewed contact with the judge at least in part for her increasing irascibility.

Frances could not hold the Bradwells responsible for Mary's obsession with shopping, however, which she had harbored since long before she met the couple. Even in the early years of her marriage, shopping excursions had soothed and distracted Mary whenever she was worried or upset. When Abe had traveled on the county court circuit, Mary would ease her loneliness by setting out to her favorite Springfield shops to purchase fabrics, ribbons, trim for a new hat—little things that comforted her and did not damage their limited family budget. In Springfield, where everyone had known her, fear of embarrassment and Abe's limited means had prevented her from running up debts, but such was not the case when she had accompanied him to Washington for his term in Congress. On one occasion, Abe had returned to their boardinghouse after receiving two unpaid bills from local merchants at his office. "I hesitated to pay them," he had said, somewhat sternly, "because my recollection is that you told me there was nothing left unpaid." At first Mary denied that the bills were hers—why she did so, when the falsehood was easily disproven, Frances could only guess—but eventually she had admitted the truth. Mary's woebegone letters to her sisters afterward revealed just how much the incident had upset her, and they knew that this had been a shameful moment for Mary. Indeed, she had tried very hard to curtail her spending for as long as she remained in the city.

Unfortunately, her resolve crumbled when she returned to Washington years later as the president's wife. Early in Abe's first term, when Mary discovered that Congress allotted $20,000 to each administration to refurbish the White House, she set about spending the allowance with unrestrained delight. Granted, as Frances knew firsthand, the White House had been sorely neglected and desperately needed improvement. Even on her first visit, when the excitement of Abe's inauguration and her amazement over her sister's rise had rendered her awestruck, Frances had observed the shabby state of the Executive Mansion—the threadbare rugs, broken furniture, torn wallpaper, and ruined draperies, from which souvenir collectors had snipped pieces until they hung in tatters.

By the time Mary learned about the refurbishing funds, Frances and all of Mary's traveling companions except cousin Lizzie Grimsley had returned home. The first lady could not even stroll down Pennsylvania Avenue without reporters setting telegraph lines abuzz with the news, so when Mary and Lizzie traveled to New York City on a shopping expedition in early May, journalists hounded their every step. Stories of them attending the theater, inspecting carriages at a manufacturer, dining, enjoying soirees, and visiting local luminaries filled newspaper columns and invited spiteful commentary. When Frances read of Mary's expenditures on carpets, china, mantel ornaments, and other furnishings for the White House, she winced in sympathy, wishing it were possible for her sister to be more discreet. She also worried at the amount she seemed to be spending, not only because the papers depicted her as wasteful, but also because Frances could not imagine how the congressional allowance could cover it.

And yet it had been impossible not to be swept up in her sister's delight when she returned to Washington from New York and wrote home, delighted and full of anticipation, to describe her purchases and where she intended to arrange them. Before the year's end, Mary had ordered custom wallpaper from Paris; a splendid carriage; a 190-piece porcelain dinnerware set adorned with the United States seal and embellished with royal purple and double gilt for the Executive Mansion, as well as a second set for herself, with her initials substituted for the nation's seal; glassware and silverware; custom carpets, mantelpieces, draperies, chandeliers, and books; and rare exotic plants for the conservatory. She arranged for furnaces, gaslights, and running water to be installed, and she ordered everything scrubbed, polished, and repaired from attic to cellar. "I am determined to transform the White House into a showplace worthy of our great nation," she told her sisters, and Frances had no doubt that she would.

But although Frances had shared Mary's excitement and longed to be invited for a return visit to tour the refurbished White House, she understood how insensitive it looked for the first lady to be spending so much on carpets and china when poor, brave Union soldiers went without tents and blankets. Regrettably, either Mary had not considered the plight of the soldiers or it had not concerned her enough to persuade her to rein in her shopping. By autumn, her renovations to the White House had not only run well over budget but earned her sharp criticism in the press. Frances learned much later that the White House gardener, John Watt, had taught Mary how to pad bills and hide expenses in his account. Ignoring the warnings of the commissioner of public buildings that she had no money left to spend, Mary continued running up debts until it became impossible to conceal them from Abe anymore. They had argued furiously on her forty-third birthday, and afterward Mary begged the commissioner to intercede with the president on her behalf. Reluctantly, he did so, and although Frances did not witness Mr. Lincoln's explosive reply— "I swear I will never approve the bills for flub-dubs for this damned old house!"—everyone had heard of it soon thereafter.

A more cautious woman would have learned her lesson, but not Mary. After the renovations were completed—and with such exquisite taste that even her harshest critics grudgingly admitted that the White House had been transformed into a beautiful, elegant, and glorious mansion, as befit a distinguished nation—Mary still indulged in extravagant shopping. Whenever she traveled to New York City, the newspapers filled up with snide reports about the first lady ransacking the treasures of Broadway stores, filling her carriage with shawls, boas, capes, handkerchiefs, parasols, fans, bonnets, boots, and gloves. Frances could only guess at how accurate the newspaper reports were, but when she read about an $80 handkerchief and a $2,000 shawl, she gasped aloud, pressed a hand to her heart, and prayed that the reporter was wildly exaggerating. Frances could not see how Mary could possibly afford all that she acquired, not when Frances's own rough calculations indicated that her sister's personal expenses over a mere few months had surpassed the entire budget for the White House refurbishments.

A member of the White House staff had been charged with the thankless task of approving all of Mary's official expenditures, but apparently no one had monitored her personal spending. Perhaps everyone had assumed that the limits of her husband's salary would restrain her, but that had not been so since their newlywed years in Springfield. Whenever the first lady had ordered luxurious goods from a fine shop on Broadway or Pennsylvania Avenue, the shopkeepers had been all too delighted to extend her credit—but eventually the bills had come due, requiring payment in full.

Mary had become very skilled at hiding her mounting debts from her husband; indeed, he had died without learning the truth. Frances had to wonder if Mary was using those well-honed skills now to conceal the extent of her spending from Robert, and from Elizabeth and Ninian. Ann insisted that Mary's avid shopping had become a mania, and although Ann had always been Mary's most severe critic, Frances found her observations difficult to dismiss. After all, Mary did spend hours every day ensconced with dressmakers or visiting Springfield's finer boutiques, and surely some purchases resulted from so many consultations and outings. A woman as canny and determined as Mary would not find it difficult to smuggle new parcels into the Edwards residence and hide them among the trunks and cartons already stored in its various rooms and closets.

Frances's suspicions heightened after Elizabeth confided in her about a recent upsetting incident at home. In mid-January, the Edwardses had received a letter from Robert inquiring about an unpaid bill in his mother's name that Springfield's finest milliner had forwarded to him at his law practice. When Elizabeth and Ninian asked her about it, Mary unleashed a torrent of vitriol against her son that Elizabeth said fairly scorched their ears. Then Elizabeth's expression grew pensive. "Mary said something else truly upsetting," she said, lowering her voice, although they were alone in Frances's parlor. Her sons Will and Ed were at work, Mary Jane was married and mistress of her own household, and Fanny was resting in her bedchamber, unwell.

"What did she say?" prompted Frances.

Elizabeth inhaled deeply, steeling herself. "She said that she had engaged two hired assassins to take Robert's life."

"What?"

"Of course, it must be nonsense," Elizabeth hastened to add. "Mary would never do such a thing, not to her only living child—"

"To anyone's child, I should hope!"

"And even if she were deranged enough to want to—and I don't believe she is—well, how could she? How would Mrs. Abraham Lincoln find a professional assassin in Springfield, Illinois?"

"I can't imagine there are many assassins-for-hire between here and Chicago." Frances clasped a hand to her forehead, disbelieving, but also deeply worried. "Goodness. She cannot be serious. She must have just been lashing out in anger, trying to get a reaction from you."

"I might think that, except that she has mentioned it on several occasions."

For a moment Frances could only stare at her, shocked. "This is madness," she managed to say. "I do mean that literally. I know you want to believe that Mary's reason has been restored, but threatening to kill Robert?"

"I don't think she would ever do it."

"The threat is madness enough." Frances felt ill at the very thought of saying anything so hateful about any of her beloved children. "We don't know what Mary might do, if she is truly mad. We should contact Dr. Patterson at once, and Robert, to warn him."

"It isn't our place to write to Dr. Patterson," said Elizabeth. "Yes, Mary lives with Ninian and me, but she is Robert's responsibility. I'll write to him, and he can inform Dr. Patterson if he sees fit."

"In the meantime," said Frances firmly, "if Mary makes any more death threats against Robert, or anyone else, promise that you will tell me, even if you don't believe she is serious."

Elizabeth agreed to do so, but made Frances promise not to contact Dr. Patterson on her own. Reluctantly, Frances accepted this condition, but she resolved to nag Elizabeth daily until she wrote to warn Robert, and also to spend more time with Mary so that the burden of observing her did not always fall upon Elizabeth's shoulders. Did she not already do more than her share of sisterly caregiving by having taken Mary into her own home—and by making room for the piles of trunks their sister insisted upon keeping near at hand?

Two days later, Frances called at the Edwards home with her daughters Fanny and Mary Jane, her sister's namesake, to invite her on a sleigh ride so they could enjoy the fresh air and the lovely white blanket of new-fallen snow. It was a clear, sunny day and only a few degrees below freezing, so if they bundled up well and sat close together beneath a pile of snug quilts, their good spirits and merry company would keep them warm while they sped along their favorite picturesque loop from the city into the countryside and back.

Delighted, Mary accepted their invitation and hurried off to change into a warmer dress and stockings before putting on her boots and wraps. Frances and her daughters chatted with Elizabeth in the foyer while they waited, and when Mary did not promptly return, Frances went to see if she needed any help. In all the bustle and strain to find spaces to store her many trunks, perhaps the warmer clothes she sought had been misplaced.

Frances found Mary sitting on the edge of her bed, pulling a second pair of warm stockings over the first. She had already changed into her warmest wool dress, and the one she had taken off lay on the bed beside her. "We aren't going to the North Pole," Frances teased.

"Laugh if you must, but you'll wish you were wearing two pairs of stockings when we're a mile out and your toes go numb." Smiling, Mary rose and smoothed her skirts. "Do you think the girls' hoods and scarves will be warm enough? They looked a bit worn. I have others they can wear."

"Their wraps are warm enough, but on the way over Mary Jane discovered a hole in her mitten. Do you have a pair she could borrow?"

"I do indeed." Mary promptly opened a bureau drawer and began searching.

"You find those, and I'll hang up your dress." Frances lifted the discarded garment from the bed. "You'll wrinkle the fabric if you leave it lying about like—"

Abruptly she fell silent. The dress was strangely heavy. Bemused, she ran her hand down the bodice to the skirt until she found a pocket, which bulged open to reveal something solid and metallic—

A pistol.

Frances might have gasped, or perhaps it was her silence that made Mary look up from the drawer. "Be careful with that," she said, a hint of annoyance in her voice. "It's loaded."

After freezing for a moment in uncertainty, Frances carefully hung the dress in the wardrobe, heart pounding, taking care not to jostle the weapon. Then she turned to face her sister. "Mary," she said with forced calm, "why are you carrying a loaded pistol around the house in your dress pocket?"

Mary drew herself up and regarded her older sister evenly. "You know why."

"I truly don't."

"Robert, of course," Mary snapped, impatient. "I will never again allow him to come into my presence. You can tell him that."

Frances's heart plummeted. "Mary, you can't mean that you would ever—he's your son!"

Quickly Mary stepped around her, retrieved the pistol, and slipped it into the pocket of her heavy wool dress. "I will do nothing unless I am provoked. You can tell him that too."

18

April 1861

EMILIE

When Emilie read her eldest sisters' and half-sisters' accounts of their glorious adventure in Washington City—the powerful address that brother Abe had delivered from the east portico of the Capitol; the splendid inaugural ball held in the "White Muslin Palace of Aladdin," an enormous temporary ballroom constructed on Judiciary Square; the thrill of staying at the White House and marveling at how wonderfully Mary's childhood dream had come true—she wished with all her heart that she and Ben had accepted the Lincolns' invitation to join them on the Inaugural Express to Washington City. Sadly, Ben had felt that it would be inappropriate to attend, for as much as he loved and respected Abe, he was a staunch Democrat and had campaigned for Mr. Douglas.

"Brother Abe doesn't care about that," Emilie had protested, crushed. "He and Mary wouldn't have invited us if they did. Ninian is attending, and he's a Democrat. Even Martha is going, and Alabama has seceded. We're family, first and always. Can we not celebrate Abe's great achievement for that reason alone and forget our differences?"

But her husband had insisted that it would have been ungracious to accept Abe's hospitality when Ben had not supported him in the election, as other brothers-in-law had done, and so with great regret, he had declined. Afterward, when the newspapers described Mr. Douglas himself accepting a place of honor near Abe's seat on the platform and holding Abe's hat for him while he delivered his inaugural address, Ben had ruefully acknowledged that perhaps they could have accepted the invitation after all. By then it was too late, and Emilie had only her sisters' enthralling descriptions of the glorious celebrations to console her.

Thus, in April, when brother Abe sent Ben a personal invitation to visit him at the White House, a thrill of anticipation swept through her. She knew that Mary longed for Emilie and Ben to visit even more than Abe did. By then, all of Mary's friends and family except for Lizzie Grimsley had returned to their own homes, and even their good and noble cousin occasionally mentioned how much she missed her children back in Springfield. Reading between the lines of her cousin's letters, Emilie surmised that Mary found herself increasingly lonely as the Washington elite continued to snub her. How strange it was to imagine her confident, generous, and vivacious elder sister feeling unsettled in her new surroundings and in the exalted role she had desired for so long! Yet never before had Mary lived among strangers who were thoroughly unimpressed with her family name, which had always carried great influence back in Lexington and Springfield. Brother Abe, preoccupied with the demands of his high office, had surrounded himself with colleagues who regarded his wife's notes about policies and appointments as annoying and meddlesome. His aides obliged her to struggle with them for control of the very White House functions for which she was the hostess. Excluded from her husband's inner circle, missing her departed sisters and nieces, disdained by the popular ladies of Washington, Mary had confided to Lizzie that, aside from Lizzie herself, her only true friend within a hundred miles was her dressmaker, Mrs. Keckly.

Deeply sympathetic, Emilie longed to visit Washington even more urgently than before, for helping to raise Mary's spirits was far more important than attending balls and levees and enjoying royal treatment at the White House. To her delight, this time Ben agreed that they should go. "This is a personal invitation not only from my brother-in-law, but my president," he said. "We both want to visit them, and to refuse would be to offend people we dearly love for no good reason."

Thrilled, Emilie flung her arms around her husband and kissed his cheek. "I'll write to Mary, and you write to Abe—right away, please, so I needn't fear you'll change your mind!"

She and Ben had only begun to make their travel arrangements when shocking news came from South Carolina. At first the reports were scattered and contradictory, but terrifying; in Lexington, men crowded the telegraph offices and hotels, demanding news and spreading rumors, but no one knew precisely what was happening, or what might have already happened. Waiting anxiously for Ben to bring home news from his well-placed sources, Emilie soon learned of the grim picture emerging of recent events at Fort Sumter.

Since December, when the crisis in Charleston Harbor had begun, Ben had opined on several occasions that if the president ordered the federal troops to abandon Fort Sumter and a second stronghold, Fort Pickens on Santa Rosa Island near Pensacola, the South could be reconciled to the Union peacefully. His father, a former governor of Kentucky, emphatically disagreed, insisting that appeasing the secessionists would only embolden them and provoke similar conflicts elsewhere. Emilie's instinct was always to side with her husband, but listening to the father and son debate, she realized that the country faced a terrible impasse: surrendering the forts would embarrass Abe, undermining the authority of his administration and thereby his power to hold the Union together, while sending provisions to Major Anderson could provoke an attack that would lead to civil war.

In all the weeks since, citizens North and South had waited, fearful or eager, for one side or the other to act. On the day after Abe's inauguration, the first item placed upon his desk had been a letter from Major Anderson, informing him that his soldiers' provisions would be exhausted within a month, even though the men had already dropped to half rations. In early April, Abe had ordered supply ships sent to Fort Sumter and Fort Pickens, and although the news had not been released to the public, he had notified the governor of South Carolina through other channels. The governor had responded with an ultimatum: he demanded that all federal troops evacuate Fort Sumter immediately. Major Anderson had refused, resolutely holding his position. On the morning of April 12, Confederate cannons bombarded the fort from artillery batteries installed around the harbor. After exchanging fire with Confederate guns for thirty-four hours—surrounded, their supplies all but exhausted—Major Anderson had been forced to surrender.

To Emilie, Lexington seemed equally divided between those who were outraged by the attack and those who rejoiced over it. While secessionists cheered the start of war, Union households draped windows and balconies with red-white-and-blue bunting and flew the Stars and Stripes from every mast and flagpole. Southern sympathizers openly sought recruits for the Confederate Army, while loyal Union men rushed to join militias. On April 15, President Lincoln issued a call for seventy-five thousand troops to suppress the insurrection, with a certain quota required from each state. Emilie's father-in-law agreed with the president that these troops, enlisted to serve for ninety days, would be sufficient to put down the rebellion, but Ben was not convinced. A graduate of West Point, class of 1851, he had served in the army until health issues had compelled him to resign. He had studied under or alongside many of the men now emerging as leaders on both sides of the conflict, and he knew that none of them would be easily intimidated or defeated.

While New York and other states throughout the Union

promptly organized volunteer troops in response to the president's call to arms, the governors of Kentucky, Missouri, North Carolina, and Virginia declared that they would furnish no regiments to go to war against their Southern brethren. Then, on April 17, two days after Abe issued his proclamation, Virginia seceded from the Union. This devastating blow to the North provoked great rejoicing throughout the secessionist South. Surely it was only a matter of time before the new independent commonwealth of Virginia added its military and economic might to the Confederacy.

Emilie and Ben knew they would be visiting the White House at a particularly fraught moment. Although Washington was the capital of the Union, it was essentially a Southern city, surrounded by Maryland to the north and east on the other side of Chesapeake Bay, and separated from Virginia to the west and south by only the Potomac River. Maryland had not seceded, but like Kentucky, it was a slave state, with regions of passionate sympathy for the South. Abe would doubtless be preoccupied with his duties, and Mary distracted with her husband's needs, but neither Emilie nor Ben was inclined to cancel. They had promised to visit, Ben could not ignore a personal invitation from the president, Mary would need Emilie's cheerful and supportive presence more than ever, and a more favorable occasion to visit seemed unlikely to appear anytime soon.

On the eve of their departure, when they took the children to Buena Vista to stay with Ma during their absence, Ma pleaded with Emilie to delay the journey, only for a few months, just until the rebellion subsided. "It says in the papers that Washington City is bracing for an invasion, that the Confederates want to make it the capital of the South," she said, her expression tense and apprehensive. "The city is surrounded by enemies, and no one knows who will arrive first, trained militia companies from the North or invaders from the South."

"I'm sorry, Ma, but I must go. Mary's expecting me," Emilie

said gently, smiling an apology and kissing her mother on the cheek. "Please don't worry. If Washington weren't safe, brother Abe would have sent Mary and the boys north to New York."

Her mother said no more, but her downturned mouth and teary eyes showed that she was not reassured.

The next morning, as arranged, a neighbor took Ben and Emilie and their trunks to the train station, from whence they traveled north to Cincinnati, then east across southeastern Ohio. They were obliged to change trains at a town on the Ohio River, so Emilie went out for a stroll to stretch her legs and take in the fresh air while Ben saw to the transfer of their luggage. The view of the broad river and the green hills of Virginia on the opposite side was enchantingly lovely, but she felt a wistful pang as she admired the scene. It did not seem real that she was gazing upon a foreign country and that, when they crossed the river, they would leave the United States. Abe would say that they had not, but Ben would counter that indeed they had.

A train whistle blew. Startled from her reverie, Emilie left the riverbank and made her way back to the station. She had almost reached the platform stairs when she glimpsed Ben hurrying toward her, so she held up her skirts slightly and quickened her pace. "Did I misjudge the time?" she asked when he offered her his arm and hastened her toward the train.

"No, it's only that—" Ben glanced over his shoulder, assisted her aboard the train, and followed quickly after. "Don't worry, but there are rumors flying around the station that there may be trouble ahead, in Baltimore."

She paused to glance over her shoulder at her husband as she preceded him into the rail carriage. "What sort of trouble?"

"You're aware, of course," said Ben as they made their way down the corridor, his voice low so that no one would overhear, "that Union troops traveling by train to Washington from the Northern states have to pass through Baltimore, about forty miles northeast of the capital."

Emilie nodded, although she had not actually given the route much thought until that moment.

"Why is that a concern?" she asked quietly, checking the numbers on the doors for their compartment. "Maryland is still in the Union. If we were going to run into trouble, I would expect it to be directly across the river, in Virginia."

The steam whistle blew as they entered their compartment and shut the door behind them; slowly, but with increasing speed, the train chugged out of the station.

"As it happens," Ben said, glancing out the small window, "our route passes through a region of Virginia that did not want to leave the Union. Even now some politicians are clamoring for their counties to secede from Virginia instead and form their own state, so that they may remain."

Emilie shook her head, incredulous. What had become of their country? The unimaginable was unfolding before their very eyes, every day. "And while Maryland remains in the Union, much of Baltimore wishes that it had not."

"Exactly so. Rumors abound that thousands of Marylanders with Southern sympathies are plotting to block the passage of Northern troops through the city, and since Baltimore does have a history of street-mob violence, the authorities must take the threat seriously." Ben rubbed his bearded jaw, frowning, as he settled back against the leather seat. "Complicating matters is a quirk of Baltimore's railway system."

"A quirk?" echoed Emilie, eyebrows rising. "Like the quirk that threatened the Inaugural Express?"

Ben nodded. "In this case, trains bound for Washington arrive at President Street Station, but then they must be towed by teams of horses several blocks west through the city streets to Camden

Station, from which they may resume their journey by rail. In times of peace, the system is merely inconvenient."

Emilie felt a chill as she finished the thought on her own. In a time of war, it was potentially disastrous. "We're aboard a passenger train, not a troop transport," she said, forcing confidence into her voice. "Surely we're in no danger."

His riveting blue eyes held hers. "Dearest, if I thought you were in any danger, I never would have let you board this train."

A warm rush of affection coursed through her. She snuggled closer to him on the leather seat, and when he lifted his arm, she tucked herself beneath it. From the first days of their marriage, she had resolved that wherever he went, she would follow, whether around the grueling county court circuit or into a city seething with political anger. She believed with all her heart that there was no safer place in the world for her than by his side.

The train sped through newly seceded Virginia and on to Maryland. Emilie and Ben passed the hours talking, reading, dozing, or gazing out the window at the passing scenery. Emilie's thoughts shifted between pleasant daydreams of dancing, dining, and visiting with Mary at the White House and tremulous worry about the simmering unrest in Baltimore. They would have to pass through the city not only once, to reach Washington, but also on the return journey—unless, God willing, the conflict had subsided by then.

Emilie was dozing on Ben's shoulder when the dawning awareness of a sudden, quiet stillness woke her. "Where are we?" she asked groggily, sitting up and covering a yawn with her hand.

"Sykesville, and we've been here a while." Ben rose, bemused. "I'm going to ask the conductor why we haven't moved on."

Suddenly uneasy, Emilie nodded, and as soon as he left, she went quickly to the window to peer up and down the platform, which was surprisingly crowded. Men, couples, and a few families with children stood amid their piled luggage or sat wearily upon trunks, their expressions and gestures full of impatience, frustration, and, here and there, traces of fear. They appeared to want to board the eastbound train, but the conductors were discouraging them. As Emilie watched, a few passengers disembarked, took in the scene, and tried to get the attention of anyone in a railroad uniform, but they did not wander too far from the train, perhaps fearing that they would not be allowed back on board. Emilie searched the crowd for her husband but did not see him, and when a sudden stir of alarm swept through the crowd from one end of the platform to the other, like a wave moving upon a beach, her heart thudded anxiously. What news was upsetting them so?

She was just about to go find a conductor and ask when Ben opened the compartment door. "Trouble in Baltimore," he said, confirming her fears. "We may be delayed a few hours."

Earlier that morning, he told her, a Union regiment, the Sixth Massachusetts, had left Philadelphia on a train bound for Washington City. The soldiers had hoped to pass swiftly and unimpeded through Baltimore, but they had been warned that in the crossing between stations they should expect to be accosted with insults and abuse, and possibly even assaulted, all of which they had been ordered to ignore. Even if they were fired upon, they were not to return fire unless their officers gave the explicit command.

The train carrying the Sixth Massachusetts had arrived in Baltimore unannounced, and cars carrying seven of its companies had been towed through the city unhindered. But word of the soldiers' presence had spread quickly, and soon a crowd had massed in the streets, shouting insults and threats. The mob had torn up the train tracks and blocked the way with heavy anchors hauled over from the Pratt Street piers, forcing the last four companies of the Sixth to abandon their railcars and march through the city. Almost immediately, several thousand men and boys had swarmed them, hurling bricks and paving stones, while dishes and bottles had rained down upon them from upstairs windows. As the mob's rage had surged, a few citizens had broken into a gun shop, and soon thereafter the soldiers had heard pistol shots. The companies had pushed onward at quick time, but when the furious mob blocked the streets between them and the Camden Street station, the soldiers had opened fire. As the mob retreated, the soldiers had finally reached the depot, only to discover that the tracks had been sabotaged, preventing them from continuing on to Washington.

"A stationmaster a few stops ahead of us telegraphed that the soldiers are frantically trying to repair the tracks, but the protesters keep regrouping and harassing them," said Ben. "The railroad won't send any more trains into Baltimore until the unrest ceases."

"How long will we be held here?" asked Emilie. "Hours? Days?"

It was impossible to say, he told her, and when she steeled herself and asked if Washington City was under attack, his reply made her shiver: the Sykesville stationmaster said he had not received any news from the capital since shortly after the riots had broken out.

They waited an hour, taking turns at the window and leaving the door open so they could query a conductor if he passed by. Eventually the compartment began to feel so close and confining that Emilie had to go outside for some air. They met the stationmaster on the platform, and when he assured them there was no danger of the train leaving them behind, they strolled off into the town in search of hot coffee and a good meal.

Upon their return to the depot, they learned that the Sixth Massachusetts had repaired the railroad tracks damaged in the melee and raced off to Washington. But any hopes that they too might soon continue their interrupted journey were swiftly dashed when the stationmaster grimly reported that at least three soldiers and nine civilians had been killed in the riots and scores more injured. The damage to property had been even worse than originally estimated: after the federal troops had escaped, frenzied Southern sympathizers had destroyed railroad tracks leading to the North, burned bridges, and severed telegraph lines, isolating Washington from the rest of the Union.

The capital city stood alone, stranded and imperiled, surrounded by enemies.

Feeling faint, Emilie tried to draw in a deep, steadying breath, but her corset restrained her. "Are the Confederates shelling Washington, as they did Fort Sumter?" she asked, a tremor in her voice.

"No, ma'am, not that I'm aware of," the stationmaster replied.

"We have family there, you see," she said, pressing a palm flat against her stomach.

"Sir," the stationmaster said, addressing Ben, "if I may suggest, you ought to find a good boardinghouse for yourself and your lady, before the best are all taken. We won't be leaving tonight, nor tomorrow, I suspect, and you'll be much more comfortable in a proper room than in your compartment."

Ben agreed, and while Emilie returned to the train to put their things in order, he went into town to find a suitable place to stay. By nightfall they had settled into a clean, comfortable suite only three blocks from the station. They hoped to spend only one night there, but one night became two and then three. They joked that they should think of it as a second honeymoon, feigning more mirth than they truly felt. They spent the days exploring Sykesville until Emilie believed she could draw a map of it from memory, and they gathered what news they could from the stationmaster, their boardinghouse dining companions, and the papers. Word that Washington City was isolated and vulnerable had sent a frisson of urgency racing through the North. While young men rushed to join regiments and engineers raced to repair the damaged bridges and railroad tracks, Northern governors ordered their newly mustered regiments to Washington and military officers contrived other ways to transport them there, since Baltimore remained impassable.

"You see?" said Ben, offering Emilie an encouraging smile. "Mary and Abe and the children are safe. It would have been front-page news if they were not, and even as we speak, regiments of fine Union soldiers are hastening to the capital to protect them."

As he spoke, his smile was as warm and his eyes as kind as ever, but a new tension in his voice made her half expect him next to say that they should give up and return to Lexington. Yet if he ever considered it, he said nothing.

At last, train service resumed, and shortly after noon on April 25, they arrived at the Baltimore & Ohio depot in Washington City. They had telegraphed ahead, but with repairs to the lines still in progress, they did not know whether the Lincolns had received their message until they found Mary waiting in a carriage for them outside the station. Their trunks were swiftly stowed, they climbed aboard, and Emilie found herself in her elder sister's arms, both of them tearful from relief as the horses swiftly carried them to the White House.

The Seventh New York Regiment had arrived at the same station only a few hours before, Mary reported. The soldiers, clad in crisp new uniforms, had marched past throngs of cheering, relieved citizens to the White House to meet Abe, and then on to bivouac in the House chamber. Earlier that afternoon, Mary had gone out with Abe, Secretary of State Seward, and Secretary of War Cameron to review the troops, and she pronounced them brave and magnificent, ready for whatever might come. More regiments were expected any hour from Massachusetts, Ohio, Rhode Island, and elsewhere, and there were rumors that some would set up camp in the Capitol rotunda and others in the Executive Mansion itself. With the military presence increasing hour by hour, fears of an imminent Confederate invasion had diminished, but Baltimore remained a dangerous nest of Southern collusion, and railroad service had yet to be fully restored.

As they drove up Pennsylvania Avenue past soldiers marching

here, drilling there, and pitching tents in orderly rows on an expanse of green meadow in between, Emilie realized that she was visiting a vastly different city than the one the other Todd sisters had toured only weeks before.

"Since you were delayed, we will have so much less time together than we had planned," Mary lamented later as she led Emilie on a tour of the White House while Ben and Abe conferred in the president's study. "There will be no balls, I'm afraid, nor levees, but the Seventh New York Regiment band will perform on the South Lawn Saturday morning, and I shall introduce you to several fine ladies and gentlemen then."

"I can only imagine how terribly busy you and brother Abe must be," said Emilie, linking her arm through her sister's. "We're happy that you have any time to spare for us. Ben was especially eager to discuss the states' rights conflict with brother Abe. You know how much Ben respects his opinion."

Mary smiled, eyes bright, as if she were bursting with some secret. "They may have more opportunities to converse in the days ahead than you imagine."

"What do you mean?" asked Emilie, but Mary merely gave a little shrug, declared that Emilie must see the greenhouses, and led her off in that direction.

Two days later, after the Seventh New York Regiment band had performed and the invited guests had departed, Emilie learned what lay behind her sister's mysterious remark.

They were sitting in the family's private sitting room when Abe rose from his armchair and withdrew an envelope from a desk drawer. "Ben," he said, handing him the envelope, "here is something for you. Think it over by yourself and let me know what you will do."

After a moment's hesitation, Ben opened the envelope and took out a thick sheet of paper embossed with the presidential seal. Reading alongside him, Emilie suppressed a gasp when she

saw that Ben had been offered a commission as paymaster in the
United States Army, with the rank of major. Even Emilie knew
that this was one of the most coveted posts in the service, and
that it was quite exceptional for a man only thirty years old to be
offered the rank of major.

Emilie knew her husband was deeply moved, and she knew
that after thanking Abe for the great honor, it pained him to add,
"But you know I'm a strong Southern-rights Democrat."

"I know," said Abe, looking amused.

"This commission is beyond anything I had expected in my
most hopeful dreams." Ben shook his head in disbelief as he read
the page again. "It is the place above all others which suits me."

"That is why I offered you the post—your qualifications, and
because I must have someone with your integrity and intelligence
serving in this role."

"You've been extraordinarily kind and generous to me." A flush
rose in Ben's cheeks. "I have no claim upon you. I opposed your
candidacy, and I campaigned for your opponent."

"That is how I know you will always do what you think is
right, and not what you think I want to hear."

"I wish I could see my way clear," said Ben, thinking aloud. After a moment, he squared his shoulders, held Abe's gaze, and said,
"I'll try to do what I think is right this time too. You shall have
my answer in a few days."

Inclining his head, the president said he would await Ben's decision.

Emilie knew Ben had resigned from the military with great
reluctance, and now that he had regained his health and the need
for experienced officers was urgent, he longed to return to the
service. Many of his former comrades were among the forces defending the capital, and Ben had sought them out in their encampments. There they reminisced about old times and talked of the
unexpected twists of fate that had put many longtime friends on

opposite sides of the swiftly intensifying conflict. Perhaps these same friends could advise him now.

After Abe left the sitting room to return to work, Ben went out for a long walk to consider how to respond. He returned more than an hour later, pensive, and although he seemed in good spirits that evening at supper with the family, Emilie sensed his ambivalence and strain.

Later, when she and Ben were preparing for bed, he revealed that while out walking, he had come upon Colonel Robert E. Lee of the Second Cavalry, whom he had known at the military academy. Seeing that the venerable soldier labored under a heavy burden of the spirit, Ben had asked, "Are you not well, Colonel Lee?"

"Well in body, but not in mind," the colonel had replied sadly. "I have just resigned my commission in the United States Army. In the prime of life, I quit a service wherein were all my expectations and hopes in this world."

"A similar dilemma confronts me," Ben had admitted. He had handed the colonel Abe's letter offering him the commission. Colonel Lee had read it in silence. When he finished, Ben had asked, "Did you know Mr. Lincoln is my brother-in-law?"

"No, I did not," Colonel Lee had said, "but allow me to say this: I have no doubt of his kindly intentions, but he cannot control the forces at work here. There must be a great war. I cannot strike at my own people, so today I wrote out my resignation and asked General Scott as a favor to make it effective immediately. My mind is too much disturbed to give you any advice, except to say that you should do what your conscience and honor bid."

When Ben finished his story, Emilie tentatively prompted, "And what is it that your conscience and honor bid you to do?"

"I'm not certain. I don't doubt Abe's good intentions, or his kindly feelings for the South. But how can one man stem the tide of bitterness and hatred driving these two opposing regions into mortal conflict?"

"Colonel Lee has followed his beloved Virginia out of the Union," Emilie pointed out. "Kentucky has not seceded. If you follow his example, you would remain with your state in the Union."

"Kentucky has not declared for either side, but the sentiment is strongly Southern. Yet my father is a staunch Union man, and I know Abe to be wise." Ben shook his head, sighing wearily. "This is not a decision I can make tonight, or even tomorrow, although I'm sure Abe would prefer my answer before we depart."

"I'm sure Mary would too."

Indeed, at dinner earlier that evening, Mary had made no secret of how she longed to have Emilie remain in Washington with her. "You are so beautiful and charming that you will be the belle at every White House reception and at every ball you attend," she had gushed, and smiling at Ben, she had added, "And we need scholarly, dignified young men like yourself to ornament our army."

Emilie knew that Ben was mindful of the tremendous opportunity that had been placed before him—the chance to embark on a brilliant career for which he was eminently qualified. He also sincerely loved Abe and Mary and was moved by their affection and gratified by their faith in him.

And yet he was torn.

The next morning Emilie and Ben bade the Lincolns a sad farewell, with warm handshakes and promises to write. "We hope to see you both again very soon in Washington," Mary murmured to Emilie as they shared a parting embrace.

"The highest position in the profession for which I was educated has been placed in my hands," Ben reflected as their train left the capital. "I would not only be the youngest officer of my rank in the army, but soon I could transfer to one of the cavalry regiments. With so many Southern officers resigning to join the Confederacy, I could likely be a full colonel within a year."

"It does seem promising," said Emilie, wondering why, then, he did not seize the opportunity at once, firmly, with both hands.

Their return journey proved much less eventful than their outbound trip, and soon they were back in Lexington, surrounded by their children, their friends, and all the comforts of home. Ben promptly sought the counsel of trusted mentors and comrades and talked passionately with them about states' rights. He learned that many friends had already resolved to side with the Confederacy.

"I feel as Colonel Lee did, that I cannot strike against my own people," Ben confided to Emilie. "I have struggled bitterly over what to do."

"I know."

"Our differences of opinion could never affect the love I feel for your sister and my brother-in-law."

"I know that too," she said gently, resting a hand on his shoulder. "They do as well."

That afternoon Ben wrote to President Lincoln to decline the position of paymaster. It was, he told Emilie afterward, the most painful moment of his life.

She believed him, for she shared his pain, just as she shared his allegiance to the South, for above all other ties of friendship and family, her first loyalty was to her husband. She would share his fate, for better or for worse, until death did them part.

19

January 1876

ANN

Although Mary refused to hand over the pistol so they could inspect it, the Todd sisters assumed that it was the same gun Mary and Abe had given to ten-year-old Tad in 1863. Their youngest son had greatly admired the soldiers he met in the White House and at their encampments around the city, and like many lads with no concept of the realities of warfare, he had become enthralled by all things martial. The soldiers Willie and Tad encountered in Washington City had been exceedingly kind to them, and after Willie died, some of Abe's military guards had adopted his bereft younger brother as their mascot, occasionally inviting him to take his rations with the troops and giving him the unofficial rank of third lieutenant. As Tad's fascination had grown, Abe had indulged him by issuing certain official requests on his behalf, such as asking the secretary of the navy to obtain a sword for him, writing to the secretary of war to request some company flags, and dispatching an army captain to find Tad a small gun that he could not hurt himself with.

Ann could not think of any gun that met that description unless it remained unloaded, but taking that perfectly reasonable precaution apparently had not occurred to Abe or Mary. From what Ann later learned from friends and family who visited the White House, Tad never injured himself with the pistol, but he had become quite a little menace with it nonetheless. Once Abe had scolded him for pointing the gun playfully at a friend, and on another occasion Tad had been forced to relinquish the pistol for a week as punishment after accidentally shooting out a window while visiting his playmates Bud and Holly Taft at their home on L Street. Abe and Mary had been infamously indulgent parents, but allowing their young son to run around with a loaded gun for a toy seemed astonishingly negligent even for them.

The ill-fated pistol had probably been buried at the bottom of one of Mary's many trunks ever since Tad's death about four and a half years before. Now Mary—legally insane, enraged at her only surviving son, by nature impulsive—carried it around in her pocket, loaded, if she was to be believed, though that may have been merely a lie intended to frighten her sisters.

To Ann, it was obvious that they must get the gun away from her. Ninian and Frances agreed, but Elizabeth wavered. "I cannot believe Mary truly intends to harm Robert," she insisted. "She has buried her husband and three sons. She would never take the life of her only surviving child."

"Even if she is not a threat to Robert, she may be a danger to herself," Ann pointed out, irritated. Elizabeth persisted in her belief that giving in to Mary in everything would calm her, help her regain her reason. But on what grounds? Elizabeth's policy of indulgence certainly hadn't helped Mary improve thus far. What *had* worked was the quiet and solitude of Bellevue under the care of medical professionals, but the progress Mary had made there was swiftly unraveling, if it had not been entirely undone already.

There was no longer any question in Ann's mind but that Mary was insane, and therefore must be relieved of the dangerous weapon immediately. To her relief, and no small surprise, Elizabeth eventually was persuaded. The question remained how to go about it. If they tried to take the pistol by force, it could go off accidentally, injuring or even killing someone. If, as head of the household, Ninian demanded it, Mary could become upset and turn the weapon upon herself. She had attempted suicide before, and the implication that she was not sane enough to carry a pistol could, with cruel irony, compel her to try again.

"I think I may be able to convince her to relinquish it," said Elizabeth, pensive. "I shall appeal to her protective nature by reminding her of the possible danger to my young grandchildren. Children are curious, as she well knows, and if a child chanced upon her gun, the consequences could be tragic."

"And if that fails?" asked Ann, dubious.

"Then I shall offer a compromise: she may keep the pistol, if she allows Ninian to lock up the ammunition in his safe."

Frances looked as skeptical as Ann felt, but they all agreed that Elizabeth should make the attempt. Elizabeth thought it best if she confronted Mary alone, so Ann did not witness the undoubtedly strange and awkward conversation that ensued, but she was not surprised when, two days later, Elizabeth admitted defeat. Mary had dismissed Elizabeth's concerns, and her suggestion that Mary relinquish the gun or even just the bullets, with a shrill laugh. "I keep the pistol close to me at all times, so there is no danger that it will fall into a child's hands," she had declared. "And in a time of danger, what use to anyone is an unloaded pistol?"

Thus thwarted, Elizabeth decided to ask Robert to write to his mother and demand that she turn the pistol over to Ninian for safekeeping. "This way, Ninian will have an excuse to confiscate the weapon without bringing Mary's wrath down upon his head or mine," said Elizabeth one snowy morning in early January when she and Frances met secretly at Ann's house. Lewis had promised to escort his great-aunt on a sleigh ride out into the country; Elizabeth would return home first, and with any luck Mary would never know that she had left the house.

"Yes, but then Mary will bring her wrath down upon Robert's

head instead," said Frances. "She has already threatened to have him murdered. It's dangerously imprudent to give her any more justification."

Elizabeth gazed heavenward and sighed. "Mary has not hired any assassins. She wouldn't even know how. In any case, she is angry at Robert, but not murderous."

"We should hire a Pinkerton agent to pose as an assassin for hire," exclaimed Ann, inspired. "He and Mary could meet ostensibly by chance at one of her favorite shops. He could confess the nature of his profession and tell her that it would be his great honor to serve the widow of the great Abraham Lincoln—you know, the sort of effusive praise she basks in—if she should ever require his services. If Mary attempts to hire him to kill Robert, the authorities would have evidence that she is not of sound mind, and she would be returned to Bellevue."

"No, Ann," said Frances, incredulous. "The authorities would have evidence that Mary plotted to commit murder. She wouldn't go to Bellevue, but to prison!"

"No judge in the nation would send Abraham Lincoln's deranged widow to prison," Ann retorted. "Not if no one was actually harmed. She would be sentenced to Bellevue, or another place like it."

"Oh dear Lord in heaven." Frances covered her face with her hands and heaved a sigh. "Sometimes I have no idea what you're thinking."

Elizabeth regarded Ann sharply. "Sometimes I think you're entirely too flippant about Mary's suffering."

"My suggestion was made in earnest," Ann protested. "Believe me, I take Mary's suffering very seriously. Sometimes I suspect I'm the only one who does. She is not well, and she belongs in an asylum. She has threatened Robert's life, and you two seem more concerned with sparing her feelings than with getting a deadly weapon out of her hands!"

"Well, then, how would *you* get the gun away from her?" said Frances.

"Oh, no, no." Ann laughed shortly. "I already told you what I would do. I would have a Pinkerton take it, but *I* am too flippant, so no one need listen to me."

"Please," begged Elizabeth, raising her hands, "let's not argue among ourselves. We all want to help Mary." She let her arms fall to her sides. "I'll write to Robert to warn him about the gun. He will either tell us what he wants us to do, or he will consult Dr. Patterson, and we shall follow the doctor's recommendations."

"In the meantime," said Frances pointedly, "you have a deeply troubled woman carrying a loaded pistol around your house."

"In the meantime," Elizabeth replied, an edge to her voice, "if I can think of another way to convince her to relinquish the gun, I shall do so." Her gaze shifted to include Ann. "I trust we will all remain committed to helping Mary, if not out of sisterly love and duty, then as repayment of our debt to her martyred husband."

Debt? Ann raised her eyebrows at Elizabeth, but when Frances nodded somberly in reply, Ann muffled a sigh and did the same. Let her sisters interpret the gesture as they wished. Of course she would continue to help Mary, in her own way, but not as repayment of any debt to Abe. She owed him for preserving the Union and for abolishing slavery, as every American did; she admired him for his accomplishments, loved him as a brother, and mourned him deeply. But to be personally indebted to him? Ann did not see it.

After her sisters left, Ann continued to mull over Elizabeth's curious turn of phrase as she went about the daily routine of the household. Elizabeth and Ninian certainly had been in Abe's debt, for after Ninian wrote to humbly suggest that he be offered a patronage position, Abe had appointed him a captain with the Commissary of Subsistence. William had been made an army paymaster, and his brother, Dr. Edward Wallace, had been appointed as the naval officer at the Philadelphia customhouse. Frances too owed Abe, in a sense, for it was through him that she had met William. Emilie's husband would have owed Abe a great deal if he had been wise enough to accept the commission Abe had offered him at the beginning of the war—a post any of his brothers-in-law would have gratefully accepted—but Ben had thrown in his lot with the Confederates and had suffered the consequences, as had their brother and half-brothers who had enlisted in the rebel army.

They had all benefited from Abe's position with regard to pride and esteem, but what had Abe ever offered Ann and Clark from his presidential largess? No patronage positions, that was for certain, not as others had received. Only Levi had been similarly overlooked, but he had fallen back into his dissipated ways and could not have been trusted with an important post. Not so Clark, a proven businessman and loyal Unionist who had deserved better. Abe had not even done Clark the courtesy of offering a satisfactory response to a simple request, something that would have been inconsequential for Abe to provide but profoundly beneficial to Clark if he had received it. All Clark had wanted, back in the winter of 1864, was for Abe to give him "simply a hint" as to when the war would end, once he was reasonably certain. If Clark had a bit of advance notice, he could strategically close out some stocks, earn a profit, and pay off some rather substantial debts. But even this little thing Abe had declined to do. Instead of promising to grant Clark's request when the time came, he wrote only that he had no hopes of an imminent conclusion to the war, but rather expected it to be fought out "to the bitter end," a statement that was true but entirely unhelpful.

No, Ann loved and respected Abe in life and would honor his memory in death, but she would not agree that she owed him any debt other than that which every faithful American owed to the president who had held the fractured nation together during its greatest crisis. Ann would help Mary, not to repay a debt, but because they were sisters; despite their differences and personal squabbles, if one Todd sister suffered, none of them could be truly happy.

But what to do? Someone could get hurt while they awaited advice from Robert or Dr. Patterson. Once again, it fell to Ann to act while everyone else dithered.

Rather than try to speak to Mary alone at the Edwards residence, where Elizabeth, Ninian, or Julia was sure to interrupt and possibly ruin everything, Ann came by the house one morning and invited Mary to go shopping. Mary's eyes narrowed slightly in suspicion, but she could not resist her favorite pastime, so she put on her wraps, took up her reticule, and joined Ann in the carriage.

They began at Mary's favorite shop for fabric, notions, and trims, where she purchased some lavender silk ribbon for a new bonnet and a spool of thread. Next they went to the milliner's, but only to browse for inspiration. They chatted pleasantly about fashion and the weather as they went from shop to shop, and as soon as Ann sensed that Mary was feeling at ease, she said, "Mary, may I ask you a frank question?"

Mary inhaled deeply as if to steel herself. "I suppose."

"Do you understand how upset we all are about your pistol?"

She gestured dismissively. "Many people carry pistols."

"You never used to be one of them."

"After what happened to my beloved husband, no one should wonder why I should want to protect myself."

"I agree." Ann paused. "However, I thought you should know what others are saying behind your back."

Mary's gaze sharpened. "And what is that?"

"I probably shouldn't say." Ann pretended to mull it over. "Do you promise not to tell Frances or Elizabeth that I was the one to tell you?"

"Yes, yes, just get on with it."

"Dr. Patterson is convinced that your compulsion to carry a gun is a sign of paranoia. Dangerous paranoia, and mania," Ann added for emphasis, for Mary was frowning skeptically. "Apparently the unreasonable refusal to give up an object, even if it is forbidden by law or the rules of a particular household, can be a sign of madness."

"Dr. Patterson said this? To whom?"

"In separate letters to Robert and Ninian."

"Naturally." Pursing her mouth, Mary wheeled about, left the shop, and headed down the sidewalk, obliging Ann to follow. "I assume they are conspiring to take it from me by force."

"Not exactly." When Mary halted and turned around, frowning quizzically, Ann said, "They intend to wait, observe, and keep a record of how many days you refuse to part with the pistol. When you exceed a certain limit, they may, if they desire, use this to justify sending you back to Bellevue."

Mary blanched. "That's nonsense. They would need another trial."

"I believe they're counting on you to dread a second trial so much that you will go quietly. Of course, the obvious way to avoid all that, to keep your freedom as well as your pistol—well, I'm sure you've already thought of it."

"Enlighten me."

"Simply give the gun to someone you trust, and declare that you sold it. They will be satisfied that you don't intend to harm yourself or anyone else, and you can have your gun quickly returned to you if you ever have a particular need for it."

Mary pondered this, a canny glint in her eye. "I suppose you're offering to hold my gun for me. How could I be certain that you wouldn't give it to Ninian to lock up in his safe the moment I gave it to you?"

"You would have my solemn promise as a sister."

"And if I asked you to return it to me?"

"I would inquire whom you wanted to shoot, and whether you intended to kill or merely maim. If I thought you were making a terrible decision, I'd attempt to help you find a better solution to whatever had you so vexed." Ann smiled a bit sardonically. "Do you have a better idea? Which is more important to you, feeling the weight of that pistol in your pocket or being at liberty to do as you please?"

Mary considered, but they both knew there was really only one choice.

Ann's expectations for her scheme's success had been rather low, so it was with great relief that she carried the pistol home, removed the bullets, and locked the pistol and ammunition in separate drawers of Clark's desk.

The following evening, when the families gathered at the Edwards residence for Sunday dinner, Elizabeth took Frances and Ann aside. "Isn't it wonderful that Mary sold the pistol?" she murmured, the relief having taken years off her face. "How thankful I am to be relieved of this worry!"

"You're welcome," said Ann dryly. "She didn't sell the pistol. I convinced her to entrust it to me until she actually needs to shoot someone, at which time I am supposed to return it, which obviously I shall not do." Elizabeth and Frances stared at her, dumbfounded. "Yes, I also told her to lie about it. Don't tell her you know the truth, or you'll create anxiety where for the moment none exists."

"Well done, Ann," said Frances, looking somewhat amazed.

"The gun is secure, everyone is safe, and that is what matters," said Elizabeth, smiling and reaching out to give Ann's hand a quick squeeze.

But that was not all that mattered to Robert.

"Your letters give me great concern, not for myself, but for the things unforeseen that may yet happen," Robert replied after his aunts wrote to tell him how the conflict over the pistol had been resolved. He reminded them that the doctors they had consulted the previous spring had warned them that no one could predict the possible derangements that could take possession of his mother, and therefore she should be placed where no catastrophe could happen.

The obvious implication was that evidently the Edwards residence was not such a place.

"I am afraid the present situation will, as it did last spring, move from bad to worse," he continued. "If it would get better, it would relieve me from an overwhelming anxiety. My mother was removed from the care of Dr. Patterson despite my concerns as to the safety of such a step, and she remains out of professional care contrary to my judgment. No catastrophe has yet occurred, but I live in continual apprehension of it."

If his mother's condition did not improve, Robert concluded, he might have to return her to Bellevue Place, despite the anguish and scandal this would undoubtedly foment. "If your influence cannot restrain her in Springfield," he asked his aunts, "what are we to do?"

What indeed, Ann wondered. She had cleverly resolved the problem of the pistol, all but single-handedly, but what about the next problem and the one after that? Because as long as Mary was free to do as she pleased, there would inevitably be more problems.

20

February—May 1862

ELIZABETH

Elizabeth first learned that her nephew Willie was seriously ill from a brief, startling report in the newspaper on February 11.

SICKNESS IN THE PRESIDENT'S FAMILY.

It was announced yesterday that the usual Saturday reception at the White House and the levee on Tuesday would be omitted, on account of the illness of the second son of the President, an interesting lad of about eight years of age, who has been lying dangerously ill of bilious fever for the last three days. Mrs. Lincoln has not left his bedside since Wednesday night, and fears are entertained for her health. This evening the fever has abated and hopes are entertained for the recovery of the little sufferer.

Elizabeth's heart thudded with apprehension. The dreadful images the words evoked were so vivid in her mind's eye that the optimistic last line offered only a hollow comfort. A quick flurry of notes sent around Springfield confirmed that neither Frances nor Ann had known about their nephew's illness either. They agreed that Willie must be in grave condition for reports of his sickness to make the papers, replacing the wildly popular coverage of Mary's latest controversary.

Earlier that month, Mary had hosted a magnificent ball in the East Room of the White House, sending out more than five hundred invitations to prominent men in government and their wives, as well as to special friends, important Washington person-ages, and visiting dignitaries. From the renowned Mrs. Keckly, Mary had commissioned an off-the-shoulder, white satin gown with a low neckline, flounces of black Chantilly lace, black and white bows, a garland of myrtle trailing down the skirt, and a long, elegant train. An elaborate menu was planned, including roast turkey, foie gras, oysters, beef, duck, quail, partridge, and aspic, complemented by an assortment of fruits, cakes, ices, and fanciful creations of spun sugar.

As word of Mrs. Lincoln's lavish plans spread, she provoked crit-icism from her usual detractors, who expressed astonishment and disgust for the vain spectacle of the ball and its hostess. "Are the president and Mrs. Lincoln aware that there is a civil war?" Ohio senator Benjamin Wade had written acidly in a widely published rejection of the invitation. "If they are not, Mr. and Mrs. Wade are, and for that reason decline to participate in dancing and feasting."

It had pained Elizabeth to imagine how mortified Mary must have been by this very public rebuke, and to learn how many Washingtonians had shared Senator Wade's opinion. A great many of Mary's invitations had been brusquely declined, or so the papers reported, and nearly one hundred had been returned with indignant notes protesting the first lady's excessive frivolity when the nation was distracted, mournful, and impoverished by the war. But in spite of such denunciations, since the event was not open to the public, invitations had remained highly coveted items. "Half the city is jubilant at being invited," one reporter archly noted, "while the other half is furious at being left out in the cold." Little wonder, after the *New York Herald* predicted that the ball would be "the most magnificent affair ever witnessed in America." Subsequent reports soon confirmed that Mary's gala had been a triumph.

A glorious White House ball, a child's frightening illness— these were the stories Elizabeth once would have heard from Mary herself, a prolific letter-writer whose pen usually overflowed with news, observations, and opinions. But the sisters had quarreled, if one could call it a quarrel when it was so entirely one-sided, and Elizabeth had not heard from Mary since her last angry missive in September.

Elizabeth would never dismiss her offense as trivial, but it seemed so small among the troubles of wartime that she still could not quite believe that one misplaced letter had caused such anger and estrangement. Mary and Julia had never been particularly close, but whether from a lack of interest or a clash of personalities, Elizabeth could not say. As Julia had grown, Mary had become more disapproving of her niece's behavior, which she considered forward, and over time, as Mary made little effort to conceal her feelings, Julia became resentful.

Even so, Mary had invited Julia and her younger sister to join her entourage aboard the Inaugural Express. Afterward, Julia and her younger sister had returned to Springfield with Frances, while Elizabeth had stayed on to help Mary settle into the White House. While they were apart, Julia had written to her mother to share the news from home, and one letter had contained unflattering remarks about her aunt Mary. If only Elizabeth had burned the letter after reading it, before it somehow became separated from her other correspondence and slipped between the bedstead and the wall of her White House bedroom, where a maid found it five months later. She presented it to her employer. Another woman would have declined to read a personal letter not addressed to herself, but not Mary. Greatly offended by Julia's insults, Mary had fired off two angry letters, one to her niece and one to Elizabeth, denouncing their duplicity and ingratitude for insulting her behind her back after she had shown them such gracious hospitality during their stay in the White House. When Elizabeth had apologized and tried to make amends, Mary had fired back another letter full of blistering insults. Vexed, Elizabeth had resisted the temptation to apologize a second time and had decided not to write again until Mary sent an apology of her own. Since then five months had passed, with no word from Mary and no lessening of Elizabeth's resolve.

Their estrangement explained why Mary had not written to Elizabeth, but not why she had neglected to write to Frances or Ann, or any other member of the family who would have sent word to Elizabeth. Could it be that Willie was so dreadfully ill that Mary dared not spare a moment away from nursing him? The newspaper had noted that Mary had not left his bedside for days. If it was also true that the boy's fever had broken, perhaps Mary would write soon, after she had some time to rest.

Elizabeth waited anxiously for a letter, but expecting none, she also studied the newspapers with care. A week after the first mention of Willie's illness, she spotted another, two sentences as bleak and ominous as any she had ever read: "THE PRESIDENT'S BOY STILL VERY ILL. President Lincoln's boy William is still in a very critical condition."

Elizabeth felt as if all the breath had been squeezed from her lungs. By now her nephew had been seriously ill for more than a fortnight, as best as she could judge. How frantic Mary must be, tormented not only by her son's suffering but also by dreadful memories of Eddie, who, before his tragic death, had also languished in a sickbed for weeks.

"I should telegraph Mary and Abe to let them know we are praying for Willie," Elizabeth said to her husband that evening, and again to Julia and Lizzy the following morning. Yet she did not send word. Mary would be too desperately busy to pause to read a telegram, she told herself, especially one from a sister with whom she no longer cared to correspond.

Late in the afternoon on February 20, Elizabeth was in the nursery amusing her two-year-old grandson with a toy rabbit while Julia had a lie-down on account of her delicate condition. At the sound of footsteps, she glanced up to find Ninian standing in the doorway, but a cheerful greeting faded on her lips as she took in his red-rimmed eyes and stricken expression.

As the observant nurse hurried over to mind little Lewis, Ninian took Elizabeth's hands in his. "Darling, come and sit with me in my study," he said hoarsely. "I'm afraid I have news that will break your heart."

Word had come down the wire from Washington less than an hour before. An acquaintance who worked in the telegraph office had hurried to inform Ninian so that the family would not be shocked when they read the morning papers.

Despite the physicians' valiant efforts to save his life, earlier that day, their beloved nephew Willie had perished. His younger brother Tad suffered from the same affliction. Abe was said to be utterly devastated, and Mary so staggered by anguish that she had taken to her bed, inconsolable and keening.

"He was the light of their lives," Elizabeth choked out as she fell into Ninian's arms, weeping. "He was such a lovely boy, so kind, so good, wise beyond his years—everything a parent might wish a son to be. There are no words for such a loss. May God comfort them."

Ninian held her and consoled her as best he could, but eventually she had to compose herself and break the news to the rest of the family. Heartbroken, Julia and Lizzy clung to each other and wept. Ninian and Julia's husband, Edward, went out to inform Frances, Ann, and their families, while Elizabeth remained at home to comfort her daughters and her bewildered grandson, and to imagine too clearly the scenes of bereavement and sorrow unfolding at the White House.

The next morning Elizabeth received a telegram from Robert, sent not from Harvard but from Washington: "Willie gone. Mother prostrate from grief. Dearest aunt please come at once."

Stunned by the request, Elizabeth was at a loss to respond. Had Mary asked for her, or was this Robert's idea? Did he know they were estranged? Would she travel hundreds of miles only to be turned away from the White House because Mary refused to see her? There were valid reasons to decline—the unpredictability of travel in wartime, the expense, her grandson's needs, Julia's difficult pregnancy. Elizabeth wanted to decline, but the past haunted her, and when she remembered the fathomless depths of her own anguish after losing her firstborn child, she was moved to pity.

"I've decided to go to Washington, to Mary," she told Ninian two days after receiving Robert's telegram. "I'll try to console her, if she'll see me. If she turns me away, at least I'll know that I tried."

Ninian put his arms around her and kissed her cheek. "We'll both go. Abe is grieving too, and he carries the weight of a divided nation on his shoulders. Let us do what we can for them."

Before she could change her mind, Elizabeth telegraphed Robert to let him know they were coming. Swiftly, she and Ninian made their travel arrangements, packed their trunks, and left instructions with her sisters to check in on Julia often and to alert William immediately if she experienced even a hint of trouble with her pregnancy.

Elizabeth and Ninian arrived in Washington one day after young William Wallace Lincoln was interred in a vault at Oak Hill Cemetery in Georgetown, where he would lie until his small coffin could be buried in the family plot back home in Springfield. As their carriage rumbled off to the White House, Elizabeth peered out the windows at the transformed capital, marveling at the changes that had been wrought since Abe's inauguration, just under a year before. Washington City had become one vast military camp, the streets filled with soldiers in uniforms, troops quartered in nearly every available space. A park she and her sisters had once visited, Franklin Square, had been converted into an encampment for the Twelfth New York Regiment, filled with rows upon rows of precisely arranged white tents, with the commanding officer's headquarters in the middle of the square and an open space for marching and drilling. A closer look and a whiff of something fetid revealed that some of the encampments were military hospitals, and numerous government buildings they passed appeared to have been converted to that purpose as well.

Upon their arrival at the White House, Elizabeth saw that it too had been transformed. The mansion had been draped in the black crepe of mourning, the curtains drawn, the mirrors covered. Even their footsteps on the new carpets Mary had selected with such care seemed muffled by a thick, oppressive shroud of grief.

While servants attended to their luggage, the butler led them to Robert, pale and red-eyed, and yet composed, with only a faint quiver of his jaw betraying the grief he kept so carefully contained for his parents' sake. He embraced his aunt and uncle, thanked them profusely for coming, and accepted their condolences with a nod and a quick look away to hide unshed tears. While the butler escorted Ninian to Abe's office, for the affairs of state would not wait while the president mourned, Robert led Elizabeth to her sister's bedchamber.

"I pray you can bring my mother out of her despair," Robert said in an undertone, though no one was near. "After Willie passed, she collapsed in paroxysms of grief, shrieking and wailing in anguish until the doctor dosed her with laudanum."

"And Tad?" asked Elizabeth, anxious. "Has his condition changed since you telegraphed us?"

"Tad is improving," said Robert as he escorted her up the stairs, "but he is terrified that he might also die. He's heartbroken, and he cries because he will never see Willie again."

Elizabeth felt a stab of grief. "Oh, the poor, dear boy." He needed his mother desperately, but Mary was too consumed with grief to comfort him.

"My father arranged for a capable nurse from one of the military hospitals to care for Tad and to look in on my mother, but for the most part, Mrs. Keckly and two other friends have been watching over her in turns, day and night." Robert's jaw tightened and he inhaled deeply, shaking his head. "Whenever she drifts out of her drugged stupor, she becomes delirious and wild with fresh despair. Aunt Elizabeth, I—I don't know what we'll do if you can't reach her."

The first remedy Elizabeth would suggest would be to cut back on the laudanum, then eliminate it entirely. They had reached the top of the stairs, but even before they turned down the corridor, she heard Mary keening, an unearthly, heartrending cry that rose and fell, sending a shiver down her back. At the bedroom door, she paused and turned to Robert. "You see to Tad, and let him know Aunt Elizabeth will be there soon. I'll see to your mother." When he nodded, she forced a reassuring smile, steeled herself, and entered Mary's room.

She found her younger sister in bed in the throes of grief, the curtains drawn over the windows, the air close and uncomfortably warm. After her eyes adjusted to the dim light, she recognized the lovely woman of color who rose gracefully from the chair pulled up to Mary's bedside—Mrs. Keckly, Mary's companion, perhaps even friend, since she had evidently become much more to her than a dressmaker. Quietly, Elizabeth reintroduced herself, only to learn that Mrs. Keckly remembered her well, despite her evident fatigue. Elizabeth thanked her for watching over her sister and urged her to go home and get some rest. Visibly relieved, Mrs.

Keckly bade her good-night, promised to return the next day, and quietly departed.

In the days that followed, Elizabeth was grateful for Mrs. Keckly's steady, calming effect on Mary as they endeavored to draw her out of her torment. Mary was alternately paralyzed by sorrow and frantic with despair, and her sudden bouts of keening frightened Tad and unsettled the entire household. Either Elizabeth or Mrs. Keckly remained with her at all times, and often they both did, gently urging her to eat, to let them wash her face, dress her, and arrange her hair, to venture down the hall to see Tad, who improved day by day under the watchful eye of Nurse Pomroy. Elizabeth managed to coax a smile from her sister when she told her how Tad refused to take his medicine from anyone but his father, so the president was frequently called out of important conferences and even cabinet meetings to administer the dose. Every time, Abe readily went.

Throughout his mourning, Abe carried on with the duties of his office with stoic surety. And yet, on the one-week anniversary of Willie's death, Ninian observed that he locked himself in the Green Room, where Willie had lain in repose before his funeral, whether to be alone with his thoughts, to remember his beloved son, or to pray Elizabeth and Ninian could only wonder. Abe observed the private mourning ritual every Thursday for several weeks thereafter, and Elizabeth was relieved to see that it appeared to offer him some solace.

With gentle and persistent coaxing, Elizabeth eventually persuaded Mary to leave her bed, to wash and dress, and to attend church services. Mrs. Keckly swiftly completed pieces for her mourning wardrobe so that she might properly receive callers, but although acquaintances came to express their condolences, Mary admitted almost no one. When the beautiful and popular Elizabeth Blair Lee called and sent up her card, Mary could not bear to send her away peremptorily, so she begged Elizabeth to receive her instead. It turned out to be one of Elizabeth's most pleasant duties, for Mrs. Lee, sister to both a Missouri congress-man and the postmaster general, was charming and friendly, and the message of condolence she had Elizabeth deliver to Mary was so heartfelt and kind that it brought fresh tears to Mary's swollen, bloodshot eyes.

"Your aunt Mary still confines herself to her room, feeling very sad, and at times gives way to violent grief," Elizabeth wrote to Julia in mid-March. "She is so constituted, and the surrounding circumstances will present a long indulgence of such gloom." She regretted the word "indulgence" as soon as she wrote it, for it implied that Mary could end her grief by sheer force of will if the people around her refused to tolerate her misbehavior any longer. Elizabeth regretted all that the word implied, and yet she did not cross it out.

Robert, as quiet in his grief as his mother was expressive, endeavored to maintain a brave, strong front and was tenderly solicitous of his grieving mother. Mary responded well to his at-tention, but eventually Robert was obliged to return to Harvard to finish out the term. Soon thereafter, in the first week of April, obligations called Ninian back to Springfield. They had intended to travel together, but Mary remained in such a fragile state that Elizabeth decided to stay on a while longer. She missed home, and she was concerned for Julia, but Mary needed her. Although Mary never once mentioned their estrangement, Elizabeth knew her sister was thankful it was apparently over.

Although Mary never left the White House, beyond its safe, sheltering walls the war went on, and word of another sudden loss reached Mary and Elizabeth there. Far to the south, General Grant had defeated the rebel forces at Shiloh in Tennessee, but it had been a costly battle, the bloodiest of the war so far, with more than thirteen thousand killed, wounded, or missing on the Union side and nearly eleven thousand casualties for the South. Among those killed was their half-brother Sam, an officer in Company I, Crescent Regiment of the Twenty-Fourth Louisiana.

It was impossible to imagine their handsome, popular younger brother, so full of life and fire and fun, lying dead on a Tennessee battlefield. Elizabeth and Mary had loved to cuddle him when he was a baby, a special privilege Mammy Sally had rarely granted. "It is just as well that I see no one," Mary confided to Elizabeth and Mrs. Keckly the day after the grim news arrived. "I would be obliged to smile and pretend that I don't care that Sam is dead, or all my enemies would come out of the woodwork, questioning my loyalty to the Union."

To the sisters' dismay, staying out of sight did not keep Mary out of her persistent critics' minds. When eulogies for Sam appeared in Southern papers, his death reminded Mary's detractors of the Todd family's ties to secessionists and stirred up the old, tired questions about her loyalties. It was an unnecessary, disrespectful, appalling thing to do when the White House remained draped in mourning black, Elizabeth thought indignantly, a display of callous disregard for Mary's unrelenting grief.

And unrelenting it was.

By mid-April, Elizabeth had become accustomed to Mary's sudden fits of weeping. She had learned to sit with her sister patiently, murmuring soothing phrases until she grew calm again. One day she and Mrs. Keckly were with Mary in the family's sitting room, comforting her in their well-practiced fashion, when Abe entered and stood just inside the doorway, studying his wife. After a moment, he took her gently by the arm, led her to the window, and solemnly pointed to St. Elizabeths Hospital in the distance.

"Mother," he said, "do you see that large white building on the hill yonder?"

Mary nodded, her eyes widening. Everyone in Washington, even Elizabeth, a mere visitor, recognized the lunatic asylum, an imposing landmark on the city skyline.

"Try to control your grief," Abe continued, his voice steady, "or it will drive you mad, and we may have to send you there."

Elizabeth muffled a gasp, and from the corner of her eye she saw Mrs. Keckly struggling to conceal her shock. That Mary might be destined for an asylum was an idea too terrible to contemplate, and Elizabeth was astounded that Abe would speak so to his grieving wife.

And yet, in the days that followed, it seemed that the warning alone had compelled Mary to try to regain control of her nerves. Mary still canceled her once-customary receptions and levees and accepted almost no callers, but her dormant fascination with politics briefly rekindled on April 16, when her husband signed an act of Congress abolishing slavery in the District of Columbia.

The measure had been hotly contested in Congress and in the press, and a great many white citizens had sent letters and petitions to congressmen, editors, and other influential men demanding that the bill be voted down. In the end, their complaints and protests went unheeded, and the measure became law.

The colored residents of Washington responded with unrestrained jubilation. Their faith in President Abraham Lincoln was renewed, as was their resolve to see slavery abolished everywhere, for everyone, forever. "This is only the beginning," Mary told Elizabeth, her eyes bright, her thoughts focused on the future for the first time since Elizabeth had returned to the White House. "Soon freedom will ring for all people, all across this great, unified nation."

Elizabeth found her sister's renewed interest in the fate of the country very promising, perhaps enough so that she no longer needed Elizabeth as desperately as before. Reluctant to leave the entire burden of Mary's care to Mrs. Keckly—who had already done more for Mary than any other friend and, Elizabeth feared, had probably neglected her business in the process—Elizabeth wrote several letters to the family back home trying to secure a replacement. "Your aunt Mary wonders if Mary Jane Wallace will not feel like coming on when I am ready to leave," she wrote to Julia, testing the waters, hoping her daughter would pass along the suggestion. "She does not yet feel as if she can be alone."

When that letter provoked no response, Elizabeth focused her appeals on Frances, determined to persuade her to send her daughter to the White House. The summer season required only a very simple, affordable wardrobe, Elizabeth assured her, in case money was the issue. Writing to her niece directly, Elizabeth said, "Aunt Mary says that she will be only too glad to defray your expenses in coming, which you can repeat to anyone who objects on those grounds." But when none of her sisters or nieces responded to her increasingly fervent pleas, Elizabeth realized that she must either leave her post vacant or remain indefinitely. But she simply could not stay away from home any longer, not with Julia's second child on the way.

Abe's urgent and obvious wish for her to remain made Elizabeth's choice even more difficult. Just as Mary did, he seemed to find Elizabeth's company soothing, so she made a point to spend time with him, to distract him, if only briefly, from his mourning and from the heavy cares of government. Once she took him to view the Executive Mansion's conservatory, which he admitted he had never visited, even though it was one of Mary's favorite places on the estate. Another time, she accepted his invitation to ride out to view the Navy Yard and Arsenal. As the carriage rumbled over the stones of Pennsylvania Avenue, she realized with a start that this was the first time she had left the White House since her arrival.

Abe praised Elizabeth for her good influence over Mary when she was caught in the throes of despondency or temper, and he confessed that he thought her presence was essential to his wife's mental health. Dutifully, Elizabeth remained to support her sister, brother-in-law, and young nephew as their needs required, but as Mary continued to improve in small ways, day by day, her longing for her own home grew more acute. Whenever she mentioned setting a date for her departure, however, Mary regarded her with an expression so stricken that Elizabeth immediately postponed her trip another week.

Then, in early May, she received an urgent letter from Ninian informing her that Julia had suffered some minor complications with her pregnancy. It was nothing life-threatening, but the fear and anxiety they caused were affecting Julia's health, and she desperately needed her mother's calming presence. Something in Ninian's turn of phrase suggested that Julia was perfectly fine and the alleged complications were only a ruse meant to give Elizabeth an excuse to come home right away. Nevertheless, it was with genuine worry that she explained the situation to Abe and Mary and immediately began arranging her homeward journey.

Mary accepted the news resignedly and with more grace than Elizabeth had expected. "Please carry my love and thanks to everyone back in Springfield," she said two days later as they shared a parting embrace in the carriage outside the train station. "We'll be leaving the White House soon ourselves, to escape the summer heat and miasma."

"Oh, indeed?" said Elizabeth, pleased. This was surely another encouraging sign. "Are you going to New York?"

"Not nearly so far. Last year I found us a summer residence on the grounds of the Soldiers' Home about two miles from the city." Mary inclined her head to the north. "It's a cool, wooded, secluded haven on a hilltop, far enough away from the Capitol and the White House to serve as a restful retreat, but near enough for Abe to travel back and forth, if he must. It's truly lovely, and I trust it will be perfectly serene. I wish you had time to see it."

Elizabeth smiled. "Perhaps the next time I visit," she said as the officer escorting them opened the carriage door to help her descend.

"Write to me in care of the Soldiers' Home," Mary called

through the window. "There I expect to have few distractions and sufficient leisure to reply promptly, so I won't neglect our correspondence as I did before."

So that was how Mary chose to explain away their months of estrangement—she had simply been too busy to write. "The Soldiers' Home," Elizabeth repeated, nodding. "And you should write to me at the same address as always. I trust you remember it?"

"Of course," said Mary, allowing a brief smile. "I think I know your home as well as any I have ever called my own."

As she should, Elizabeth thought as she gave Mary a small, parting wave and turned toward the station. Elizabeth had told her sister once, long ago, that she should consider the Edwards residence to be her own home for as long as she liked. Elizabeth had never revoked that privilege, nor would she ever.

21

January–May 1876

FRANCES

Although Mary had relinquished the pistol and ceased making absurd threats against Robert's life, her anger persisted and her demands to have her bonds restored only increased. When a fortnight of excessively frigid and snowy weather in late January kept her away from the shops, she spent hours in Ninian's library poring over his law books, taking notes and comparing statutes. Privately her sisters speculated that perhaps she intended to follow the narrow path blazed by her friend Mrs. Bradwell and become a lawyer, although Ann pointed out rather unkindly that this would require years of study and Mary was off to a late start.

"Leave her be," Frances advised. "Study occupies her mind and distracts her from her resentments. She may surprise us all and become the second-most-famous lady lawyer in the land."

Mary did surprise them, but in a far less dramatic and pleasing fashion. On the first day of February, when the Todd sisters took advantage of a relatively mild day to gather in Elizabeth's parlor for tea and sewing or knitting, Mary left them for a moment and returned with a crisp, neatly written manuscript several pages long. "There is no legal reason why my bonds must be kept from me one day longer," she declared, holding out the document to Elizabeth, who seemed too startled to take it, and then to Frances, who did. "My selfish son is entirely mistaken. I have found precedent in the law by which they may be restored to me."

"It was not only Robert who told you that, but also Governor Palmer," Frances pointed out as she leafed through the document. She was not familiar enough with legal language to parse the various clauses and subsections, and she was surprised that Mary understood it any better. "Why would you doubt your own lawyer, especially someone as renowned as he?"

"He must have overlooked this," said Mary. "This sort of law practice isn't his specialty. I certainly don't mean to accuse him of colluding with my son."

"Don't you? That's cause for rejoicing," said Ann in an undertone that her sisters were meant to overhear.

"Mary—" Elizabeth paused, apparently searching for the proper words. "Would you like Ninian to review your brief, or your lawsuit, or whatever it is?"

"It's a legal study, and indeed I would like him to read it," said Mary. "I would also like him to represent me in court, if my son does not relent and I am obliged to sue him."

As Ann heaved a sigh, exasperated, Elizabeth suggested that Mary leave the document on Ninian's desk so he could examine it that evening after dinner. Mary went off to complete the errand and returned looking well satisfied with herself. The pleasant mood of their sewing circle was spoiled, but they forged on for another hour, carefully steering the conversation away from any topics likely to remind Mary of her many grievances against those whom she believed had wronged her.

The following afternoon Elizabeth stopped by Frances's house to report that Ninian had examined Mary's paper thoroughly and found several errors in the application of the law that rendered her argument moot. Not unexpectedly, Mary had refused to believe this, and so an appointment with Governor Palmer had been arranged for two days hence. "I almost hope Mr. Palmer finds a mistake in Ninian's review," said Elizabeth wearily. "Then Mary could have her bonds back and this endless struggle would be behind us."

"This meeting will surely resolve the struggle either way," said Frances. "If the governor agrees with Mary, so be it. Let her have her bonds back. If he agrees with Ninian, Mary will just have to wait until June for her sanity hearing, as she already knows. It's unlikely that she could come up with another legal maneuver to reclaim her bonds between now and then, so she will probably turn her attention to preparing for her appeal."

"I hope you're right," said Elizabeth, dubious. "Mary has always demanded that things be exactly as she wants, exactly when she wants them. It's hard to imagine that she would let the matter drop after forcing it upon us for so many months."

Frances acknowledged that Elizabeth made a fair point, but she still believed that Mary would abandon her cause when she had irrefutable proof that it was lost. Her lawyer's opinion about her new legal brief would convince her. Mary was clever and persistent, and no fool. Frances had always admired this about her, even when those qualities were inconvenient.

Two days later, to no one's surprise but Mary's, Governor Palmer sided with Ninian, showing citations from law books to support his position. Soon thereafter, as Frances had predicted, Mary turned swiftly away from the pursuit of her bonds. Unfortunately, instead of withdrawing to Ninian's library to prepare for her upcoming sanity hearing, she renewed her verbal assault upon Robert. She sent him letter after letter demanding that every item of hers currently in his possession be returned to her immediately or, she threatened, she would hire movers and arrange a police escort to forcibly remove them from Robert's home.

Frances supposed that Robert could have fought his mother on this demand, especially since a great many of the items she listed were gifts she had presented to Robert and his wife years before her sanity trial. Silver that graced their table, paintings displayed on their walls, jewelry and clothing they had worn, books they enjoyed—Mary wanted it all back, every page and piece and scrap.

On February 7, Frances received an urgent summons from Elizabeth and hurried to the Edwards residence as soon as she could. Upon her arrival, she discovered her eldest sister standing in her front hall looking dazed and distressed. Surrounding her, filling the foyer and the hall and spilling over into the parlor, were trunks and cartons and crates, all recently arrived from Chicago, containing every last item on Mary's detailed lists. The packing documents ran to a startlingly thick sheaf of pages.

"I have absolutely no idea where we're going to put all of this," said Elizabeth, dismayed. "We barely managed to stow the last lot. We squeezed so many trunks into one corner of the attic that the housemaid who used to sleep in the bedroom beneath it resigned out of fear that one day it would all come crashing through the ceiling and crush her in her bed. Now what shall we do?"

"I could store some trunks at my house," said Frances, gazing about, impressed in spite of herself at the sheer volume of Mary's hoard. "If Mary will part with them. Where has Robert been keeping all this? Does he rent a second house simply for storage?"

Elizabeth nudged a small carton aside with her foot and pressed the back of her hand to her forehead. "That is an option I had not yet considered. As farfetched as it is, I'm tempted. I cannot abide a cluttered house."

In the days that followed, Frances and Ann helped Elizabeth and Mary find places to stow Mary's worldly goods. Ninian, clearly disapproving, wanted nothing to do with the project, but he grudgingly assisted when they needed help with a particularly heavy or cumbersome object. Frances surmised that one of her sisters, or perhaps Ninian himself, must have complained to Robert about the overwhelming mess he had made of the Edwards residence, for Elizabeth soon received a letter apologizing for how his obligation to satisfy his mother's demands had disrupted the household. "Although I considered these things as much my own as if I had bought them, I have returned them to her, desiring to satisfy her as far as I can," he explained. "Her entire demand is so unreasonable in the light of any possible use these things could be to her in her present situation that it is plainly irrational and the emanation of an insane mind." He concluded by alluding once again to the possibility of returning Mary to Bellevue, but Frances knew Elizabeth would never abide by this solution, however reasonable it seemed to everyone else.

By the end of February, most of Mary's belongings had been stored out of sight. A visitor would never have suspected they were there, nor imagine the sweat, stress, and short tempers that had gone into the laborious task of concealing them. Nearly every closet and storage room, as well as the attic, now resembled a puzzle box, with cartons and trunks carefully stacked just so in order to use every available square inch of space. In consequence, Mary could only with extraordinary difficulty get to any of her belongings, but that was her own fault. She had refused to let Frances or Ann store anything in their homes, which would have allowed her to more easily enjoy those things she had insisted upon having.

The other Todd sisters were ever mindful that Elizabeth bore the brunt of Mary's needs and eccentricities. Perhaps to offer her a respite, Emilie wrote to Frances in early March, wondering if she should invite Mary to visit. "If you think Elizabeth could spare her, I would love to entertain Mary here for a month or so," wrote Emilie. "It would be ideal if she could come in Spring, when travel is more agreeable and Lexington is in bloom. Katherine, Ellie, Ben Jr., and I long to see her. Could you please take her measure and let me know if I should send a proper invitation?"

Frances thought this was a wonderful idea. Mary had loved to travel once, and she enjoyed being pampered and amused, which was undoubtedly what Emilie and her children had in mind. The Helms had not worn themselves out with months of worry and conflict; they were fresh and rested and forewarned. Mary would enjoy the novelty of a change of scene and new conversation, and the temporary easing of their responsibilities would allow Elizabeth and Ninian to rest and restore themselves until they were ready to welcome Mary back.

But when Frances approached Mary with the suggestion, her younger sister recoiled as if she had been struck. "Return to Lexington?" she said, aghast. "I couldn't possibly. I adore Little Sister and I'm gratified that she longs to see me, but I could never return to Lexington."

"Certainly you could," protested Frances, astonished. "Lexington is your home, your birthplace. It's breathtakingly beautiful in spring, as you surely must remember. We have so many friends and relations who would be delighted to see you again—"

"Yes, that's precisely the point. There will be a great many people in Lexington eager to gape at the mad Mrs. President, the Todd sister who left Lexington so proudly, so full of promise, and went from the White House to the asylum. I could not bear so many pitying glances and careful conversations everywhere I might go."

Frances's heart sank. "Emilie shall be so disappointed if you refuse."

"I trust you will break it to her gently then."

Mary's hard look and the decisive set of her mouth told Frances that any attempt to cajole her into accepting the invitation would fail utterly. Feeling sorry for Emilie and sorrier still for Elizabeth, Frances told Mary she would invent a plausible excuse for declining the invitation. Then, resigned, she went home, took pen in hand, and told Emilie exactly what Mary had said.

Emilie replied that she understood perfectly and that she was grateful for the attempt. "Perhaps Mary will change her mind and visit me in early summer," she wrote, suggesting that she may not have understood perfectly after all.

With no visit to Little Sister to look forward to, Mary was free to concentrate on her ongoing animosity toward her son. Frances knew that in an attempt to defuse his mother's anger, Robert had tried to find men his mother trusted to take over his conservatorship, but understandably, no one was willing to undertake the role. By the middle of May, Mary had contrived a new way to punish her son: she repeatedly threatened to intentionally bankrupt herself and depend entirely upon government support for the rest of her days, just to shame and spite him.

Robert bore this new attack with the same steady but pained resolve with which he had endured all the others. "I should hardly think of my mother as fully restored to sanity, as Aunt Elizabeth does," he wrote wryly to Frances after she warned him. "The sane way to punish me for trying to look after her best interests would be not to plunge herself into poverty, but to make a will and leave me nothing in it."

Nothing proved his mother less fit to manage her own financial affairs than threats to bankrupt herself to spite her heirs, Robert added. If his mother wished to prove that she needed a conservator indefinitely, she should continue to do exactly what she was doing.

Mary would have only herself to blame at her sanity hearing in June if her vindictive threats convinced the judge to affirm the original decision and return her to Bellevue.

22

September 1861–December 1863

EMILIE

F ive months after declining the commission to serve as pay-master of the United States Army, Ben packed his kit and kissed Emilie and the girls good-bye. He lowered his head as if in prayer as he rested his hand upon Emilie's abdomen, the slight rounding still unnoticeable beneath the layers of gown and petticoats. Then he set out for Bowling Green to join the Confederate Army. Upon his arrival, he accepted a commission as colonel with the First Kentucky Brigade under General Simon Bolivar Buckner, who had been his instructor at West Point and had become a good friend.

"This separation I sincerely hope will not continue long," Ben wrote to her soon thereafter, "but dear Em, I have gone in for the war & if God spares my life I expect to battle to the end of it. I feel that I am fighting for civil liberty & in that cause I feel that all men capable of bearing arms should be in the service."

Five months later, he was promoted to brigadier general, and three weeks after that, he was tasked to organize the Third Kentucky Brigade, in Breckinridge's division. Less than a year had passed since he had declined Abe's commission and the rank of major, knowing that such promising opportunities rarely came by twice in a lifetime. Now Ben had risen even higher than the post he had declined, and after the Confederate Army triumphed, Emilie could only imagine how much higher he might soar.

If Ben could commit his life to a cause, so could she—and her cause was her husband and children. Perhaps that was not as impressive as the struggle to create a new nation, but to her it was infinitely more precious. She and Ben had promised each other on their wedding day that they would not let his career separate them, so after she recovered from the birth of Benjamin Jr. in May 1862, she resolved to follow him into the South, joining the wives of other officers who moved from camp to camp as their husbands did.

Ma tearfully begged her not to go, and her younger sister Kitty was terribly afraid of what might befall her and the children, but Emilie would not be deterred. "I won't be on the battlefield, but in the town nearest the brigade's encampment," she assured them. "The nearest *safe* town."

After arranging for a wet nurse, Emilie kissed her precious baby good-bye and entrusted him to his loving grandmother and aunt at Buena Vista. Then she packed one trunk for herself, another for her daughters, and a third full of essential supplies that Ben had mentioned were sorely lacking in the South. They traveled by rail to Elodie's home in Selma, Alabama, from whence Emilie intended to choose another safe destination closer to Ben.

Elodie was thrilled to see them. She had recently married, and her new husband, Colonel Nathaniel Henry Rhodes Dawson, was away serving with the Fourth Alabama Infantry. Twice widowed, he had entrusted to Elodie's care his two daughters, ages seven and two, one from each of her predecessors. Even with the help of a capable mammy, Elodie was feeling overwhelmed by her new responsibilities and was grateful for the companionship of a beloved elder sister who also happened to be a more experienced mother. A short ride away stood the charming Italianate cottage of Martha and her husband, Major Clement B. White of the Alabama State

Guard. The three sisters spent many companionable hours watching the cousins play together, reminiscing about bygone days in Kentucky and Illinois before war split the family apart, and yearning for their absent husbands.

Emilie had been in Selma only a few weeks when a telegram from Louisiana brought dreadful news. On August 5, Ben's regiment had been advancing on Baton Rouge when a band of Confederate irregulars had encountered pickets outside the Union lines. When the Yankees had fired upon them, the irregulars had fled, colliding into the approaching Confederate troops and setting off a barrage of friendly fire. In the chaos, Ben's horse had fallen, pinning him to the ground. Though badly injured, he was expected to recover. The same could not be said for his aide-de-camp and brother-in-law, Alexander Todd, who had fallen to a Confederate bullet.

The three Todd sisters wept in one another's arms—dear Aleck, only twenty-three, so handsome and courtly, so full of promise, and poor Ma, eight hundred miles from her cherished son, on the other side of enemy lines. Did she even know she had lost another son to this terrible, devouring war? First Sam, now Aleck—who would be the next Todd to fall? David, a sergeant with the Twenty-Seventh Louisiana Infantry? George, their elder half-brother serving the Confederacy as a regimental surgeon?

Emilie's grief for her lost brother was compounded by worry for her husband. Even after he wrote to assure her that he was mending well, she desperately longed to be at his bedside, nursing him tenderly, with the tireless attention only a devoted wife could give. When Ben sent word that he had been reassigned to command the post in Chattanooga during his convalescence, she swiftly arranged to join him there and bade a sad farewell to her sisters, promising to write and praying they would meet again soon.

Emilie's joy at being reunited with her beloved Ben was immeasurable. "My darling wife," he murmured as he embraced her.

"I hardly believe you're here—an angel alighting on this wretched earth." He looked years older than when they had parted in Kentucky, yet his blue eyes shone with affection as he swept his daughters into his arms, and when he teased them and made them giggle, his smile was as bright as she remembered. He had a hundred questions about his namesake, who was growing healthy and strong back at Buena Vista, but even as Emilie shared every detail she could remember, her heart ached from longing and regret. She had not cuddled her baby in her arms in months, and most of what she told Ben about him she had learned from Ma's and Kitty's letters.

Although they were in the same city, Ben's days were consumed by the unrelenting demands of war and their hours together were few and far between. One day, after leaving Katherine and Ellie with another officer's wife so she could explore Chattanooga, Emilie came upon a large number of wounded soldiers being carried into a school that had been made into a makeshift hospital. A few men reclined on desks that had been pushed together, but most lay on the bare floor, moaning in pain. Some clutched at her skirt as she passed, pleading for water, for medicine to assuage their fevers, for their mothers. Everywhere she looked she found brave young men with little food, no medicine, no beds, no blankets, nothing to provide them the least comfort. Deeply troubled, she visited the other public buildings that had hastily been transformed into hospital wards and saw that it was the same everywhere—scarce supplies, inadequate staffing, and appalling conditions that did almost nothing to foster healing and recovery.

Indignant, Emilie stormed to the quartermaster's office, only to learn that the neglect was not the fault of anyone in Chattanooga: only half of the hospital supplies they had requisitioned had arrived. Desperate telegrams to Richmond had yielded nothing, for essential goods were becoming scarce throughout the Confederacy. "We got bolts of oilcloth and plenty of straw," a sympathetic but harried clerk told her. "Might be you could spread the straw on the ground and lay the cloth on top of it. Beats a cold, hard floor anyway."

Emilie thanked him, certain that they could do much better for their brave heroes than that. Haunted by the men's anguish, she sought out her closest friends among the nomadic officers' wives and asked them to bring other industrious ladies to a meeting at Ben's office later that afternoon. When more than two dozen had assembled, she divided them into groups to sew the oilcloth into cots to fill with clean, fresh straw. "Let us resolve to have every one of our wounded men off the ground and into a cot within a fortnight," she proclaimed. Her ladies applauded, then quickly took needles in hand and got to work.

By the time Ben was named commander of the Kentucky Brigade after General Hanson was killed at the Battle of Stones River, Emilie and her ladies had made more than twelve hundred cots and hundreds of blankets. No patient arriving in Chattanooga spent more than a few hours on the unforgiving ground, and that only when a vast number of wounded flooded the city all at once.

Unfortunately, Ben's promotion brought their reunion to an end. As he prepared his troops to leave Chattanooga for Jackson, Mississippi, nearly 400 miles to the southwest, Emilie and the girls traveled 160 miles to the southeast to board with a distant acquaintance in Griffin, Georgia, until Ben established new headquarters. While he led the Kentucky Brigade to the reclaimed state capital, where they would join Major General Johnston's stealthy advance upon the rear of General Grant's forces surrounding Vicksburg, Emilie settled her daughters into their new lodgings, two small but pleasant rooms in a town of fewer than three thousand residents about forty miles due south of Atlanta.

Far from the front, Emilie and the girls were safe and well provided for. Their landlady was courteous, another tenant had children for Katherine and Ellie to play with, and although meat was scarce, meals were considerably improved by the summer bounty of the expansive kitchen garden. Emilie was relieved to be spared the scenes of suffering and death that had assaulted her senses in the military hospitals—the mangled bodies, the piteous moans, the stench of blood and rot and evacuated bowels—but she missed the useful work that had filled her hours and given her a sense of purpose. The ladies of Griffin organized their own projects for the war effort, and Emilie joined in where she was needed, but she was no longer energized by the thrill of urgency, of necessity. She knew she should be grateful to be restored to a quiet domestic life, and yet she awaited Ben's summons with more resignation than contentment, her patience diminishing day by day.

The weeks passed slowly, dull and ordinary except when rumors of raging battles spread through the town. Then tension and fear simmered to a boil until at long last the telegraph lines crackled with news from the front, bringing relief to some households and despair to others.

In mid-September, the pattern of her days suddenly shifted when her landlady gave her one week's notice to find other accommodations. They had not expected Emilie to stay so long, the landlady admitted somewhat abashedly, and another tenant needed the rooms for her children, who had been crowded four to one bedchamber too long. "I understand," said Emilie, smiling to hide her distress. "I should have realized we had overstayed our welcome. I'll make other arrangements immediately."

After making inquiries and finding nothing suitable nearby, Emilie realized that nothing held her in Griffin. Any safe Southern city would do, as long as it had telegraph service so that Ben could summon her and a railroad station so that she and the girls could hurry back to him when his summons finally came. Longtime family friends from Kentucky residing in Madison, Georgia, had urged Emilie to bring her daughters and stay as long as she liked, and in every letter, Elodie and Martha prevailed upon her to return to Selma.

Given that she had so little time to decide, the pull of sisterly affection drew her back to Alabama. With a day to spare before her eviction, Emilie packed their trunks and telegraphed Ben in care of headquarters to inform him of their move, hoping against hope that her message would reach him in the field.

Perhaps out of guilt, Emilie's erstwhile landlady escorted them to the train station and had her driver see to their luggage. The depot bustled with anxious travelers, and since their train was delayed, Emilie had ample time to study them: weary women, some with children like herself, many swathed in the black crepe of mourning; gentlemen too elderly to enlist, with fragile, white-haired wives on their arms; and soldiers, their uniforms in various stages of disrepair, some eager and cracking nervous jokes, others hollow-eyed and silent. The soldiers sat or sprawled wherever they could find room as they awaited transport, indifferent to propriety. One fellow lay on the floor almost at Emilie's feet, so whenever she turned about to keep her restless daughters in sight, her skirt brushed against him, yet never once did he stir. As an hour dragged past, she felt increasingly unsettled until something in the angle of his head suddenly struck her as very wrong and she realized with absolute certainty that he was dead.

Heart plummeting, she took her girls by the hands and led them away. She searched for a station agent, but before she found one the train chugged up to the platform and she had to usher the girls aboard before every seat was taken. Once aboard, she told a conductor about the dead soldier, but he merely shrugged and moved on, as if this horror was nothing new.

After a long, uncomfortable, exhausting journey in the over-crowded train, with Katherine bored and Ellie tearful, both longing to run and play, they at last arrived in Selma. The sight of Elodie waiting for them on the platform, beaming with happiness, lifted her depressed spirits. "I've never been so happy to see you," Emilie said fervently, nearly falling into her sister's embrace. Elodie hugged her and promised that a tasty meal awaited them at her home, followed by a hot bath and a good night's sleep, after which everything would look brighter.

Emilie had just finished dressing after her bath and was squeezing water from her thick, dark hair when a soft rap sounded on the door. Before she could respond, the door opened and Elodie stood before her, her face pale, her expression an unsettling mix of disbelief and misery.

"Yes?" Emilie stood, and her damp hair, unbraided, fell nearly to her waist. "What is it?"

Wordlessly her sister held out a telegram. Seized by a sudden chill, Emilie declined to take it, so Elodie placed it in her hand and closed her fingers around it.

Emilie forced herself to look. At first glance, she was confused; it appeared to be two days old, with one message appended to another, a note from General Bragg explaining the first part, which in stark letters said—

"Atlanta Ga, Mrs. General Helm in Griffin. Find her and send her up in train today. The general is dead."

Then she could read no more. She collapsed upon the bed and the paper drifted to the floor. She felt her sister's arms around her, felt her own tears wet on her cheeks and aching sobs tearing from her throat, but as if from a great distance, because she could not survive this blow if she were fully present for it in all its brutal clarity. The truth that her beloved Ben was gone forever was one she would have to half disbelieve if she were to take her next breath, and another one after that, and another.

She lost an hour to anguish, insensible from grief, until it finally broke through that Elodie had read the rest of the telegram and was telling her something vitally important—Ben would be laid to rest in Atlanta on September 23. "Tomorrow,"

Elodie was saying. "I'll accompany you if you wish to go, but we must leave now."

"Of course," Emilie murmured, sitting up, pushing her hair out of her face. "Yes. I must say good-bye."

Martha was swiftly summoned to look after all the children. Elodie packed a satchel and replaced the few items Emilie had taken from her trunk, and before she quite knew what was happening, she was back at the station leaning heavily on her younger sister's arm, too stunned and heartbroken to weep. She should have worn black, she realized distantly when they were an hour east of Selma. Black crepe was what widows wore, black dresses and heavy black veils, and here she was in navy blue with tiny brown flowers, wholly inappropriate. Ma would be scandalized.

Suddenly she longed for her mother and her infant son so desperately that she almost could not breathe.

The train was forced to make extended stops at several stations along the route owing to unspecified trouble farther down the tracks. They sat four or five hours outside of Auburn, the only sound an occasional distant rumble that could have been thunder or artillery. The steady thrum of insects in the darkness rose and fell as Emilie drifted in and out of sleep. The train started up again at dawn, jolting her awake to find her head resting on Elodie's lap, her heart hollow, her face wet with tears.

The sisters arrived at the Citizens Graveyard just as Ben's funeral was beginning, too late to see him in his coffin, too late to give him one last kiss. When she cried out in disappointment that a parting look had been denied her, Elodie murmured that it was better this way, it truly was, for Ben would want her to remember him as he had been when they parted in Chattanooga, not as he was now. "Keep that parting kiss in your memory always," said Elodie, clasping her around the waist, keeping her on her feet.

Emilie closed her eyes and remembered.

After the funeral, Emilie and Elodie stayed for a week at the home of Colonel Dabney, who had taken charge of Ben's remains before the funeral. "Come home with me," Elodie urged, tears in her eyes. "You and the girls can stay with me until the war is won."

"I want to go home," Emilie said, voice breaking. "I just want to go home to Kentucky and Ma and little Ben."

In the end, Emilie and her sisters agreed that it would be best if she and her daughters stayed in Madison with their longtime friends from Kentucky, Mr. and Mrs. Bruce, until they could return to Kentucky. She was told that her mother, her father-in-law, and several military colleagues of Ben's were appealing to General Grant and President Lincoln to issue a pass so that she and her daughters could cross the lines. But communications between the enemy governments were fragmented and fraught with suspicion, so it was not until late November that Emilie learned that Abe himself had granted Ma a pass. At that very moment, she was on her way from Lexington, and when she arrived, Martha too would come to Madison and help escort them home.

Ma arrived in early December, determined but tremulous with grief and concern. When Ma took her in her arms, it was almost as if Ben had died a second time as Emilie's pain and sorrow, tamped down over time by the effort to keep up a brave front for her devastated daughters, broke through to the surface again. Ma rested from her long journey for a day, but their yearning for home and the urgency to return before some unseen calamity rendered their pass invalid compelled them to depart the day after.

Escorted by Ma and Martha, Emilie and her daughters traveled by train and coach to Richmond, the capital of the Confederacy; from there they took the flag-of-truce steamboat down the James River to Fort Monroe in occupied Virginia. The weather had been cold and damp for most of the voyage, and the bracing winds off the open sea chilled Emilie to the marrow as they gathered on the deck while federal officers came aboard to inspect the ship for contraband and to examine the passengers' papers. The lieutenant who studied Ma's pass shot her a look of pure astonishment upon discovering that it was affixed with the signature of the commander in chief himself.

"Everything is in order, sir," said Ma, when the officer seemed to scrutinize their papers too long.

"Yes, ma'am," he replied. "There's only one thing more. We have orders to require an oath of allegiance to the United States from everyone who wishes to come ashore."

"May I request a parole on to Washington?" asked Emilie, taken aback. "I shall return if I am required to take the oath."

"Beg your pardon, ma'am, but my orders say everyone is obliged to take the oath. I cannot parole you to Washington City or anywhere else without it."

"I cannot do it," said Emilie, shaking her head. "You cannot ask this of me."

"Ma'am, I—"

"I have just left my late husband's friends and brothers in arms, ill and poorly clad, with tears in their eyes and sorrow in their brave hearts for me over my great bereavement," she said, tears gathering, a tremor of grief and fury in her voice. "They will believe that I have deserted them and that I was not true to the cause for which their beloved commander gave his life. I assure you, it is not from bravado that I refuse, but out of loyalty to my husband. To betray his memory, sir, would be treason."

Another officer had joined them while she spoke, and the men kindly but firmly tried to persuade her, emphasizing that they could not make exceptions, not even for the sister-in-law of the president. Eventually the exasperated lieutenant declared, "I will have to telegraph the president your decision."

He strode off. Forbidden to disembark, Emilie and her companions endeavored to make themselves comfortable on the deck, admiring the scenery, pointing out interesting sights to the girls in the harbor and on the shore, a tantalizing, forbidden land.

Hours passed before the officer returned, smiling and waving a telegram. "Here's the president's reply," he said, handing the paper to Emilie.

She read it aloud. "'Send her to me. A. Lincoln.'"

A wave of relief swept through her. Quickly it was decided that Emilie would take Katherine with her to the White House, while Ma, little Ellie, and Martha would find lodgings in Baltimore. As soon as arrangements could be made, Ma would take Ellie home to Kentucky, while Martha would remain in Baltimore until her pass expired, to visit friends and acquire necessities unavailable in the South.

They parted with embraces, thanks, and promises to write.

When Emilie arrived in Washington City, young Katherine by her side, she found the capital of the North utterly transformed since she had last seen it in April 1861. What had once resembled a military parade ground had become one vast hospital, filled with the stench and moans of sick, wounded, and dying soldiers, on a scale she could not have imagined despite her experience with the makeshift hospitals in Chattanooga.

Mary and Abe met Emilie and Katherine at the front door of the Executive Mansion, welcoming them with warm embraces and tears in their eyes. At first, the adults were too grief-stricken to speak; they had all suffered such terrible losses that for a long moment all they could do was to embrace one another in silence and tears. Emilie's heart went out to her sister and brother-in-law to see how the burdens of his office had taken their toll on them both, but especially Abe, whose kind eyes and warm smile belied the lines that worry had etched on his face, his sunken cheekbones, his intensely melancholic aura.

Duty soon summoned Abe back to his office. While Katherine ran off to play with her cousin Tad, Mary led Emilie upstairs to the family's private quarters, where they sat in the parlor and let their tears fall unheeded as they spoke of their children and of old friends in Springfield and Lexington. They said nothing of the pain and politics that divided them, nothing of the future, which seemed empty of anything but despair. Emilie chose her words carefully, loath to say anything that might inadvertently injure her sister's battered heart. From the hesitant way Mary introduced new topics, Emilie knew she was picking her way through the same uncertain terrain.

They dined alone, and afterward Mary led her on a tour of the White House, which she had refurbished magnificently. The East, Green, and Blue Rooms were beautifully illuminated, and in the Red Room, Emilie admired the portrait of George Washington that Dolley Madison had cut out of the frame and carried off to save it from the British. "Dolley Madison's first husband was a Todd," Mary remarked, repeating a fact Emilie knew well.

Emilie was offered a lovely bedroom that had been redecorated for a visit from the Prince of Wales. Its purple draperies and wall hangings were rich and sumptuous, but to Emilie they seemed grim and funereal despite the bright yellow cords that bound them. Katherine had a smaller but much brighter room next door. Although Emilie had expected to rest uneasily in the Union capital, surrounded by Yankees, they both slept well and awoke refreshed, Katherine cheerful and lively, Emilie full of calm acceptance.

That calm remained with her throughout the day, but deserted her later that evening. At midmorning, Emilie and Mary were engrossed in conversation when a strikingly beautiful colored woman entered the room, a sewing basket on her arm. Her eyes widened almost imperceptibly to see the two sisters seated together on the sofa, clutching hands and choking back tears.

"Ah, Mrs. Keckly," said Mary, rising, her hand still in Emilie's. "Allow me to present my dear sister, Mrs. Emilie Helm."

"How do you do, Mrs. Helm," said Mrs. Keckly cordially, with a polite bow of the head, but Emilie was too undone to do more than nod and press her lips together in a pained semblance of a smile.

Mary crossed the room, placed a hand on Mrs. Keckly's elbow, and guided her back toward the door. "My sister and her daughter arrived only yesterday, and we have so much to discuss. Would you come back tomorrow—no, the day after? And would you please—" Her voice dropped to a murmur. "What I mean is, we would not like it whispered about that Little Sister is staying with us."

Somewhat bemused, Mrs. Keckly agreed and bade them farewell. Thus did Emilie come to realize that while Abe and Mary would not deny that she was visiting, they did not want it widely known to the public. Though this made her uncomfortable, Emilie understood: many in Washington would look askance at a Confederate widow residing at the White House. She did not wish to make matters more difficult for the Lincolns, who had enough to contend with without troublesome relations stirring the pot.

As if to prove that they had no intention of hiding her away, when Abe went to bed early with a bad cold, Mary invited their cousin John Todd Stuart to join them for dinner. Emilie had not seen him since she was a belle of eighteen, and at first she dreaded to see how he would treat a rebel cousin. He was so kind and courteous, however, that she was quite at her ease by the time they retired to the Blue Room for coffee. Her wariness returned in an instant when a maid delivered cards from two callers and Mary agreed to receive them. Excusing herself, Emilie left the room and went to choose a book from Abe's study, but a few minutes later Mary found her there and asked her to return. "Our visitors came especially to see you, Little Sister, to inquire about mutual friends in the South," she cajoled. "Could you perhaps help ease their worries?"

Emilie was reluctant to accept—it was painful to see friends, and meeting strangers felt even worse—but she did, arranging her veil over her face as she followed her sister back to the Blue Room. There Mary introduced New York senator Ira Harris, father of one Union officer and stepfather of another. The second gentleman was General Daniel Sickles, a former US congressman from New York and founder of the famed Excelsior Brigade of the Army of the Potomac. Although he had lost a leg at Gettysburg, he remained on active duty, and rumor had it that he deeply resented General Grant for refusing to appoint him to a combat command.

"When I heard that you were at the White House, just arrived from the South," said General Sickles, "I told Senator Harris that you could probably give him some news of his old friend General John Breckinridge."

"I'm sorry, Senator," said Emilie, turning to him, "but as I have not seen General Breckinridge for some time, I cannot give you any news of his health."

"Thank you all the same, madam," replied Senator Harris, bowing. He then proceeded to ask her several pointed questions about the Confederate government and military, its resources and general morale. Increasingly wary, she offered only polite, noncommittal answers, until in his vexation he declared, "Well, we have whipped the rebels at Chattanooga, and I hear, madam, that the scoundrels ran like scared rabbits."

"It was the example, Senator Harris, that you set for them at Bull Run and Manassas," she replied tightly.

A faint flush of embarrassment had risen in Mary's cheeks. "Senator Harris," she ventured, "I wonder if you have heard of the Contraband Relief Association. My dear friend, Mrs. Keckly, founded the organization to—"

"And you, madam," Senator Harris interrupted, turning upon her. "One might well ask you why your son Robert isn't in the army. He is old enough and strong enough to serve his country. He should have gone to the front some time ago."

Mary blanched and bit her lip, steadying herself. "Robert is preparing even now to enter the army," she replied. "He is not a shirker, as you seem to imply, Senator, for he has been anxious to go for a long time. If fault there be, it is mine, as I have insisted that he should stay in college a little longer. I believe an educated man can serve his country with more intelligent purpose than an ignoramus."

The senator rose from his armchair, harrumphed, and pointed at Mary. "I have only one son and he is fighting for his country." Fixing his glare upon Emilie, he added, "And, madam, if I had twenty sons, they should all be fighting rebels."

"And if I had twenty sons, Senator Harris," Emilie retorted, trembling, "they should all be opposing yours."

Blinded by tears, heart pounding, she fled the room and stumbled away, desperate to reach the privacy of her room where she could weep unobserved, but Mary caught up to her and embraced her. Emilie felt her sister's tears fall upon her head as she wept on Mary's shoulder.

They said nothing more about the incident that night, but the next morning Mary told her that after she and Emilie had fled, General Sickles had gone to Abe's bedchamber to harass him on his sickbed despite cousin John's attempts to intervene. After the general indignantly reported what had unfolded in the Blue Room, Abe had grinned at John and said, "That child has a tongue like the rest of the Todds."

Infuriated, General Sickles had slapped the table with his palm. "You should not have that rebel in your house."

At that, Abe had drawn himself up, solemn and dignified in spite of his illness. "Excuse me, General Sickles, my wife and I are in the habit of choosing our own guests," he had said, regarding the general with all the courtesy due him as a wounded veteran. "We do not need from our friends either advice or assistance in the matter. Besides, the little 'rebel' came because I ordered her to come, not of her own volition."

Emilie was both touched and astonished to hear how courteously Abe had defended her. "Of course he did," said Mary, surprised. "Union or Confederate, family must come first. If everyone
felt this way, we might not have had any war at all. Oh, Little
Sister, I could fill pages and pages if I listed all the families I know
that have been divided by this war. I would start with our own
and go on and on until it broke my heart."

Abe was too noble, and Mary too defiant, not to defend her, but
Emilie realized that every time they did so, their political enemies
would use it against them.

Later that afternoon, Emilie and Mary were drinking tea in the
family parlor while Tad and Katherine sat on the rug before the
fire looking through a photograph album. "This is the president,"
Tad said proudly, pointing to a portrait of Abe.

"No, that is not the president," said Katherine, her brow furrowing in confusion. "Mr. Davis is president."

Scowling, Tad shouted, "Hurrah for Abe Lincoln!"

"Hurrah for Jeff Davis," Katherine shouted back defiantly.

Just as the mothers were about to intervene, a chuckle from the
doorway alerted them to Abe's presence. "Pa, you're the president.
Tell her," Tad demanded, shooting his younger cousin a look of
indignant fury.

Amused, Abe sat down on the sofa and drew a child onto each
knee. "Well, Tad, you know who your president is," he said reasonably, "and to your little cousin, I am Uncle Abe." He chatted
with them calmly until they stopped glaring at each other, but
Emilie, chagrined, knew it would not be the last disagreement
between the two.

In the days that followed, even as Emilie worried that she and
Katherine were wearing out their welcome, Mary and Abe each
took her aside privately to encourage her to stay. "I hope you can
come up and spend the summer with us at the Soldiers' Home,"
Abe suggested once as they walked together in the conservatory.

"You and Mary love each other, and it is good for her to have you with her."

"Perhaps," Emilie replied, although she thought it unlikely. "After being away from little Ben so long, I don't know when I might be ready to travel again."

Abe nodded, rueful. "I feel worried about Mary," he confided. "Her nerves have gone to pieces. She cannot hide from me that the strain has been too much for her."

"She does seem very nervous and excitable. I think she fears that other sorrows may be added to those we already have to bear." Emilie hesitated before adding, "I believe if anything should happen to you or Robert or Tad, it would kill her."

Abe shook his head, his sorrowful expression deepening. "If anything does happen to me or my boys, would you promise to look after Mary? This is a great favor, and perhaps too much to ask, but it would ease my mind."

"Of course I promise," said Emilie, "but nothing will happen to you, and you mustn't think that way."

He gave her a sad half-smile and thanked her.

That night, after Emilie had retired to her chamber and was preparing for bed, a knock sounded on the door. "Little Sister, may I come in?" Mary called softly.

Emilie quickly rose to let her enter, and when she did, Emilie saw that Mary was smiling though her eyes were full of tears. "I want to tell you, dear Emilie, that one may not be wholly without comfort when our loved ones leave us."

Was she referring to the solace of prayer? "I'm not sure I understand."

Mary drew closer, clasping and unclasping her hands. "When my noble little Willie was first taken from me, I felt that I had fallen into a deep pit of gloom and despair without a ray of light anywhere. Had it not been necessary to cheer Mr. Lincoln, whose grief was as great as my own, I could never have smiled again, and if Willie did not come to comfort me I would still be drowned in tears—"

"What?" Emilie broke in, startled. "Willie—"

"Yes, he comes to comfort me, and while I long to touch him, to hold him in my arms, and I still grieve that he has no future in this earthly realm—he lives, Emilie!" she cried, a strange, eerie thrill in her voice. "He comes to me every night and stands at the foot of my bed with the same sweet, adorable smile he always had. And he does not always come alone."

"What—what do you mean?"

"Little Eddie is sometimes with him, and twice he has come with our brother Aleck. He tells me he loves his Uncle Aleck and is with him most of the time." Mary clasped her hands to her heart. "You cannot imagine the comfort this gives me. When I thought of my little son in the vastness of eternity, alone, without his mother to hold his little hand in loving guidance, it nearly broke my heart."

Mary's eyes were wide and shining, as if she were in the presence of the supernatural. Emilie shivered when Mary drew closer to kiss her cheek before bidding her good-night and leaving the room, the strange, unsettling smile still upon her lips.

The next morning Emilie remained so disturbed by Mary's midnight revelations that she could not bear to repeat them, but she did warn Abe that Mary was nervous and overwrought from being under a tremendous strain. Abe again asked her to stay longer, but Emilie knew the time had come for her to take Katherine home, to reunite their little family and wait out the rest of the war.

On the morning of her departure, Abe provided her with a pass that allowed her to return to Kentucky, relieved her of all penalties and forfeitures, and restored her rights. "You know this only protects you from past transgressions," he added wryly. "It will not safeguard you from crimes you may commit in the future."

"I understand," said Emilie, allowing a hint of a smile as she tucked the precious document into her reticule.

He studied her for a moment, his expression earnest and grave. "Little Sister, you know I tried to keep Ben with me. I hope you don't feel any bitterness toward me, or believe that I am to blame for all this sorrow."

Emilie took a deep, shaky breath. "Let neither of us blame the other. My husband loved you and was deeply grateful to you for the commission you so generously offered, but he had to follow his conscience. He had to side with his own people—and I had to side with him."

They parted in forgiveness and gratitude, with fervent wishes to meet again in happier days, when the sorrows of the past would diminish beneath the bright hope of the future.

23

May–June 1876

ANN

Elizabeth claimed to believe that Mary's reason had been restored, but Ann and Frances agreed with Robert that she remained in the grip of mania and depression. Robert wrote to his aunts that he dreaded what might become of his mother if she were able to spend her money and travel with no restrictions, but with each letter, his tone became increasingly resigned. At the end of May, he confided to Ann that Justice David Davis had advised him to let the conservatorship cease, uncontested, at the end of the stipulated year. Even if his mother did squander her fortune, as her compulsion to shop perhaps made inevitable even if she had not threatened to do so deliberately, she would still be able to live on her annual pension of $3,000 from the United States government. "Justice Davis concludes that it would be better for my happiness to give a free consent to the removal of all restraint on her person or property and trust to the chances of time," Robert wrote. "I am inclined to agree. It will be a leap of faith, but perhaps all will be well. As for my mother's unmitigated anger with me, I sincerely hope that Aunt Elizabeth is correct, and it will cease once control of her bonds is returned to her."

Ann hoped so too, but she was skeptical. Nothing she had observed over the past year—or indeed, throughout all the years she had known Mary—suggested that her sister would simply let bygones be bygones once she had what she wanted.

On Thursday, June 15, Ninian traveled to Chicago to represent Mary in the long-awaited hearing to remove her conservator and to restore her rights and property. Unlike her insanity trial of the year before, Mary was not required to be present, and so she did not attend. Before Ninian departed, he reminded her sisters that this would not be a trial to declare her sane, but only to confirm that she could control her assets.

"Perhaps that's for the best," Frances replied. "Mary would never accept a verdict declaring that her sanity was restored, for she never believed she had lost it."

The hearing at the Cook County courthouse would be a relatively simple affair. Mary's petition requesting the dismissal of her conservator would be submitted, Ninian would testify regarding Mary's fitness to assume control over her property, Robert would consent to step down from the role, and an accounting of her estate would be provided. In addition to Robert and Ninian, also present would be Robert's attorney, Leonard Swett; the county court judge; the court clerk; and a jury of twelve citizens rather than a panel of learned physicians. To avoid a spectacle in the courtroom, Robert had asked the court to keep the hearing confidential. "They cannot ban reporters," he had mentioned to Ann in his last letter, "but at least they can keep out the crowds of loafers expecting some entertainment."

The hearing convened at two o'clock, and not quite three hours later, a messenger knocked on Ann's door bearing a note from Elizabeth. She and Mary had both received telegrams from Ninian after the proceedings, which had taken less time than the swearing-in and seating of the jury. Mary had been declared restored to reason and capable of managing and controlling her own estate. Robert would accompany Ninian to Springfield on the morning train to return her bonds to her in person.

"Restored to reason?" Ann echoed, puzzled. Ninian had emphasized that this hearing was not intended to resolve that question. Mary would be thrilled, no doubt, to have her bonds back, but she would take great offense at the phrasing of the verdict that had returned them.

Elizabeth had ended her note with a plea for Ann to come to the Edwards home early the next day to help distract Mary as they awaited the men's arrival—and perhaps more importantly, to help diffuse the tension when the mother and son met. "Mary has been so furious with Robert for so long that I cannot imagine she will receive him with affection and cordiality," Elizabeth wrote. "He will endure whatever comes with uncomplaining stoicism, but I hope that with her sisters present, she will endeavor to control her temper. Perhaps once she has her bonds in hand, she shall forget her anger and reconcile with him."

Ann thought reconciliation was unlikely, but otherwise she agreed with her sister's reasoning, so she sent the messenger back with a note assuring Elizabeth that she would be there.

Frances had been invited too, as Ann discovered when she arrived the next morning and found her three sisters in the parlor, chatting about a recent letter from Emilie while they knitted and sewed. A warning look from Elizabeth behind Mary's back told her not to mention the hearing; Ann offered a barely perceptible nod in reply as she took her usual seat. It was unlikely that her sisters had any news to share about the hearing that Ann had not already read in the morning edition of the *Chicago Tribune*. In Ninian's testimony, which Ann had found a bit puzzling, he was reported to have said, "Mrs. Lincoln has been with me for nine or ten months, and her friends all think she is a proper person to take charge of her own affairs." Which friends? Ann wondered. The Bradwells? Certainly not her sisters. "She has not spent all that she was allowed to spend during the last year," Ninian had said, though not for lack of trying, Ann thought as she read the article.

"And we all think," he concluded, "she is in a condition to take care of her own affairs."

The jury must have found Ninian's testimony and Robert's willingness to be relieved of the conservatorship convincing, for they had retired only long enough to sign the verdict before returning to declare, amid other legal jargon, that they had found that "the said Mary Lincoln is restored to reason and is capable to manage and control her estate."

Again that phrase had been used, even though not a single physician had examined Mary and she had not even been present for anyone to question directly. Ann was no lawyer, nor was she married to one, but the proceeding did not seem quite right to her, although it very well may have been perfectly legal.

The article concluded with an inventory of Mary's property, which Robert had presented to the court. Ann was pleased to see that Robert had increased Mary's holdings by $8,000 during his tenure as her conservator, and that he had waived the standard ten-day notification period so that the verdict could be enacted as soon as possible. Ann dared to hope that Mary's heart would soften when she was presented with the facts of how she had prospered thanks to her son, but it was a thin hope.

Ninian and Robert arrived shortly after eleven o'clock, and at the sound of them crossing the threshold, the sisters set aside their handwork and exchanged wary glances. Frances and Elizabeth instinctively rose, but Ann stayed put, watching Mary as she drew herself up in her chair and fixed an imperious gaze on the doorway.

Ninian entered first, with Robert close behind, carrying a leather briefcase fastened with a strap. They greeted the ladies, and Elizabeth went to kiss her husband's cheek, but when Robert approached his mother, she bolted from her chair, scrambled behind it, and held up a hand. "Don't come any closer," she commanded.

Robert halted. "Good morning, Mother," he said evenly, indicating the briefcase. "I've come only to return your bonds to you.

I knew you were anxious for them, and bringing them myself was the fastest way to deliver them."

"Give them to your uncle," Mary snapped. "I see on your face the reluctance with which you yield them up, my poor pittance which you so ignominiously fought for."

"On the contrary," Robert said, handing the briefcase to Ninian, "I am relieved to be rid of them."

Mary laughed, sharp and incredulous. "Nonsense and lies. You were not satisfied with the fortune I bequeathed you when I first made my will, so you brought false charges against me so you could steal my money!"

Her voice rose with every word until she was nearly shouting.

"Mary," Frances broke in, "that's simply not true. As your conservator, Robert increased your wealth. Is that the behavior of a thief?"

Mary ignored her. "Look at this white hair," she commanded, gesturing to her head. "You have caused this, with the torment you inflicted upon me this past sorrowful year."

A muscle worked in Robert's jaw, but otherwise he was stoic. "Everything I did was in what I believed to be your best interest."

"My heart fails me when I think of the contrast between you and your noble, glorious father, and my three precious sons who have gone before." Mary's face flushed, and she trembled as she clutched the back of her chair with both hands. "God is just, and retribution must follow those who act wickedly in this life! Sooner or later, compensation surely awaits those who suffer unjustly, if not here, then in a brighter and happier world."

"Mary, please calm yourself," Elizabeth implored.

"I am sure our lost loved ones are anxiously awaiting the reunion after which no more separation comes," Mary shrilled, her gaze locked on her son's face, which had gone stony and pale. "But you will not be able to approach us in that other world on account of your heartless conduct to me. Your father worshiped me, as well as my blessed sons did, and they will not let you draw near us in the world to come!"

"Mary," Ann exclaimed. "How could you be so cruel? Shame on you!"

"It's all right," said Robert, his voice low and weary. "I've done what I came here to do, and I need not stay. Mother, the children would like to see you, Mamie especially. I will leave it up to you when, or if, you would like to arrange to see them." Nodding to his aunts and uncle, he turned and left, and a moment later they heard the front door open and quietly, firmly close.

"Did you hear that?" Mary asked, sinking down upon the sofa beside Elizabeth, trembling, looking around at her sisters for confirmation. "Did you hear how he threatened to withhold my grandchildren from me?"

"He did nothing of the sort," Ann retorted.

"I have been deeply wronged, and by one for whom I would have poured out my life's blood," Mary lamented. "His wickedness cannot be allowed to triumph."

"Mary, please, do be calm," said Elizabeth, taking her hand. Frances sat down on Mary's other side, resting a hand on her shoulder and murmuring soothing phrases. Muffling a sigh, Ann glanced from her sister to the doorway, tempted to hurry after Robert, but instead she sat in a chair across from her sisters so that the burden of calming Mary did not fall to Elizabeth and Frances alone. A vague shadow of anger and disgust passed over Ninian's face as he excused himself and carried off the briefcase, no doubt to put the bonds in his safe until Mary needed them.

For nearly an hour and a half, Mary tearfully expounded on the allegedly terrible sins Robert had committed against her, a pitiable, brokenhearted woman who had been called upon to give up all her dearly beloved ones until they were reunited in heaven. Although Ann remained, and fetched water and a fresh handkerchief upon request, she stopped listening to Mary's rant after a while, indignant on her nephew's behalf and exhausted by Mary's tempers and pertinacity. All of her demands had been met. Could she not be gracious in victory?

Later, after Mary had retired to her bedchamber afflicted with migraine and exhaustion, Elizabeth led Ann and Frances to Ninian's study, where she asked him for his firsthand account of the trial. He told them little they had not already learned from his telegrams and the newspaper reports, but he acknowledged that everyone in the courtroom had seemed surprised by the jury's verdict. "They were not called upon to try the question of Mary's sanity," he said, frowning and shaking his head, "and I regret very much that the verdict stated that she was 'restored to reason.'"

"Mary objected to that phrase too," Elizabeth said. "She said no one can restore what was never lost."

Ann thought that if the jury could have seen Mary's ugly display in the Edwardses' parlor, they might have returned a different verdict altogether.

Mary's sisters were disappointed that regaining possession of her bonds had not mitigated her anger toward Robert, but Ann was not surprised. Even so, they little understood the intensity of her antipathy until Robert forwarded a letter to Elizabeth, a caustic list of demands and accusations that his mother had sent him three days after he returned her bonds.

Springfield, Illinois.
June 19th, 1876

Robert T. Lincoln
  Do not fail to send me without the least delay, all my paintings, Moses in the bulrushes included—also the fruit picture, which hung in your dining room—my silver set with large silver waiter presented me by New York friends, my silver tête-à-tête set also other articles your wife appropriated & which are well known to

you, must be sent, without a day's delay. Two lawyers and myself, have just been together and their list, coincides with my own and will be published in a few days. Trust not to the belief, that Mrs Edwards' tongue, has not been rancorous *against you all winter & she has maintained to the very last, that you dared not venture into her house & our presence. Send me my laces, my diamonds, my jewelry—My unmade silks, white lace dress—double lace shawl & flounce, lace scarf—2 blk lace shawls—one black lace deep flounce, white lace sets ¹/₂ yd in width & eleven yards in length. I am now in constant receipt of letters, from my friends denouncing you in the bitterest terms, six letters from prominent,* respectable, *Chicago people such as you do not associate with. Two prominent clergy men have written me, since I saw you—and mention in their letters, that they think it advisable to offer up prayers for you in Church, on account of your wickedness against me and High Heaven. In reference to Chicago, you* have the enemies *& I chance to have the* friends *there. Send me all that I have written for; you have tried your game of robbery long enough. Only yesterday, I received two telegrams from prominent Eastern lawyers. You have injured yourself, not me, by your wicked conduct.*

Mrs A. Lincoln

My engravings too send me. Send me Whittier Pope, Agnes Strickland's Queens of England, other books, you have of mine.
M. L.

"I never said anything rancorous about Robert to Mary," Elizabeth protested when Ann finished reading the letter. "I certainly never banished him from my home! How could she say such outrageous things?"

"She never thought Robert would dare forward the letter to you," said Ann, returning it to her, "or that you would show it to me. And Frances and Ninian, I presume."

"Yes, of course, I did." Elizabeth clasped a hand to her brow, sighing, shaking her head. "Frances is most upset by the insults and accusations of thievery, Ninian by her threat to publish this list of allegedly stolen property."

Ann closed her eyes and heaved a sigh. She sincerely hoped that going to the press with accusations of theft was merely a ploy to pressure Robert, but with Mary, one never knew. "And the six letters from eminent Chicagoans denouncing him?"

"Ninian does not believe they exist, and neither do I."

Ann was inclined to agree. Robert had been almost universally praised in the press for his steadfast, honorable conduct throughout his mother's ordeal, and it seemed unlikely anyone would put their name to a letter condemning him. Yet Mary's friends included the meddlesome Bradwells and others like them. If Mary truly wanted to create a firestorm of trouble for her son, it was within her power to do so.

"I must return this to Robert in the afternoon mail," said Elizabeth, giving the letter one last look of distaste before slipping it into her pocket. "He has already shown it to his lawyer, and although Mr. Swett made a copy, Robert would like the original back."

Ann pursed her lips and nodded, barely managing to hold back words she knew she would later regret. Was it too much to ask that they handle their disagreements quietly, within the family? Had they not had their fill of public scandal—nearly all of it due to one headstrong, impossible, very troubled sister?

Someone had to call Mary's bluff, or she might never cease her threats and accusations. Neither Robert nor Ninian nor Elizabeth had managed to do it, but perhaps Robert's lawyer would.

There was only so much they could be expected to endure out of sisterly duty and respect for her martyred husband.

24

April–May 1865

ELIZABETH

A pounding on the door late at night heralded the sudden, terrible, irrevocable transformation of their world.

The fearsome noise roused the entire household, and all gathered in the foyer to hear the dreadful news the messenger had brought to Ninian. Earlier that evening, while Abe and Mary were attending a play at Ford's Theater, a dark-haired man had broken into the state box and shot Abe in the back of the head at close range. A friend seated nearby had attempted to apprehend him, but the assailant had slashed him with a knife, injuring him badly, and then leapt down to the stage and fled through a rear exit. Mortally wounded, Abe had been carried across the street to the Peterson boardinghouse, where physicians were fighting to save his life.

Elizabeth groped for a chair, stunned, ears ringing. Her blood felt as if it were frozen in her veins, and her lungs as if they would collapse for want of air. Distantly, she heard that an attempt had been made on Secretary of State William Seward's life as well, and that he and his son had been stabbed multiple times and were close to death. Guards had been posted around the homes of Vice President Johnson and other members of the cabinet.

"Is Abe expected to live?" Elizabeth heard herself say. Ninian looked to the messenger for an answer, but the boy, pale and stricken, merely shrugged.

Elizabeth imagined Mary wild with grief, keening ceaselessly as she had when Willie died. And what of Robert and Tad—where were they? Although she and Mary had had another falling-out and had not spoken in ages, Elizabeth longed to comfort her sister and nephews, but hundreds of miles separated them and a telegram would have to wait until morning.

Never had the nighttime hours dragged so slowly. Every minute seemed an eternity, and Elizabeth could do nothing but wait and weep on Ninian's shoulder and watch the eastern sky through the window for the dawn.

Morning came at last, gray and somber. When he was not pacing, Ninian stood at the window, gazing down the sidewalk and muttering under his breath about the long overdue messenger. Sometime after seven o'clock, a distant church bell began to toll, and then another joined it, and another, until all the bells in Springfield resounded with the terrible news. *Abe is dead*, Elizabeth thought, stunned and disbelieving. A moan escaped from her throat, and she collapsed into Ninian's arms, anguished and weeping.

The morning papers told the terrible story, but Elizabeth was too heartsick to take in more than a few scattered details. Celebrated comedienne Laura Keene, whom President Lincoln had gone to see perform that night, had identified the assassin as the actor John Wilkes Booth. After Abe had been shot, Mary, who was holding on to his arm at the time, had cried out, "Oh, why didn't they shoot me? Why didn't they shoot me?" In great distress, she was said to be at her husband's bedside along with several members of his cabinet. The surgeons were doing all that could be done, but it would not be enough. "The president is slowly dying," came a grim report dispatched at 1:15 a.m. "The brain is oozing through the ball hole in his forehead. He is, of course, insensible.

There is an occasional lifting of his hand, and heavy, stentorious breathing—that is all." Another dispatch from 3:00 a.m. stated that the president's condition was unchanged.

The mournful bells had offered the dreadful postscript, which telegrams and afternoon papers soon confirmed. Abe was gone. Days after Richmond had fallen and General Lee had surrendered at Appomattox, Abe had been cruelly killed, having led the nation through a devastating war only to be denied the blessed reward of peacetime.

In the bleak, grief-numbed days that followed, Elizabeth rarely left home, and then only when she had no choice. Springfield, so recently the scene of merry celebrations as the end of the war appeared on the horizon, had plunged into mourning. Never had a nation plummeted so suddenly from joyful hope to utter despair. The merry bands fell silent. Flags that had waved proudly in victory were slowly lowered to half-staff. Grief-stricken citizens took refuge in churches and in the company of friends. Others found strength in righteous anger, demanding justice and retribution. Government offices and shops were darkened and closed. Every public building in Springfield and nearly every residence, be it grand or humble, was draped in the black crepe of mourning for the city's favorite son.

As going out in public was unbearable, Elizabeth's sisters and their families often gathered at the Edwards home to console one another, to share news from Washington, and to avoid the press. Ann's husband had happened to be in New York on business on that fateful Good Friday, and he had rushed to Washington to see how he could be of service to Mary and her sons. "Clark will let us know what he learns there," said Ann. "Mary may not see him— the papers say she will see almost no one but her children and a few trusted friends and advisers—but Clark will certainly meet with Robert."

Ninian, too, departed for Washington as soon as he could pack a suitcase. "Will you not join me?" he asked Elizabeth. "You know how Mary is. I'm certain she needs you desperately."

"She has not summoned me," Elizabeth replied, her voice curiously flat. "Nor has Robert."

This tragedy was not like three years before, when Willie had died and Robert had begged Elizabeth to come even in the midst of her estrangement from Mary following their quarrel over Julia's insulting letter. Then their silence had lasted several months. This time their estrangement had been so unyielding that they had not spoken in almost two years.

In August 1861, after Ninian had humbly asked for a patronage position, Abe had commissioned him as a captain with the Commissary of Subsistence, putting him in charge of purchasing, issuing, and accounting for rations and other supplies for the army. Even before the appointment was official, men from the Springfield Republican establishment had written to Abe to complain about his choice, claiming that Ninian was closely associated with men who had committed "the most stupendous and unprecedented frauds ever perpetrated in this country." Ninian was entirely innocent of any wrongdoing, of course; the obvious impetus for their protests was their ongoing resentment that Ninian had become a Democrat ten years before and their desire to have one of their own men in the influential post. After investigating the matter, Abe had found no reason to deny his brother-in-law the appointment. Ninian had accepted the role and then fulfilled his duties faithfully, but his rivals had not relented: they continued to accuse Ninian of using his post to enrich himself. Abe had given the complaints all due consideration but had remained loyal to his brother-in-law.

Then, in the spring of 1863, the complaints suddenly had become more numerous and more vehement. In May, Abe had written to Edward—Julia's husband, who also happened to be the editor of the *Illinois State Journal*—to interview him about new accusations of corruption against his father-in-law. "No formal charges are preferred against him, so far as I know," Abe had noted, "nor do I expect any will be made; or, if made, will be substantiated. I certainly do not suppose Mr. Edwards has, at this time of his life, given up his old habits, and turned dishonest." Yet Abe had grown weary of the continual harassment from Ninian's critics, provocations he said Ninian could have spared him had he kept more complete, incontrovertible records. Abe must have known that Edward would show the letter to his father-in-law, since he had not been instructed to keep it secret. Upon reading it, Ninian had immediately written to Abe to defend his actions, to plead for his job, and to remind Abe of their long friendship and history of mutual trust, but to no avail. Within a fortnight, Abe had bowed to political pressure and replaced Ninian.

Shocked and certain that Ninian had been greatly wronged, Elizabeth had written to Mary imploring her to intercede with her husband. Mary had fired back a scathing refusal, defending Abe's decision and rebuking Ninian for putting the president in a politically vulnerable position. "If your husband has done nothing wrong," Mary had declared, "he should have taken greater pains to prevent the *appearance* of wrongdoing."

"If?" Elizabeth had exclaimed, astounded, when she read the letter. Offended, she immediately had written back to dispute Mary's unfortunate phrasing and to give her the opportunity to apologize and amend. Soon thereafter, Mary had replied to confirm that she knew the definitions of all the words she had used in her letter and not one had fallen from her pen by accident. She then had proceeded to reel off several paragraphs of slanderous accusations, any one of which Ninian could have ably refuted if he had been given the opportunity.

Indeed, Elizabeth had shown him the letter so that he could do precisely that, but he had merely sighed and said, "This is not worth the dignity of a response." He had meant that he would not respond, but Elizabeth had decided that, if it was beneath his dignity, it was beneath hers too. She had never replied to the offensive letter, Mary had never sent another to apologize, and so silence had fallen between them.

Elizabeth understood that Ninian had been the one most harmed by the incident, not herself. Now he was determined to go to Washington to pay respects to his brother-in-law and president, and to comfort his widow and children. If he could put past differences aside, shouldn't Elizabeth try, for the sake of her sister and her nephews?

"It was only a job, darling," said Ninian gently, as if he read her thoughts. "My pride suffered, but that was nothing compared to what we suffer now."

But it was more than the loss of a post, Elizabeth wanted to object. By replacing him, Abe had all but confirmed that he agreed with the slanderous charges. And rather than gently and regretfully decline to intercede, Mary had thrown those charges back in Elizabeth's face, adding a few sharp accusations of her own.

It was only a job—and yet it wasn't. Ninian could forgive Abe, but Elizabeth could not yet forgive Mary. Then there was the practical reality of what might happen if Elizabeth attempted to cross the threshold of the White House. One newspaper report after another stated that Mary had not left the Executive Mansion since her husband's assassination and that she would see almost no one. Elizabeth dared not endure the shame and embarrassment of traveling hundreds of miles to console her bereaved sister only to be left standing on the doorstep.

"When we were estranged before, Robert summoned me," Elizabeth reminded her husband, her voice catching in her throat. "He and Mary could easily summon me again, if I were wanted. I must assume that I am not."

Even as she spoke, she could not quite accept that after all they had been through, it had come to this. Her sister's worst fears had been realized—she had lost her husband to a terrible act of violence, committed right before her eyes—and yet Elizabeth mourned at home instead of packing a trunk and racing to Mary's side.

It felt so wrong, and yet Elizabeth did not see how she could do otherwise.

Ninian was still making his way to Washington when Ann heard from Clark that Mary was frantic with misery—wailing, keening, inconsolable. Mrs. Lee and Mrs. Welles, the wife of the secretary of the navy, sat at her bedside in turns; Mrs. Keckly, too, stayed with her almost every day and slept in her room every night. Robert, shaken and heartbroken, looked after his mother and her affairs with tender solicitude, but poor young Tad, devastated by the loss of his beloved father, was terrified by his mother's outbursts. "There is no comforting Mary," Clark wrote somberly. "She is suffering such paroxysms of grief that only laudanum offers her any respite, and even that is fleeting. I suspect that witnessing the sudden and awful death has somewhat unhinged her mind, for at times she has exhibited symptoms of madness."

Compounding Mary's distress was pressure from Springfield civic leaders to return her husband's remains to Springfield for burial. This she agreed to do, but she became livid when informed of their plans to erect a mausoleum in the center of town to better accommodate the multitudes of grateful citizens whom they expected to visit Springfield to pay their respects in the years to come. To this Mary was adamantly opposed, for it contradicted Abe's own desires, which he had shared with her only weeks before his death. As she explained to Clark, on one of their visits to General Grant at City Point, Virginia, she and Abe had toured a cemetery, and the conversation had turned to their own final resting places. When they passed a serene place where spring flowers were blossoming on the graves, Abe had said, "Mary, you are younger than I. You will survive me. When I am gone, lay my remains in some quiet place like this." Burying him in the center of Springfield would be the very antithesis of Abe's wishes.

As his widow, Mary could rightly claim greater authority in this matter, and as the Springfield monument association began making decisions without her, she became so livid that she abandoned the isolation of her bedchamber to thwart their plans. Clark, who was president of the board of managers of Oak Ridge Cemetery on the northern outskirts of Springfield, described for her a beautiful hilltop in the center of the graveyard, a peaceful, pastoral setting suited for contemplation and quiet mourning. Mary set her heart on that idyllic place, and when the civic leaders balked, she threatened to have Abe's remains interred in Chicago or in the crypt of the US Capitol rather than allow them to trample over her privilege to choose her husband's final resting place. Eventually the monument association acquiesced, and Clark arranged for a temporary receiving vault to be built near the Oak Ridge knoll until a suitable monument could be constructed.

Although Mary had roused herself for that battle, she remained too overcome with grief to attend Abe's private funeral ceremony in the East Room of the White House, nor did she accompany the funeral procession that carried his remains to the Capitol, where he lay in state in the rotunda so that thousands of grieving citizens could file past and pay their respects.

On Friday, April 21, nearly a week after Abe's death, a nine-car funeral train bedecked with bunting, crepe, and his portrait on the engine left Washington on a seventeen-hundred-mile journey westward to Springfield, carrying three hundred passengers and the remains of the president and his young son Willie. The *Lincoln Special* traveled at only five to twenty miles per hour out of respect for the thousands of mourners who had assembled along the rail lines, lighting the way with bonfires at night. The train made scheduled stops in twelve cities, where tens of thousands gathered to mourn and to bid farewell to the Great Emancipator, the savior of the Union. Appointed to accompany the president home to Springfield were Ninian and Clark, as well as Clark's

brother Charles Alexander Smith, Justice David Davis, the Todd
sisters' cousin Brigadier General John Blair Smith Todd, Abe's
longtime friend and bodyguard Ward Hill Lamon, and other distinguished gentlemen.

On May 3, Elizabeth, Frances, and Ann were among the
mourners who gathered at the Chicago & Alton depot to meet
the funeral train as it pulled slowly into the station. Although the
population of Springfield was fifteen thousand, the crowd num-
bered almost seven times that. As the train halted at the platform
and the pallbearers approached, all fell silent and still. Then, as
the coffin emerged from the railcar, the agonizing silence was broken by a sob, and then another, until the sounds of muffled lamen-
tation were almost too much for Elizabeth to bear.

Soldiers from the Veteran Reserve Corps carried Abe's coffin
into a gleaming black hearse, each side adorned with a silver oval
medallion engraved with his initials, encircled by a wreath, and
flanked by two inverted torches, all fashioned from silver and
framed by thirty-six silver stars representing the states of the
Union. As a band commenced a dirge, six black horses pulled the
hearse in a slow, formal procession toward the city square.

As members of the family, Elizabeth, her sisters, and their
children were given places near the front of the cortege. Glancing ahead through her dark veil, Elizabeth glimpsed her husband
close behind the hearse with the other dignitaries who had accompanied the casket from Washington. Throngs of men, women,
and even children clad in mourning black lined the route, their
sobs and muffled groans audible above the slow and melancholy
music. On the west side of the city square, they passed the building in which the Lincoln & Herndon law practice kept offices; the
windows were shrouded with crepe and a banner had been un-
furled across the top of the building that read, HE LIVES IN THE
HEARTS OF HIS PEOPLE.

Elizabeth felt someone take her hand—Frances. Elizabeth

squeezed her sister's hand in a silent message of encouragement, pressing her lips together to fight back the aching sobs building up behind her heart. If she broke down now, in front of the hundred thousand grieving onlookers, she feared she would not be able to get through the rest of the ceremony.

The hearse halted on the north side of the state capitol building, where the cornices and pillars supporting the deep black dome were swathed in white and black, with black drapery falling from the eaves and columns. Also heavily draped in black was the entrance through which the soldiers carried the coffin before proceeding upstairs to Representatives' Hall. They placed the coffin upon an elegant catafalque covered with black velvet, embellished with thirty-six burnished silver stars, trimmed with silver fringe and sprigs of myrtle, and surrounded by white flowers and evergreen boughs. White lace and gold stars that glowed and sparkled in the gaslights adorned the ceiling. Engraved upon the walls above the tall doors were two inscriptions: WASHINGTON THE FATHER, LINCOLN THE SAVIOUR, and SOONER THAN SURRENDER THIS PRINCIPLE, I WOULD BE ASSASSINATED ON THIS SPOT.

The words struck Elizabeth almost like a punch to the heart, and for a moment she could not breathe. Then a faint memory stirred, and she remembered that Abe had expressed a similar thought in his speech at Independence Hall in February 1861, when the Inaugural Express had stopped in Philadelphia. How impossibly long ago it seemed, and yet she remembered the scene so vividly that she could almost hear the cheers and applause of his listeners ringing out anew.

The inscription was only a paraphrase of Abe's words. Nevertheless, it had staggered her.

The procession began to pass by the catafalque, and as the sisters approached the coffin Elizabeth was reunited with Ninian, and Ann with Clark. Elizabeth's heart thudded as she drew closer and glimpsed Abe's features and saw how greatly they had altered.

She had hoped to carry away a memory of him in repose, at peace at last, but too much time had passed since his death and she scarcely recognized him.

Heartsick, she continued past the coffin, leaning upon Ninian's arm for support. Tens of thousands of mourners were expected to pass by the catafalque during the twenty-four hours Abe would lie in state, but Elizabeth left the statehouse immediately, withdrawing to her own home until the concluding ceremonies the next day.

"Mary never could have endured this," a voice murmured close to her ear as she left the hall, startling her. It was Ann, tears shining in her eyes, her face pale and drawn. "It was just as well that she did not come, even for appearance's sake."

Throat constricting, Elizabeth nodded, although she was not entirely sure what Ann meant. Elizabeth had not heard anyone fault Mary for not accompanying the remains of her husband and son aboard the *Lincoln Special*, for not attending one funeral after another over twelve days through seven states and 180 towns. That was more than any grieving widow should be expected to bear.

The next morning, after the final viewing, the sealing of the casket, the solemn music, the procession of ten thousand mourners from the capitol past the black-draped Lincoln residence to Oak Ridge Cemetery, the sermons and heartfelt eulogies, and the interment in the vault at the foot of a wooded knoll, Elizabeth's thoughts again turned to Mary, as they had throughout that long, melancholy day. Mary had not returned to Springfield for the funeral, but surely she intended to do so eventually. Elizabeth wondered when this would be and what her sisters could do to ease her homecoming.

Although Robert had not joined the entourage aboard the funeral train, at Justice Davis's urging, he had come for the burial, traveling on a more direct route and arriving in time to join the final procession. When Elizabeth found a private moment to speak with him, she was startled to learn that his mother had not decided when she would leave the White House, nor where she would go when she did.

"She cannot stay in the White House indefinitely," said Elizabeth. "The Executive Mansion belongs to Mr. Johnson and his family now."

"Given the circumstances, Johnson has kindly not evicted my mother so that he might move in," Robert said. He looked haggard and grim, as well he might, since the burden of his devastated family and his father's legacy had landed heavily on his young shoulders. "At present he is staying in a well-guarded house on Fifteenth and H Streets. He works out of a small office in the Treasury Building, forgoing the use of the White House residence, offices, and reception rooms that are rightfully his."

"That is generous of him."

"Then it is the only generosity he has shown my mother," said Robert, an edge to his voice. "President Johnson has not called on her, nor has he sent a single note to express his sympathies."

"How unbecoming of a gentleman," Elizabeth said, bemused. Then she added, "But Mary does intend to come home to Springfield when she leaves the White House, does she not?"

Robert grimaced. "I don't know. I overheard her tell Mrs. Keckly that she could not bear to return here."

He and his father's closest friends had urged his mother to do exactly that, Robert explained—to return to Springfield and the home she still owned, at least until his father's estate was settled. He had died without a will, so although his property would eventually go to his widow and children, they would not receive their shares until the legal knots were untangled. And yet his mother adamantly rejected the idea of returning to her former hometown. She believed that she had burned too many bridges and become the subject of gossip. Moreover, she was estranged from her sisters and half-sisters. Most of all, she could not bear to set foot in her once-happy home on Eighth and Jackson, where she feared she would be tormented by memories of the early years of her marriage and the husband and sons she had lost.

Elizabeth felt heat rise in her cheeks, and she could scarcely meet Robert's eyes. Now she knew why neither Mary nor Robert had summoned her to the White House to tend to Mary in her anguish. "Despite our differences, if Mary comes home, I shall welcome her as a sister," she said, fighting back tears. "We can leave the past in the past."

"Perhaps you and my aunts can," said Robert, resting a hand on her shoulder comfortingly. "I'm less certain about my mother. Please do not let this distress you. My mother is not herself. In time, she may realize that it is indeed best for her and Tad to be in the familiar home she once cherished, among family and longtime friends."

Elizabeth nodded, not trusting herself to speak. If Mary did not return to her own home, where would she go? Surely not to Lexington, for many of the same reasons she objected to Springfield. She and Ma had never gotten along, and even Emilie, who had once so admired and adored her, had broken with the Lincolns the previous autumn after Abe refused to grant her a permit to sell Confederate cotton to support herself and her children. Elizabeth could not imagine that Mary would turn to any of their half-sisters living in the South, for obvious reasons. So if not Springfield, where?

For six weeks Mary remained at the White House, too devastated and overwhelmed to leave, but eventually, reluctantly, she decided to settle in Chicago. As Robert explained to his aunts, she insisted that his father had intended to retire there after his second term, and it was a city that had always been good to him, a place reminiscent of triumph, not despair. It was in Chicago that Abe had received his first nomination as the Republican candidate for president, and Chicago where he and Mary had accepted the hearty congratulations of throngs of supporters at the Tremont Hotel after the election. The city was also reasonably close to Abe's tomb in Springfield, where Mary thought she might seek solace in the years to come—but for short visits only, never to stay indefinitely.

Robert intended to go into exile with her, he wrote to Elizabeth, his dejection evident despite his straightforward tone. He was now the head of the family, and it was his responsibility to look after his mother and younger brother. Elizabeth understood and respected her nephew's decision all the more knowing how much it must pain him to abandon his promising future in the East. Only a few weeks before, he had been a proud and gallant Union officer, courting the lovely young Miss Mary Eunice Harlan, a senator's daughter, and intending to study the law. Now, for the sake of his mother and brother, he would leave that life behind.

Despite their estrangement, Elizabeth was surprised and a little hurt when Robert told her whom Mary had begged to accompany her on the journey to her new home and to stay with her until she settled in—not any of the Todd sisters or a cousin, but Mrs. Keckly, her dressmaker and confidante. Elizabeth told herself that she should be grateful that Mary had chosen her companion wisely and that the estimable Mrs. Keckly had agreed to go. Elizabeth had been impressed with how patiently and faithfully Mrs. Keckly had looked after Mary in her wild and frantic grief after Willie died, and according to Robert, her care for his mother had surpassed even that great kindness after his father's death. Evidently there was something about Mrs. Keckly's particular strengths of character that made her uniquely qualified to tolerate Mary's eccentricities and tempers and to comfort her in her deepest despondency.

Perhaps, in Mrs. Keckly, Mary had at last found a companion who would never disappoint her.

25

June–October 1876

FRANCES

Mary's vitriolic missive of June 19 so incensed Robert's lawyer that he immediately fired off a blistering letter to Ninian, as Mary's host and guardian, to refute her absurd accusations. Her letters were clear evidence of "the utter wreck of Mrs. Lincoln's mind," Mr. Swett declared, for they were full of hateful phrases "such as none but an insane mother would write to her son." His client had done absolutely everything possible to ensure his mother's health and safety, and if, after all Robert had sacrificed, his mother still insisted upon trying to ruin him by threatening lawsuits and scandalous publicity, Mr. Swett himself would pursue having Mary confined as an insane person, regardless of Robert's desires or those of anyone else in the family.

Frances could not fault Mr. Swett for his furious response, especially since she knew Mary had sent other letters to Robert after that provocative one, letters in which she called him a villain and a "monster of mankind" and demanded additional items that she had given to her son and his wife as gifts. Ann agreed wholeheartedly with Mr. Swett, and to Frances's surprise and no small relief, Ninian and Elizabeth did too. They wrote to both Robert and his lawyer to assure them that Robert had their confidence and sympathy, and that they never once believed he had acted improperly or selfishly, but always to best ensure his mother's security and comfort.

Exhausted, and desperate to bring the conflict to an end, Frances, Elizabeth, and Ann approached Mary as a united front to gently but emphatically explain that no good could come of her relentless demands and threats. If, as a member of the bar, Mr. Swett resolved to call for a new insanity hearing, there would be very little the family could do to prevent him. Mary quaked at that, but she insisted that Mr. Swett's letter was "filled with voluminous falsehoods" and that he was as debased and villainous as his client. "It is unfair and unkind for you three to band together against me," she lamented, tears in her eyes. "Is that sisterly? Is that just?"

Without waiting for an answer, she fled the parlor and shut herself away in her room, leaving her sisters frustrated and worried that they had only made matters worse.

"Why can she not relent?" groused Ann, flinging herself into a chair and folding her arms over her chest. "She knows that all these bits and bobs she gave to Robert and his wife are their rightful property, and she has no use for them anyway. She already has what she really wants—control of her assets and legal proof that she is not mad, though I for one dissent from the court's opinion. Why can she not just declare victory and walk off with her prizes?"

"She has always excelled at holding grudges," said Elizabeth, sighing. "She wants to punish Robert for having her committed, and I don't think she will stop until she has satisfaction."

"But what will satisfy her?" Ann persisted. Elizabeth only shook her head and shrugged.

Later that night, at home in her empty bed, Frances wished with all her heart that William were there to advise her, to speak to Mary on her sisters' behalf. Mary had trusted him implicitly as the physician who had so valiantly tried to save the life of her precious Eddie, and often, when her sisters' words had failed, he had been able to speak in a particular reasonable tone that had calmed her tempers. What would William say now? Frances wondered. What would he do to reach his distressed sister-in-law?

Sleep eluded her as she pondered the question, but eventually she drifted off, and in the morning when she woke she realized her sisters' mistake: they never should have taken Mary by surprise in Elizabeth's parlor, three against one, when she had assumed they were gathering to knit and sew together as always. Mary almost never admitted wrongdoing in front of Ann, and she certainly would not have done so with Elizabeth and Frances looking on.

Then, too, they all should have been mindful of the sorrowful date inexorably approaching—the fifth anniversary of young Tad's death.

In the autumn of 1868, soon after Robert married Miss Mary Eunice Harlan, Mary had taken Tad to tour the celebrated capitals and landmarks of Europe that she and Abe had once planned to visit together after his second term. She had gone because she had believed she could live more economically abroad, because she could not bear the familiar places that evoked so many memories of her late husband, and because she craved the peace and solitude that anonymity in a foreign land would bring. For two and a half years, Mary and Tad had lived in Europe, meeting old friends, exploring wondrous sites, partaking of luxury on a budget in Germany, Austria, Scotland, England, France, and Italy. While Tad had attended school in an excellent German academy, Mary had visited health spas seeking relief from various pains and discomforts, enjoying the royal treatment she received as the widow of the great President Abraham Lincoln.

While she was abroad, Mary had become a grandmother, and eventually her longing to see her granddaughter, as well as eighteen-year-old Tad's ever-increasing homesickness, had compelled her to return to her homeland. Mary had been anxious about the ocean crossing and its effects upon their health, worries that had proved prescient when Tad's weak lungs suffered in the storms and damp. Upon his arrival in Manhattan, he had been diagnosed with a serious chest ailment and put on bed rest at a hotel.

When his doctors had pronounced him fit enough to travel, Mary and Tad had continued on by train to Chicago, where they had stayed with Robert and his family until accommodations could be found for them at the Clifton House, a nearby hotel. But rather than improving, Tad's symptoms had only worsened. Increasingly desperate, Mary had nursed him tirelessly and consulted the best doctors, but small improvements in Tad's condition had invariably been followed by serious declines. Despite all her efforts, on July 15, Tad had died from a dropsy of the chest.

Another death, another precious son lost, another devastating blow. Frances had sent condolences on behalf of herself and her children, but she had neither expected nor received a reply. Robert had once confided to her that he had heard his mother declare, in despondent moments after his father's death, that if not for Tad, she would have gladly joined her husband in the grave. By her own admission, only Tad and her responsibility for him had kept her from taking her own life.

In a sense, Mary had warned her sisters what she would do when she believed she no longer had anyone or anything to live for. Why had they not listened?

Before confronting Mary about her threats to ruin Robert, Frances should have remembered that her sister had always struggled with the bitter annual reminders of her greatest losses. On the anniversaries of those tragic events, she could become distraught, melancholy, quick to anger, or inconsolably tearful. Frances could not believe it was happenstance that Mary's most intense episode of derangement, the one that led to her institutionalization, had coincided with the tenth anniversary of Abe's assassination. In a matter of days, it would have been five years since Tad had perished. Was it any wonder Mary was overwrought and irrational?

Despite their sister's fragile state, the ongoing conflict had to be resolved before any more damage was done. Elizabeth hated confrontation, Ann enjoyed it a little too much, and Emilie was too far away. It was up to Frances to reason with Mary, to convince her either to forgive Robert or at least to stop tormenting him—and if Frances earned her sister's eternal enmity for her trouble, so be it. She had to try.

On the morning of July 15, Frances borrowed Ann's carriage and rode to the Edwards residence. After a private chat with Elizabeth, she went outside to the garden, where she found Mary sitting on a bench in the shade of a plum tree. Lewis, sprawled out on the grass nearby, was reading to her from a volume of poetry by John Greenleaf Whittier. Lewis's voice was clear and warm, and the poem lovely and heartfelt, but Mary's expression was sorrowful, her gaze distant.

Frances inhaled deeply to brace herself as she approached. Lewis was the first to notice her; he sat up, smiled, and wished her a good morning. Mary nodded but said nothing.

"Elizabeth said we may cut some of her flowers, and Ann has lent her carriage," said Frances. "I thought we could ride out to Oak Ridge Cemetery and place flowers upon Tad's grave."

Mary shot her a wild look. "No. No. I couldn't bear it."

"Perhaps you should, Great-Aunt Mary," said Lewis. "I shall escort you, if you like."

Mary managed a small, tender smile. "You're very kind to offer, my dear, but even with your strong arm to lean upon, I dare not."

Frances's heart sank. "I'm sorry," she said, pressing a hand to her waist. Her corset suddenly felt much too tight. "I know what an unhappy day this is for you, and I thought paying our respects might help."

"Nothing can help this, this fathomless despair." Mary paused and then amended her response: "Knowing that you remembered, and that you care, that does help a bit."

"Lewis," Frances asked, "would you please fetch Great-Aunt Mary a glass of water?"

"Of course." He bounded to his feet and loped off toward the house.

After he disappeared inside, Frances seated herself on the bench beside her sister. "Mary, I understand how brokenhearted you are, but—" She hesitated. "You have one son remaining to you. I know you've had your differences—immeasurable and great in number. And yet he is your only living child. Could you not try to reconcile?"

Mary shook her head. "Absolutely not. If one of your children had done to you what *he* has done to me, perhaps you could understand."

Frances chose her words carefully. "It's true that you have been through an ordeal that I cannot fully comprehend. And yet I must believe that love endures between you and Robert. If you cannot reconcile today, would you please consider a cessation of hostilities before all hope of reconciliation is quashed?"

"All hope is already—"

"No. Don't tell me that because I won't believe you." Frances steeled herself. "Very well. There are other reasons to stop threatening lawsuits and scandalous publicity. First, it is unkind and beneath you to ruin your son. Second, you will harm yourself worse than you will ever harm Robert."

Mary eyed her, frowning. "I fail to see how."

"Then I must remind you of a very unpleasant subject that your sisters have never dared to bring up in your presence— your attempt to sell your wardrobe in New York nine years ago." Nearly everyone in the country referred to the incident as "the Old Clothes Scandal," but Frances would spare Mary that.

"I needed money," said Mary tightly. "Surely, of all my sisters, you understand what it is like not to be able to make ends meet."

"I do indeed," Frances replied evenly. "I can even admire your frugality. Why shouldn't you sell off your finery, your exquisite gowns and sumptuous lace shawls, if you no longer need them?

Those dresses and other lovely clothes were too beautiful to be locked away in trunks forever, and you needed money more than you needed a fancy White House wardrobe."

Mary's eyes narrowed slightly in suspicion. "Exactly."

"But that wasn't your only purpose, was it?" Frances persisted. "Certainly, you would have gladly accepted profits from the sale of your clothes, but you also hoped that reports that you were obliged to sell your wardrobe because of your impoverished circumstances would shame the Republican establishment into providing for you."

Mary frowned and tore her gaze away. "I see you've read that dreadful book."

"Yes, I confess that I have read Mrs. Keckly's memoir, but at the time I needed only to glimpse the scathing newspaper headlines to see how badly your scheme failed. Instead of shaming the Republicans, you embarrassed yourself—and it pained me to see how you suffered for it." Frances placed a hand on her sister's shoulder, but Mary kept her face resolutely turned away. "Mary, you must see the similarities between then and now. You must see, as I do, that this misguided effort to shame Robert will result in an equally unhappy ending—for you."

A long moment passed in silence.

"Given the malice of the press toward me and the perfidy of men," said Mary grudgingly, "you may be right."

Frances seized her advantage. "You brought up Mrs. Keckly's memoir—the private letters she printed, the intimate conversations she repeated. Consider how much that hurt you. And although we all loathe to remember him, let us recall just for a moment the dreadful Mr. Herndon, his vile lectures, his vicious biography—"

"So-called biography," Mary interjected sharply. "Those wretched volumes were so full of slanderous falsehoods that they are more aptly considered works of fiction."

"Lies and truths alike wounded you," Frances reminded her. "Now consider what you have been threatening to do to Robert. Would you truly be willing to inflict such pain upon your only surviving son? Because if, after all you have suffered yourself, you would be capable of—" Frances's throat constricted. She withdrew her hand from her sister's shoulder and clasped her hands together in her lap. "I must believe you are better than that, Mary. It would break my heart if you proved me wrong."

Mary sat in silence for a moment, her back turned, her shoulders shaking as if from suppressed sobs. "I will think about what you've said," she said hoarsely, rising. "In the meantime, if you would be so kind as to lay flowers on my dear Tad's grave today, I would be grateful."

"Of course," said Frances. "Are you sure you won't come with—"

But Mary was already hurrying to the house and did not look back.

When her sister had disappeared through the back door, Frances rose, retrieved the garden shears from the basket beneath the kitchen window, and began cutting flowers for the gravesite. She had not been working long when she heard footsteps on the stone path and turned to find Lewis striding toward her. "I was on my way with the glass of water when I saw from the doorway how urgently you were speaking to Great-Aunt Mary," he said sheepishly. "That's when I realized you didn't really want the water; you just wanted to be alone. Is everything all right?"

Frances assured him it was, or at least, she thought it would be. She apologized for the ruse and invited him to accompany her to the cemetery. He nodded, sympathetic, and did not ask why his great-aunt Mary wished to remain behind.

Two days later, Elizabeth told Frances and Ann that Mary suddenly and without a word of explanation had informed Ninian that she no longer intended to file a lawsuit against Robert or to denounce him in the press. She would be satisfied with the repayment of certain debts Robert owed her for the purchase of her former residence on West Washington Avenue in Chicago.

"When I pressed her for a reason, all she would say was that she was exhausted," said Elizabeth, eyebrows drawn together in worry. "What do you suppose she meant by that?"

"Perhaps that she'll resume her attack after a good night's sleep," said Ann scornfully.

But Ann was mistaken. Weeks passed, summer faded into fall, and although as far as her sisters knew, Mary made no effort to reconcile with Robert, she no longer threatened to ruin him.

Frances hoped the burgeoning peace would bring Mary some tranquility of heart, but she seemed restless and discontented, except when Lewis took her for carriage rides, went out walking with her, or read aloud to her from her favorite poets. When her sisters gently asked her what troubled her, Mary confessed that she could no longer bear living in Springfield, where every familiar scene and favorite place evoked painful memories of happier bygone years and everyone regarded her as a madwoman who ought to be locked away in an asylum and forgotten. "I feel it in their soothing manner," she told her sisters when they protested that it was not so. "If I should say the moon is made of green cheese, they would heartily and smilingly agree with me. I love you all, but I cannot stay."

"Would you be happy in the midst of strangers?" asked Elizabeth.

Mary put her head to one side, considering. "Not likely, but I would be much less *un*happy."

Despite this fair warning, Frances was stunned when Mary announced that she intended to return to Europe. Would she not then be tormented by memories of her travels with Tad?

She would stay in cities where she already had friends, Mary explained, and their company would mitigate any sorrow she might feel when reminded of loved ones she had lost. Faithful Lewis had already agreed to accompany her on the train from Lexington to Philadelphia and on to New York, where on the first day of October she would board the steamer *Labrador* and set sail for Le Havre, from whence she would travel by steamer to Bordeaux, then by rail to Pau, a health resort in the French Pyrenees. She insisted that her sisters keep her travel plans secret so that Robert could not prevent her from going, for she feared he might return her to Bellevue if that was what was required to detain her. No amount of argument would convince Mary that Robert had absolutely no intention of committing her to an asylum ever again, so they kept her secret, though not without misgivings.

"I go as an exile, and alone," Mary declared as she left the Edwards residence and climbed aboard the carriage to the train station, with Lewis as her solicitous escort.

Frances and Ann had come to see her off, and as the three sisters watched the carriage disappear around the corner, Elizabeth said, "She will soon grow weary of isolation in a foreign land, and she will come home."

Ann nodded knowingly, but Frances, heartsick, thought it was far more likely that they would never see her again.

26

May 20, 1875

MARY

She was not insane. This Mary knew with all her heart and soul and being.

She was distressed and despondent, yes, but what rational woman would not be in her circumstances? Bereft of her great love and her three cherished sons, abandoned by her sisters, betrayed by her dearest friend, scorned by the world, ridiculed by those who had once respected her, and now hauled into court by her only surviving child and denounced as mad—

What woman of sound mind would not succumb to despair? Who would not see all too clearly that she had no reason to go on?

She could not be confined to an asylum. There, among the morbidly insane, she truly would go mad. She had lost almost everything else, but she had clung fiercely to her reason, her understanding. She would not submit to having those stripped away from her too.

Robert had come by her hotel suite that morning on his way to work—to see how she was doing after the previous day's ordeal, he claimed, but in truth, to gloat, to take grim pleasure in her misery. Upon his departure, he had warned her that he would return later with Mr. Swett to escort her to Bellevue Place.

Her son and his lawyer might very well try, but she intended to be gone by then.

They had placed three guards on her: a stern-faced woman who stayed inside her hotel room and two men, at least one of whom she suspected was a Pinkerton, stationed outside her door. She had overheard Robert instruct them not to let her leave the hotel under any pretense, but also not to physically restrain her in any way. She could have laughed at how Robert had tied their hands. How did he expect the guards to hold her there if she wished to depart—by the power of persuasive speech? No, he assumed she would confine *herself* there, cowering in her room. Robert believed her to be humbled, intimidated, too fearful to disobey him, and too mad to plan an escape. He would learn how very wrong he was, in this and other matters.

The lady guard had been placed in Mary's room to prevent her from jumping out the window or otherwise harming herself, so when Mary picked up her reticule and announced that she must see the concierge to arrange to send an urgent telegram to her sister, the matron merely frowned, nodded, and adjusted her stance. Heart pounding, Mary stepped into the corridor and told the two men the same story. They too frowned and studied her, but when she turned to go, they made no move to stop her. She quickened her pace, muffling a laugh of delight when she made it to the stairwell without being accosted. Swiftly she descended, pausing once at a landing, certain she heard footsteps a flight above as if someone were in pursuit. The sounds stopped when she did, so after a moment's fearful hesitation, she hurried on her way.

Of course she did not stop to speak to the concierge; she had to make haste, and there was no need to carry her ruse that far. She had passed the Squair & Company drugstore in the lobby many times since she had checked into the Grand Pacific Hotel a month before, and she had stopped in occasionally, so this visit would not strike the pharmacist as unusual. Stepping up to the counter, she forced a smile to hide the tremor in her voice and ordered a three-ounce bottle of laudanum and camphor—to apply to her shoulder for neuralgic pain, she added, when Mr. Squair momentarily hesitated.

"I shall need a half-hour to prepare the concoction, madam," he said. "Shall I send the bellboy up to your room with it when it is ready?"

Mary fought back the urge to chide him for the delay. "No, no thank you. I have other errands. I shall return for it."

Quickly she turned and left the drugstore. Crossing the lobby, she paused to glance over her shoulder as she reached the front entrance, a prickling on the back of her neck warning that she was being watched. She hastened outside, hailed a cab, and rode one block to the Rogers & Smith drugstore on the corner of Adams and Clark Streets. Instructing the driver to wait, she entered the shop, joined the queue, and waited impatiently while the pharmacist served two other customers. To her consternation, when it was finally her turn, a clerk summoned Mr. Smith into a backroom before she had a chance to place her order. The pharmacist promptly returned, frowning oddly, and when she asked for the laudanum and camphor, he apologized and explained that they were out.

"Of which compound?" she asked, suspicious.

"Camphor," he replied, too quickly.

"I see," she snapped, and wheeled around only to nearly collide with one of her guards. For a moment, she froze in shock, but she quickly recovered her composure. What did it matter? It was all nearly over anyway. "I need to purchase a few essentials before my travels later today," she informed him imperiously. "Please do excuse me."

Knowing he would not lay hands on her, she quickly sidestepped him and hurried from the store and into her cab. "Dale Pharmacy," she instructed the driver, "two blocks down Clark Street."

Minutes later, she entered the drugstore only to find three bemused customers waiting at the counter but no druggist in sight. Edging around an aisle of shelves, she glanced through the open doorway into the back office only to stop short, her heart in her throat, upon discovering Mr. Dale conversing solemnly with Mr. Squair, their brows furrowed, their voices low.

Panicked, she drew back, but as she inched toward the door she realized that if Mr. Squair was here, he would not be at his own shop. Hurrying back to her cab, she urged the driver to return at once to Squair & Company.

Her pulse racing, she fought to maintain an appearance of calm when she entered the shop for the second time that morning and politely inquired of the young, bespectacled assistant druggist whether her order was complete. "Only a few minutes more, madam," he promised, raising a finger and darting into the backroom. He promptly returned, rang up the purchase, and handed her a small, brown bottle labeled LAUDANUM & CAMPHOR. She felt a surge of triumph, but quickly concealed it, thanked him, and left the store.

As soon as she reached the sidewalk, she uncorked the bottle and drank the entire concoction down, shaking it upside down above her mouth to get every last drop. Immediately a wave of relief swept over her, cooled by only the faintest undertow of regret.

She returned to her hotel room, nodding in passing to the lone guard posted outside her door and the matron standing by the window. She lay down on her bed, fully clothed, to await the end.

She expected to drift off peacefully into a dreamless sleep from which she would never wake, but five minutes passed, and then ten, and she felt no different, except that her pulse had steadied as the nervous excitement of her mission subsided. As the seconds ticked by, her heart began to pound once again, and she felt tears gathering. Could she not succeed even in this?

The assistant druggist, probably a novice, must have worked up a diluted solution. Fuming, she rose from the bed, took her reticule in hand, again talked her way past the full complement of guards, and returned to Squair & Company. The pharmacist had resumed his post, and his eyes betrayed a flicker of wariness when she sternly informed him that his assistant's concoction had done absolutely nothing to ease her shoulder pain. She ordered a replacement bottle, declaring, "I shall come behind the counter to observe you as you mix the compounds, just to be sure it is done properly this time."

"I apologize for the error earlier today, madam," said Mr. Squair. "However, the laudanum is kept in the cellar. The stairs are dark and steep, and customers are absolutely forbidden to go down there."

"Very well," snapped Mary. "Just please, be quick about your business."

She paced near the window as she waited, ignoring the curious glances of other customers, until Mr. Squair returned with a new bottle, labeled LAUDANUM POISON.

"Be very careful with it," he advised. "It is highly potent."

She thanked him curtly, quit the store, and, on reaching the hotel lobby, swiftly uncorked the bottle and drank down every drop of it. She closed her eyes, sighed, and clasped the fist holding the empty bottle to her bosom. Now it was done.

She opened her eyes, and her heart plummeted.

Robert was approaching her from across the lobby, flanked by her two male guards. Her son's face was stricken and pale, and just as she was wondering why he had come hours earlier than expected, she saw Mr. Squair around the corner, arms folded over his chest, chin lowered and mouth set in determination, and she knew that these men, all these men, had conspired with her son against her, and there was no hope now of going to sleep and waking in Abe's arms, not with these men empowered to determine her fate.

She had delivered herself into their hands, but they could not hold her forever. She would not submit. She had powerful friends, and Abe was watching over her. They would see. She was Mrs. President, and she would not submit.

27

July 1882

ELIZABETH

On July 15, 1882, the eleventh anniversary of Tad Lincoln's death, Elizabeth fought back tears as she telegraphed Robert in Chicago: "Your mother collapsed of a stroke. Insensible and failing. Come at once if possible to bid farewell."

Next she sent similar telegrams to Emilie in Lexington and Margaret in Cincinnati, knowing they would want to be notified even though they could never reach Springfield in time to say good-bye.

Then she hesitated, debating whether to telegraph their brother George in South Carolina. Even amid a family that included numerous former rebels, George was notorious, estranged even from his siblings who had supported the South. Elizabeth had exchanged a few letters with him after he had signed up as a surgeon with the Confederate Army, but she had broken off contact entirely after it became widely known that he treated Union prisoners of war, especially colored troops, with shocking brutality, violating his Hippocratic Oath and all the rules of human decency. During the war, he had also publicly declared that his brother-in-law Abraham Lincoln was "one of the greatest scoundrels unhung." Mary had never forgiven him for it, nor had he sought forgiveness. It would be a betrayal even to invite him, though it made no difference now to Mary, who was not conscious enough to realize an invitation had been considered. So Elizabeth sent no telegram to

George. He would not have come anyway, and he would learn of Mary's death from the papers all too soon.

Did she have days left, or merely hours? The doctors could not say with any certainty.

Frances, Ann, and Lewis had been keeping vigil by Mary's bedside ever since they realized that she was not likely to rise from her sickbed. In that time, several of Mary's other grandnephews and grandnieces had passed in and out of the Edwards residence, looking in on their great-aunt Mary. They prayed silently with heads bowed in the parlor and helped the Todd sisters however they could.

So few of their siblings remained to mourn Mary's passing. Sam and Aleck had been killed in action during the war, and in 1871 David had at long last succumbed to the injuries he received at Vicksburg. Levi had died of liver failure in 1864, decades of heavy drinking having finally exacted their inexorable toll. Martha had perished of a brief illness in 1868 when she was but thirty-five years old, and Kitty, the youngest of them all, had died of heart disease when she was only thirty-four. Most recently, Elodie had died in childbirth in 1877. At sixty-three, Mary had long outlived them, and yet to Elizabeth, five years older, Mary's imminent passing still seemed to have come much too soon.

Before death had parted them forever, war and time and circumstance had scattered the sisters and brothers far from their Lexington birthplace. None had traveled farther than Mary.

On her last trip abroad, Mary had not wandered about Europe as widely as before, but had mostly remained in the resort town of Pau, making occasional sojourns to other cities in France and Italy. Her letters home had been quite cheerful and optimistic; she was either received anonymously, which relieved and relaxed her, or treated like honored aristocracy, which delighted her beyond measure. She occasionally complained of various ailments—fatigue, neuralgia, chest colds, aches and soreness—and also rather suddenly lost a significant amount of weight, which she considered a cause for celebration rather than concern.

After the first year, however, the tone of her letters turned melancholic. She dwelt upon her past losses as much as the impressive views of Herculaneum, the Bay of Naples, and Mount Vesuvius. By October 1879, she had begun to express a deep longing to return to America, referring to herself as an oppressed, heartbroken woman and her long absence from her homeland as an exile. All that kept her from returning, she confided to Elizabeth, was her profound terror that Robert would seek to have her committed the moment she set foot on American soil.

"That is preposterous," Robert protested when Elizabeth told him of his mother's fears. "Please assure her that under no possible circumstances would I do so. I have no reason to think that such interference is now or will hereafter be proper. Even if it were, I would do nothing. If I could have foreseen what a torment this entire experience would be for me, nothing would have induced me to go through with it. The ordinary troubles and distresses of life are enough without that."

Elizabeth passed on Robert's assurances—in her own, more encouraging words—but Mary demurred. Nevertheless, she had begun sending Robert's daughter occasional presents from France and Italy, and Elizabeth decided to interpret this as a faint glimmer of hope, however improbable, that Mary might one day reconcile with her son.

In December 1879, Mary seriously injured her spine after falling from a stepladder while trying to hang a painting. Her physicians set her in plasters, but even after they were removed, she suffered intense pain and weakness along her left side and found it difficult to walk. Six months later, the lingering debilitation caused her to trip and fall down a flight of stairs, worsening the damage to her back so that certain movements inflicted excruciating pain.

Mary was too unwell to live alone any longer, so despite her anxiety over Robert's intentions, she had to return to America.

In October 1880, she sailed from Le Havre to New York aboard the steamer *L'Amerique*. Lewis met her at the dock, but she felt too ill to continue on, so he checked them into a suite at the Clarendon Hotel. There she was examined by Dr. Louis A. Sayre, a world-renowned orthopedic physician and a childhood friend, who diagnosed her condition as an inflammation of the spine, disorder of the kidneys, and a "great mental depression," requiring proper medical treatment and "the sympathy of family and friends."

When Elizabeth read Lewis's telegram, the doctor's recommendation struck her as a stinging rebuke. If sympathy could have cured Mary of her mental afflictions, she would have been well long ago, but sympathy and love had never been enough. For many years and possibly still, Mary had required the thoughtful attention of a skilled physician specially trained in diseases of the mind. That was precisely the kind of care she had had from Dr. Patterson at Bellevue Place, where she had greatly improved. If not for the Bradwells and their misguided mission to rescue her from mortal embarrassment, Mary would have remained in the asylum until she was fully restored to reason, rather than thrust back out into the world before she was ready and subjected to new injuries before the old wounds had scarred over.

When Mary became well enough to travel, Lewis escorted her on the train from New York to Springfield, where Elizabeth and her granddaughter Mary Edwards helped her settle into her old room. Elizabeth hid her dismay at her sister's debilitated condition, her pain, her limited mobility, her depressed spirits, and her failing eyesight. How had Mary managed so long on her own, so far away across the sea?

As the weeks passed, Elizabeth, Ninian, and Lewis discovered that although Mary usually seemed perfectly rational and pleasant, she still suffered from troubling manias and delusions. She insisted upon sleeping on one side of the bed in order to leave her husband's side undisturbed for him, and sometimes she alarmed companions by giving a sudden start and asking if they too had just heard his voice. She kept sixty-four trunks of clothing in the Edwards residence, and she would spend hours each day opening, unpacking, sorting, and repacking them, grimacing in pain as she bent and knelt in her work, yet doggedly persisting, driven by some compulsion that Elizabeth could not understand.

And yet there were bright moments, glimmers of the woman Mary might have been had she not been tormented by loss and abandonment ever since their mother's death and their step-mother's rejection so many years before. She adored Lewis, and she was amiable and merry and charming in his company. She was generous to Frances, who had suffered financial hardships since William's death a few years after the war. Mary kindly gifted her hundreds of dollars for necessities and the payment of debts, refusing to consider it a loan; while still abroad, she had sent Frances hundreds of dollars' worth of fine woolen goods to replace the faded, threadbare clothing she otherwise would have worn until the patches needed patches.

Then, in May of 1881, after months of gentle but persistent cajoling on Elizabeth's part, she agreed to meet with Robert.

Eleven-year-old Mamie had been begging to see her grandmother ever since Mary returned from abroad, eager to thank her in person for the lovely gifts she had sent from France and Italy, to read poetry together, to listen, enchanted, as her grandmother regaled her with stories of her travels. Elizabeth invited Robert to bring Mamie for a visit, and then, instead of leaving his daughter at the front door and going off to spend time with his aunts, Robert accompanied Mamie inside and joined her and his mother as they sat in the parlor and took tea in the garden. It was a strained détente, but it was a beginning, and as the weeks passed it took a firmer hold. By winter, Mary and Robert were exchanging cordial letters, and although Mary remained estranged from Robert's wife, the arrangement between mother and son suited them both.

How fortunate it was indeed, Elizabeth thought as she left the telegraph office, that Mary and Robert had reconciled before it was too late. She could not bear to imagine how Robert might have suffered in the years to come if he and his mother had not made peace, if their last parting, now swiftly approaching, had been made from a cold distance rather than in amity and love.

Robert arrived in Springfield early the next morning. Tears in his eyes, he quickly greeted Elizabeth with a kiss on the cheek, then hastened to his mother's bedchamber. Fighting back her own tears, she joined him and her sisters in the vigil that would surely reach its inevitable conclusion before the day's end.

Soon Mary's suffering would be over, Elizabeth told herself. That was how she must think of her sister's passing. At last Mary would find the peace and solace that had eluded her in life.

Would peace come to the sisters she left behind?

When Elizabeth's own last day came, she hoped she would be able to look back on her life and know that she had done right by her sisters. As the eldest, she had always wished to do her duty, relying upon the wisdom of others for guidance. If she had been too indulgent, her consolation would be that she had erred on the side of humanity.

All her life, through the ebb and flow of the years, through estrangement and friendship, through times of bright hope and times of bleakest despair, Elizabeth had loved Mary, always, and had needed her. Who but a sister could a woman count on to truly understand her, even when they did not understand each other at all?

Though passions had strained, they had never broken their bonds of sisterly love. The war with all its divisiveness and rancor had not done that, nor would even death.

For whatever the world took away from them, even taking them from one another, love would abide.

Author's Note

Mary Todd Lincoln died in Springfield, Illinois, on July 16, 1882, at the age of sixty-three, on the thirty-third anniversary of her beloved father's death and one day after the eleventh anniversary of her son Tad's death. Modern physicians and historians theorize that she died of a stroke, possibly caused by a ruptured blood vessel in the brain, and that complications of untreated diabetes contributed to her final illness and death.

On July 19, Mary's body lay in repose in the parlor of the Edwards residence, the same room in which she had married her beloved Abraham almost forty years before. Lying in a casket draped in black velvet and surrounded by fragrant flowers, she was attired in a beautiful white silk dress, a posthumous gift from her sister Elizabeth. On her finger she wore her wedding band, engraved with the phrase LOVE IS ETERNAL—a tenet that had sustained her throughout her long, lonely years of widowhood.

So many mourners attended Mary's funeral—including family, friends, dignitaries she had known as first lady, and countless sympathetic strangers—that the First Presbyterian Church of Springfield could not accommodate them all. After the opening hymns from the choir, a scriptural reading, and prayer, Reverend James A. Reed offered a biographical sermon. "In introducing his subject," the *Chicago Tribune* reported, "Mr. Reed drew a comparison in which the life and career of Abraham Lincoln and his now deceased spouse were contrasted with the growth and decay of two pines which he had observed standing side by side on a rocky ledge in the Allegheny Mountains":

> The trees which he recalled to mind grew from the same rocky crevice, their roots intertwining and gaining subsistence from the same source, and the trunks almost joined at the base, so as to appear as two branches springing from one trunk. Near the ground one of these trees had been blasted, and, as if in sympathy, the companion had wasted slowly away, until in a few years it too had died. It seemed to have been killed when the fatal blow fell on its mate, and its after subsistence was merely a living death. Similar was the course of life with the illustrious Lincoln and his mate as pictured by the speaker. Mrs. Lincoln, he thought, might be said to have been killed by the fatal bullet which ended the life of her husband.

Hymns and prayers followed the sermon, and then a long, solemn procession conveyed Mary's remains to the monument on the lovely wooded knoll at Oak Ridge Cemetery, where she was interred with her beloved husband and sons Eddie, Willie, and Tad.

In death, Mary Lincoln at last received a measure of the sympathy and kindness often denied her in life. "By the death of Mary Todd Lincoln . . . there is removed from the stage of life a figure always invested with a certain historic and tragic interest," the *New York Times* observed. "It would be well for those who have been disposed to judge harshly of some of the personal characteristics of Mrs. Lincoln to remember that few women have ever been more devoted to their husbands, and that few have ever suffered so awful a shock as she when he was killed by her side."

Elizabeth's death six years later at the age of seventy-four was as sudden as Mary's had been prolonged. One morning a week after she and Ninian celebrated their fifty-sixth wedding anniversary, Elizabeth welcomed two friends for a brief visit and invited them to join her for lunch later that afternoon. After her callers departed, Elizabeth set out on an errand, but fainted and collapsed in the yard. "She returned to the house unassisted," the *Chicago Tribune* reported, "and was helped to the sofa where she expired within five minutes. Her husband, who is in feeble health, was at her side. He is greatly prostrated, and some anxiety is felt about him." Those fears proved prescient: Ninian died eighteen months later, at age eighty, at the home of his son Albert Stephenson Edwards. He was buried beside his beloved wife in Oak Ridge Cemetery in Springfield.

In March 1891, Ann Maria Todd Smith died at the age of sixty-seven in San Francisco, where she was visiting her sons Edgar T. and Allen H. Smith. Her remains were returned to Springfield, where she was interred beside her husband, Clark, who had died in 1885.

Frances Todd Wallace passed away at her home on Second Street in Springfield in August 1899 at the age of eighty-two. "She was essentially self-reliant and strong, but kindness and love ruled her life," an obituary lovingly eulogized her. "She was never so happy as when doing some good for others. The precept that it is more blessed to give than to receive was exemplified in her daily life. Her quiet home was a central place for the entire neighborhood, and young and old alike loved to seek her society. The delight she felt in the companionship of her neighbors was reciprocated to the fullest degree. Her reminiscences of people and events of the old times were of a most interesting character, and her memory to the last was remarkable in their [*sic*] fidelity to details as well as the force and vividness of the impressions conveyed."

Less than a year later, Frances's younger brother, George Rogers Clark Todd, died in South Carolina at the age of seventy-four, estranged from his siblings to the last. Four years later, in

March 1904, Margaret Todd Kellogg died of heart failure in Daytona Beach, Florida. "A Distinguished Lady's Death," the headline lamented, noting that Margaret had traveled to Florida for her health two months before, accompanied by her three daughters and a son-in-law, who was also her physician. "Mrs. Kellogg came from one of the most renowned and distinguished families in American history," the article noted, with some inaccuracies, "being the sister [sic] of the late lamented and martyred President, Abraham Lincoln, who was cruelly assassinated in April, 1865, at the closing of hostilities in the unhappy but sanguinary conflict between the North and South. She like her noble brother [sic], was loved and adored for her ennobling traits of character and God-loving, Christian devotion."

Mary and Abraham's beloved Little Sister, Emilie Todd Helm, survived all of her siblings and half-siblings, passing away in February 1930 at her home, Helm Place, on the Bowman's Mill Pike in Kentucky at the age of ninety-three. Two days later, the *Louisville Courier-Journal* warmly eulogized her in a piece titled "Little Sister":

> It was a happy turn of fate that Mrs. Ben Hardin Helm, Mary Todd Lincoln's half-sister, should have been spared these many years and that she was able, both verbally and by her diary and correspondence, to correct many false impressions of circumstances surrounding the lives of Abraham Lincoln and his wife in a day when public interest in them runs high. Many books have been written about the Lincolns, husband and wife, in these last ten years, and not the least of them was that of Katherine Helm of Lexington, based largely on her mother's recollections, letters and writings.
>
> Mrs. Helm's death, at the age of 93, removes a woman who was well beloved by the "boys" in gray, at many of whose reunions she had been an honored guest. She was an

impressive figure at that time when, after General Helm was killed at Chickamauga and she was granted a pass through the lines from Atlanta, Union officers at Fortress Monroe sought to force her to take the oath of allegiance. Tearfully, yet firmly, the young widow refused. The authorities communicated with Lincoln, who had granted the pass. "Send her to me," wired the President, and Mrs. Helm went to the White House, to be reunited with her sister.

"I had just lost my husband," she wrote in her diary. "Mary had lost her son, Willie, and we both had lost three fine, young brothers in the ranks of the Confederate Army."

Lincoln was very fond of "Little Sister," as he had called Emilie Helm ever since that day in 1847 when, returning from Congress, he visited the Todd home at Lexington and gave her that pet name as he caught her up and held her at a terrifying height from the floor. Mary Todd was very fond of this child, and because of her confidences, the younger sister was able in later years to refute the cruel story first told by William Herndon that Lincoln had failed to appear at his own wedding, supposedly planned for January 1, 1841.

It was in April, 1861, that Lincoln offered Ben Hardin Helm, then 30 years old and ten years out of West Point, a paymaster's commission in the Union Army, with the rank of major. That same day in Washington Ben Helm talked to Robert E. Lee and learned he had resigned his commission. Helm's father, Gov. John L. Helm, was a slave owner, but a Union man. Mary wanted her beautiful sister to live in the White House with her. The place offered was much coveted and Helm realized his opportunity might readily lead to advancement. He thanked Lincoln and asked for time. Returning to Kentucky he was convinced by Simon Bolivar Buckner that he should cast his lot with the Confederacy, and so he wrote the President, after "a bitter struggle with myself." Two years later Lincoln broke the sad news of Ben Helm's death to his wife, then in New York, and Senator David Davis described the President as much moved by the tragedy. "Davis," he said, "I feel as David of old did when he was told of the death of Absalom."

"Lincoln's affection was even deeper for 'Little Sister,'" the remembrance concluded, "even though while at the White House and until the surrender she remained a 'loyal little rebel' to the last."

Rebels and Unionists though they indeed had been, in the end the Todd sisters proved to be, above all other loyalties, sisters.

Acknowledgments

Mrs. Lincoln's Sisters is a work of fiction inspired by history. Certain events and people that appear in the historical record have been omitted to better serve the story.

I am deeply grateful to Maria Massie, Rachel Kahan, Alivia Lopez, Molly Waxman, Camille Collins, Cynthia Buck, and Jennifer Hart for their contributions to *Mrs. Lincoln's Sisters* and their ongoing support of my work. Geraldine Neidenbach, Heather Neidenbach, and Marty Chiaverini were my first readers, and their comments and questions about early drafts of this novel proved invaluable. As ever, Nic Neidenbach generously shared his computer expertise to help me in crucial moments.

I am indebted to the Wisconsin Historical Society and their librarians and staff for maintaining the excellent archives on the University of Wisconsin campus in Madison that I rely upon for my research. The sources I found most useful for *Mrs. Lincoln's Sisters* include:

BAKER, JEAN H. *Mary Todd Lincoln: A Biography*. New York: Norton, 1987.

CLINTON, CATHERINE. *Mrs. Lincoln: A Life*. New York: HarperCollins, 2009.

EMERSON, JASON. *The Madness of Mary Lincoln*. Carbondale: Southern Illinois University Press, 2007.

EPSTEIN, DANIEL MARK. *The Lincolns: Portrait of a Marriage*. New York: Ballantine Books, 2008.

FLEISCHNER, JENNIFER. *Mrs. Lincoln and Mrs. Keckly: The Remarkable Story of the Friendship between a First Lady and a Former Slave.* New York: Broadway Books, 2003.

FURGURSON, ERNEST B. *Freedom Rising: Washington in the Civil War.* New York: Knopf, 2004.

GOODWIN, DORIS KEARNS. *Team of Rivals*. New York: Simon & Schuster, 2005.

GREEN, MAUREEN HELM. "Emilie—Abraham Lincoln's Sister in Law." *Kentucky Ancestors*, vol. 4, no. 1, 2008, pp. 4–16.

HELM, KATHERINE. *The True Story of Mary, Wife of Lincoln*. New York: Harper & Brothers, 1928.

HOFFMANN, JOHN. "The Lincoln Ox Yoke at the University of Illinois." *For the People*, vol. 16, no. 2, 2014, pp. 1–7.

KECKLEY, ELIZABETH. *Behind the Scenes*. New York: G. W. Carleton & Co., 1868.

MIERS, EARL SCHENCK, ED. *Lincoln Day by Day: A Chronology.* Washington, DC: Lincoln Sesquicentennial Commission, 1960.

TURNER, JUSTIN G., AND LINDA LEVITT TURNER, EDS. *Mary Todd Lincoln: Her Life and Letters*. New York: Knopf, 1972.

I consulted several excellent online resources while researching and writing *Mrs. Lincoln's Sisters*, including the Abraham Lincoln Papers at the Library of Congress (www.loc.gov/collections /abraham-lincoln-papers/); the archives of digitized historic newspapers at Genealogybank.com (www.genealogybank.com) and Newspapers.com (www.newspapers.com); and census records, directories, and other historical records at Ancestry (ancestry.com).

As always and most of all, I thank my husband, Marty, and my sons, Nicholas and Michael, for their enduring love, steadfast support, and constant encouragement. You make everything worthwhile, and I could not have written this book without you.